TIM

"Look, Angel, I c............ ....ing but a little more than a week."

"A week?" She pulled back in shock.

"Believe me, I'd give you a lifetime if I could." He laughed, but there was no humor in his dark, tormented eyes. "A lifetime. I've outsmarted myself; I've got forever, but I can only promise the woman I love a few more days."

"It's okay, Johnny," she whispered. "I trust you. If that's all the time we've got, I won't ask any questions; I'll take it and be glad for it."

With a soft cry of anguish, he took her in his arms, pulled her to him and kissed her.

For a second she resisted; then she melted against him. She could hear her own pulse pounding in her ears. "Johnny," she cried, "this can't happen. I told you I don't belong in this time."

"You belong wherever I am," he insisted.

Then she forgot everything but the sensation of being in his arms. . . .

Books by Georgina Gentry

APACHE CARESS
BANDIT'S EMBRACE
CHEYENNE CAPTIVE
CHEYENNE CARESS
CHEYENNE PRINCESS
CHEYENNE SONG
CHEYENNE SPLENDOR
COMANCHE COWBOY
HALF-BREED'S BRIDE
NEVADA DAWN
NEVADA NIGHTS
QUICKSILVER PASSION
SIOUX SLAVE
SONG OF THE WARRIOR
TIMELESS WARRIOR
WARRIOR'S PRIZE

Published by Zebra Books

ETERNAL OUTLAW

Georgina Gentry

Zebra Books
Kensington Publishing Corp.

http://www.zebrabooks.com

I love movies, but never the handsome, suave heroes. My soul thrills to the rugged and tortured tough guys, the secretly vulnerable, tender ones whose hearts can belong to only one woman. This story is dedicated to the antiheroes of the silver screen who, one by one, without knowing it, have secretly starred in so many of my stories:

John Garfield
Humphrey Bogart
Lee Marvin
Jack Palance
Charles Bronson
Clint Eastwood
Bruce Willis
Tommy Lee Jones

Prologue

Kansas
Late afternoon
October 5, 1892

Johnny Logan was bleeding to death and he knew it. It was all he could do to stay on his paint stallion as it slowed to a walk. Only a couple of miles behind him in the frontier town lay a botched bank robbery, citizens and fellow outlaws dead or dying in the streets. Soon Johnny would be dead, too . . . unless the posse got here first.

He put his hand to his bloody, gunshot arm and winced as the horse stopped. God, he hurt so! Crimson blood dripped dark and wet onto the saddle, down the stallion's black-and-white hide and into the prairie dust. What a miserable end to a miserable life.

Johnny struggled to stay conscious, hanging on to the saddle horn, his head whirling. *Where was he?* He looked around at the desolate prairie. He saw a broken chair, some empty boxes, garbage, shattered dishes and other refuse.

He threw back his head and laughed. "A garbage dump! This is Coffeyville's ash heap! How ironic! How funny!" His laughter choked off into a weak cough as he reeled in the saddle, the stallion looking back at him as if questioning his sanity. "Don't you get it, Crazy Quilt, old boy? I'm just human trash myself. Fittin', ain't it, that I should die here?"

The horse snorted and stamped its hooves as if awaiting orders to move on.

Johnny glanced at the sun soon to set on the western horizon. "You're right, boy," he mumbled, "gotta get outa here; law's lookin' for me. Reckon all the others are already dead."

Johnny attempted to urge his horse forward, but he no longer had the strength. Instead, he felt himself falling. He hit the ground hard and shuddered a long moment, willing himself back into consciousness despite the pain. He lay in the midst of the rubble, his blood-smeared horse now munching stray blades of grass growing through the trash.

If he could just stand up and get back on the horse . . . Johnny struggled, but he was growing weaker by the moment. He couldn't even get up, much less mount and ride across the border into Indian Territory, where he might find refuge among the Kiowa. It would be dark soon and Johnny was afraid of the dark; silly weakness for a tough, half-breed gunfighter. No matter, he thought, he wasn't going to be alive to see the sun set.

"What a rotten end to a rotten life," he muttered and tried to staunch the flow of blood from his arm, but he didn't even have a bandanna to tie around it. "The fastest gun in the West dies amid a pile of trash."

Well, he was human garbage himself; the unwanted half-breed bastard of a mixed-blood Kiowa Indian girl and a frontier soldier. He didn't even have a real name; Logan's was the name of the saloon where, as a starving urchin, he'd been fed in exchange for sweeping up and emptying spittoons.

Johnny licked his cracked lips in desperation, cursed God and screamed at the sky, "I don't want to die! I want to live! I'd do anything to live!"

Abruptly, a tall, lean rider seemed to appear out of nowhere, loping toward him. It must be the sheriff or a bounty hunter. If it was a posse, they'd string him up right here. Johnny managed to turn his head and look around, chuckling softly. "No tree," he whispered. "Can't lynch me; no tree."

The stranger reined his shadow gray horse to a halt and leaned on his saddle horn, looking down at Johnny. "You've left a blood trail. I'm surprised no one but me has noticed it yet."

Johnny stared up at him. The somber stranger's voice was deep as a tomb, and it seemed to echo through the stillness. His eyes glowed dark and hard as obsidian over a small mustache and a mouth like a hard slash. He was dressed all in black with the finest boots, western hat and a long frock coat. Something about him sent a chill up Johnny's back. "Don't— don't I know you?"

The sinister stranger nodded and lit a cheroot as he stared down at Johnny in the twilight. A diamond ring on his hand caught the final rays of sunlight. "We've known each other a long time. I didn't figure you recognized me when we played cards last night in the Lady Luck Saloon. You cheat as badly as you rob banks. No wonder you're a loser; you don't have any real talent for evil."

"Hot; so hot. Help me," Johnny gasped and ran his tongue over his dry lips again. "You've got a canteen; give me just a sip of water."

The other shrugged as he dismounted. Funny, Johnny thought, he didn't throw a shadow across the ground in the fading light.

The stranger grinned. "You'll think hot and thirsty when you get where you're going."

"Going? I can't even ride. I—I don't want to die." Johnny begged, holding out a bloody hand in appeal, "Please, get me to a doctor. . . ."

The gambler yawned and squatted down next to Johnny, then looked at the setting sun. "Stop whining, Logan. You've always been brave, no matter what."

"I—I've never been this hurt before."

"It's almost over; you'll be dead when the sun sets."

Johnny stared up into the soulless dark eyes and then at the ghost-gray horse. An eerie, troubling memory came to him of an old preacher on a street corner in a lawless trail town shouting scripture at the sinners passing by.

. . . and I looked up and beheld a pale horse and his name that sat upon him was Death and hell followed with him.

Johnny fumbled for his Colt. "Whoever the hell you are, help me, damn you, or I'll—"

"You'll what?" The gambler blew cigar smoke into the air. "Your pistol is empty."

"How—how do you know—?"

The other only smiled.

Of course his Colt was empty. The bank robbery had been an inferno of gunfire. Johnny knew who this rider was now. Ironic. He had not planned to die like this. Handsome, tough gunfighters went out in a blaze of bullets in some wild saloon with half the town and all the pretty, adoring whores watching. "You—you've come for me?"

The other nodded and tossed away his cigar. "Of course there is an option. . . ."

Johnny looked at his life running out, mixing with the dust beneath him. "Anything," he gasped. "I'd do anything. . . ."

"Fine." The stranger pulled a paper from his black frock coat and knelt next to Johnny. "Here's a contract; good for one hundred years with an option to renew."

Johnny began to laugh through his pain. "A joke; it's a joke. I'm dreamin' all this."

"Just sign it," the gambler snapped. "I'm running out of patience and you're running out of daylight."

Johnny looked toward the dying sun. "What's the catch?"

"No catch." The other unrolled the ancient-looking parchment and laid it next to Johnny's hand. "People make bargains with me all the time."

Johnny felt so very weary and in pain. "Nobody ever did nothin' for me and I don't do nothin' for no one."

"Sweet guy; about like my other clientele."

This couldn't be happening. Something about a contract. "I—I don't have a pen."

"Just dip your finger in your blood and sign."

"What?"

"Either sign it or let your miserable short life end here amid the garbage; I'm late already and I've got thousands of eager customers waiting." The forbidding stranger turned toward his horse.

"Wait! Come back; I'll sign." Johnny didn't care any more what was on the paper. All he knew was that he wanted to live. He dipped his forefinger in the warm scarlet stream dripping down his arm and, slowly and painfully, scrawled his name across the paper.

"Smart hombre," the other grinned. "All your dreams of long life and riches are about to come true."

"Nobody gives nothin' for free," Johnny gasped incredulously. "What do you get out of this?"

The other looked at him, and the triumphant expression in the soulless eyes sent a sense of dread through Johnny's very heart. "Why, don't you know? I get you!"

Chapter One

Jiminy Christmas, just what had she let herself in for? Angelica Newland turned uncertainly to climb back onto the city bus, but it was already roaring away down the busy expressway in a haze of exhaust fumes.

"Think of this interview as an adventure," she muttered to herself, looking at the imposing black marble and glass skyscraper looming before her. "You know you don't have what it takes to get this job as a fancy executive assistant."

Angie looked again at the address. Yes, this was the right building: *666 Logan Parkway. 666.* Without thinking, she crossed herself, then felt foolish. She had never been religious, but old habits died hard, and she knew her late grandmother would have warned her not to consider a job in a building with that address.

The Oklahoma breeze blew wisps of her dark blond hair out

of her French twist. She probably looked a sight, but nothing much could improve her plain looks anyway, she thought. Angie squinted at the magazine in her hand. A darkly handsome man dressed in a tuxedo with a leading Hollywood beauty on his arm stared back from the cover of *Business International Monthly*. The headline splashed across the cover read: JOHN LOGAN VI: THE MYSTERIOUS OUTLAW OF WALL STREET, CONTROLS HIS EMPIRE FROM CATTLE COUNTRY WHILE LIVING THE ELUSIVE LIFE OF AN INTERNATIONAL PLAYBOY.

"I might as well get this over with," Angie thought aloud, swallowing her misgivings as she put the magazine in her purse and marched through the heavy brass and glass doors, blinking pale blue eyes temporarily blinded by the bright sun outside.

The building was as rich and foreboding inside as it was on the outside. It made her feel frumpy and plump, nothing at all like the elegant women she saw crossing the rich marble halls, hurrying to beautifully decorated offices.

She searched out the directory by the elevators. "Executive Offices: 66th Floor." Angie took a deep breath and straightened her navy blue dress, wishing it wasn't so plain as she stepped into the elevator to be whizzed up at dizzying speed. She'd felt drawn by some unseen force to apply for this job, but now she regretted the impulse. She pulled out the magazine again.

It was his eyes, she decided. John Logan VI's dark eyes seemed weary and sad, belying his reputation as a cutthroat business exec.

"Jiminy Christmas, he's used to beauties. He won't hire me." Angie stuffed the magazine back into her purse. She'd already read it twice. According to the article, for six generations his family had built its sprawling empire, beginning with railroads and gold mines and, later, cattle and oil. The outlaw of Wall Street, they called him. John Logan VI had a reputation for being hard and ruthless and very, very successful.

"Just a dream boss," she muttered to herself as the elevator stopped. "Angie, you are an idiot!"

She got off on the sixty-sixth floor. The corridors surrounding the elevator were full of hurrying people. Angie paused at a central desk where a nervous young man with thinning red hair tried to deal with three phones that all seemed to be ringing at once. The name plate on his desk read: ALBERT RENQUIST.

"Excuse me, but could you direct me to Mr. Logan's office? The Jiffy Girl Employment Agency sent me."

The man juggled one phone at his ear while reaching for another, his expression dubious. He ignored her for a long moment while he dealt with the phones and a fax machine that clicked at the end of his desk. She was only too painfully aware of his disapproving scrutiny as she waited. So what if she was ten pounds overweight? Well, okay, fifteen pounds. She was going to start a new diet this very week to see if she could take it off.

Finally, he gave her his attention. "Jiffy Girl sent *you?*" He sounded incredulous.

She stuck out her chin defiantly. "I said as much. Is he in?"

He blinked, evidently not used to a woman who stood her ground. "No one ever knows whether Logan's in or not; sometimes we go for months without seeing him. Let me check." He dialed, and immediately his tone became subservient. "Renquist here, sir." He asked a few overly polite questions, then hung up. "Mr. Logan is expecting you." He sneered and gestured toward a giant pair of walnut doors at the end of the hall. "I'll buzz you through, although you don't look like executive assistant material to me."

"Thank you. I'll tell Mr. Logan you said so." Angie turned and strode toward the doors.

"Please don't do that," he called after her. "He's—he's a difficult man to work for."

Angie paused, looking back over her shoulder. The balding twerp seemed reasonably cowed. John Logan must be a real SOB. "I won't tattle on you," she assured him and strode toward the big walnut doors, seeing her reflection in the gleaming brass and glass of the walls as she walked, more than a little conscious of that extra weight. It had always been a problem, no matter how little she ate. "If I were only five foot nine, long-legged and gorgeous," she murmured with a sigh, "I might have a chance at this job."

But did she really want it? Even more, she regretted her impulse in asking Jiffy Girl for this interview. But Angie had been getting desperate. School had barely started and already it didn't look as if she'd be getting enough substitute teaching jobs to live on. She had to take some drastic steps or she would soon be flat broke.

"Hold that thought," she reminded herself, taking a deep breath for courage before she grasped the brass knob and walked through the heavy doors.

She was in a small, richly decorated office with a fine walnut desk and a sweeping view of downtown Oklahoma City. The big doors closing behind her cut off the frantic noise of business and hurrying feet into sudden silence. The office was empty, and Angie realized she was facing another door off to her left that was slightly ajar. From there she could hear a slight murmur of conversation.

Angie bit her lip, wondering if she was supposed to wait here or if she would be given instructions via the intercom. She pulled at her skirt, straightening it, and wondered if she should have dressed in something other than a no-nonsense navy blue dress. At least the dark blue was thinning, helping to hide her plumpness.

She waited, fidgeting and wishing this interview was over. *Talk about a fool's errand. . . .*

After a long moment, she walked to the door, and knocked gently. "Mr. Logan?"

No answer. Inside, she could still hear the slight murmur of conversation. Was he interviewing someone else, or was he trying to intimidate her by letting her cool her heels in the outer office? Why had she felt almost driven to apply for this job?

Well, she had that interview with the dentist in Moore this afternoon; she'd have a chance there.

Angie took a deep breath and walked in. So this was the office of one of the richest men in the world. In awe, she looked around at the fine antique furnishings, the expensive Western paintings on the walls. Somehow, she had a feeling those Remington bronzes on the tables were originals. Priceless Navaho and Persian rugs muffled her footsteps.

A high-backed leather chair was turned away from her and toward the wall of gleaming windows behind the big walnut desk. Past the windows, she could see the skyline of downtown Oklahoma City against a pale blue sky.

A murmur of conversation drifted to her, and Angie realized there was a man in that high-backed leather chair, his black cowboy boots propped up on a low filing cabinet as he talked on the phone. Expensive, custom-made cowboy boots, she realized, and small feet for a man. *Small feet on a man means a big . . .*

Angie turned crimson as she remembered her Southern grandmother's saying.

The man had a magazine in his hand. She could see his arm, clad in a dark gray silk suit. "I don't give a damn if the ad agency does think this will sell fine jewelry," the voice snarled in a deep, Southwestern drawl. "I hate the damned ad; pull it!" He slammed the magazine down on the desk so hard, it bounced. "I own that magazine, too, don't I? Fire the editor! I hate ads featuring women that look like they're starving! I don't care if it *is* a fashionable look! I own your ad agency, don't I? After you do all that, I'll expect your resignation in the mail, pronto!"

The hand slammed the phone down so hard, it rattled, and she heard him sigh, as if annoyed. His chair creaked as he turned toward the giant windows and the view of Oklahoma City behind his desk.

Intrigued, Angie tiptoed closer and peered at the open magazine. It was a typical fashion layout, she thought; a gaunt beauty wearing expensive gold and diamonds and the latest couturier gown. The silver-blond model looked flat-chested and starving.

Without thinking, Angie said, "Well, I don't blame you! It's nice to see someone making a political statement against fashion models who look like they're recovering from bulimia."

The big leather chair whirled around. "Where in the hell did you come from?" It was the man from the magazine cover, every bit as intimidating and darkly handsome in person. No, he really wasn't handsome; he was virile and dangerous-looking, and somewhere in his mid-thirties. *A lot of American Indian blood,* Angie noted. Instead of a regular tie, he wore a fine turquoise and silver bola with his Western suit.

As a former Air Force brat, Angie wasn't easily intimidated, but this glowering big male made her take a step backward. "I—the Jiffy Girl Agency sent me, and I just want to say you have a lot more principle than *Business International Monthly* says you do if you'll try to change a fashion trend that's landing thousands of young women in hospitals trying to imitate it."

He didn't say anything, just continued to glare at her as if he couldn't believe her effrontery. His eyes were black as jet and just as hard. A tiny mole twitched on the left side of his sensual mouth.

"What I mean is," Angie rushed on, "they said you were a real old-fashioned robber baron, but you must have some principles, because I heard you say to jerk the ad, and then that you were willing to close the company, and—"

"I have few principles," he growled, "and you have more guts than any woman I ever met." He leaned back in the big leather chair and folded his hands across his wide chest, staring at her.

Angie was so startled by his admission, she gulped. "No wonder they call you an outlaw—"

"Don't call me that!" he roared at her. "I just sued and ruined that rag for calling me that! I'm not an outlaw; I'm respectable and successful! My company doesn't do anything most of the international companies don't do, but I'm fair game for the tabloids because I'm always brutally frank, Miss— Miss—?''

He wasn't going to intimidate her, she vowed to herself, but her knees seemed to be shaking. "Newland. I was merely suggesting that those magazine ads annoy me, too, and plump women vastly outnumber skinny ones, so that's more money that's spent on clothes and jewelry—''

"Hush." He made an annoyed gesture.

"What?''

"I said hush; you chatter more than a squirrel.''

Angie hesitated, trying to read his dark, rugged face as he leaned his elbows on his desk and steepled his fingers, staring at her with that intimidating, steely gaze. No, he definitely wasn't handsome, but he had an arresting, virile quality, like all those antiheroes in the old movies she loved so well.

"You could at least ask me to sit down.''

"I said hush." He gestured toward a chair and reached out to pick up what was evidently her application. "Now, Miss . . . ?''

"Newland; Angelica Newland," she said, deciding from his stoney expression that she was going to be out of here in record time.

Logan's cold, dark eyes scanned her résumé with no hint of the sad weariness that had drawn her on the magazine cover. He was probably a good poker player, she thought.

"Well, Miss Newland—''

"Mrs.," she corrected, "but I'm divorced—''

"Now why does that not surprise me?" He drummed his fingers on his desk.

The expression on his dark features told her that this was no time to go on about Brett's drug and job problems, or how she tried and tried to straighten him out while he spent all her salary. Actually, she was now a widow. Brett had OD'd more than a year ago, but she seldom told people that. She felt guilty for being alive and not saving him from himself.

"I suppose I was out of line commenting on the ad," she began, "but I can see why you objected to it—"

"Can you, now? I'm not politically correct," John Logan snapped. "I objected to the scrawny girl in the ad because she was too skinny to appeal to me or any other man, for that matter, and men are the ones who buy expensive jewelry and trinkets for women."

"Oh." Angie sighed without meaning to; of course it was true. She wondered who John Logan VI bought fine jewelry and furs for.

He glanced up at her loud sigh. "Angelica? Pretty fancy name."

"My mother found the name in France or someplace; my father was in the Air Force and was always being transferred around the world. He retired here at Tinker Air Force Base before he died."

"I didn't ask you all that." His dark eyes bored into her. "Do they call you Angel?" A hint of a mocking smile played across his hard mouth.

"Not hardly! Angie, most of the time."

He studied the papers before him. "Hmm. Twenty-four years old. You're an elementary-school teacher?"

"I would be if I could find a job." She shifted in her seat as his eyes took in every detail of her, "I haven't even managed to find a permanent position, so I've been substituting, but not enough to make a living."

"At least you're frank about it. Do you have any experience at all in being a personal assistant?" He tossed the application on his desk.

"To be honest, none, but I need a job."

Now he really did stare at her. "Your honesty is refreshing; hardly anyone ever tells me the truth. They tell me what they think I want to hear."

Angie took a deep breath. "Maybe it's because you bully everyone so much, they're terrified of you."

His eyebrows went together in a black line across his rugged, dark face. "What did you say?"

"Never mind." Angie stood up. "You don't need to bother with the formalities; I've had enough interviews to know that this one's finished before it starts. Just write NFD across my papers like the others have done—"

"I will say when this interview is ended!" John Logan thundered. "Sit down and hush!"

"I will not hush!" Angie was too annoyed and tired and discouraged to care anymore. She started toward the door, throwing her words back over her shoulder. "This is my thirteenth interview this week and this is only Thursday morning. I'm very tired of filling out applications only to lose the job to some thin, ditsy bottle blonde with long legs and big silicon boobs."

She struggled with the doorknob a moment, then realized he probably controlled it from his desk for security reasons. "Please open the damned door and I'll do us both a favor and go interview that dentist out in Moore."

"I said the interview isn't over until I say it is, so come back here."

Angie turned to confront him, determined she would not cry. He would enjoy that triumph too much. "Does everyone jump when you say 'frog'?"

"Most of the time." He drummed his fingers on his desk and stared back at her, a slight smile playing around his hard mouth. "Money does that for a person."

"I don't think you have enough money to hire me, Mr. Logan." She stood by the door and glared back at him.

"You are a fiesty thing, aren't you?"

Fiesty? She hadn't heard that word since she'd sat through twenty reruns of *Gone With the Wind.* "Mr. Logan, I am going to report you to the management of Jiffy Girl."

He shrugged. "Be my guest. I think Jiffy Girl was swallowed up by Logan Enterprises in a stock acquisition last summer. Now sit down and we'll finish this interview."

He must be determined to humiliate her, but she would not let him, no matter how much money the SOB had. Angie marched back over and took a chair across from him.

He had picked up her papers again and was reading them. "Oh, yes, here it is. 'Angelica Newland Security Update.' " He continued to study the application, but his hard, hostile face was so inscrutable, she couldn't read his expression. Now he looked at her for a long moment. "My inside information tells me you're divorced but also widowed, have no blood relatives, and survived a bad car wreck several years ago that killed your mother and younger sister."

She nodded, not wanting to relive those memories. They had told her she had died momentarily, and only a fast paramedic had brought her back to life. "I don't see what that has to do with my applying—"

"In my position, Mrs. Newland, I have to be cautious. I check out everyone whom I might hire clear back to grade school." He looked at the papers again. "Hmm. Graduate of Oklahoma State University, high grades, training in CPR and first aid?"

"I thought as a teacher, I might need it in a playground or athletic field emergency."

"Very commendable." However, his tone made it sound more sarcastic than anything else. "Father a retired air force officer," John Logan read aloud, "but he's dead, too?"

Angie nodded. "I told you I was an Air Force brat, but my folks were divorced when I was small."

"Why did you come back to Oklahoma?" His dark eyes bored into her.

Angie hesitated. He'd think her silly if she shared the idea that she'd felt drawn . . . no, compelled by some inner force to return to this city. It wasn't something she could explain.

"I don't know for sure. I was pretty rootless; then when I saw all that about the bombing of the Federal Building, I was reminded all over again how special the people of this state are."

"I think so," he said. "Your father's dead?"

Angie nodded. "Trying to keep up with his young trophy wife was what gave him a heart attack in Florida."

"Trophy wife?" His dark eyebrows arched upward.

"You know; less than half his age."

"And pretty?" he asked.

"Certainly! No one would ever write NFD on her job application." Angie said it with more bitterness than she meant. Evie was probably just the kind of woman John Logan would choose.

The thought discouraged and annoyed her. She started to get up, but he waved her back down, regarding her for a long moment. Then he stood up, and came around the desk. He was tall and broad-shouldered. That looked like an expensive custom-made suit he wore, but it had a Western cut. He sat down on the edge of the desk, only inches from her. She could smell the expensive shaving lotion from here. His dark eyes bore into hers, making her shift uneasily in her chair. The tiny mole by his mouth jerked as he frowned. "Tell me what 'NFD' means?"

"Everyone in the business world knows that." Angie raised her chin defiantly and bit her lip. She wasn't going to give him the satisfaction of making her cry, but she was reduced to blinking rapidly.

"I reckon my staff has kept me ignorant of such things," he said and looked at her curiously.

Of course he was too important to deal with the minor details of employment, even at his own company.

"It—it means 'Not Front Desk,' " Angie explained, reliving the humiliation. "When you see the interviewer write that across your papers, you know you won't get the job; you're not pretty or flirty enough to put out front, dealing with male execs and salesmen as they come through. They hide you in a back office; that is, if you get an offer at all.''

She thought she saw a smile tug at the corner of his grim mouth. ''That's against the law, isn't it?''

''It's supposed to be,'' Angie shrugged, ''but they get away with it; most people never learn the code.''

''Hmm. And knowing that, the agency still sent you over to interview for an executive assistant position?''

''They tried to discourage me,'' Angie blurted out. ''They said they'd sent you a dozen applicants and you'd hired two in the past three weeks and then fired them. But I felt compelled to come, for some reason—''

''Desperate enough to consider working for the outlaw of Wall Street?'' He leaned closer, surveying her again, his face grim. Now he pulled a large, ornate gold pocket watch from his vest and looked at it.

''What a beautiful antique watch!'' she said without thinking.

''It is, isn't it?'' He studied it as if he had not noticed it in a very long time. ''The first John Logan bought it from the proceeds of one of his early, ah—railroad ventures.'' He slipped it back in his vest, and it dawned on Angie that the watch had been a not-too subtle hint at how much time he had already spent with her. He was a busy man and he was telling her so.

She hesitated. ''I didn't mean to take so much of your time. I'll be going—''

She got up, but he reached out and caught her arm in a strong grip. ''You disappoint me, Mrs. Newland; I reckoned you were a little sassier than that.''

Sassy? She hadn't heard anyone use that word since her dear grandmother died. She pulled out of his grasp. ''Stop tormenting me. Just lie and tell me the position is already filled, and maybe offer me a file clerk's job.''

''I don't need a file clerk; I need someone to handle all these damned appointments and meetings I'm supposed to show up at, and all that blizzard of paperwork. I'll admit I'm a hard man to work for.''

"Difficult," Angelica thought aloud. "The agency said difficult."

He laughed, and it had the sound of a man who didn't laugh much. "I haven't had anyone be honest with me in so long, I've forgotten what it's like. I was just about to have some coffee. Would you like some?"

Angie hesitated. This was the strangest job interview she'd ever been on. He was toying with her for his own bored amusement, not realizing or caring that she'd used up her unemployment benefits and the rent on her furnished room was due. If she didn't find a job this week, she'd have to start selling off her father's antique coin collection, the only thing the pretty trophy wife hadn't gotten in the will. "Thank you. I—I didn't have time for a cup this morning." She wouldn't tell him she didn't have an extra dollar for coffee in her purse.

"Good. I'll see if I can figure out how this damned contraption works." He left his desk and went over to a sideboard, then began to fiddle with an automatic coffeepot. He obviously didn't have any idea what to do with the thing.

"Here, let me," Angie said without thinking. Putting her purse down, she went over, took the coffeepot from his hand, and filled it at the bar sink, then set it up.

"I keep a chef on payroll, but I fired him, too," Logan grumbled, stepping back and letting her do it. "He kept making some damned slop called cappuccino, and I like the regular stuff. They tell me I don't dare ask a secretary to make coffee any more."

"I don't have any problem with making coffee for a boss," Angie said as she reached for cups. "What do you like in yours?"

"I like it strong and with three spoons of sugar," he said, and returned to sit down in the expensive leather chair behind the big desk.

"Didn't your mother ever tell you all that sugar would rot your teeth?" Angie asked.

"Leave my mother out of this," he snapped in a bitter tone.

"That was presumptuous of me; I'm sorry."

"Don't be. She—never mind." His expression was closed and hostile. The silence seemed to hang heavy as the coffee began to brew and the scent drifted through the room. He seemed bored, and she fidgeted and tried to think of some bright, interesting bit of conversation, but flirty small talk wasn't Angie's style.

She put three spoonfuls of sugar in his coffee and brought it to him; then she got herself a cup, put some cream in it, and took it back to her chair. "I know I'm not sleek and sophisticated," Angie began apologetically, "but I'm a hard worker."

"You look fine to me," he said. "I don't know what it is with you damned women, wanting to look scrawny." He watched her and sipped his coffee. "Most of the women I know pick at their food like sparrows. Now, Lillian Russell could put away a slab of steak better than any man—"

"Who?"

"She was a Broadway star of the turn of the century," Logan said and paused, "or so I've heard."

"Oh, you're a history enthusiast?" Angie smiled at him over her coffeecup.

Logan actually smiled, as if he'd heard a joke. "You might say that."

Now there was only silence as he studied her. She wasn't quite certain if she was supposed to thank him for the interview and leave or ask him if there were any more questions he wanted answered. He stared at her for a long moment. "Tell me, Mrs. Newland, just why I should hire you?"

Angie wiped her mouth. "I haven't the faintest idea, except that I need the job and you're evidently difficult to work for. I realize I may not be front desk material—"

"That is a matter of opinion." Logan shrugged broad shoulders. "At least you're not a bag of bones in a tight miniskirt. You also seem to have some brains, which is more than I can say for the others I've been sent."

Surely after the way they'd clashed, he wasn't about to offer her a job? She looked at him over her coffeecup.

He glared at her across the desk. "I am about to do something I know I'll regret later, but I'm damned tired of interviewing people."

"Most executives in your position would let some underling do the interviewing," Angie said.

"Damn it! I know that. How do you think I ended up with those two gorgeous nitwits who didn't last? Renquist hired them."

Angie put down her cup. "You—you're offering me the job?"

"If you want it; although, like I said, I know I'll regret it." He leaned back in his chair and put his cowboy boots up on the desk again.

Small feet, big . . .

"Why are you blushing?" he demanded.

She had a sudden vision of this big, virile man naked and felt herself burn even more. "I'm not sure I can tell you."

"Can't or won't?"

"I'm not sure; maybe both."

"People don't usually buck me this way, Mrs. Newland."

She looked at him squarely. "I need a job, Mr. Logan, but I won't be bullied; I put up with enough of that from my husband."

"Mrs. Newland," his face was grim, "I have checked into your finances; you can't possibly turn down this job; not at the salary I'm offering."

Damn him, his investigators had done a thorough job after all. "All right; but I'm afraid this is going to be a relationship from hell."

Now he grinned, but there was no mirth in his hard, dark eyes. "If you only knew. Can you start today?"

"Yes." She was immediately apprehensive. Some unknown force had compelled her to interview for this job, but she hadn't really expected to get it. *Jiminy Christmas, what was she letting herself in for?*

Chapter Two

It was Friday morning and it was still hard for Angie to believe she'd landed this dream job in this elegant skyscraper. *Or was it going to be a nightmare?* She brushed that nagging thought aside as she went up in the elevator. Renquist scowled at her from his bank of ringing phones, but Angie only smiled and nodded. She went into her office and put her brown lunch bag into the bottom drawer of her desk. Today, she was starting her new diet. She'd brought a salad and a piece of broiled chicken breast. She looked down at her plain brown suit and sighed. When she lost some weight and got her first paycheck, she was going to reward herself with some new clothes.

Was John Logan VI even in his office? His door was closed, but her fax machine had spit out a hundred messages overnight and the phones were all ringing. She turned on her computer and dug into the workload, hardly looking up. Her stomach rumbled, but she tried not to think about food. She must take off those extra pounds.

She buzzed Logan on the intercom and got no response. Maybe it wasn't working.

She knocked on his office door. "Mr. Logan?"

No answer.

Hesitantly, she stuck her head inside his office. He sat behind his desk, staring wistfully out at the landscape of rolling prairies in the distance. "Mr. Logan, you have three invitations to charity balls in this morning's mail, a plea for funds to redo some historic building, and a reminder of a dinner at the country club."

He scowled. "Send them all a generous check and decline for me."

"Oh, and Mrs. Ruthford Van Hinesworth called about the debutante dance—"

"The snotty old bat is hoping to interest me in her simpering sorority daughter. Tell her I'll be out of the country and I'm so sorry."

"Yes, sir." *So he wasn't married.* She looked at the custom-made cowboy boots propped up on his desk and the finely tailored Western suit and said without thinking, "I don't know many cowboys like you."

"That's more true than you know, lady." He stood up and paced around his office. He was a big, wide-shouldered man, she thought. "I'm getting restless again. I may take off for a few months, or even a couple of years; go to Europe or my place in Scotland, or just go up to my ranch for awhile, where I can ride horses and get away from all this."

A ranch. Angie had always yearned to own a ranch and live the simple country life. "How big is your spread?"

"I don't remember"—he shrugged—"couple of thousand acres maybe, up in the Osage country near Tulsa."

"Sounds wonderful!" Angie sighed.

"You ride, Mrs. Newland?" He eyed her curiously.

"A little. Being an officer's daughter used to have a few privileges. Of course, I can't afford it anymore."

In her office, the phone was ringing again. John Logan scowled at her. "I do hope you're going to answer that eventually?"

"Oh, yes, sir!" She scurried away, upset with herself that she'd been daydreaming about what it would be like to ride across a thousand-acre ranch with John Logan by her side. Was she out of her mind? This rich and forbidding man would eventually combine his fortune with some other big Oklahoma oil-and-cattle empire by marrying some wealthy society beauty. Angie didn't qualify on any count.

She busied herself dealing with all the mail piled up on her desk, sorting through the letters that seemed to need Logan's personal attention and those that needed to be filed. It was amazing how many phone calls there were.

She punched the intercom. "Mr. Logan, Zurich on line one and a teleconference wanting to schedule from London."

"Damn, most of this stuff usually goes to the board of directors," he shouted back. "Re-route it so I don't have to talk to those twits."

"I'm sorry, sir, I didn't realize that. Oh, there's an E-mail on the computer; are you supposed to have lunch with some international bankers meeting in Tulsa today?"

He swore. "Damn, I forgot about that. Those prissy types will want French food or snails or something, and I feel like Mexican food. Mrs. Newland, first call my 'copter to pick me up, then call El Sombrero in Tulsa and reserve their private dining room. The twits can eat tamales with me or starve."

"Will there be a problem with reservations this late?" she asked.

"There'd better not be," John Logan snapped. "I own that chain of Mexican restaurants. Get hold of Pedro, the manager; he'll handle it."

"Yes, sir." Quickly, she ran to grab the Rolodex off her desk. Pedro at El Sombrero offered to close the whole restaurant for Logan's guests, if needed. "No, I don't think that will be necessary," Angie assured him. "Mr. Logan just wants the private dining room, and he said something about tamales."

The man at the other end laughed. "*Sí*. Tell Johnny there's plenty of tamales, and we just refilled the sugar bowls for his coffee."

This underling's informal attitude toward the menacing business exec startled her. John Logan must have another side Angie and *Business International Monthly* didn't know.

She hung up and flipped through the Rolodex. *Logan, Inc., Aircraft. Of course the outlaw owns his own flying service. J. R. Ewing of* Dallas, *you've been outclassed by this Oklahoma rogue. Is there anything Logan doesn't own or can't buy?*

She dialed the number and in minutes, a fancy blue helicopter with big *J.L.* initials on the side flew past her window to the helipad.

Angie ate her lunch at her desk and tried to compensate by picturing herself thin and pretty. Just like her sister had been. But then, Barbara had been a cheerleader, too. Slender, popular and vivacious, that had been Barbara, with a terrific life before her. Why had God taken her and Mother while sparing the plain, plump sister? She'd heard people whispering that at the funerals. Angie had asked herself that a thousand times. There didn't seem to be any rhyme or reason to it, even though her long-dead Grandmother said God didn't leave anything to chance; there had to be a plan in it.

Angie brushed her thoughts aside and began typing a list of charities that were on the Logan Enterprise contributions list. When she saw how many of them there were, she felt a little differently about John Logan. Maybe his cold, callous demeanor was a front to protect himself from all the evil or greedy people who tried to take advantage of him. Funny, for a man who had all the money and power in the world, he didn't seem very happy.

Late in the afternoon, she heard the chopper returning, but he didn't buzz her office and she had too much work piled up on her desk to even look up. She finished sorting his mail finally, taking past quitting time to do so. It wasn't as if she had any reason to rush out of here to the dull little rented room on the south side. The weather was extremely hot for early September and the little window air conditioner hardly worked at all.

The sun was low on the horizon when she finished sorting the faxes and reached for her purse. There probably were few people left in the building by now; she'd stayed later than she'd meant to. Perhaps she'd better check with Logan and see if he had any instructions for tomorrow. Angie knocked on his office door. "Mr. Logan?"

No answer.

"Mr. Logan?" She opened the door slowly and stepped inside. There wasn't anyone there. The fading twilight threw distorted shadows across the rich Western paintings and Navaho rugs. From somewhere came the faint sound of music.

She remembered that the helipad attached to a veranda and a penthouse. Angie crossed the gleaming wood floor toward the other doors. "Mr. Logan?"

The door to his penthouse was slightly ajar. Maybe she should just leave him a note. For all she knew, the rich bachelor might be entertaining a lady in his private quarters. "Mr. Logan?"

No answer. From somewhere inside, faint, thready music drifted on the still air: ". . . *after the ball is over, after the break of morn, after the dancers leaving, after the stars are gone. . . .*"

Angie took a tentative step inside. She looked around and took a deep breath. The room was the most beautiful place Angie had ever seen, but with a definite man's touch. Tall ceilings, rich wood paneling, the finest of Western paintings and sculptures, chairs covered in spotted steer hide, a big fireplace in the corner. On the table, an antique phonograph with a shiny metal horn played away on an ancient wax cylinder: ". . . *many*

*a heart is aching, if you could read them all; many the hopes
that have vanished after the ball. . . .''*

"Mr. Logan?"

"Out here. Damn it, what do you want?"

His disposition certainly hadn't improved any. Angie followed the sound of his voice out onto the open veranda. There were potted trees and a breathtaking view of the skyline and the coming sunset. A warm Oklahoma breeze blew across the patio sixty-six stories above the ground, bringing the scent of wheat fields and prairie.

John Logan stood by the railing, a drink in his hand, silhouetted against the setting sun. Looking down at the traffic far below, he seemed to have forgotten she was there. Angie paused uncertainly in the doorway and watched him, the way he was looking down. There was a misery and a lonesomeness in his rugged profile that pulled at her heart. She had a sudden feeling he was contemplating jumping. "Mr. Logan, are you all right?"

His head jerked around sharply. "Of course I am," he snapped. "Why are you still here? It's past office hours."

"I'm sorry," Angie stammered, "but for a moment there, I was afraid—"

"Afraid what?"

"Nothing." *Was she a complete idiot?* He was one of the richest men in the world; he had everything his heart could desire—money, luxury, adventure, probably the most beautiful of movie stars and society women awaited his calls with eagerness. How presumptuous of her to even think he might be considering . . .

He laughed and sauntered toward her, weaving slightly. "You think I might fall and you'd lose your good job? Don't worry, Mrs. Newland. I'm the luckiest man in the world; if I fell, I probably wouldn't even break a leg."

"From the sixty-sixth floor?" She could smell whiskey on him, along with the scent of expensive cologne, leather and fine tobacco as he sauntered past her into the living area of the penthouse.

"Would you like a drink?" He poured himself a tall one, his face shadowed and weary in the growing dusk, as if he had the weight of the world on his wide shoulders.

"You don't have to offer me hospitality, Mr. Logan. I was just checking to see if there was anything else you needed. I left a list of phone calls. Two magazines want to do interviews—"

"I never give interviews. That *Business International Monthly* thing was unauthorized. Send the phone calls on to the general manager in London." He gulped his drink and poured himself another, humming along to the phonograph.

Angie looked around at all the fine leather-bound books on the shelves, waiting for him to dismiss her. In the silence, the old phonograph played away: *". . . after the ball is over, after the break of morn . . ."*

"Such a great antique!" Angie said, a little awkward in the silence, wondering if he had forgotten she was there.

"Antique, yep, that's me," he muttered, sipping his drink.

Angie laughed, although she wasn't quite sure what the joke was. "No, I meant the phonograph. You don't see many like it these days—"

"Bought it new." He seemed lost in thought.

"New?" Angie was certain she'd misunderstood him. "But it must date back to the turn of the century—"

He looked up sharply, disconcerted. "I meant, a dealer found it in a warehouse for me, never been opened. Rare find."

"I'd say so," Angie said.

The song had run out and was scratching over and over at the end of the wax cylinder. In the silence, there was no other sound. Logan sipped his whiskey. "You ever hear of King Midas?" he asked.

He must be drunk, because that didn't make much sense. "You mean, the greedy king who wished that everything he touched would be turned to gold?"

Logan nodded and frowned, then gulped his drink. "The lesson here, Angel, is to be careful what you wish for; you might get it, and the price may be higher than you think."

She thought of the tabloids, the ringing phones, the constant faxes, the stress of making multimillion-dollar business deals, the lack of privacy, and almost felt sorry for John Logan VI. Angie suddenly felt very uncomfortable. Whatever emotional problems this man was having, she wasn't sure, as a personal assistant, that it wasn't presumptuous of her to comment. She cleared her throat softly, but his mind seemed to be far away. He put the needle back on the cylinder.

"After the ball is over, after the break of morn . . ."

"Do you waltz, Mrs. Newland?"

Before she could answer, he put down his drink, swept Angie into his arms and waltzed her around the room in the dim light of the coming nightfall.

Angie was too dazzled by his strength and warmth to do anything but let him hold her, slowly dancing her around the room. His breath was warm against her hair. Without meaning to, she closed her eyes and relaxed her body. It seemed to fit into the hard planes of his. She could feel his heart beating against her. She wondered about the hard bulge under his jacket.

"You dance well," he mumbled. "So many women don't know how to waltz anymore."

Was she out of her mind, dancing in the darkness with her drunken employer? Angie pulled away from him self-consciously. "As an officer's daughter, I learned some of the social graces."

He was looking at her in a way that made her very aware that she was a woman, that he was a virile, perhaps dangerous male and they were alone in an almost dark room. He moved slightly, and she saw the gleam under the jacket and realized abruptly what the bulge had been. "Mr. Logan, are you—are you carrying a gun?"

"A pistol; it's not called a gun." He reached inside his coat and pulled out a fine but well-worn old Western Colt. From here, it looked as if it had notches in the butt. "Don't look so shocked, Mrs. Newland. It's legal to pack a pistol in this state."

Angie blinked. "I know; I'm just not used to a man wearing a pistol so casually."

He hefted it in his hand. "I'd feel naked without it."

With all his money, he must feel vulnerable to thieves. "Mr. Logan, I'm leaving now. Can I do anything; get you anything before I go?"

He sighed and shook his head, then slipped the Colt back into the holster under his jacket. "No, I don't think so." He was once again cold and remote. "I was out of line, Mrs. Newland. I—I'm just tired; business pressures and all."

She didn't want to like this arrogant man, yet her heart went out to him. "Maybe you need to get away for awhile, Mr. Logan. I could make reservations for you. Can your business run without you?"

He laughed without mirth. "The way my accountants have it set up, if I disappeared forever, Logan Enterprises could keep running without missing a beat. I'm just a figurehead."

He looked so desolate that without thinking, Angie reached out and almost put her hand on his arm. Then she drew back, knowing this remote and mysterious man would resent such familiarity. "But you have your family—"

"No, my parents were lost at sea more than a dozen years ago with their yacht. I'd been living and going to school in Europe up until then. Father was afraid of kidnappers, so even the press hardly knew I existed until I caught a plane home when I heard the news."

"I'm sorry," Angie said. "You don't have any brothers or sisters?"

He shook his head. "I'm alone in the world."

"Me, too." She started toward the door and paused. "I'm surprised you aren't married."

His eyes grew cold and he straightened his shoulders. "Mrs.

Newland, you overstep yourself. All the women I meet seem to be either stupid little ninnies or after my money.''

How could she have thought there was any warmth to this man? The outlaw of Wall Street; what an arrogant, dislikable son of a bitch. ''You're right, Mr. Logan, of course. My apologies. Now, if if there's nothing else, I'll be going.''

He didn't answer. He was staring off at the horizon, his face incredibly sad. ''Did you ever see a movie called *The Highlander?*''

''What?''

''Never mind.'' He shrugged and refilled his glass. ''You can leave, Mrs. Newland.'' His tone was one of curt dismissal.

She turned on her heel and left the penthouse. As she closed the door behind her, the faint strains of the Gay Nineties tune still echoed through the deserted sixty-sixth floor of Logan Towers. *The Highlander* she thought in confusion as she got her things. *That was a strange movie about a man who had the power to live forever.* It didn't seem like a movie a tycoon like John Logan would like. Ah, well, he was evidently drunk.

Angie caught the last bus on the evening run to the south side of Oklahoma City and warmed a can of soup in the microwave. The rented room was crowded and hot, and the neighbors upstairs were fighting again. The whole building smelled of greasy fried food and stale beer. When she got her first paycheck, she was going to get herself an apartment. Maybe eventually she could even buy a car, although she didn't have any place to go except to work, and the bus would get her there. She didn't have a boyfriend, or even any real friends to speak of. With her father in the Air Force, the family had moved so often, she'd stopped making friends; it was too painful to leave them. Her own loneliness had led her into a too-hasty marriage.

Marriage. She was only too aware of her own loneliness as she reached for a Western romance novel to carry her away from her dreary surroundings for a little while. Yet she had a difficult time keeping her mind on the story. She kept seeing

John Logan's dark, virile profile in her mind. The outlaw of Wall Street didn't seem very contented with his way of life, she thought. But John Logan's money and power weren't what intrigued her; it was the man himself. What had drawn her to interview at Logan Towers? And what was it about the moody, lonely executive that had caused her to take this difficult job? Angie had a sinking feeling she was going to regret it.

Angie lay in bed sleepless Friday night, listening to a noisy party down the hall. Although it sounded loud and crude, the kind of people who didn't appeal to her, still the sound of partying made her feel lonely. She hardly knew a soul except for Brandi Closner downstairs. Angie's rent was almost up and she'd already given notice she intended to move, but she hadn't had time to look for another place. If she disappeared off the face of the earth, nobody would notice or care.

Angie didn't really have any plans for Saturday night, and certainly not a date, but Brandi Closner caught her in the downstairs hall in the early afternoon. Brandi's dark roots were showing under the flaming red hair and she had a bad habit of popping her gum. "Hey, like I didn't see you at the party last night."

"I—couldn't make it." Angie couldn't bring herself to lie, but she didn't want to say she hadn't been invited. Not that she would have gone anyway. She probably wouldn't have fitted in; that crowd might have considered Angie terribly old-fashioned and naive.

"Hey," Brandi said, "I was going to Frontier City tonight, but my Eddie decided to go on a run with his biker buddies instead. Why don't you and me go?"

Angie blinked at the surprising invitation from a girl whom Angie barely knew. She didn't think she had much in common with Brandi, who seemed to be a real swinger. "I don't think so. I thought I'd stay home and wash a few things out."

"You're kiddin' me. What a bummer of an evening you got."

Angie saw the sympathetic look in Brandi's eyes and realized how pathetic she must appear to the other girl. She didn't have any urge to go to an amusement park, but she couldn't bear one more night of sitting in her room watching an old movie on television when somewhere, someone was making love, sharing an adventure. "I've changed my mind, Brandi, let's go. You have a ride?"

"A friend will drop us." Brandi grinned and popped her gum. "Call you later to firm it up."

"Great!" Angie said with an enthusiasm she did not feel. Somehow she felt she'd just made a big mistake.

Angie didn't feel any better about it that night as she and Brandi walked through the noisy crowds and lights of the amusement park. Oklahoma City's only amusement park was colorful and exciting, but Angie couldn't work up any enthusiasm for the rides. She was all too aware of how dowdy she must look to Brandi in plain jeans and a blouse, when Brandi was wearing a bare midriff and skintight shorts.

"Like, this is gonna be a ball." Brandi popped her gum. "Maybe we'll meet some fellas."

Angie took a deep breath. "Look, Brandi, I don't know about going off with some guy you meet for the first time—"

"Hey, relax, will ya? You worry too much." The other girl shrugged and winked at a big guy wearing a muscle shirt and tattoos as he passed. "That would serve Eddie right."

It crossed Angie's mind that Brandi wouldn't have a qualm about deserting her if she found some attractive male to leave with. In that case, how was Angie going to get home? She wasn't sure there was any bus service this far out on the highway.

Brandi glanced at her watch. "Hey, it's time for the gunfight. There's this one real stud muffin gunfighter."

"Gunfight?" Angie blinked.

"This is Frontier City, you know," Brandi said. "They have fake gunfights on weekends; you know, like the Old West."

"Okay." She turned and followed Brandi through the crowds toward the area that looked like a real Old West street. The area was roped off for the drama. Three horses were tied in front of the fake saloon, and from inside, an old piano played "Oh, Susanna."

The crowd grew quiet with anticipation.

Two unshaven actors lounged against the hitching rail. "We all set to knock over the bank?" one of them said.

"First," the other answered, "I plan to ambush the Ringo Kid; killing that gunfighter means more to me than robbing the bank."

"Ringo?" The other whistled low and long. "That's one man I wouldn't mess with; nobody handles a Colt like he does."

The first one laughed. "You think I don't know that? I don't intend to take him on man-to-man. I've got Zake up on the roof and Joe over there by the livery stable. When I challenge Ringo, I expect all three of you to cut down on him before he can draw. Then we'll rob the bank."

Brandi punched Angie's arm. "Here's where the hunk comes out of the saloon," she whispered. "Man, oh man, is he something I'd like to take to bed!"

All eyes turned expectantly toward the saloon as the bearded one yelled, "Ringo! You in there? Come out in the street for a showdown!"

For a long moment, there was no sound save the snort of a tied horse and the old piano playing the Stephen Foster tune. Except for the silent, waiting crowds, it would have been easy for Angie to believe she really was in an old Western town more than a hundred years ago. A thrill ran up her back. When she read Western romances, Angie sometimes fanticized about escaping back to that time period; living on a ranch, loving a man who rode a horse and handled a gun like Clint Eastwood.

The swinging doors of the saloon creaked as a big, dark man dressed in black, his gun tied low, pulled a bandanna up over his face as he stepped through and paused on the wooden porch.

Perhaps he intended to rob the bank himself on his way out of town. At any rate, he looked as deadly and dangerous as a real gunfighter. There was something so authentic about him, the audience could easily believe everything they saw being played out was real. Brandi punched Angie's arm. "Ain't he something, though?"

Angie stared at the actor playing the gunfighter. "Jiminy Christmas!"

"What's the matter?"

Angie was too stunned to answer. Brandi was right; the man was a real hunk. Even with his face obscured by the bandanna, there was something familiar about that big, rugged frame and the way he walked. Angie took a deep breath of surprise as she recognized him. There was no mistake; it was John Logan.

Chapter Three

Angie stared at the masked gunfighter, speechless with surprise. He didn't seem to see her; he was watching the other actors with an intensity that made it seem almost as if he was a real killer.

John Logan had missed his calling, she thought. He looked more authentic than any of her favorite Western movie actors.

The street was silent save for the nicker of a horse tied to the hitching rail and the tinny old piano playing in the background.

Abruptly, the other players drew down on Logan, but his hand went to his holster with lightning speed. The three outlaws bit the dust, one falling off the roof of the stable and groaning. Logan did some fancy trick shooting then, knocking some bottles off the roof of the saloon while the crowd cheered and applauded. All the actors took a bow.

Angie hadn't moved, staring in disbelief at the man playing the Ringo Kid. He moved with all the deadly ease of a real gunfighter, she thought.

Brandi didn't seem to notice her silence. "Hey, like that was a real blast, wasn't it? I'm goin' for a soda and some popcorn; see ya later."

The girl sauntered away before Angie could protest. At that moment, Logan seemed to see Angie for the first time, and she saw him start in surprise. Then he recovered himself and pushed through the crowd toward her. "Mrs. Newland?"

"Jiminy Christmas! Is it really you, or do you have a twin brother?"

He reholstered his pistol with a practiced hand. "Never expected to see you here."

"Ditto!" Angie regained her composure. "Now tell me there's a reasonable explanation as to why one of the richest men in the world is working part-time at an amusement park."

"Shh!" He put his finger to his lips. "Hush, Angel, someone will hear you. I do it for fun and donate my salary to charity. Does that surprise you?"

She shook her head. "Mr. Logan, everything about you is unusual. What surprises me is how good a shot you are."

He smiled a rare smile. "For a couple of hours on Saturdays, it makes me feel like I'm really back in the Old West." He sounded wistful as he pulled out a big gold watch and looked at it. "I've got to change; the park will be closing soon. You out here with someone?"

"Uh, sure." How could she admit she didn't have a date on Saturday night? "Having a great time, too."

Was that a flicker of disappointment in his dark eyes? No, probably boredom. She couldn't be sure with his face still hidden.

Over by the saloon set, one of the gunfighters yelled, "Hey, Johnny, you comin'?"

"Be right there." He waved at them.

Angie looked up at him for a long moment. "Nobody around here knows who you really are, do they?"

"No." He shook his head and his grim expression left no room for argument. "And you'd better not tell them."

"How have you kept this quiet so long?"

Logan pushed his Stetson back. "Most of the people I do business with never come to amusement parks. Well, see you Monday."

Angie nodded and watched him stride away. He looked more at ease out here, dressed in Western clothes with a Colt on his hip, than he did in the office. The outlaw of Wall Street working part-time at an amusement park and giving the money to charity. What a strange guy; yet so vulnerable and lonely in his own way. Angie swallowed hard. *Stop it, you little fool,* she scolded herself. *He doesn't think of you as a woman; only as an employee.*

Reluctantly, she turned away and pushed through the crowd, looking for Brandi. *Where had that girl gotten off to?* It was late and the crowds were starting to leave. Angie wouldn't put it past Brandi to go off with some guy she had picked up.

"Hey, Angie, over here! I got us a ride!"

Angie turned toward where Brandi yelled and waved, feeling a flood of relief as she started toward the redhead. The feeling turned to uncertainty as she noted the men standing with Brandi in the dark shadows. There were two of them, big unshaven guys in black leather.

"Angie, this is Moose and Leo. They're gonna give us a ride home on their bikes."

"Hey." The brutes nodded, and Leo said to Brandi, "You didn't tell us she was a blonde."

She could smell marijuana and beer on the man. Angie tried to smile, but she didn't like the way these tattooed hulks looked her over. "Gee, I don't know, Brandi. I—"

"What's the matter, honey?" Leo grabbed her arm. "Ain't I good enough?"

Angie shook off his hand. "Brandi, I really think we should call a cab—"

"A cab? Get real!" Brandi snorted. "You know what a cab would cost out here?"

"Besides," Leo leered at Angie, "we know where there's a party goin' on; all the beer we can drink."

"I think you've already had plenty," Angie said. "I just want to go home." She took a step backward, but Leo grabbed her and pulled her toward him.

"What's the matter, honey? I'll take you home after the party."

The other two laughed, but Angie's temper flashed and she jerked away from him. "Brandi, you can leave with this pair if you want, but I'll find my own way home."

Brandi frowned and bristled. "Well, ain't you the snotty bitch!"

Leo grabbed Angie's arm again. "You're goin' with me, honey. I'll make you glad you did."

"Get your hands off me!" Angie slapped him.

With a curse, he grabbed her, dragging her to him. Angie opened her mouth to scream, but he clapped his hand over her lips. She bit his fingers.

"Ouch! You bitch!" Leo drew back to hit her and a deep, cold voice from the darkness said, "I wouldn't do that if I were you."

Angie's head jerked up and everyone froze in place. The moonlight silhouetted the big man.

Recovering, Leo let go of her, and Angie lost her balance and fell to the ground.

Leo said, "Now, buddy, who asked you to mix in?"

Angie looked up, gasping at the sight of John Logan standing there, feet wide apart, casually dressed in jeans, a Western shirt and a denim jacket. He looked every bit the old-fashioned gunfighter, except he no longer wore the pistol and the mask. When Logan spoke again, it was in a soft, deadly whisper. "This place has good security," he said. "All I have to do is yell, and we'll have a half-dozen park guards all over us."

"Hell," Leo sneered, "if you got to yell for help, I bet Moose and I can take you."

"I wouldn't bet on it," Logan said, and before anyone could react, his hand flashed out, fast as a snake's strike, and clipped Leo across the neck.

Leo went down like a falling tree.

Now Logan turned to Moose. "You want some of this?"

Moose backed away, shaking his head. "No, man, this ain't nothin' to me; we didn't know we was messin' with your woman."

Leo sat up, moaning.

"Get your friend and get out of here," Logan ordered.

Brandi looked from Logan to Angie with big eyes as Moose helped the groaning Leo to his feet. The three of them hurried away in the darkness.

Angie looked up at Logan with a sigh of relief. "Thanks, I—"

"So that was the date?" Logan snorted. "I figured you'd have better taste than that." He reached down, caught her small hand in his big one and pulled her to her feet with a gentleness that surprised her.

"I never saw that guy before," Angie protested. "We caught a ride out with one of Brandi's friends and then she picked up that pair of guys." Angie realized she was trembling.

Logan took off his Western jacket and, reaching around her, draped it over her shoulders. It was still warm from his big body and it smelled faintly of leather, aftershave and tobacco.

Angie looked around. The park would be closing soon and she wondered if she had enough money for cab fare.

Logan lit a slender, expensive cigarillo. "You got a ride home?"

She could feel her face burn with humiliation. "I—I'll get a cab."

"Clear out here? Come on, I'll drive you." He sounded annoyed.

"You don't need to feel obligated—"

"Obligated? Of course I'm obligated." He puffed the smoke and she watched the cigarillo tip glow in the darkness. "I can hardly leave an employee in a mess like this."

An employee. Of course he wasn't thinking of her as a woman; she was only an employee. She didn't really want him to see the run-down place where she lived, but she didn't know what else to do.

"Come on, Angel." His tone was almost gentle, and he brushed a loose strand of hair away from her face. Then he took her arm and they started toward the gate.

"You hit that big guy like you've been in a million saloon brawls."

He glanced sideways at her and frowned. "It was stupid of me. He finds out who I am, he'll sue me for big bucks." He rubbed his knuckles, and a rare smile flitted across his lips. "Felt good, though. Haven't been in a fight in quite a while."

She couldn't imagine when a high-society type like John Logan VI ever got a chance to street brawl, but she didn't say anything as they walked out to the parking lot and he opened the door of his black pickup truck for her.

He tossed away his smoke as he got in and started the engine. "You hungry, Angel?"

She was, but she didn't want him to feel obligated to feed her just because he was stuck with giving her a ride home. "No."

"Then you can watch me chow down." He pulled out of the parking lot and headed south on I-35.

Angie leaned back in the seat, watching his profile in the darkness, his strong hands on the steering wheel. "Where are we going? I'm not dressed for some fancy—"

"Nothing fancy—just one of my favorite spots down in Stockyards City." He didn't say anything else until he cut off the freeway onto I-40. In a few miles, he turned off on Agnew and drove into the packinghouse area of Oklahoma City, where ranchers had always brought their beef in to sell.

He pulled up in front of the old Cattlemen's Café at the corner of Exchange and Agnew. "You ever been here? Best beef in town. President Bush came here for a steak when he was in Okie City."

She started to ask if Logan had had supper with any president and decided he probably had. She wondered how many employees Logan took out for a steak. This guy was getting more mysterious and unpredictable all the time.

Logan went around to open her door. He put his big hands on her waist, lifted her down. Such old-fashioned chivalry impressed her. Most of her dates wouldn't even think to open a door, much less help a girl out. The warmth of his hands on her body made her pulse quicken. She said, "You want your jacket back?"

He shook his head. "Not now. You might get cold."

Across the street from the Cattlemen's, Langston's big western wear store displayed boots, Stetsons and jeans in its windows.

Angie looked around. "I'm not really familiar with Stockyards City; I love this street."

"My last date wasn't impressed." Logan actually grinned at Angie, and the tiny mole by his mouth twitched. "Houston oil society; her old man and I were making a merger."

"Did you two make your own merger?" she asked before she thought.

He shrugged. "Of a sort. Women come and go, but good business mergers are something you can count on."

Was he letting her know not to get her hopes up? As if a plain, dumpy girl could even dream that a man like this . . .

"The Cattlemen's Café was won on a hand of cards in a poker game," Logan said.

Angie laughed, "I suppose you sat in on the hand?"

"Nope, but I think my father did. Nobody likes steak as much as oil men and cowboys."

They went inside. It was unpretentious, and the jukebox was playing a Garth Brooks song about friends in low places. Most of the diners were dressed in Western clothes, but there were a few business suits in the crowd. The waitresses greeted Logan like an old friend and looked Angie over with curiosity as they found a booth.

She took a deep breath. The smell of broiling meat drifted through the café and made her mouth water. "I think I'll just have a salad."

Logan frowned. "I bring you to the best steak house in Oklahoma City and you want salad?"

Angie felt guilty about the calories, but she ended up ordering a sirloin steak and iced tea, while Logan had the T-bone and a cold beer.

Now that they were here, she felt extremely conscious of the fact that she'd put her rich employer to a lot of trouble and was having a difficult time thinking of things to say. She noted women at other tables were looking Logan over appreciatively, but his attention was on Angie. "How'd you enjoy the show?"

"You can really handle a gun," Angie said.

Logan shrugged. "If you only knew."

"What?"

"Never mind."

An older waitress brought the food. "Hey, Johnny, who's the lady?"

"Oh, I work for Logan Enter—" Angie began, thinking Logan wouldn't want anyone to think she was his date, but Logan interrupted her before she could finish.

"This is Angel," Logan cut in smoothly. "We've been out to Frontier City. Angel, this is Marge."

"Glad to know you," Angie said to the smiling motherly type who put a big plate of sizzling steak in front of her.

"Likewise. Johnny's one of our favorites around here." Marge slid a rare T-bone in front of him and left.

Angie looked at him. "They don't know who you are either, do they?"

Logan shrugged and glared at her. "No, and don't you tell them. I'd just as soon everyone thought of me as a local cowboy."

"But—"

"Hush, Angel, and eat; your steak's getting cold."

Well, it wasn't her business if John Logan VI wanted to work on Saturday nights at a Western amusement park and hang out with the cowboys in Stockyards City. Angie dug into her food. The steak was rare, and mouthwateringly delicious.

When she looked up, Logan was watching her and grinning. "If you aren't hungry, I'd hate to see you when you were."

She felt a flush rise to her face. "I've been trying to diet."

He shook his head. "I told you I'm sick of seeing women pick at their food. Besides, today's women are too damned skinny."

Could he possibly mean that? No, he was being polite, Angie thought. "I don't think I've thanked you yet for taking on that Leo for me."

Logan shrugged and cut a hunk out of his T-bone. "I'd do it for any lady."

"You're chivalrous; something pretty rare in today's men. I don't think that reporter who wrote about the Wall Street Outlaw got to know you very well," Angie said.

Logan frowned at her. "I'm as ruthless and merciless as he said I was, Angel; that's how the Logans have ended up on top. We don't care who we stomp on to get there."

She paused and looked at him for a long moment. The stone-cold eyes had just a hint of vulnerability. "I don't believe that."

"Believe it, Angel, and don't be thinking anything different." He gave her a fierce scowl and returned to his steak.

Angie fell silent and took a bite of baked potato. He must suspect that she was beginning to take a personal interest in him and he was warning her off. He was right, of course; a man like John Logan couldn't get romantically involved with a girl like her.

In the background, Vince Gill, another Oklahoma boy, sang about love.

Logan finished his steak and pushed back his plate, then sipped his beer. The waitress came over. "Hey, Johnny, get you anything else? Food okay?"

"Great as usual, Marge."

Marge looked Angie up and down and Angie smiled at her. "That was really good."

Marge wrote out the check and said to Angie, "I never seen Johnny bring a girl in here before."

Logan frowned at her. "I was just giving the lady a ride home, Marge. A guy at the park got fresh with her."

"Oh"—Marge nodded—"well, now, that's the cowboy way, ain't it?"

Angie was reminded all over again that she'd inconvenienced her employer. She waited until Marge had left before she said, "Mr. Logan, I can get home from here all right, honest."

"It's late," Logan said. "I'll drop you off."

They got up, and Angie noted out of the corner of her eye that he left a generous tip for the waitress. He paid the check and they went outside.

An old, threadbare man came out of the alley next door. "Hey, cowboy, got a dollar for some coffee?"

"Sure. Pass the favor on, buddy."

In the moonlight, Angie saw Logan slip the old man a twenty-dollar bill.

They got in the pickup and drove away.

Angie said, "You never fail to surprise me."

"What? You mean me giving that broken-down old bronc rider a dollar?"

"It wasn't a dollar; it was a twenty."

"Okay, so it was a twenty; what of it?"

"I don't think you're near as hard and ruthless as the press says you are. I saw the list of charities Logan Enterprises supports."

He made a sound of dismissal. "It's tax deductible; that's all."

"Why wouldn't you want people to know? Your image could certainly use a little polishing—"

"I said, keep quiet about it." His voice was firm; it wasn't a request, it was an order.

"Okay. But it was still a nice thing to do."

"Besides, maybe I'm just soothing my guilty conscience for all my past sins as an outlaw," Logan said, and he didn't smile.

"If you say so."

"Good girl. Now tell me where you live."

She told him, and he drove without comment until they pulled up in front of the old rooming house. "Angel, this is a pretty rough part of town for a lady alone. I'll see you get an advance so you can afford to move."

She didn't look at him. "I've already given notice here; I'm looking for another place."

He came around and opened the door, helped her out. They were standing close together and she could smell the scent of tobacco and leather and fine shaving lotion.

"Oh, don't forget your jacket."

"Sure." He put his hands on her shoulders.

Angie looked up at him and had the exhilarating but troubling feeling that he was trying to decide whether to pull her to him and kiss her. Abruptly, she had never wanted anything as much as she wanted him to crush her to his massive chest and cover her mouth with his.

However, he would regret it later, she knew, so she took a deep breath and forced herself to step away from him, take off his jacket and hold it out. "You don't need to walk me to the door."

Their hands brushed as he took the jacket and he, too, must have felt the magnetism because his rugged face mirrored emotion and indecision. "You sure?"

She'd didn't want to have to invite him in for a drink. Besides the fact that her place was small and shabby, she might be tempted to forget he was her boss and just remember that he was tall and virile and exciting. It would be too easy to fall in love with this man, and that would mean heartbreak. "No, I'll be okay." She started up the sidewalk, then turned to look back at him. "Thanks again for stepping in with Leo."

"It's the cowboy way." He tried to make light of it. In the moonlight, he looked so handsome. She could see his full lips and the tiny mole and his dark, tortured eyes.

He wanted to come in; she could see the loneliness in those eyes, yet she dare not crumble to her own desire. Tonight he might be lonely, but Monday, the CEO of Logan Enterprises would be embarrassed for hitting on an employee and would terminate her.

"Well, good night, Angel."

She looked back at him, hesitating. She fought an urge to go into his arms, kiss him. She could almost feel his powerful embrace; taste the heat of his mouth. She wanted to run her hands through that black hair, put her face against that broad shoulder. "Good night, Mr. Logan, and thank you again for dinner and rescuing me."

She turned and almost ran up the sidewalk. Behind her, it seemed a long time before she heard him start his engine and drive away. No, he didn't drive away; he screeched his tires and roared away as if he was upset or angry.

Now what could upset a rich, successful man like John Logan?

Angie went into her cramped furnished room and closed the door, feeling hot tears gathering in her eyes. "Angie, you're going to have to quit this job," she said to herself. "You don't need the heartache John Logan can bring you."

Easier said than done, her mind argued as she got ready for bed, knowing she was facing a sleepless night. The problem was, she was beginning to care about the strange, lonely millionaire, and common sense told her this could never be. How much better off she would be to admit it now, rather than stay and risk the chance of being badly hurt.

Angie spent a sleepless night and a long, dreary Sunday. She tried to watch television and read a romance novel, but she couldn't keep her mind on either. All she could think of was the way John Logan had looked, so natural and at ease dressed like a cowboy, and the attraction she felt for him. When she finally slept Sunday night, she dreamed he was just a plain cowhand and the two of them were riding across the prairie on their Oklahoma ranch; making love in the shade of a scrub oak tree. It was as wonderful as any Western romance novel she had ever read.

Monday morning, she entered Logan Towers with her mind made up to quit the job. She would wait until Logan had a quiet moment to tell him she was leaving. However, when she got there, the phones were ringing and the fax machine had at least fifty messages from over the weekend. She wasn't even sure he was in his office.

Angie dug into her workload, hardly looking up. She didn't see or hear anything from inside the executive office, but she had plenty to do. Late this afternoon, she would give notice. She couldn't tell him that she might be falling in love with him; he'd probably laugh at that. At least she'd stay until Jiffy Girl found a good replacement; not just any assistant would do for this strange and hostile millionaire.

That decided, she ignored her rumbling stomach, trying to

keep her mind on her work. If she'd lose a little weight, maybe she could find another job.

Angie was deep into sorting a pile of invitations to a dozen social functions when Renquist entered her office, staggering under the weight of a big dusty box he dropped on her desk. "Someone found this in an old company warehouse, with Logan's name on it. You'd better ask him what to do with it."

She nodded coolly, remembering how rude the man had been to her when she came for the interview. "I'll ask him."

"He's a strange one, isn't he?" Renquist volunteered.

She wondered what he'd think if Renquist knew about the part-time job at the amusement park, but she only shrugged. "I don't know what you mean. Mr. Logan may be a little different, but he's under a lot of pressure, I'm sure."

"I've worked here for years," Renquist lowered his voice, "and you know what? Logan never seems to age a day. I think when he disappears, he goes to Hollywood for a nip and tuck, if you know what I mean."

"So what?" Angie felt suddenly protective of Logan. "Lots of people who are successful have had plastic surgery. I'd have liposuction myself if I could afford it."

Renquist grinned, started to say something, then seemed to see the warning in her blue eyes about making a joke at her expense. "I think maybe he goes to Switzerland and gets those goat hormone shots to keep him young—"

"That doesn't sound like Logan to me," Angie said, her tone icy, "and anyway, it's not our business."

"It certainly isn't."

They both started and gasped, looking toward Logan's office doorway. The big man himself stood there, glowering at them, his rugged face as dark and threatening as a thunder cloud.

Chapter Four

"Mr. Logan." Renquist gave him a timid, fake smile. "I didn't know you were there."

"Obviously! You're fired, Renquist. Clean out your desk."

"But—"

"End of discussion," Logan said. "Let Mrs. Newland get on with her work and you get out of my building."

Renquist hesitated, as if attempting to decide whether to beg for his job, but the mogul went back into his office and slammed the door.

"Damn that uppity Injun!" Renquist snarled. The little man turned and stalked out of Angie's office.

Jiminy Christmas. She hoped Logan understood she hadn't bad-mouthed him. He must have to put up with a lot of hate and envy from backbiting people. Angie sighed and surveyed the big dusty box Renquist had dumped on her desk. Could they be important files? She put the phones on hold and ignored the clicking fax machine for a few minutes to dig through the box. To her surprise, it was full of tattered newspaper clippings about the Logan dynasty. They came from newspapers around the world and most were so old, they were yellowed and brittle. Some of them actually fell to pieces in her hands.

Curious, she laid the fragments on her desk, piecing the oldest of them together so she could read it. The newspaper dated back to the Gay Nineties. Its photo was primitive and dim, but the resemblance was there. The headline read:

JOHNNY LOGAN STRIKES GOLD IN THE KLONDIKE!
RUSH TO THE ALASKAN SLOPES STARTS!

Another, dating back to April 1912 read:

RICH FINANCIER SURVIVES SINKING OF Titanic!

There was a photo of a man identified as John Logan II, Logan's great-great-grandfather, on the dock in New York City, being interviewed about how the luxury ship had hit an iceberg. The resemblance was amazing, even down to the tiny mole on the left side of the mouth.

Angie dug through the news clippings, fascinated. There was one from the 1930s about how John Logan III had survived the fiery *Hindenberg* dirigible disaster. The photo showed John Logan's great-grandfather talking to reporters about how he was just returning from overseas business when the massive dirigible caught fire and exploded. Amazing how much the Logan men all looked alike.

"This family must be the luckiest people in the world," she thought, and then paused on the next clipping.

The family luck had run out. This newspaper was from the early 1940s. The headline read:

LOGAN LUCK RUNS OUT! NOW IT CAN BE REVEALED!

John Logan V had revealed that his oil pioneer father, John Logan IV and his wife had disappeared under mysterious cir-

cumstances in Europe. The son was quoted as saying he sus-
pected the Nazis had killed the pair at the height of World War
II and destroyed the bodies because the oil giant had refused
to sell them strategic fuel needed for their war efforts. The son,
John Logan V, who had lived out most of the war in hiding in
Europe, would now take over the Logan empire.

There was a photo of the missing man and the son, John
Logan V. "Amazing family resemblance," Angie said aloud,
"even to the little mole on the left side of the mouth."

Finally, there was a clipping from the mid-Eighties, telling
that John Logan V and his wife, a European heiress, had been
sailing alone and were lost at sea when their yacht sank. Their
son, John Logan VI, whom most sources did not even know
existed, would be returning from his ranch in Argentina to take
control of the family empire.

"Poor Mr. Logan. He doesn't have anyone either," she said.

"What the hell are you doing?"

Angie jumped at the angry voice behind her and turned to
face the executive himself, standing in the doorway.

"I—someone sent over a box of old newspapers from a
warehouse. I was sorting through them—"

"Snooping, you mean?" He strode over to tower above her.

"That's it! I quit!" Angie stood up and reached into the
bottom drawer of the desk for her purse. It was heavy. Damn,
she'd forgotten she'd stuck Father's coin collection in her purse,
intending to go by the bank and rent a safety deposit box. "I
was trying to do my job, Mr. Logan, and you are the most
suspicious, distrusting—"

"Where are you going?" He reached out and grabbed her
arm.

She tried to pull away from him, but he was as strong as he
was big. "What does it look like? I'm quitting! You think
everyone is out to get you. You're paranoid, Mr. Logan; I
actually feel sorry for you!"

He let go of her. "Look, let's talk about this. Maybe I was

too hasty." He sounded almost humble, which seemed most unusual for John Logan.

"I don't think we can work together." Angie shook her head. "Maybe you'd be better off with another assistant." She started for the door.

"Hey, I—I blew up; okay? Don't go."

Surprised, Angie paused, looking back at him. John Logan evidently didn't know how to apologize. His shoulders sagged, and he looked vulnerable and weary.

"I don't know," she said uncertainly.

"Look, I was upset at the sight of all those news clips. There's some pretty unhappy memories there."

She had had tragedy in her life, too. "I can understand where you're coming from."

He nodded. "Renquist see those?"

What a strange question.

Angie shook her head. "No, just the box. Judging from the dust on the top layer, no one has opened it in a long time."

"Good." He pulled out the big gold pocket watch. "Shred them and then ring down for my limo. There's a meeting of some oil men and they'd like me to offer some advice."

Angie took a deep breath. "Shred them? But Mr. Logan, don't you want to look through them? There's a lot of personal history and—"

"I said shred them. Never know what old family skeletons might surface that would give the tabloids a field day." His voice was as cold as his eyes.

Her instincts told her to turn and go out the door, but something seemed to hold her back; something deep inside told her she could not walk away from this man. She felt obligated to stay, even as she had felt somehow compelled to apply for this job. She came back to her desk. "I don't think there's anything in this box that might cause you trouble; I looked the clippings over pretty close."

"You did?" He sounded upset. "Look, let me have that box."

"I can shred them if you wish," Angie argued, a little annoyed, "if you'd trust me to—"

"Angel, I don't trust anyone." He picked up the box. "That's how men who make it to the top and stay there survive."

You poor, miserable SOB, Angie thought, but she didn't say it. "All right, sir. I'll ring down for your limo."

"Thanks, Angel." He gave her a long, thoughtful look as he went into his office carrying the box. She got up to close the door behind him, watching as he began to run the old newspapers through the shredder by his desk. *What on earth did he think was in there that might cause him trouble? The man was paranoid.*

Angie returned to her desk and dialed Logan's driver. Logan didn't come through her office, but she knew he had a private elevator. It was noon, and she ate the salad she had brought and thought about the steak Logan had bought her Saturday night. Today he acted as if none of that had ever happened. Hours later, she thought she heard him come into his office. She didn't see him for the rest of the day.

The early morning sun shone brightly on her desk when she stood up and flexed her muscles, then went to the window. She hadn't slept well last night. Angie looked down at the traffic. Below her, an expensive, sleek gray sportscar pulled into the Logan Towers drive. A tall man dressed in black stepped out of the car, handed the keys to the doorman, turned toward the building, paused and looked up. His gaze seemed to lock on Angie's and she shivered. Even from here, there was something cold and calculating about the man.

"That car must have cost a bundle," she said aloud and returned to her work. The buzzer on her desk went off, and someone from Security said, "A Mr. Nick Diablo on his way up to see Mr. Logan."

"All right; I'll buzz him through."

A long minute passed before she heard the outside buzzer. She pushed a button to open the big walnut doors. It was the man she'd seen on the street below, and something about him sent a chill through her. Her first thought was that she'd finally met a gangster or a professional gambler. He wore an expensive black suit and Italian loafers. With the suit, he wore a scarlet silk shirt, open at the throat, with several heavy gold chains around his neck.

"Hello, honey. Tell Johnny I'm here, will you?" The stranger ran a well-manicured finger across his neat mustache.

"My name is not 'honey.' " Angie did not smile. He was handsome in a greasy, dangerous sort of way, his eyes as black and hard as obsidian. "Do you have an appointment?"

She stood up, her shadow from the bright morning sun slanting across him. Odd; he didn't seem to throw a shadow of his own.

"I don't need an appointment. We're old friends. Just tell him, okay?" Diablo smiled at her and checked his wristwatch. It was expensive gold, Angie noted, with diamonds marking the hours. He also wore a gold and diamond pinkie ring on a soft, manicured hand and reeked of too much aftershave lotion.

Angie punched the intercom, wondering how long it would take to get Security up here if this guy was a crackpot. Then she remembered that Logan carried a gun, that old-fashioned Colt. She also knew Logan could handle himself in a fistfight. "Mr. Logan? A Mr. Diablo to see you."

The intercom came on. "Who?"

"A Mr. Diablo," Angie said and looked the man over again with a frown, lowering her voice to a whisper. "You want me to call Security?"

The stranger leaned on her desk and smiled. "Oh, honey, I don't think Johnny will want you to do that. Tell him Nick is

here, and we've got a contract to renegotiate; he'll remember.''
Diablo's mouth smiled, but his hard eyes did not.

Mafia, Angie thought. *Logan's mixed up with the mob.* "Mr.
Logan, did you hear that? A Mr. Nick Diablo to see you.''

Logan opened the office door, his dark face puzzled and
annoyed. "Diablo? I don't know any—''

"Hello, Johnny. Long time no see,'' the oily stranger said.
She watched Logan's eyes as he ignored the outstretched
hand. First they were puzzled; then they widened in surprise
as he finally seemed to recognize the stranger. He actually
paled and took a deep breath. If he hadn't been clutching the
door, he might have fainted. Angie felt stunned. She had never
expected anyone could frighten Logan so. For a long moment,
the two men looked into each other's eyes.

Angie looked from one man to the other. "Mr. Logan, if
you'd like me to call Security—''

"Oh, I don't think that's necessary.'' The stranger grinned.
"Do you, Johnny?''

The color came back to Logan's face and he shook his head.
"No, of course not. Come in and we'll talk. Angel, see that
we're not disturbed.''

"Angel?'' Nick Diablo laughed and winked at her. "That's
funny, considering. . . .''

"Shut up, Nick.'' Logan made a gesture, as if to discourage
the stranger from saying more. Diablo followed John Logan
into his office and the door closed behind them.

The hair raised on the back of Angie's neck. She didn't like
the stranger's looks, and his appearance had brought fear to
Logan's eyes. Logan had struck her as a man not afraid of
anything, but he'd paled at the sight of this mobster type. Was
Logan in any danger? Was this why he carried a pistol? What
should Angie do to aid her boss? She left the intercom on and
listened in. If Logan needed help, she wanted to be able to
alert Security immediately.

Holding her breath, Angie leaned close to the intercom to catch every word.

"So, Johnny, you don't seem very pleased to see me."

Logan's voice was angry and annoyed. "I didn't expect to ever see you again."

"Why not? We've got a contract, remember?"

"But the time ran out several years ago; I figured the contract was null and void now." Logan sounded apprehensive.

Nick Diablo laughed. "You must not have read the fine print; there's always fine print in my contracts."

"I'll break it, then. I've got the best lawyers—"

"No, *I've* got the best lawyers," Diablo retorted. "Everyone knows that. You could at least offer me a drink."

There was the sound of a crystal decanter being opened. "All right, we'll have a drink. As far as I'm concerned, you're too late; we have no contract. You should have come to renew seven years ago when it was up for renegotiation."

"I was too busy." Diablo didn't sound concerned. "Business is very good; almost more than I can handle. And with Hollywood, Washington, D.C. and the rest of the world eager to do business, it's easy to forget a due date. Remember, Johnny, you wouldn't have this rich lifestyle and all that goes with it, if it wasn't for me."

"Cut the small talk." Logan sounded upset and seemed to be pacing the floor. "What is it you want?"

"Well, to ask whether you want to sign again, of course."

She thought she heard Logan sigh, and when he finally spoke, he sounded very weary and full of regret. "Do I have a choice?"

"Of course you do; we all make choices that set our course in life. I figured it's a done deal; you wouldn't want to lose this great life you have."

"Sometimes I think it's not so great." Logan sounded bitter, resigned; maybe even a little scared.

Diablo laughed. "On the other hand, you know the alternative."

"No, not that. I—I'm afraid to die. I'll sign."

The mob. The mob was going to kill Logan if he didn't hold up his end of some contract. Angie debated whether to call Security, then decided this wasn't something they could deal with without the news media hearing about it. Bad publicity could send Logan Enterprises's stock tumbling on Wall Street.

"Smart boy!" Diablo said. "Now, to do this right, you'll have to go back."

"Back?" Logan sounded startled.

"Where you signed the original. That way, if you should change your mind and decide not to renew—"

"Are you nuts?" Logan's voice rose as he lashed out, "Of course I'll sign again; anybody would."

"Good." The sound of a chair scraping, as if Nick Diablo was getting to his feet. "Thanks for the drink, Johnny. I'll see you at the exact time and place."

Angie heard the door open and reached to flip off the intercom as the sleazy stranger came out of Logan's office. Mr. Logan didn't come out. The man sauntered over and leaned on Angie's desk, grinning. "How about a drink when you get off work?"

Angie bristled. "I don't think so."

"Hey, honey, I could do things for you; I know people in Hollywood."

"Get lost," Angie said.

He wasn't smiling now. "You're making a big mistake, sweetheart. I've got more money and power than Johnny Logan; in fact, I *own* Johnny Logan."

Was her attraction to Logan so very apparent that even a sleazeball like this could see it? "Mr. Logan doesn't seem like the type to do business with you."

Diablo grinned, and the scent of his shaving lotion was overwhelming; like a fancy whorehouse, maybe. "You'd just be surprised who does business with me, sweets. What would tempt you? Whatever anyone wants, I can get . . . for a price."

"I want you to get out of my office."

"Don't play hard to get with me, doll." Diablo winked at her and fingered his penciled mustache. "Everyone has her price. What's yours?"

"Get out of here before I call Security."

He grinned. "I'm turned on by a woman who's hard to tempt, but sooner or later, I'll get you, sweetheart." He sauntered out of the office. Funny, with the morning sun slanting through the giant windows and shining on him, he still didn't throw a shadow across the white marble floor.

Angie realized she was shaking. She went to the window and looked down at the street. In a few minutes, she saw Diablo get into the shiny gray sports car and pull away. Whoever that man was, he was rich, powerful and evil. She went back to her desk and sat down, wondering what to do next. She was hungry, and it was hours yet to lunch time. She thought about running downstairs to get some no-fat yogurt on her break. Or maybe she needed to stick around in case Logan wanted her to call the F.B.I. or something.

She punched the intercom. "Mr. Logan?"

No answer.

Alarmed, she got up and knocked on his office door. "Mr. Logan?"

"Come in, damn it!"

She stuck her head around the door. "I—I'm sorry to disturb you, but I was about to take a coffee break and thought I'd better see if you were all right."

"Now, why wouldn't I be?" He didn't look all right. He still looked pale, and he had a tall tumbler of bourbon in his hand. And that hand trembled.

It alarmed her that he was drinking this early. "I was concerned about that fellow who was just here."

"Forget about that," Logan snapped. "You never saw him."

"If you say so."

He looked ghastly as he gulped his drink.

Angie hesitated. "Are you sure you don't want me to call the F.B.I. or something?"

"They can't do anything; he's too powerful. I was crazy and desperate or I never would have . . ." His voice trailed off and he looked up at her keenly. "How much of that conversation did you hear?"

She'd never been a very good liar. Angie bit her lip. "All of it. I left the intercom on, thinking you might need me to call Security if things got out of hand."

He patted his shoulder holster. "I had my pistol, remember?" Then he laughed without humor. "Trouble is, with Nick Diablo, a weapon isn't much good."

She thought about the whole powerful crime family that must back a gangster.

"Look, Angel, I'm going to have to go on a business trip."

"That contract—?"

"Don't interrupt, just listen," he ordered, looking off as if his mind was far away. "I'll be gone until after the first week of October."

He looked so worried, her heart went out to him. "Mr. Logan, if there's anything I can do—"

"Nobody can do anything," Logan whispered. "He owns me. I've got no choice; not if I want to live."

"You're exaggerating," Angie said. "Surely the Justice Department or someone—"

"They'd lock me up in an insane asylum if I told them about this." Logan paced the floor in his expensive cowboy boots, his dark eyes wild with emotion.

"No, I'll be a witness," Angie said. "I'll tell them what I've heard."

He stopped and turned to face her. "That's right; you know everything."

She nodded, hoping to comfort him, give him a feeling of support, though in truth, Angie didn't feel she knew much of anything about either Logan or his business deals.

"I've got to go up to my ranch overnight before I take that business trip," Logan said after a long moment. "Why don't you come with me and bring all that paperwork along? Maybe we can get some work done up there, away from these damned phones and fax machines."

She opened her mouth to say no. The last thing she needed was to be alone with John Logan, not with the attraction she was feeling for him. Yet he seemed so vulnerable and in such emotional turmoil. She forgot that only hours ago, she had been considering quitting this job. Instead, she found herself saying, "I can do that, I guess."

"Good!" Logan said, avoiding her eyes. "But don't tell anyone you're going, or anything else; security, you know."

"Okay," she said uncertainly. This was against her better judgment. Everything in her told her to quit and walk out; let someone else deal with Logan Enterprises's shady mobster dealings. But he looked so vulnerable and alone.

"It'll be all right," she said softly.

He sighed. "It hasn't been all right in a long time."

"We'll go up to your ranch where you can think straight and you'll figure out some way out of this mess."

Logan watched her. "I wish I could believe that, Angel." Her blue eyes were an open book, like looking into her innocent soul. But she knew too much; enough to destroy him, maybe, if she put it all together—the news clippings, and what she'd overheard with Nick Diablo. Much as he wanted to, Logan couldn't trust her with his secret; he'd never dared trust anybody. Sooner or later, DNA or fingerprints or even something as simple as Social Security records might trip him up, but he'd been so very careful up to now. The girl seemed smarter and sassier than most. She might put two and two together and he didn't dare risk it.

No, much as he regretted it, for his own safety, he had to do it. Angelica Newland was going to go with him up to the endless rolling prairie of northeastern Oklahoma, where there'd be no witnesses. *And she wasn't coming back.*

Chapter Five

Angie had a gut feeling she shouldn't be getting involved. But she thought only of John Logan, whether he was in serious trouble with the mob, and her undeniable attraction to him. Logan packed a bag while she waited. Then they went down in his private elevator and got his black pickup truck without anyone seeing them.

They made a quick run by her place.

As she got out, Logan said, "Bring a bathing suit; it may be warm enough to swim."

Angie hesitated, thinking she didn't want him to see her in a bathing suit. "All I've got is an old one."

"That's better yet," Logan said. "You won't have to worry about getting it muddy."

"Muddy?"

He nodded. "There's a big lake on the ranch the Indians call Bottomless Lake."

He pulled out the big gold watch with a worried frown, and Angie took the hint and hurried to her room. She packed an overnight bag while he waited in his truck and in minutes, they were on their way, headed up I-35 toward Logan's ranch.

"Jiminy Christmas!"

"What's the matter?" He looked over at her in alarm.

"Oh, nothing really." Angie shrugged. "I brought my dad's antique coin collection this morning, intending to put it in a safety deposit box for safekeeping. It's still in the bottom of my purse."

He looked relieved. "That's not much of a problem. You can do that when we get back."

"Yes, but the coins are heavy," Angie grumbled. "Oh, well, I guess you're right; it's no big deal."

She tried to make chitchat as they drove, but Logan seemed preoccupied and worried. He responded only with an occasional grunt and a sideways glance, as if he was wrestling with some tough decision. He put a CD of Oklahoma's own Reba McEntire in the player. Angie settled down to do her own thinking as the prairie whizzed past. She sneaked a look at him, his dark brow wrinkled with worry, and wondered if he might try to seduce her tonight.

Get real, Angie, she scolded herself. *This guy is strictly business, with a lot of big stuff on his mind because of Nick Diablo. If he just wanted a woman, with his money, he could have cover models and cattle heiresses lining up to go to bed with him. All it would take would be a phone call.*

"You hungry?" he asked suddenly.

She had learned not to be coy with this man; he liked straightforward women. "I could eat a bite."

They were passing rows of fast-food places with parking lots full of cars and eighteen-wheelers. "Uh, these places are crowded and it's early yet," Logan said without looking at her. "We can fix lunch when we get to the ranch."

"Sure." *Was he afraid of being spotted by a hit man, or just afraid of being seen with her?*

In less than three hours, they were headed up a country road and then down a long gravel drive to a rambling ranch house built of native stone. A collie dog came barking to meet them.

"How many ranch hands do you have?" Angie asked as Logan stopped in front of the place.

"Right now, only old Juan and his wife, but I called ahead and told them they could have a couple of days off. I wanted complete seclusion for us to work." He got out of the truck, greeting the dog with enthusiasm. "Hey, Lassie, old girl! How have you been?"

Angie got out of the truck, laughing. "Lassie? Is that the best you could do?"

He turned from playing with the dog, favoring her with a rare smile. "It's as good a name as any. The dog belongs to Juan. With all my travels, owning a dog is a bother." He sounded a bit wistful.

Now he grabbed the bags out of the back of the pickup. "Come on in. We'll have a bite and then go riding. You did say you ride, didn't you?"

Angie followed him. "Not really well. I could use the practice."

"Then you'll have to be careful." He threw a warning back over his broad shoulder, "Some of the trails through the hills can be dangerous; people have been killed on them."

"Thanks for the comforting news," Angie said.

They paused in the big main room of the ranch house, and Angie looked around, awestruck. "This is what you call a small place?"

The room had soaring ceilings, leather furniture and a big stone fireplace. A rack of deer antlers hung over the mantel.

Logan shrugged, his gaze on her reaction. "It'll do. I don't get up here nearly as often as I would like."

"I love it!" Angie sighed. "I always wanted to live on a ranch."

"Here, I'll put your stuff in your room."

Angie followed him down the hall. Her room looked comfortable, with a stone fireplace and Navaho rugs on pinewood floors. "This is great."

"I was afraid you'd expect something more posh."

She shook her head. "A ranch is my idea of heaven." Without thinking, she blurted, "You ever bring another woman up here?"

"No." She could see in his dark eyes that he was telling the truth. She didn't know if that was good or not. As they stood there in silence, she was abruptly aware that they were in a bedroom, with a big comfortable bed plainly evident. His expression told her he was aware of it, too.

Angie cleared her throat. "If you'll point me to the kitchen, I'll see what I can throw together for lunch."

That broke the tension and he led her back through the big living room to a large, country-style kitchen. "Can you cook? Most girls today can't."

"Sure." She didn't tell him that her mother had insisted on Angie taking Home Ec in high school because since she wasn't as pretty or vivacious as Barbara, Mother was afraid Angie would have to count on homemaking skills to land a husband.

"Good." He nodded. "While you throw something together, I'll change and saddle up a couple of horses, bring them around to the house."

Jiminy. what could she cook? After Logan left the kitchen, Angie searched the refrigerator and cupboards. By the time he got back, she had scrambled eggs with melted cheese and hot jalapeño peppers, and homemade biscuits were baking in the oven.

She noted he wore faded jeans, a Western shirt, the holster and pistol and well-worn boots on his small feet. That brought back her grandmother's saying and she flushed.

"What's the matter?"

"Nothing; heat from the oven. Don't you ever go anywhere without a gun?"

He shrugged. "I feel naked without it. Besides, we might run across a big snake."

"That's a pretty apt description." She thought about Nick Diablo as she dished up the food.

"What?"

"Never mind." If he wasn't worrying about the sleazy mobster, she didn't want to remind him.

Logan looked pleased as he sat down. "You're really an old-fashioned girl, aren't you?"

"I suppose I am," Angie said as she poured them each a glass of milk and watched with satisfaction as he dug into the food.

"Soon as we eat, we'll go for a ride up Logan's Point," he said and abruptly looked troubled. "Then, if you're up to it, there's a lake, too. You bring a suit?"

She nodded, still dreading the thought of him seeing her in a swimsuit. *What was bothering Logan?* He didn't lose that troubled expression the whole time they were eating. He kept glancing at her as if he was struggling with a tough choice.

When they finished, she stacked the dishes in the sink and changed into jeans and sneakers. She didn't own a pair of boots anymore. They went outside into the warm early afternoon. A pair of black-and-white paint horses stood tied to a hitching rail out by the kitchen door.

"What beautiful horses," Angie said and stroked the neck of the mare.

Logan actually smiled. There was no doubt he was fond and proud of these horses. He patted the big paint's muzzle. "The first John Logan owned a paint stallion called Crazy Quilt," he said. "We've had some of that stallion's descendants in the family ever since. You need a boost?"

"Well, now that you mention it, yes," she admitted.

He came around and checked her saddle. "Wouldn't want you to fall," he muttered. "Logan's Point is a bad place to have something go wrong with your gear."

They were standing there, inches apart, Angie with her back pressed up against the mare. Logan looked down at her, standing so close, she could smell the faint scent of expensive cologne. For a long moment, she thought he was going to take her in his arms, and if he did, she didn't think she would be able to control her own response if he kissed her. They stared into each other's eyes, as if loathe to break the magnetic feeling between them.

Lassie came trotting around the house, barking and wagging her tail. That broke the tension.

"Okay, old girl." Logan laughed. "We're ready to go, too."

Angie hesitated. "I—I'm probably heavier than most of the women you—"

"Well, I should hope so. Today's beauties are too skinny." He boosted Angie up into her saddle easily, surprising her again with his strength. For a rich executive, he was all muscle and power. They didn't make men like this one much anymore, she thought.

Logan swung up on his big paint and reined it around to follow the barking dog. He had lifted Angie as if she was a petite and delicate girl. Funny, around Logan, she *felt* petite.

He rode out at a walk and she followed him, amazed at how naturally he sat a horse, as if he'd been born to it.

"Be careful," he threw back over his shoulder, "you're wearing sneakers, not boots, and if your foot should slip through the stirrup and something spooked your horse, you might get dragged to death."

"Thanks for the warning; I'll be careful."

They set out, following a trail away from the house and up through the low hills of the picturesque northeastern Oklahoma countryside, Lassie cavorting and barking ahead of them. Logan glanced back at her now and then, looking troubled. "Remember, we're all alone on the ranch today," he warned as she rode up beside him, "and miles from town. If an accident happened out here, you'd just be out of luck."

Angie laughed. "Jiminy Christmas! Why are you so preoccupied with accidents? I figure you can handle any emergency.
Besides, I told you I'd be careful."

"Did you tell anyone where you were going?"

She shook her head. "You told me not to. I don't think we're
in any danger of being followed by Nick Diablo and his bunch,
and we made sure nobody saw us leave Logan Towers."

He seemed to sigh in relief and took off up the trail at a
slow lope. Maybe she had eased his mind, Angie thought. He
might not have even told his ranch foreman he was coming or
bringing a guest, so unless someone had tailed them, no one
in the whole world knew they were here. And this giant ranch
seemed pretty isolated.

Angie gave herself over to the pleasure of the ride. There
was something about the scent of a horse, the creak of a saddle
and the warm early fall afternoon that all blended into a
delightful day.

Now they were headed up into some steep hill trails with a
lot of loose rock. Angie began to feel a little apprehensive. In
truth, she was out of practice, and this steep trail was taxing
her riding ability. Logan, expert rider that he was, was loping
up the trail ahead of her. Angie gritted her teeth and hung on.

The trail twisted so that it became a narrow ribbon of loose
rock overlooking a shallow canyon. Angie felt perspiration
break out on her face as she looked to the side and realized
that with one false step she could tumble off the mare and over
the edge of the bluff. The canyon was deep enough for the fall
to kill her. She wasn't about to admit defeat and tell Logan
she wasn't up to riding this fast. He'd think less of her, maybe,
if she did, and suddenly, what he thought mattered a lot to her.

Logan loped on ahead of her, not looking back, although
surely he must realize a girl with limited riding ability and
wearing sneakers was in a precarious position on this steep
trail. One false step by the mare and . . . no, she must not think
about that. A few hundred yards up ahead, she could see a

level pasture. If she could reach that area, Angie would be safe enough.

Even as she thought that, her saddle twisted and Angie fell. She screamed as she went over the lip of the canyon, grabbing desperately for anything to stop her fall. She caught a frail wild cedar branch growing out of the rock. It wasn't going to hold her, she knew that. In a few seconds, it would come out by the roots and she'd tumble to her death.

A loose girth. That fact flashed through her mind as she struggled to hang on. *How could that be? Logan himself had checked her saddle before she mounted.*

Above her, she heard Lassie barking frantically, and then Logan appeared, loose rock showering down around her as he stood on the lip of the little canyon. He didn't do anything, only peered down at her.

He must be frozen by horror, she thought, and she reached out a hand toward him. "Mr. Logan, please. . . ."

At that point, he hesitated a long moment, then scrambled partway down the rocks, reaching down to her. "I'll grab your hand, Angel; then you let go of the bush, okay?"

For a split second, she remembered the loose girth. *No, he wouldn't do anything like that.* She nodded. "I trust you, Mr. Logan."

He swore under his breath, as if he was angry about something. Then his big hand closed over her small one and she was no longer afraid.

"All right. Let go of the tree," he said. "I've got you."

I've got you. She looked up at him, feeling the strength of his fingers. When she let go of the branch, only Logan's grip stood between her and a fatal fall.

Maybe she shouldn't trust this man, but in only a few days, he had come to mean so much to her. She gazed into his eyes, and then she let go of the cedar limb. Now his strong grip was the only thing between her and death.

Logan hesitated a split second and she saw indecision in his dark eyes. She looked up at him, trusting him completely to save her.

He muttered a curse under his breath and then braced himself against a rock and lifted her to safety by sheer iron muscle.

Why was he so angry?

"Thanks!" she breathed. "I thought I was a goner!"

He looked annoyed, but she wasn't sure why. "I told you to be careful!"

Her spirits fell, knowing he was probably thinking about a multimillion-dollar lawsuit if she'd been hurt. "I'm sorry," Angie said. "My saddle slipped, and I don't ride as well as you do."

He didn't look at her as he strode over and checked her mare's saddle. "Damn, you're right. Sorry about that, Angel. I thought I'd tightened it, but something slipped."

"That's okay." She was ashamed that she'd even suspected he might have . . .

"You're a fiesty thing; I'll give you that." He walked to his own horse, got a canteen, then returned to her side. He poured water from the canteen over his bandanna and wiped her face ever so gently, then handed her the canteen.

The water was cold and clean and Angie drank deep.

"It was my fault," he said again, and he avoided her eyes.

"It doesn't matter." Angie shrugged. "You literally held my life in your hand; you know that?"

"Yeah, I know." He leaned against a rock and lit a slender cigarillo.

The silence was suddenly awkward. Maybe he thought she blamed him for the slipped girth. "Mr. Logan, it was no big deal."

He didn't answer.

"It's really hot, isn't it?"

Logan hesitated, then seemed to steel himself as he took a deep puff of smoke. "You feel up to a swim?"

"Well, sure, why not?"

"Now, if you don't feel like it—"

"I'm not some prissy cover model." Angie laughed.

"All right, then; you asked for it." He smoked and didn't look at her. "You a good swimmer?"

"Not really." Angie smiled. "But hey, I've got you along in case I start to drown."

He winced and ground out his smoke, carefully checking to make sure it was out to keep from starting a prairie fire. "Let's go."

Angie stepped on a big rock and mounted up. He seemed preoccupied and annoyed, she thought. No doubt she had scared him with her near brush with death.

He swung up into the saddle, looking for all the world like one of her film idols. Charles Bronson or Clint Eastwood never looked more natural on a horse. "We'll take an easier trail back to the ranch."

"Good. I wouldn't want to chance that trail twice," Angie said, relieved and still a little shaky.

With Lassie barking and chasing butterflies through the wildflowers ahead of them, they started across the rolling prairie. They rode in silence, broken only by Lassie's barking and the occasional call of a bobwhite. As for Angie she remembered again and again the feel of his big hand closing over her small one, the way his great strength had lifted her to safety.

Up ahead lay a small grove of pin oak trees. As they neared it, she saw the ground was covered with scarlet orange Indian Blanket blossoms and a riot of sunflowers.

"It's beautiful!" Angie exclaimed. "Where are we?"

Logan reined in and leaned on his saddle horn. "Our old family graveyard. This ranch was one of the first things the original John Logan bought. Reporters are always sneaking past the 'No Trespassing' signs to take photos here when they do those unauthorized articles about me."

Angie looked down at the elaborate gravestones, some of which were tilted ever so slightly. "John Logan and Little

Deer," she said aloud, and looked over at Logan with a question in her eyes.

"My great-great-great grandmother," he explained. "Johnny Logan was part Indian himself, Kiowa, and his wife was Cheyenne." He dismounted and held up his hands to Angie.

She hesitated a long moment before she slid off into his arms. They were standing so close, she could feel the heat of his big body against the suddenly erect tips of her nipples. She looked up at him and saw the building intensity of his eyes. She wanted him to kiss her; oh, how badly she wanted him to kiss her. He didn't.

Logan took a deep breath and stepped away from her. In those tight jeans, she was certain she could see the swell of his arousal. He turned to survey the graveyard.

Angie had to swallow twice before she could speak. "Such— a peaceful place."

"You think so?" Logan snorted. "I'm terrified of dying."

"Don't be silly; it's part of life. We must accept that."

"Not me." He shook his head and lit a slender cheroot with a trembling hand. "I've been too close to it."

"I have, too," Angie said.

He turned to stare at her. "What was it like?"

Angie shrugged. "It was like passing through a doorway from one room to another. I didn't feel any fear, but I couldn't go; there was something I had to return to take care of."

"What?"

"How should I know? I guess I will when the time comes to do it. Or maybe I only imagined it." Angie walked over to look at the old gravestones. Next to those were two more.

" 'John Logan II and Beloved Wife, Nellie,' " Angie read aloud. " 'John Logan III and Beloved Wife, Blanche.' Honestly, Logan, aren't there ever any girls in your family?"

"No, and I don't have any siblings, either." The dark man shook his head.

She got the hint. This was a very private, secretive man. "I didn't mean to pry."

"Then don't," he snapped.

Angie looked around at the peaceful scene. "Doesn't it give you a sense of rightness, of continuity, to think someday your son will see that you are buried here next to the others?"

Logan shuddered. "I'd do anything to keep from dying."

"You need to see a counselor," Angie blurted before she thought. "You've got a real phobia about that."

His expression turned icy. "I'm not used to employees offering personal advice."

She felt her face burn. "I'm sorry. You're right; I was out of line."

Logan shrugged. "Anyway, so far, there is no John Logan VII, so I'd better hurry and pick a wife so there'll be someone to pass this empire on to."

"You don't sound very enthused about it." Angie looked up at him.

"I'm not. If I don't marry money, I have to worry about whether the female is after mine." He leaned against a rock.

"Such a romantic you are." Angie laughed and averted her eyes, not wanting him to think she would ever presume. . . . "Too bad there's no stone for your parents and grandparents."

"Can't be helped," Logan said. "You read those old papers and know their story."

"It's still sad that you couldn't bury them here next to their ancestors," Angie said.

"Yes, isn't it? Well, let's go."

Johnny watched the blonde swing into the saddle. He didn't offer to help her. If he put his hands on her waist, he wouldn't be able to stop himself from pulling her down to the grass and mounting her in the heated wanting that had been building ever since he had first seen the voluptuous girl. She was big-breasted and softly curved, with a full mouth that begged for a man's lips. Funny, she thought she was plain.

He must not think about how much his body desired her; he must think what a danger she could be to him. He watched her mount up, turn the mare and start up the trail. Then he swung into the saddle and nudged his own horse forward, cursing himself because in a weak moment he had rescued Angelica Newland instead of letting her fall. He hadn't meant to; it was the way she had reached out to him, that plea and complete trust in those blue eyes as she put her life in his hand by letting go of that branch. Nobody had ever trusted him before.

Yet she knew too much, and he couldn't risk her putting two and two together. Well, he would have other chances today. And, of course, there were always the icy depths of Bottomless Lake.

He glanced back at the gravestones as he rode away. No one but him knew there wasn't a single body buried in this graveyard.

But after today, there would be.

Chapter Six

Angie noted that Logan seemed preoccupied as they rode back to the ranch house and put the horses away. It was the middle of the afternoon and the Oklahoma sun had turned the day hot.

"I'll put on my suit and meet you at the truck," she said.

He nodded. Logan was worried about this thing with Nick Diablo, she thought sympathetically. There just had to be something he could do to get out of that bad contract. Maybe later they could do some brainstorming and come up with a plan. She wanted to help him, though she didn't want to admit even to herself that there was any other reason besides the fact that she was a loyal employee.

Her blue bathing suit was an old one-piece and quite modest. Angie didn't go swimming often; she was too self-conscious. She wasn't sure she had the nerve to wear the bathing suit in front of Logan, but she didn't know how to turn down the swim invitation without making an issue of it. She put on a short terry beach robe and thongs, and headed out to the truck.

Logan was waiting there in faded cutoffs and tennis shoes, his old chambray shirt open to the waist revealing a broad, tanned chest. Just looking at him made unbidden thoughts come to her mind. He looked lithe and strong; more like a cowboy or athlete than a rich exec. What would it feel like to cuddle up to that muscular body? She felt her face flush and turned away so she wouldn't have to explain.

"You sure you want to do this?" He cleared his throat nervously.

He'd already seen her in her bathing suit, so the worst was over as far as Angie was concerned. "If you don't want to—"

"No, it—it's a great idea. I've got a cooler of soda and beer in the back of the truck," he said and didn't look at her.

Lassie came bounding around the corner of the ranch house and jumped up into the back of the pickup, barking loudly.

"This will be fun," Angie said as Logan opened the door for her.

He gave a grunt as he got in and started the pickup, and they drove away.

"Where is the lake?"

He frowned. "Up in an isolated part of the ranch. Some of the local Indians say it's almost bottomless; anybody drowns, they might not ever find the body."

Angie smiled. "Well, I've already cheated death once today; I feel lucky."

He didn't say anything. They drove to the lake, several miles from the house.

Lassie jumped down the minute the truck stopped, barking and chasing ducks along the shore.

Logan came around and opened her door, not looking at her. He busied himself getting the cooler out of the truck bed. "There's a floating platform out in the middle of the lake. I thought we might swim out there and sunbathe."

Angie slipped off the terry robe. The lake was bigger than she had expected and it looked black, signifying its depth. She walked over and leaned to put one hand in the water. "It's really cold; spring-fed, I'll bet."

"Yes," he agreed. "Good place to get a cramp."

She shielded her eyes with her hand and squinted against the sun, looking out across the water at the floating platform. "It looks like a long way."

"Not so far," he assured her, peeling off his shirt and tennis shoes.

What a chest, Angie thought. The muscles rippled under his brown skin. He must have a personal trainer, she thought. Abruptly, she pictured him naked, and her face flushed.

"Are you getting a sunburn?" he asked.

"Uh, no."

Logan seemed preoccupied and troubled. "You ready for that swim?"

"You're not going to wear your pistol?" Angie teased.

"No, I'm not going to need it for what I've got to do this time. Besides," he forced a smile, "it would get wet. Last one there is a rotten egg," he challenged and made a running dive into the lake.

"No fair!" Angie forgot her hesitancy, threw off her thongs, waded out into the cold water and began to swim toward the distant platform. The water was so deliciously icy and exhilarating, it took her breath away.

Ahead of her, Logan was cutting through the water with strong, clean strokes. Behind them on the shore line, Lassie ran up and down, chasing frogs and barking in the midafternoon sun.

Ahead of her, Logan had reached the platform and was hanging onto the side, looking back at her. "You coming, slowpoke?"

She didn't have enough breath to answer, just kept swimming ahead. For a long moment, the space between her and the platform seemed a million miles. *I'm in trouble,* Angie thought as her breath came shorter, but she was stubbornly determined that Logan wasn't going to have to rescue her twice. She kept swimming, though more slowly now. She was close enough to see the inscrutable expression of Logan's dark face and wondered if he could tell she was having a difficult time of it? Obviously not, because he only watched her without expression, not offering to swim out and assist her.

Angie wasn't sure she would make the last few yards. She was out of breath and getting muscle cramps. *Bottomless Lake*, she remembered. *Some bodies never found.* John Logan didn't need an accidental drowning to add to his many problems. She exerted her last bit of energy and swam up to him, caught his arm.

"For a minute there," Logan said, "I thought you were in trouble."

She wasn't about to admit it, though she was gasping with the effort of the swim. "If you thought so, why didn't you offer to help?"

They were both treading water, close enough to touch. "I thought your pride would be hurt if I did," he said. "I figured you wanted to make it on your own."

The current pushed them so that abruptly, their bodies touched all the way down. Angie saw the sudden intensity in his dark eyes, felt his maleness go rigid. He slipped his arms around her and pulled her against him, his eyes looking down into hers. Angie held her breath, feeling her nipples brushing his bare, brown chest through her bathing suit. For a long moment, she thought he was going to kiss her. She felt his strong arms around her, and it occurred to her suddenly that if he so chose, he could hold her under easily.

"A penny for your thoughts," he whispered.

Was she crazy? Logan had no reason to drown a mere office girl. That thing with the saddle really had been an accident. "I was just thinking how strong you are," she said and looked deep into his eyes.

"And I was just thinking how fragile you are," he answered, "and that you don't swim very well."

What an odd remark. For a long moment, they looked into each other's eyes and she wondered why he had said that? "But you're a great swimmer, aren't you, Mr. Logan? So I'm not worried."

"Don't start counting on me, Angel; I've learned you can't count on anyone but yourself in this life." He heaved a great sigh and pulled away from her, climbed the hanging ladder up onto the platform. He looked down at her a long moment, then reached down to lift her to sit on the side.

"This is a great place to lie in the sun," he said.

And to make love, Angie thought, remembering the electrically charged moment when they had embraced in the water. Angie faced the cold fact that he was a virile man and she was the only female readily available. If he wanted to make love to her, would she let him? Lovemaking with her husband had been so dull and mechanical, she had never enjoyed it; not even once. But this man made her want to pull him down on top of her, mesh with him in a primitive, frenzied mating that she had only experienced in her dreams.

Logan lay down on his back, his arm thrown out, his engorged maleness all too apparent.

Maybe it didn't matter that he didn't really care about her. She cared about him; that was enough for Angie. She lay down next to him. She hesitated, then lay her head on his arm.

Logan started in surprise, but he didn't pull his arm away. They lay there a long moment, enjoying the feeling of the sun on their cold, wet bodies. The lake lapped rhythmically against the side of the raft. Somewhere in the distance Lassie romped and barked, and a lake bird called. This was really an isolated, peaceful spot.

"Angel?" It was a question.

Instead of answering, she turned her head and looked into

his dark, troubled eyes. "Yes, Logan." It wasn't a question; it was an answer.

Logan drew a deep intake of breath and rolled up on one elbow so that his powerful body was between her face and the bright sun. Then he kissed her, his mouth covering hers dominantly, his tongue thrusting between her lips. His big, calloused hand cupped her chin and she arched into him, returning his kiss. His hot mouth sucked her lower lip gently, then more fiercely. Angie gasped and pressed her generous breasts against his hard, naked chest. He was breathing hard, kissing her more deeply as his hand moved from her face to her throat, and then hesitantly to the top of her swimsuit.

Angie didn't object to his cupping her breast. Her nipple hardened in response to his touch. Then his big hand went under the top of her suit, running his thumb over her bare nipple. She was surprised at her pulse-pounding reaction. Never had she responded with much enthusiasm to her husband's lovemaking. Maybe Brett hadn't been very good at this, but since he'd been her first and only man, she had no basis of comparison. Logan was an expert lover; she knew from the way her body was responding to his. He had moved so that he was lying partly on her body; she could feel his swollen manhood against her bare thigh.

His fingers were caressing her breast under her bathing suit and she wanted even more. She had never reached a climax with Brett, so she wasn't even sure what it was she wanted so desperately. In her mind, they had the suits off and were making heated, passionate love on this sun-warmed platform out in the middle of an isolated lake with no witnesses but some shorebirds and a happy Collie.

His tongue played with hers as his hand stroked her breast. She reached up to grasp his muscular shoulder, encouraged him to move even more completely on top of her. His hand was now outside her suit, moving slowly down her belly. She felt the heat of his fingers on her bare thigh, even though her eyes were closed. Then his fingers slipped under the leg of the wet suit and touched her femininity.

Angie gasped and stiffened; then she spread her thighs a little more and let him stroke her there. His kisses had become even more heated, she could hear his breath coming in deep gasps and his heart pounded hard against her breast. She hadn't known there could be this much excitement to sex. More than anything in this world, she wanted him on her and in her.

About that time, her roaming hand touched a ropy scar on his upper arm and her eyes blinked open.

He seemed abruptly aware of her hand and pulled back. ''Don't touch that.''

She looked under her fingers. There was a white welt of a scar on his muscular shoulder. She had been so preoccupied with his broad chest before that, she hadn't noticed it. ''John, it doesn't matter; it's not much of a scar.''

He was obviously upset. He threw her hand off his arm and sat up. ''I was . . . up in Alaska, hunting Kodiak bears with a bunch of other guys and a guide. A big male charged out of the icy tundra. I had it in my gunsights, but I was waiting for it to get close enough to make sure I couldn't miss. The novice hunter behind me panicked and pulled the trigger; hit me instead. The noise scared off the charging bear, but I nearly died out there on the ice before they could get a medic flight in.''

''You didn't need to tell me,'' Angie said softly. ''I didn't ask.''

''No, but you wanted to know.''

He had a perfect, muscular body except for that jagged white scar.

The magic had ended. Logan had withdrawn into himself; she could tell by his stiff body and the way he pulled away from her. Now she might never know if she would have stopped him if his advances had gone any further. She could still taste the heat of his mouth in her memory, feel his hard, supple body against hers. "I'm sorry I mentioned it," Angie said, and she meant it.

He shrugged. "At least you brought a halt to this. I forgot myself; you're an employee. I had no right to take advantage of you."

"You weren't taking advantage of me!" She was almost angry now as she sat up, disappointed and frustrated. She wanted the fulfillment of what his mouth and hands and body had been promising. "I guess what you're really afraid of is that I might sue you for sexual harassment."

"That, too."

"Jiminy Christmas, I don't believe this!" Her face was burning; she had almost thrown herself at the man and he'd backed off. Was it because she had broken the magic when she noted the bad scar, or was it because she wasn't slender and beautiful? "I'm going back to the truck."

"You're still too tired," he warned. "You're liable to drown. I didn't think you'd make it the first time."

"Just watch me, mister!" Recklessly, Angie dove off into the water and came up gulping cold water and coughing.

Lassie stood wagging her tail and barking on the distant shore. Angie set her sights on the black pickup truck and started swimming.

She was less than halfway there and beginning to slow. *Bottomless Lake,* she thought. *If I drown here, they might never find my body.* Her lungs felt as if they were on fire with her efforts and each arm seemed to weigh a ton as she lifted it to make another stroke. She wasn't going to make it. Her head went under once and she came up coughing and gasping for air, her body a leaden weight that seemed to be pulling her under.

Angie managed to turn and look back at Logan. He stood on the platform, watching her, his lean, dark body silhouetted against the sun. Their gazes locked and she pleaded silently with her eyes.

"Hang on, Angel, I'm coming!" He dived in and swam toward her, his strong body knifing cleanly through the dark depths. In seconds, he was beside her, his big, athletic body treading the icy water.

"You were right. I—I'm not sure I can make it," Angie gasped.

He hesitated only a split second; then he reached out and caught her arm. "Here, hang on to me; I'll get us both there."

She grabbed his shoulder, awed by the power and hard muscle of the man as he began to swim, keeping them both up as he struck out for shore. When they reached the shallow water, Angie was almost done in and she stumbled when she attempted to stand up.

He caught her and swept her up in his arms, both of them dripping wet as he carried her to shore. Brett couldn't have lifted her, but Logan acted as if she weighed nothing at all. Near the truck, he let go of her legs and she slid down his body, standing up and leaning against him. He looked down into her eyes, and for a moment the fire between them blazed again.

Logan pulled away with an oath. "Angel, I predict you're going to bring me nothing but trouble."

She looked up at him, appealing to him. "No, I won't, John; I'm on your side."

He pushed her away. "Nobody's on my side."

"Me and God," she said.

"No, least of all, God." He turned away, went to the cab of the truck, got her robe, came back and wrapped it around her. Then he returned to the truck for his Western shirt. "I must be getting soft," he muttered, so low she could barely hear him. "Two chances and I just couldn't do it."

What was he muttering about?

"John," she said, "I know you're worried sick about this gangster—"

"Who?" He paused in putting on his shirt.

"Nick Diablo."

He came back over to her. "Is that what you think he is, a gangster?"

"Isn't he?"

Logan laughed, but his eyes didn't share his amusement. He dug a thin cigarillo out of his shirt pocket and lit it with a shaking hand. "You complicate my life, Angel. In all these long, long years, I've never let a woman complicate my life."

"I don't mean to," she answered, puzzled as she pushed her wet hair away from her face.

"You're too damned innocent and unworldly."

She felt herself blush and hung her head. "Brett called me naive."

Logan made a dismissive gesture. "I never met anyone like you before. Already, you know enough to cause me lots of trouble—"

"I would never do anything to hurt you," she answered softly.

He gave her a long look; there was a glimmer of hope in it. "I almost believe that."

"Believe it, John."

"And to think I almost ... Come on, Angel, get in the truck."

"Aren't we going to swim anymore?" She tied the sash of her robe and got in while he put the cooler in the back and whistled for the dog.

"Hell no!" he roared at her. "You almost drowned; you know that? We're not riding, either."

Puzzled by his anger, she watched him toss away his smoke and slam the pickup gate behind the dog. He got in and started the truck, pulling away in a shower of gravel.

"I don't understand what you're so mad about," Angie said.

"Hush. I'm about to do something very foolish—something I'm probably going to regret."

They drove in silence back to the ranch. He got out without

looking at her. "Get dressed and get your things together," he ordered. "I'll meet you back here in about five minutes."

"But we just got here!" Angie yelled after his departing form.

"Angel, don't argue with me!" he flung back over his shoulder, "I don't intend to give myself time to change my mind!"

Angie could only blink and stare after him as he strode into the house. Lassie gamboled around her feet. "Well, puppy, it was nice knowing you. I must have done something terrible to infuriate your boss. I suppose Juan and his wife will be back soon to look after you."

With a sigh, Angie went inside to dress and pack. She put on her jeans and sneakers, tied her damp hair back into a ponytail. When she came back out to the truck, Logan stood there fully dressed in Western clothes, wearing his pistol like a gunfighter, tied down and low on his hip. His gold watch was in his hand. "Hurry up or you'll miss it."

"Miss what?" Angie didn't argue; she got in the truck. Logan put his watch in his pocket and threw their luggage in back. He got in and drove away like demons rode his coattails. He didn't say anything, just hunkered down over the steering wheel and drove like a maniac away from the ranch.

Angie didn't know what to think or say. "Does this mean I'm fired?"

"Don't even talk to me, Angel, or I might regain my senses and look after my own hide like I've always done."

"What have I done to anger you?"

He glanced sideways at her and kept driving. "You've been too damned trusting and innocent."

She was even more puzzled. "I don't know what you're talking about."

"I know that, so hush up."

They were racing along the country road, dust flying up as they passed fields of grazing cattle. The big *J.L.* brand sign hung from every fence post they passed. "Where—where are we going?"

"Don't talk to me," he cautioned. "My better judgment might take over and I'd turn this truck around, take you back and hold you under in the lake!"

She laughed at his joke, but he didn't.

Ahead of them, she saw the outline of a small town and then a weather-beaten sign: OSAGE, OKLAHOMA, WELCOMES YOU! 212 FRIENDLY PEOPLE!

Logan slowed as he drove down the sleepy town's main street. He pulled out his watch again. "You'll just make the four o'clock bus."

"Bus to where? I don't want to take a bus!"

"Angel, I'm sending you back to Oklahoma City." He pulled to the curb and looked at her. "I've got things to do and I won't put you in danger."

"But—"

"Don't talk, just listen!" He reached out and cupped her chin with one big hand. "Keep your mouth shut and don't tell anyone anything. I'll take care of business and be back in Okie City the second week of October. Then we'll see if we can do anything with this relationship."

"Business? Are you talking about Nick Diablo?"

He hesitated. "The less you know, the safer you'll be."

"But I want to go with you!" Angie protested. "Maybe I can help!"

"Call me an old-fashioned male chauvinistic pig"—he shook his head—"but I don't put women in danger."

She tried to protest, but Logan didn't answer. He was already out of the truck, putting her small suitcase on the curb. As she watched, he hurried into the small café with a faded sign outside that read: BUS TICKETS.

She wasn't going to move two inches, Angie decided, until she got some answers from John Logan. She looked down the street and saw the gray bus turn off the highway in a cloud of dust and rumble down Main Street.

Logan ran out of the café, waving the bus down. "Passenger here!"

She leaned out the pickup window and yelled, "John, I'm not going! Tell me what this is all about!"

"Angel, if I told you, you wouldn't believe me, so just go back to the city, keep your mouth shut and wait." He picked up her little suitcase, jerked her door open and grabbed her by the elbow, pulling her from the truck.

She tried to resist, but he was so much bigger and stronger than she was, he propelled her along the sidewalk toward the waiting bus even though she dug in her heels and tried to resist. Around them, curious townspeople turned to watch the drama. As Logan dragged her up to the bus she was more than a little conscious of faces pressed against the dirty windows, watching them.

The bus doors opened with a whoosh. Logan reached to put her suitcase inside and then lifted her up on the step and handed her the ticket.

"Angel, I'll see you in about a month." His expression turned grim. "If something goes wrong, call my lawyer. He's got my will; everything goes to charities. Then call the chairman of the board of Logan Enterprises in New York City and have him contact the London and Paris offices."

"But what will I tell them?"

"Tell them I'm probably dead."

"Dead? But John—"

"Hush, sweet," he commanded. "For once, stop being sassy and listen to me. They'll have to wait seven years, I think, before I can be declared dead, but everything will run on without me; I'm just a figurehead anyway."

"What about the ranch?"

He shrugged. "It becomes a summer camp for troubled boys with old Juan and his wife running the place."

"John, this is crazy!" She struggled to step off the bus, but he grabbed her as if she weighed nothing and lifted her back up on the step.

"Do as I tell you," he ordered.

She couldn't resist his strength; she was going to have to outsmart him. "Okay"—she ducked her head meekly—"anything you say."

"Good girl!" He touched the tip of her nose, turned and hurried away. She watched him stride toward his pickup.

"Lady," said the bus driver behind her, "you'll have to move off that step before I can close the door."

"Just a minute," Angie stalled, watching Logan get in the truck. Then it pulled away from the curb. Behind her, passengers grumbled behind her about the delay, but she didn't move. The pickup headed up the highway toward the north.

Sweet. He had called her sweet. Maybe it had slipped out, but it meant something. Was there even the slightest possibility that he might have a tiny bit of feeling for her? Not that it mattered whether he cared for her or not. Angie cared about him and she was going to do whatever she could to help him out of this terrible predicament. Angie turned and smiled at the bus driver. "I've changed my mind. Can I get a refund on my ticket?"

The driver glared, the passengers mumbled, but Angie grabbed her purse and suitcase and hopped off the bus. She wasn't going to Oklahoma City; she was going to follow Logan. *If he was in trouble, he needed her help!*

Chapter Seven

Angie stood on the side of the road, staring after Logan's black truck, disappearing now over the northern horizon. *Where could he be going?*

She flagged down a passing eighteen-wheeler full of bawling cattle. The trucker wore a faded red cap with ATLAS FEEDS across the front and a toothpick dangled from his mouth. He rolled down his window. "Hey, honey, what's the matter?"

She gave him her brightest smile and pointed. "Where does that road go?"

"Coffeyville. You need a ride?"

"Sure." She had never heard of the town, but didn't have any better ideas.

"Hop in." He gestured and seemed to notice her suitcase. "Fellow leave you stranded?"

"You might say that." Angie threw her suitcase and her heavy purse up on the seat and climbed in. The old truck roared away. She waved at the townspeople gaping openmouthed as the truck picked up speed. "What's Coffeyville?"

"Really nice little town just over the state line."

Kansas? Logan wouldn't be going to some little town; he was probably headed on through to Kansas City or maybe St. Louis to catch a plane. She was on a fool's errand, she knew, but whatever trouble he was in, she had to try to help him. Maybe she'd at least get close enough to trail the pickup; after that, she hadn't the foggiest idea what to do next. "I guess I should have stayed on the bus like he told me."

"What's that?" the trucker yelled over the roar of the engine.

"Nothing." She watched the road ahead as the truck ate up the miles; hoping against hope to catch a glimpse of Logan's truck ahead of them. Of course, if she did and Logan saw her, he'd be furious that she'd disobeyed him. Well, he'd said he liked her spunk. "Scarlett O'Hara lives!" she said.

The trucker looked at her as if she'd lost her mind. "Are you all right, lady?"

"Never mind."

They passed a sign that said WELCOME TO KANSAS! In minutes, the cattle truck slowed, pulling into the outskirts of a town.

The trucker yelled over the roar of the engine. "This where you want off, lady?"

"I don't know yet." As they drove through town, Angie began looking frantically for some sign of Logan's truck. There must be a million black pickups, and at least a dozen of them were on the streets of Coffeyville. Her common sense told her Logan wouldn't stop here. It would be crazy to schedule a meeting with mobsters in a little Kansas farm town. On the other hand, meeting here might be smart; Coffeyville would never be the place the F.B.I. would send in a surveillance team. "Hey, stop the truck!"

With mounting excitement, she stared out the dirty window at a black pickup with *J.L.* in a circle on the door. It was in a feed store parking lot just off the main drag. The trucker screeched to a halt and she grabbed her suitcase and purse, heavy with her father's antique coins. "Thanks for the ride."

"Don't mention it, honey." The trucker pulled away, cattle in the back bawling and milling.

Angie stood on the street and looked around. This looked like a small, pleasant farming community. However, like too many of them, some of its downtown buildings were empty and forlorn. Taking a deep breath for courage, she walked toward the pickup.

At any moment, she expected him to come striding down the sidewalk and give her hell for getting off that bus. There was no sign of Logan. Maybe he had ducked into a nearby café for a cup of coffee. She didn't know what to do except get in the truck and sit there until Logan returned. He'd be angry, but she'd make him see how much he needed her help. She tried the door. It was locked.

A teenage boy with bad skin lolled against the corner of the building. Angie said, "You see the guy who came with this truck?"

He yawned and scratched himself. "Big guy, part Indian?"

Her heart beat faster. "Yes, that's him."

"Heard him tell my dad he'd pay him to keep the truck here at our feed store. Said he'd be back in a month to get it."

Jiminy Christmas, why hadn't she thought of this? No doubt he'd changed vehicles here to throw anyone following him off the trail and then gone on to his destination. "You see which way he went? Maybe he got in another vehicle?"

"I don't know, ma'am. I thought I saw him walking down the street." He gestured vaguely. "I didn't ask no questions."

Her hopes rose. She turned just in time to see a distant, broad-shouldered man dressed in Western clothes disappearing into a shop a couple of blocks away. *Logan?*

Angie picked up her purse and suitcase, almost running up the street. If she kept him at a distance, maybe Logan wouldn't realize he was being tailed. She stopped in confusion. Which one of these shops had it been? Darn it, she had lost him. There were several boarded-up buildings, a ladies' wear, a hardware store. No. she didn't think that was the door she'd seen him go in.

She tried to picture the scene in her memory; no, it had been farther down the block. She started walking until she came to a faded sign that read:

> ### OLD-TIME PHOTOGRAPHS
> *Recapture the Past*
> *Fun and Entertaining*

Angie walked over and peered through the dirty plateglass window. The place looked deserted and none too prosperous. Evidently, the majority of local townspeople didn't find much fun and entertainment here.

Could Logan have gone in there? From here, all she could see was some ancient photography equipment, a red velvet Victorian settee, a big oval mirror in a walnut frame with claw feet and some faded and dusty old costumes hanging about the walls. It seemed like a very unlikely place for a mobster meeting. She had either been mistaken or there was a secret exit out the back.

Very hesitantly, Angie walked in and looked around. Everything was coated with a layer of dust, as if no one had touched anything for at least a hundred years. She took a deep breath and smelled decay and mildew. She also smelled something else; the faint scent of Logan's expensive aftershave. Maybe he was in a room in the back.

"Logan?" The place was so quiet, her voice and footsteps echoed eerily as she crossed the worn floor. There was something about this place that gave her the willies. Angie shuddered and walked through a side door, colliding with a giant spider web when she walked through. With a startled cry, she jumped back, brushing the clinging web away. It was an empty dressing room.

Maybe Logan had gone out the back door. A moment's search told her there was no back door. He couldn't have come out through the front; she would have seen him. Maybe she'd been mistaken as to which building he'd entered.

Angie shook her head in puzzlement. *If he hadn't been here, why did she smell the faint scent of his fine cologne?* It was an expensive brand that only a handful of men used. She looked down at the dusty floor. Except for her own footprints, the only others were a man's boots; small boots. They led up to the giant antique oval mirror and stopped there.

What the dickens? Logan wasn't the vain type. Try as she might, she couldn't imagine the big, rugged man standing before the glass admiring himself. The image staring back at her from the dusty mirror was faint and distorted. She studied the oval antique. There was something strange about it, with its dark walnut frame and claw feet. Angie put down her suitcase, shifted her heavy purse to her shoulder, reached out and put her hand on the glass. The late-afternoon temperature was warm, but touching the glass sent a chill through her body.

Only then did she notice that someone had scrawled the numbers 666 in the dust of the glass. Without thinking, she crossed herself, then felt foolish. "You've seen too many old horror films," she said.

There had to be a logical explanation. Maybe it was a cryptic message. Maybe Logan had left a clue for someone to meet him back at his address on Logan Parkway. It wasn't much, but it was the only idea she had. Absently, Angie began to trace the numbers with her finger.

Abruptly, the glass seemed to melt into liquid eddies and her hand touched empty air. Now instead of seeing her own dim reflection in the glass, she could see the town's street framed by the ancient walnut.

Only the town looked different from the one she had just

left. As she stared through the mirror, she also saw beyond the plateglass window. People in Gay Nineties costumes passed by on the brick sidewalk, and a buggy pulled by a bay horse trotted past on the street. As she stared, three cowboys on horseback rode past. "What is going on here?"

Her words echoed through the empty shop, but no one answered her. This was some kind of magic trick, Angie thought. Maybe this wasn't a photography shop at all, but a magician's supply house.

"Why in the heck would Logan go into a magician's supply shop?"

The answer was obvious; this was some kind of front for the mob, where they laundered money or passed messages back and forth. Probably even the nice people in this little town didn't realize what was going on under their very noses.

Angie stared through the mirror frame at the passing scene outside. Yes, it looked like a typical Gay Nineties Western town. "David Copperfield," she whispered, "you could take lessons from these folks in Kansas."

There must be a secret door out of here that Angie hadn't found; otherwise, where could Logan have disappeared to? In her mind, she explored all the possibilities, and they all came back the same; it had to be the mirror. "Maybe it's like that door Dorothy opens in *The Wizard of Oz*," she said to herself, "where Dorothy steps through and suddenly finds herself in a strange new world all bright with technicolor."

How this thing worked, Angie had no idea, but she was about to find out. Taking a deep breath for courage, she shifted her heavy purse to her other shoulder, hiked up her jeans leg and stepped through the frame to the other side.

She waited, holding her breath. If she'd expected that midgets would suddenly appear with a burst of music, along with a yellow brick road, she was disappointed.

"Maybe it's computer-generated." Angie looked around. The only difference she could see was that now the shop looked new and shiny, as if it was doing a lot of business. Angie walked slowly to the front door and opened it. Outside, women passed by in long dresses with wasp waists and big leg-of-mutton sleeves. Some of them carried lace parasols. A buggy pulled up to the hitching rail out front. A man in spats and a derby hat got out of it and walked down the street. A small boy in knickers ran past, pushing a hoop with a stick. Most of all, it was quiet, except for the whinny of a passing horse, the singing of birds in the trees.

"It's some kind of illusion," she said to herself. "How do they do this?"

And yet, when she reached out to pat the horse tied to the hitching rail, it was real enough. She felt its velvet muzzle brush against her hand.

Mystified, she looked up and down the street. The buildings looked bright and new, although some of the signs were different. "Why is it so quiet?"

She looked around and realized for the first time that there were no cars; none. There wasn't even a pickup truck in sight, although, somewhere in the distance, she heard the faint whistle and chugging of a train.

Mystified, Angie walked down the brick sidewalk, still clutching her purse. The whole town looked like a Western movie set. Two prim old ladies in black dresses and veiled hats passed by and gave Angie disapproving frowns. "Such nerve!" one whispered to the other as they passed. "Has the girl no shame?"

Angie looked down at her clothes. She wore an average pair of jeans, sneakers and a denim shirt. Maybe they weren't talking about her. She looked behind her, expecting to see some bimbo in a tank top and tight miniskirt, but there wasn't anyone behind her.

Oh, well, the pair must be eccentric. She had more intriguing things than that to think about. Angie stopped and looked around. There had to be a reasonable explanation for all this.

Maybe they were filming a Western movie or new television series here today and had cleared all the cars off the street. The director was going to be upset if Angie blundered into a scene and messed up their filming.

How did Logan fit into all this? If she could find him, the mystery would be solved, although he'd be angry with her for following him. Angie started walking, looking in every direction for him. From some open window, an antique phonograph played, *"Ta-ra-ra boom-de-ay! Ta-ra-ra-boom-de-ay!"*

The man in the derby hat and spats came out of a harness store and glared at her before stomping away. "Disgusting!"

Other people were turning to stare and then whispering together as she passed, and she looked down, puzzled. Did she have toilet paper stuck on her shoe, or were her jeans unzipped? She couldn't figure out what they were upset about.

She passed an old-fashioned barber shop with a striped pole and looked in the door. Inside, a quartet of men with handlebar mustaches were harmonizing: *". . . after the ball is over, after the break of morn . . ."*

Yes, it was a film set, all right. There wasn't any other explanation for this Gay Nineties street. Angie looked around, expecting to see film crews in the vicinity or hear someone yell, "Cut!"

There wasn't anyone except the actors in their historic costumes. Maybe it wasn't a movie shoot; maybe the town was having a historical reenactment. Everyone was supposed to dress authentically for those, she knew; maybe that was the reason everyone kept turning to stare at her. She passed two old men whittling on a bench in front of the general store. "Look at that hussy!" one said to the other, "wearing men's pants!"

"It's the beginning of the downfall of the American family," the other grizzled geezer predicted dourly. "No tellin' what'll happen if they all get the vote like them suffragettes want!"

This reenactment thing was being carried just a bit too far,

Angie thought. She almost confronted them, then realized how silly she'd look when they explained about the reenactment. Besides, she had more important things on her mind, like finding Logan.

She paused on the corner and looked toward the late afternoon sun slanting in the West and didn't have a clue what to do next. If Logan had stepped through that trick mirror, she wasn't certain where he might have gone. By now, he might have left this town. Maybe she should go back through that photography shop and see if his truck was gone.

The thought crossed her mind that she might be asleep and dreaming all this. She could remember many occasions that had seemed so real, she'd been surprised when she'd awakened in her own bed and realized it had all been a dream. Maybe she was asleep at Logan's ranch and dreaming everything that had happened since they'd gone swimming and Logan had been overcome with a sudden change of mood.

Tentatively, she pinched herself. "Ouch!"

"Are you all right, ma'am?"

Angie started, turning to see an old lawman with a beard and goatee staring at her, head cocked in disapproval, the late afternoon sun glinting off his badge. "I'm Marshal Connelly."

She must look silly. "I—I was just pinching myself to see if I was dreaming."

His bushy eyebrows went up.

"I mean, I stepped through that mirror," she hastened to explain, "not realizing your town was having a historic re-enactment—"

"A what—?" Now he really was staring at her.

She had a feeling he was going to find the rest of it even stranger, and Logan sure didn't need any trouble with the local law. Abruptly, she thought about her suitcase. Oh, darn, she'd left it in that shop. "I—I've lost my luggage. I've got to go look for it."

"Oh"—he nodded in understanding—"I wondered why

you were dressed like that. All right, ma'am, you go on now, you hear?''

She nodded and turned back up the street. Her watch read 5:30 P.M.

Still clutching her purse, she hurried toward the shop. As she had feared, the door was locked, with a sign reading CLOSED hanging in the window. She rattled the knob and cursed under her breath. *Darn it, now what was she supposed to do?* If she could find the phone number, maybe she could call the owner at home and get him to come down and open up. Fat chance! Things were going from bad to worse. First, Logan missing, and now her suitcase locked in the shop.

''This has to be a dream,'' she muttered to herself. ''One of those dreams of frustration where everything goes wrong.'' Either that, or she was losing her mind. She didn't want to think about that.

What to do and where to get help? She looked up and down the street. Most shops were now closed, and people were disappearing off the streets as the September sun sank low on the horizon. Maybe she should find the police station and ask for help. Then she thought about the mustachioed marshal who had looked at her so disapprovingly. No, she'd better not do that.

What to do? ''Think, Angie,'' she told herself. ''Take a deep breath, be calm and think!''

The only thing that occurred to her was that she should find herself a motel room, spend the night and start fresh in the morning. Up and down the street, flickering gas streetlights came on. This town must be like Williamsburg, she thought; everything has to be authentic.

She started back down the street, and in the distance saw the faint glimmer of light from windows. Outside the windows, she could just barely read a sign that read: HOTEL. Angie was suddenly very tired. She probably wasn't even thinking straight, she told herself. ''Once you've had some rest, you'll figure out what to do next,'' she assured herself and started walking toward the sign.

Angie walked over to the hotel in the growing darkness. It might be the only one in this little town; Logan might even be staying here.

She walked in, paused. It looked like a set for every Western movie she'd ever seen. Behind the desk, a young man with a handlebar mustache and sleeve garters stared at her clothes.

They surely wouldn't take an out-of-town-check and she didn't have much cash. In her hurry, she hadn't cashed in her bus ticket. Oh, wait a minute; she had a credit card. Angie went up to the desk. ''I know I'm dressed sort of casual, but my luggage is ah—lost. It's a long story, but I need a room for the night. Do you take plastic?''

''What?''

He must be hard of hearing. Angie reached in her purse and pulled out her credit card, slapped it on the counter. ''I've got both Visa and MasterCard.''

The young man picked it up, staring at it as if he'd never seen a credit card before. Then he handed it back to her, shaking his head dubiously. ''I don't know what kind of trick you're trying to pull, you hussy, but Coffeyville is on to you city slickers. I didn't just come in on a punkin wagon, you know.''

''The card is good,'' Angie said in a huff. ''I might overstretch my credit now and then, but I made a payment this month, so if you'll just call—''

''Call what?'' His mustache wiggled over his curled lip.

''Wherever it is that shops call when they check credit cards; I don't know.''

''Credit? We don't give credit.'' He pointed to a sign hanging on the back wall. ''Had some gamblers skip out owing us money.''

That explained it, Angie thought, or maybe since this was such a small operation, the owners just didn't take credit cards.

She put the card away and did some quick thinking. She

hadn't seen an ATM machine anywhere and she didn't want to go out in the dark to search for one. Angie had to have a room for the night and she had no cash. Except for her father's antique coins. "How much is it?"

"Two dollars."

"Are you kidding me?" Angie blinked at him.

He drew himself up proudly. "I realize that's a little more than is usually charged in these parts," he sneered, "but this is a nice hotel."

This had to be a joke. Still, the man didn't laugh when she laid two silver dollars on the counter. Instead, he handed her a big, brass key. "Top of the stairs and to your right."

"This whole town is a loony bin," Angie whispered to herself. She started to leave the desk, hesitated and turned back. "By the way"—Angie leaned over the counter—"you don't happen to know John Logan, do you?"

The clerk froze and his mustache quivered. "Johnny Logan? You know Johnny Logan, the gunfighter?"

"Well, he's only that on weekends," Angie explained. "The rest of the time, he's a—businessman." Like in Oklahoma City, the strange millionaire might not want his real background known.

Big beads of sweat stood out on the clerk's pale face and he mopped his brow. "Tell—tell Johnny I treated you well; that I wasn't disrespectful."

The man looked terrified. Angie had a sinking feeling; were there things about John Logan he hadn't told her? Was his wealth really traceable to the mob?

"Does he usually stay here?"

"No, ma'am."

"Do you have any idea where I can find him?"

The man ran his finger around his collar, as if it was choking him. "No, ma'am."

Jiminy Christmas, what was wrong with this guy? It didn't look like she was going to get any more information from him.

Right now, she was so tired, she couldn't think. Maybe if she got a good night's rest, she could straighten it all out in the morning. Better yet, maybe she'd wake up back in her own bed in Oklahoma City and realize the whole thing had been a dream; even the part about Logan kissing her on the floating boat dock.

She sighed wistfully, remembering that special moment, and started for the stairs. As she walked through the lobby full of potted ferns and Victorian furniture, she noted an old man on a red velvet settee reading a newspaper. She slowed and glanced at the headlines, afraid she might see Logan's photo on the front page, along with an article about a federal sting and gangsters. Instead, the headline read:

*Grover Cleveland Campaigning Hard for the
Presidency*

Grover Cleveland? Her eyes must be playing tricks on her. Angie squinted to see the date at the top of the paper; then she blinked and looked again. There was no mistake; the date read: *September 5, 1892.*

Chapter Eight

Angie cleared her throat. "Excuse me, sir?"

The old man lowered the paper. He had chewing tobacco stains on his white beard. His eyes widened as he looked her up and down. "If my wife sees me talking to a hussy like you, I'll be in trouble. Please leave me alone."

"I'm not a hussy!"

"Well! I reckon you are, seein's as how you're wearin' men's pants and accosting strangers in hotel lobbies. And I thought this was a respectable hotel!"

She must not give him a piece of her mind; the old gentleman was probably suffering from Alzheimer's. "I'm sorry, but I just wanted to know; is that an old paper?"

He nodded, and frowned, folding the paper.

Relief flooded through Angie and she smiled. *Of course! The newspaper was a movie prop!* And the actors had been rehearsing a scene. "Is there a shoot tomorrow?"

The old man's face blanched. "Lord, I hope not!"

The clerk must have been eavesdropping, because he yelled from the desk, "She's a friend of Johnny Logan's."

Immediately, the old man stood up, bowing and scraping. "Oh, I'm so sorry, ma'am. Tell Johnny it was a mistake; we all send him our regards."

His sudden change in attitude left Angie bewildered. Either this whole town was nuts or she was. She realized the old man and the desk clerk were staring at her. Maybe she'd be suspicious, too, of a stranger who checked into a hotel without any luggage and asked a million questions. Just what was going on here that everyone acted so strangely? Well, there wasn't anything she could do about it tonight. Angie paused and considered going back out for a pizza, but she was tired.

She returned to the desk clerk. "There's a dining room?"

He blinked. "This is a very fine hotel, miss, and the way you're dressed—"

"Never mind." Angie made a dismissive gesture. "If you'll hand me the Yellow Pages, I'll have some Chinese takeout or a pizza sent in."

"What?" His handlebar mustache wiggled and he looked at her as if she'd lost her mind.

"Pizza," she repeated.

He stared at her and scratched his head.

"Pizza! Pizza!" She was out of sorts and almost shouting. "Don't you speak English?"

He nodded, backing away.

"I'm sorry; I'm tired," Angie apologized. It was possible that a little farm town in Kansas might not have a Chinese restaurant or pizza parlor. She hadn't even seen a McDonald's or a Wal-Mart. Yes, indeedy, this was a very backward town.

"Ma'am, if you're hungry, since you're a friend of Johnny Logan's, I'll send a girl up with a tray."

Angie smiled. "Room service. Now, that's more like it. I'd like something with low cholesterol and maybe some yogurt."

"What?"

He must be hard of hearing. Angie was tired of dealing with these very strange people. "Never mind. What did the dining room serve tonight?"

"Fried chicken and roast beef."

"Sounds good. I'll have a roast beef sandwich and a wine cooler."

He was staring at her again.

"Make that a glass of milk."

That he understood; he nodded.

Angie started for the stairs, paused. "Oh, do you have cable or satellite?"

The young man and the old man looked at each other and shrugged.

What was it with this town? "Oh, you've got Pay-For-View. Very well, I'll pick a movie and put it on my tab."

"Lady," said the young man, "I wouldn't want to insult a friend of Johnny Logan's, but you don't make much sense."

"I don't make much sense?" She almost yelled it at him. "Never mind, I'm too tired to watch television anyway."

She started up the stairs.

The desk clerk called after her, "I'll send that sandwich right up, ma'am, and remember to tell Johnny how nice I was to you."

"Yeah, right." She went upstairs to her room, walked in and looked around in the dim glow of a fancy painted gaslight on the wall. "If this is the best hotel in Kansas, I'd hate to see the others," she said aloud.

There was a bed, a golden oak chest of drawers and a bowl and pitcher on a washstand. There wasn't even a television. The walls were covered with Victorian flowered wallpaper. She sat down on the bed and discovered it sported honest-to-goodness metal bedsprings that complained noisily when she moved. Maybe she could call Logan's ranch or his answering service and see if he'd left any messages for her. She looked around. No phone.

"I am either dreaming or losing my mind. Even the crummi-est hotel should have phones." Of course, this was the boonies of Kansas. Or maybe this room was to be used in a shoot tomorrow and it had to look authentic. Darn, she'd meant to ask the clerk what movie was being shot here. With Logan's money, he might be a financial backer, which would be a reasonable explanation of why he was here. She thought about Nick Diablo. Maybe the crime syndicates had entered the film industry.

There was a knock on the door. Perhaps it was Logan, having heard she was here. Relief flooded through her as she went to the door. "Who is it?"

"Bessie, ma'am, bringing you some supper."

Oh, yes, room service. "Just a minute."

She didn't have much cash for a tip unless she used her father's antique coins, but as weird as these people were, she didn't know if they'd put a tip on her bill or not. Angie opened the door to a young country girl who was much plumper than Angie. She wore a long dress. This realism thing was getting old fast. "Bring it in, Bessie."

The girl brought in the tray and set it on a golden oak table, her brown eyes wide with curiosity. "Are you really a friend of Johnny Logan's?"

Why was everyone so fascinated with John Logan? He must own most of the land around here. Angie nodded. "Yes. I work for him." She handed a handful of dimes to the girl.

The girl looked at the money in her palm, then back to Angie. "They'll put the meal on your bill, ma'am."

"No, it's a tip," Angie explained. "I realize it's not much, but I'm without much cash, and—"

"This is all for me?" Bessie looked both horrified and awe-struck.

"Well, yes."

"Thank you, ma'am, thank you." Bessie fled as if she expected Angie to try to take the money back.

"Well, everyone in this town is a character." Angie sighed and sat down to eat.

Boy, whatever this hotel lacked in decorating, it made up for in food. The bread and the pickles tasted homemade and the beef was tender and juicy. There was also a big slice of dark chocolate cake to go along with the tall glass of cold milk. "I shouldn't eat all this, but maybe I'll walk it off tomorrow," Angie said to herself and dived in. The food was so good, it almost made her forget that she was here to solve a puzzle about Logan's mysterious disappearance. Well, she couldn't do anything about that tonight.

Dinner finished, Angie sighed with pleasure and decided to give up and go to bed. Maybe if this was only a dream, she'd wake up in her own bed in the morning. No, maybe if she was lucky, she'd wake up in Logan's bed at his ranch. The thought made her blush. She began looking for the bathroom. There wasn't one. Instead, there was a bowl and a pitcher.

Angie went out into the hall, searching, and discovered a bathroom with a clawfoot tub and an old-fashioned toilet with a wooden tank high on the wall. It flushed with a pull chain. "No five-star hotel rating for this place," she grumbled. "I'll bet the movie stars have sleek R.V.s parked out in a field somewhere so they don't have to stay at this dump. This is worse than the old place in *Psycho*."

None of that mattered; she could be a good sport for a few hours. Returning to her room, Angie lay down on top of the covers and slept soundly.

Daylight streaming through the window awakened her. She sat up, listened to the metal bedsprings creak and remembered where she was. "It's time to get the hell out of Dodge, or Coffeyville, or whatever."

Angie found a comb and a lipstick in her purse and tried to make herself look presentable. If she didn't get any new information about Logan this morning, she might as well use that bus ticket, go to Oklahoma City and wait as he'd ordered her to do.

She went down the stairs and found the dining room off the hotel lobby. All right, so she wasn't properly dressed for a formal hotel dining room, but she was hungry. Angie walked in and waited to be seated. A number of people were eating breakfast, all dressed in period costumes. *They're filming a scene,* Angie thought, *or maybe this is just where they feed the crew and these are the extras.* Any other time, she would have been eager to find out who the star was, but today, she was too preoccupied with Logan.

Why were all these people turning to stare at her so coldly? Hadn't they ever seen a girl in blue jeans before?

The head waiter came over to her, his nose in the air, his face a cold mask. His hair was parted down the middle and greased so shiny, she wondered if she could see her reflection in it? "I'm sorry. We don't serve your kind in here."

"My kind? Now just what is that supposed to mean?"

Before the waiter could answer, the little old man from last night limped into the dining room and tugged at the waiter's sleeve. "She's a friend of Johnny Logan's."

The waiter started, then regained his composure. "Why didn't you say so, miss? Right this way!" He escorted her with a flourish, leading her to a good table near the window while everyone stared. Outside, cowboys rode past on horses, and a wagon with a farmer on board moved slowly down the dusty street. Filming must have started early, Angie thought. Then it occurred to her that with the way everyone in the dining room was dressed, the cameras must be about to move in here. She'd ruin their shoot.

"Look," she said to the waiter, "just give me a bite and I'll get out of here in a hurry. I'll settle for a Pop Tart and a cup of decaf."

"I beg your pardon?"

"Well, if you don't have Pop Tarts, what about a bowl of chocolate sugar loops?"

He looked at her as though he didn't understand plain English. Angie glanced around. Everyone else was having eggs and bacon. She cringed at the thought of all those calories, but pointed at the menu. "Okay, give me that."

He nodded and went off, leaving Angie attempting to ignore the stares. When she sneaked looks at the other women, a lot of them were every bit as pudgy as she was.

"Besides shooting a Western, they must be having a Weight Watcher's convention," she said to herself.

The waiter brought her a plate piled high with eggs and bacon, and homemade biscuits dripping butter and strawberry jam. Angie took a long look. "I have died and gone to heaven where nobody counts calories! Thank you, God!"

She dug in and savored every morsel. The coffee was real coffee, too. She sipped it and thought of Logan, wondering if someone was making his coffee this morning, good and strong, the way he liked it, with three spoons of sugar.

The waiter brought the bill. Angie looked at it. Twenty-five cents. "There must be some mistake."

The waiter blanched. "Madam is not happy with the bill?"

"The amount must be a mistake," Angie said.

"Then for a friend of Johnny Logan, the breakfast is free."

"What? No, I intend to pay. It's just that the amount—"

"It's too much, right? For you, madam, it's on the house."

Angie tried to protest and pay the bill, but the waiter insisted the meal was free. People were turning and staring at the exchange.

"Madam, I insist, for a friend of Johnny's, the meal is free. Tell him I said so."

John Logan must have bought this town; that was the only explanation. And maybe he owned this hotel. Wasn't that how Aspen, Colorado, became such a big thing? Hadn't some millionaire bought Aspen and turned it into a ski resort?

Satisfied with that explanation, Angie left the dining room, feeling the stares of the other diners as she went. The first thing to do was reclaim her luggage so she could put on some clean clothes, if she could find somewhere to take a bath. She'd intended to take one this morning, but when she'd gone down to the old-fashioned community tub and opened the door, she'd surprised a bearded cowboy sitting in the tub, cutting his toenails.

She started down the street toward the photography shop. What to do after that? *Oh, Logan, where in the heck are you?*

Other shops were open already on this warm fall morning, the proprietors out sweeping the brick sidewalk or polishing glass windows. However, when Angie rattled the door at the photography shop, she discovered it was still locked. She put her face against the glass and peered in.

Near the plateglass windows was the big, oval mirror, the key that had opened her access to this weird adventure. Maybe if she stepped back through, she'd be in a normal town again, complete with telephones, pickup trucks, boom boxes and fast food. She had to help Logan before that gangster did something terrible—like put Logan's small feet in a bucket of cement.

Somewhere down the block, a car backfired. At least, it sounded like a car to her. However, around her, people screamed and dived for cover. A rider galloped past on a horse, drunk and shooting.

Jiminy Christmas, she'd gotten right in the middle of a shoot. Any moment now, a director would yell "cut!" and come scream at her for ruining his scene.

The cowboy galloped past, and people got up, brushing the dust from their clothes. A small boy came by selling newspapers. "Extra! Extra! Chicago's world fair soon to open!"

Angie handed him a half-dollar. "Give me one of those."

"Gee, lady, I'm not sure I can break this—"

"Keep the change." Angie grabbed the paper.

His eyes grew wide. "Gosh, thanks, lady."

Angie stared at the paper. The date on it read September 6, 1892. The front page had a story about the new invention called a Ferris wheel that would be a wondrous entertainment at the Columbian Exposition World's Fair in Chicago. Little Egypt, the belly dancer, was expected to shock everyone with her writhing display.

A thought crossed her mind; a thought so bizarre, she couldn't deal with it. "Young man, what's the date?"

He paused and looked at her as if she'd lost her mind. "Why, September sixth."

"I mean, really?"

He stared at her clothes. "September 6, 1892. You been stuck out on a farm for awhile?"

Angie closed her eyes and swayed on her feet. Either she was losing her mind or everyone was in on the joke except her. No, that couldn't be. She read time-travel romances, but she knew time travel wasn't possible—was it?

"Lady, are you all right?" The little newsboy sounded anxious. "I could get you some smelling salts if you're about to swoon."

Smelling salts? Swoon?

"I—I'll be fine." Angie sat down on the brick curb by the horse trough in front of the shop. Horse trough? She ran a dozen possibilities through her mind and discarded most of them in panic. Maybe this was one of those new virtual-reality amusement parks and they were testing it out in Kansas. Logan could afford to invest in an expensive venture like that. Whatever the reasonable explanation was, Angie didn't want any more of it. She returned to rattle the doorknob of the photography shop again and pressed her face against the window. Even from here, she could see her distorted reflection in the oval mirror. None of this made any sense. Maybe she was losing her mind. She ran a half-dozen possibilities through her mind and decided there was no reasonable explanation.

She thought about those time-travel romances she had read.

In many of them, all the heroine had to do to get out of a time period was reverse the process. Could she have time-traveled? Angie breathed a sigh of relief. If so, the answer was simple; once she got inside the shop, she would step back through the mirror. That would return her to her own time period.

She still had her heavy purse hanging over her shoulder. If she wasn't such a law-abiding citizen, she'd consider throwing it through the plateglass window and crawling through to get to the mirror. No, she shook her head. Besides the fact that it was wrong, the police might get there before she could reach the mirror. She could only imagine what jail must be like in this town.

Behind her, a rough voice asked, "Hey, honey, you look good to me."

Angie turned to face a rough-looking hombre in dirty Western clothes. "Not hardly!" She took a deep breath. He could use some of Logan's fine cologne, too; or maybe just some soap.

"I love it when women play hard to get!" He grinned at her, and she noticed he was missing a front tooth. "I know where we can get us some whiskey. Let's you'n me go have a drink."

"To quote a country song, buddy, what part of no don't you understand?"

He advanced on her, tipping back the ragged brim of his hat with the barrel of his pistol. "Don't get uppity with old Duke, sister; you can't be much, wearin' them tight men's pants!"

"They aren't men's pants." Angie drew herself up with dignity. "And if they're a little tight . . . well, that's none of your business."

He'd been drinking, too. As he moved toward her, she could smell the sour scent of whiskey on his breath. She wished she had a breath mint to offer him. Angie took a step backward; feeling the weight of her heavy purse hanging from her shoulder. Maybe she could swing it and knock him down or . . . no, she'd better give up that idea. This guy was wearing a pistol low on his hip and tied down, gunfighter style. Then she remembered the magic words that had caused people to cower in fear when she'd said them; "John Logan."

"What?" The ruffian stopped uncertainly. "You know him?"

Angie gave a quick sigh of relief. "I certainly do. In fact, I work for him."

"Doin' what?" He grinned and winked, "I reckon I can guess, purty as you are. I heard old Johnny was back in this area and we're due for a showdown."

"What you really need is a new script writer," Angie frowned. "This dialogue stinks!"

"Who you sayin' stinks, gal?" He advanced on Angie. "That half-breed Logan and I are enemies, and now I got his woman at my mercy!"

This seemed a little too realistic, and besides, he was drunk. A warning bell went off in Angie's head. You never could predict what a drunk would do. She backed away. "I just work for Logan."

"Don't give me that, honey." He grinned. "I already heard a pretty girl who dressed funny has been mentioning his name all over town. I'm gonna use you as bait to get the guy."

"Let go of me!" She tried to jerk away, then remembered what he'd just said and paused. "Pretty? They said I was pretty?"

"Just like Lillian Russell! And they is right."

Well, darn, she'd finally found a time period where plump women were the ideal and she was going to have to contend with a stinking drunk.

"Hey, Duke!" Someone yelled from a doorway, "You better let Johnny's woman go; he's acomin'!"

Duke started, then grinned. "You hear that, gal? Your lover is gonna get shot; then everyone will know who's the fastest gun in the West."

Jiminy Christmas, and she was going to be caught in this

gun duel in front of the locked photography shop. Could Logan really be coming?

Even as she started to move away, Duke reached out and caught her arm. He pulled her hard against him and took his pistol out of its holster, then stuck it up under her breast. "You keep quiet now, you hear, purty thing?"

A horse and rider rounded the corner at a slow walk. The horse was a magnificent black-and-white paint stallion. The rider was big, wide-shouldered and dressed all in black. She would have known him anywhere, even though his face was shadowed by the black Stetson. "Logan, look out, he's got a gun!"

The rider reined in, his hand on his thigh. The people on the street scattered like frightened chickens into buildings or cowered behind trees and horse troughs. The street grew so quiet, she heard a cricket chirping somewhere behind her.

The rider ignored her; his dark eyes watching the drunk. "Duke," he said in a low, harsh voice, "I told you to clear out of town by sundown; I reckon you don't speak English."

"Shut up, Johnny!" Duke snarled and pulled Angie even closer. "It was me that said this town wasn't big enough for the both of us. Now as you can see, I got your woman. You get off that fine horse, I intend to mount him, too!"

There was a sharp intake of breath from the watching citizens in the doorways. Angie felt perspiration break out on her face. The pistol poked her sharply in the breast. Even if Logan shot the drunk, Duke's pistol might go off and finish her.

"Please, John," she whispered, "be careful what you do!"

The expression on the dark, rugged face didn't change. "Duke," the rider said, "you're a rotten coward, hiding behind a woman. Step away from her and I'll give you a chance to make a name for yourself."

"That's all I been wantin'," Duke snarled, but he didn't turn her loose. Angie was shaking. Even if this was a movie or a dream, it all felt so real. What could she do to help Logan?

Every old Western movie she'd ever seen flashed through her mind, as well as all those romance novels. Heroines always did something to save the hero. Well, maybe she could do that, too.

Angie brought her elbow back up under Duke's ribs as hard as she could, even as she dodged out of the way, yelling, "Scarlett O'Hara lives!"

With an oath, Duke dropped the pistol and stumbled up against the storefront.

The rider's hand went to his holster. "All right, Duke, you wanted to find out who was the fastest; now you'll get that chance. Pick up that Colt and you call it."

Duke's unshaven face went pale with fear. "I—I didn't mean to touch her, Johnny. I didn't know she belonged to you!" He was bending over again, doubling up as if in pain. From where Angie stood, she saw the sudden reflection of the sun on steel in his boot.

"Look out!" she screamed. "He's got another gun!"

Logan's Colt cleared leather even as Duke jerked the hidden pistol from his boot. The sound of the shot roared in her ears. Duke got off a shot, but it went harmlessly into the horse trough nearby, and a tiny stream of water ran out to soak the ground while horses reared and neighed at the noise.

Duke clutched his chest, stumbled and half-turned at the impact. He pulled the trigger again, but the shot went wild and shattered the front of the photography store, sending a shower of glass across the brick sidewalk.

The sudden smell of burnt powder and fresh blood made Angie cry out in alarm. People ran and screamed as Duke fell, leaving a smear of blood down the shattered store window. In the confusion, the spotted stallion lunged forward and Logan leaned over, lifting her up on the saddle before him. "Hush up, woman. You're enough to wake the dead!"

His big chest was a comfort and she clung to him as the

paint stallion reared. "John, we've got to get out of this loony place. We've got to go back through the mirror to reality—"

"I said hush!" He turned his horse and galloped away, holding her tightly against him.

The mirror. Angie struggled in his arms to look behind them. The wild shot had broken more than the plateglass window; the antique mirror lay shattered in a million pieces.

"Oh, jiminy! John, what have you done? Now we're both stuck back in this time!"

He didn't answer, or maybe he didn't hear her. He only cradled her against his hard body and spurred the big stallion away from the scene. As they galloped down the street, Angie got a quick glimpse of the horrified faces of townspeople. The two old-timers were sitting whittling and staring in open-mouthed surprise. Even the mustachioed quartet had come out of the barber shop to gawk.

She had a million questions to ask, but none of the answers mattered to Angie; nothing mattered but that she was in Logan's arms. She buried her face against his chest as they rode. "Thank God I found you," she whispered.

He didn't answer, only held on to her with one strong hand and rode expertly, galloping the paint stallion out of town.

It was a wild ride and the horse was lathered and blowing when Logan slowed to a walk. "You all right?"

"Yes." She looked up at him, so glad to see his dark, forbidding face. "I suppose there's a reasonable explanation as to why you dumped me in Osage and then came up here to play John Wayne."

His rugged face furrowed in confusion. "Who?"

"Look, John, let's lay it on the line. I know I'm overstepping my place, but whatever kind of trouble you're in, I want to help."

"You're a nosey wench, missy, and you have no idea what kind of trouble I'm in. Besides, I don't need any help from a slip of a girl." He kept riding.

She looked up at the tiny mole near his mouth. "I can hardly be called a slip of a girl, but I like the image anyway."

"They tell me you've been mentioning my name all over town; I want to know why." He drew in under the shade of a cottonwood tree and looked behind them. When he seemed assured that no one was following, he dismounted and held up his hands for her.

Angie hung on to her purse and slid off into his arms, remembering the feel of his embrace. "Why? That's a crazy question. I've been trying desperately to find you."

He looked puzzled. "Why?"

"You know why!"

He shook his head, reached to take a blanket from his bedroll and spread it on the ground. "Sit down and rest, girl; you've had a bad scare."

Okay, so he didn't want to talk about it yet; maybe he was afraid to trust her. She sat down on the blanket and watched him as he began to unsaddle his horse. "John," she said, "I know you're in trouble and I want to help."

"You said that already." He finished staking the beautiful paint out to graze and sat down on the blanket. "Look, I appreciate your offer, but I don't need anyone."

"Mr. Logan—"

"You can call me Johnny. You don't know what kind of hombre I am; not someone you should get mixed up with."

"Let me decide that." She gave him a spirited, level look.

"You're a fiesty thing, Miss—?"

"After what's happened between us, I think you could at least call me Angel like you used to." She almost blushed, remembering their embrace at the ranch lake.

"Angel; yes, that's a good description if I ever heard one. Okay, my beautiful Angel, just what am I going to do with you now?" He pulled out the big gold watch and checked the time.

"Well, I see you didn't lose that antique coming through the time barrier."

"Antique? I bought this just a few weeks ago."

Angie raised her eyebrows in puzzlement. "That's not what you told me before."

"Before?"

He had either forgotten his previous explanation or he had lied to her. Somehow, that hurt, showing as it did that he didn't quite trust her.

He checked the time again before putting his watch in his vest. "I've got to meet some people late this afternoon."

Was there going to be a showdown between him and the mob? She was so scared for him, she overlooked the confusion over the watch. "Okay, we've got some time then; maybe we can figure a way out of this mess."

"We?"

"Don't you understand that I've gone to a lot of trouble to try to help you?"

"Again, why?"

After what had happened at the lake, he had to ask? He was a lonely, suspicious man who didn't trust anyone, and maybe most people had disappointed him.

"I'll show you why." Her emotions overwhelmed her and she reached out and took his rough face between her two hands and kissed him.

He started in surprise; then he pulled her hard against him, taking control of the kiss. His mouth covered hers, his tongue darting between her lips to tease and torment.

Slowly, Angie lay back on the blanket and pulled him with her. He smelled of tobacco and horses and leather. She had never wanted a man before—Brett had never managed to arouse desire in her—but at this moment, she knew the full meaning of the word. Her skin felt on fire, especially between her thighs. Angie returned his kiss, putting her own tongue between his lips. He moaned suddenly and sucked her tongue even deeper.

She could feel his manhood hot and hard against her body. She reached down and put her hand over it outside his trousers. Grandma had been right: small feet, big . . .

His callused hand came up, covering her breast, and she pressed against his palm, encouraging him. He struggled awkwardly with the buttons of her blouse and she reached up to help him. Thank goodness she was wearing a bra with front hooks. She unsnapped them and her big breasts came free and swelled with desire under his searching fingers. His eager hand on her nipple sent a surge of heat racing through every nerve. Angie arched her back, offering him her breasts for his pleasure.

He needed no second invitation. He lay half on her supple body, sucking her nipple with slow, sensual motions, his tongue licking across the tip like a flame. With a shuddering moan, Angie caught his face between her hands, moved it to her other breast. "Yes, John!" she sighed. "Yes!"

He obliged, pleasuring first one breast and then the other until she was writhing with desire beneath him. She had never ached for a man before, but all she could think of now was getting both their clothes off.

Angie reached out to unbutton his shirt and slip her hands inside. She slipped his shirt off his wide shoulders, caressing him with her fingertips as she reached up and caught his nipple between her teeth.

"Oh, Angel, you must have dropped from heaven!" He gasped and pulled her face hard against his chest while she bit and teased his nipple even as her hands explored his lean body. "I want you," he whispered, "like I never thought I could want a woman!"

She smiled up at him through half-closed eyes and pulled his shirt down his arms. Abruptly, her eyes widened. "Oh my God!" She sat up suddenly.

He was breathing in great gasps. "What's the matter?" He tried to take her down to the blanket again, but she resisted.

''The scar! You don't have the scar!'' She was almost shrieking now, scrambling to pull her blouse closed.

''What the hell are you talking about, lady?'' He glared at her, trying to take her into his arms, but she resisted.

''The scar; the white, jagged scar the *real* Logan has on his arm! *You* aren't John Logan!''

Chapter Nine

Hell, he hadn't expected Angel would follow him through that mirror and back into this time period after he'd put her on a bus back to Oklahoma City. She'd been too fiesty to obey him. Now he didn't know whether to be angry or admire her for her spunk. One thing was certain: Angel would be a danger to him if she found out his secret and managed to return to the twentieth century to tell it. Anyway, she'd never believe him if he told her he didn't have the scar because he wouldn't be shot until October 5. Maybe he'd better continue to pretend not to know her until he figured out how to handle this unexpected complication.

"Didn't you hear me?" she demanded in a louder voice. "I don't know who you are, but you're not John Logan!"

"Sure I am! What's the matter with you?"

"Liar!" Angie pulled her blouse closed, scrambling to her feet. "There's something wrong here; you've got his gun and watch and you look like him, but you don't have the scar!"

"Now, Angel—"

"Don't you call me that! That's what John calls me. Now back off!" She swung her purse at him menacingly. "You're a rat, taking advantage of me like that!"

"Ow! What have you got in that purse, an anvil?" He backed away as she struck him on the shoulder.

"How dare you take advantage of me!" She swung her purse again.

"Me taking advantage of *you!"* He was in a fury now, his face dark as thunder. "Lady, you throw yourself into my arms, pull your clothes off and offer—"

"I was offering to John! Oh, you unchivalrous—!"

"I *am* Johnny Logan!"

"Not *my* John Logan; unless maybe you've got amnesia. Maybe you were hit on the head going through the mirror."

He stared at her blankly. "I don't know anything about a mirror."

She hesitated, then began to cry as the horrible truth dawned on her. "It can't happen, but there's no other explanation. Jiminy Christmas, I've traveled back in time! You must be the first John Logan!"

"Hell, as far as I know, I'm the *only* Johnny Logan!" He reached out for her, but she pushed him away.

"I can't get mixed up with you!" She stood up. "Don't you understand? You're his great-great grandfather!"

"Who?"

"Who are we talking about?" She almost screamed it at him as she straightened her clothes. "John Logan, that's who!"

"Lady, you are loco." The gunfighter sighed and shook his head. "You offer me that gorgeous body, and when I'm hot as fire, you crawl out from under me!"

"You rotten—you think I'm gorgeous?" She paused a split second in buttoning her blouse; then she decided he was just trying to get her pants off. "You don't understand," she began patiently. "Logan's ancestor has to end up with a Cheyenne girl named Little Deer."

"Little Deer?" He reached into his leather vest for a slender cigarillo. "I don't know any Little Deer!"

"But you will someday," Angie explained. "I know you're not going to understand this, but I don't belong in this time period. I came back here trying to help John. If the two of us get mixed up together, we might change history, and that would be a mess."

"Would it now?" He looked tired, frustrated and annoyed as he struck a match and lit his smoke.

Angie looked in the direction from which they'd come. "Somehow, I've got to return to my own time. John is back there somewhere and he's in trouble."

The gunfighter raised one eyebrow at her as the tiny mole by his mouth twitched. "What's the guy to you?"

Angie paused and thought for a minute. "I—I'm not sure, I care about him; that's all. I work for him."

"Most employees wouldn't be this loyal or dedicated." He stared at her as he smoked, as if trying to understand her motives.

Angie shrugged. "Maybe not." She didn't want to explain or explore her feelings for her boss right now; certainly not with his ancestor. "Anyway, I'm sorry about the mistaken identity, Johnny."

"Not half as sorry as I am, Angel." He gave her a wry smile, stood up, dropped his cigarillo and crushed it out. "I'm unchivalrous enough to wish I'd had another five minutes before you decided I was the wrong man."

Angie blushed a hot crimson. "He's inherited your small feet; you know that?"

"I'm sick of hearing about this supposed descendant; I don't understand what this is all about, except that you've been chewing loco weed or you're just plain crazy."

"That's highly possible," Angie conceded as she reached out and put her hand on the man's shoulder. She could feel the corded muscles there. He was every bit as sexy and magnetic as John Logan VI. It must run in the genes. If she had met this Johnny back in her own time, and before she met Logan . . . no, she must not think of that. "Anyway, John has a scar on his shoulder from a hunting accident; that's how I knew you weren't him."

"And I'm supposed to believe that?" The gunfighter reached up and jerked her hand from his shoulder. "I'm sick of hearing about this hombre. Would you believe I don't give a big God damn?"

"You shouldn't use God's name like that," Angie said primly. "It's wrong; my grandmother said so."

"Really?" He put his hands on his gunbelt and glared at her. "And what would dear Grannie have said about you luring a man to tussle half-naked in broad daylight on a blanket?"

Angie felt her face flame, remembering her unaccustomed passion. "She—she probably would have said we should get married first."

"Married? Not me, Angel." He looked up at her, his face tense, his black eyes hard. "I don't know where you came from or what kind of game you're playing, but I should have left you in town."

"And just why did you take me?" she challenged.

The gunfighter hesitated. Finally, he said, "Because I wanted you; that's why. I saw you there, all helpless and wearing those tight men's pants—"

"Why does everyone think they're men's pants?" Angie almost screamed at him.

"Ladies don't dress like that."

"Oh, pooh!" Angie dismissed him with a curt nod. "I can't spend any more time here; I've got to find a way back to my own time." She reached for the saddle blanket. "You've even got the ancestor to his horse. Well, I'm going to take him and ride into town."

He blocked her path. "Take Crazy Quilt? I think you won't! You know what we do to horse thieves in the West?"

Angie glared at him. "I didn't say I was going to steal it; I was just going to borrow it."

"And leave me stranded out here at the mercy of every bushwhacker and rustler who comes along?"

"You're beginning to sound like a bad old B Western movie," Angie snorted. "Let's hear you say, 'There ain't room enough in this town for the both of us!' "

He took the saddle blanket out of her hand and frowned darkly. "I'm beginning to think that's right. So now what is it you want from me, Angel?"

"I want to get back to my own time and help your great-great-grandson."

"Your own time?" The half-breed pushed his hat back on his black hair. "Lady, believe me, I'm as eager to get rid of a loco girl as you are to go. Anyway, you must be more than just an employee; you must care about the guy."

She hadn't faced up to that until just now. "I don't know for sure, Johnny," she acknowledged with a nod, "but maybe I care too much. Now lend me your horse."

His expression changed, and for a moment, he seemed about to speak. Then his eyes hardened and took on a guarded expression. "I don't trust you. You'd go back and lead a posse to me. You aren't going anywhere except with me!"

Okay, so this Johnny Logan wouldn't lend her his horse, so what was Angie to do? She'd have to go along with whatever he wanted to do while she made a plan.

He saddled up the paint stallion and swung up. Then he looked down at her. "You comin'?"

"Do I have a choice?" Angie glared at him, thinking how much he looked like his great-great-grandson.

"Sure you do." He tipped his black Stetson to the back of his head. "You can stand right here 'til hell freezes over, or you can start walking, hoping to run across a farm or someone passing by in a buggy."

"Oh, you jerk! You ought to at least take me into some town."

He held out his callused hand to her. "As you saw, I'm not very welcome in any town in Kansas."

"I don't think I have to ask why."

"Ouch! That hurt!" He favored her with a wry smile.

"I meant for it to." Angie thought over her options, and there were none. Being left stranded alone on the prairie was not too appealing. She took the gunfighter's hand and he lifted her up easily to sit behind him on the saddle skirt.

"Hang on," he ordered. "We're gonna be hittin' some rough country."

Reluctantly, Angie scooted closer to him, putting her arms around his lean waist. The half-breed was a big, virile man; she could feel the hard muscles ripple under the black shirt.

Johnny took off at an easy lope across the prairie, stopping now and then to rest his horse. Once he led the stallion to cool it out, letting Angie sit in the saddle.

Could she just grab the reins and take off? She toyed with the idea, but Johnny looked up at her and frowned. "Don't even think it!"

"Now, why would I be thinking anything?" Angie gave him an innocent smile, but he didn't smile back.

"I've learned not to trust women," he muttered.

"You're more like your descendant than you know," she complained.

"I said shut up about him." Johnny swung up into the saddle, and she slipped her arms around him again. She was getting weary. Without thinking, she laid her face against his broad back, half dozing.

He reached down and, in a gentle motion that surprised her, patted her hand. "We're almost there, Angel; you'll be all right."

In the early afternoon, he reined in a short distance from a grove of willow trees. "Hello, the camp!"

A distant voice called, "Who goes there?"

"Hey, Emmett, it's me, Johnny!"

Johnny clucked to his horse and rode on into the camp. Men came out from behind trees, all carrying rifles. There were four of them, Angie noted, a dark one and three who looked enough alike to be related, with dark blond hair and blue eyes. All were unshaven and scruffy-looking.

"Hey, Johnny"—the dark one pulled at his mustache—"who's the girl?"

"None of your business, Dick." Johnny's voice held a warning as he dismounted. "Don't give her another thought; she's off limits."

One of the blond trio laughed. "Aw! I thought you was bringin' us a treat!"

"Shut up, Bob," Johnny said, "you'll scare the lady."

"Lady?" One of the blond trio laughed. "Since when do ladies be seen with the likes of you?"

Angie bristled as she looked down into the wolfish, eager faces. "Do you guys know the meaning of sexual harassment?"

"No. Does it mean you're passin' out sex?" The one called Bob scratched his head and looked puzzled.

"In your dreams!" she said.

The men exchanged puzzled looks.

Johnny reached to help her down. "I better warn you hombres, she's a little loco; don't pay her no never mind."

"I am not loco!"

Johnny snorted and rolled his eyes.

The one called Bob wore fancy cowboy boots. He stared at her with fascination. "I ain't never seen a girl in men's pants before. Who are you, girlie?"

"Bob, don't ask her," Johnny grumbled as he knelt by the fire and poured himself a cup of coffee from the big iron pot. "She'll tell you the craziest story you ever heard. Are we out of sugar again?"

Bob nodded. "Sorry, Johnny."

"It is not a crazy story!" Angie retorted and brushed past the men to pour herself a cup of coffee. "Somehow, I've been thrown back into this time period from 1999, and I've got to figure out a way to get back. I think maybe it all has something to do with the Millennium."

The scruffy ones looked at each other blankly, then looked at Johnny.

He only shrugged and sipped his coffee. He had the devil's own luck that they didn't understand any of this. It occurred to Johnny that she not only was a danger to him if she returned to the twentieth century, she might be a danger to him now if anyone believed her story of time travel. One thing was certain: She must not be allowed to change history and, in doing so, keep him from resigning that contract. He needed time to decide what to do. "Don't ask me to explain any of it; I told you she was loco."

Bob grinned. "Loco or not, she can warm my blankets any time! What about you, little brother?" He turned toward the third of the trio.

Johnny stood up suddenly. "Bob, I'm warning you—you and Emmett and Grat—don't touch her!"

"All right, all right." Bob made a soothing gesture and stepped backward. "You know I can't outdraw you, Johnny. Why didn't you just say she was yours?"

"I'm telling you now!" Johnny's tone was like a rattle-snake's warning rattle.

Angie started to say she didn't belong to anyone, especially not this questionable ancestor of her employer. But she decided that maybe being labeled Johnny Logan's woman protected her from these four rough-looking men. These were gangsters? They looked more like the villains from an old Saturday-matinee Western.

"Well," said the younger brother, Emmett, his blue eyes brightening, "at least now we got someone to cook."

Angie glared at him. "Now, what makes you think I can cook?"

Bob snorted. "All women can cook; it comes natural."

"Buddy," Angie said, "if you lived a hundred years from now, you'd be in for a rude awakening."

The grumpy-looking older one said, "You're right, Johnny. She's crazy as a loon."

The one called Dick frowned. "You shouldn't have brought her here, Johnny. Now she knows our hideout."

"I took her on impulse." Johnny shrugged and sipped his coffee. "I got into a scrap in Coffeyville with Duke Babcock over her; had to kill him."

"Aw, Duke's been on the prod for years," Bob of the fancy boots said. "I hope what she's putting out is worth the trouble."

"I am not putting out!" Angie snapped.

"She's no threat, but she is trouble; sassiest female you've ever met."

She glared at him, wishing her looks could burn holes in his big body. "I'm not sassy; only assertive."

"You ought to beat her a little," Dick advised. "Then she'd be obedient enough."

Johnny looked around slowly at the other men. "I'll kill the man who raises a hand to her." His tone left no doubt that he meant it.

"I didn't mean nothin'," Dick whined. "I was only tellin' you how to keep her in line."

Johnny looked over at Angie. "High-spirited women and horses are a lot alike; you handle 'em gently so you don't break the spirit. Then you get a pleasing ride."

"Thanks a lot!" Angie snorted. "I suppose you've handled a lot of horses?"

"And women." He had the most roguish smile.

The others whooped like schoolboys.

"That's tellin' her, Johnny!" Dick said.

She didn't say anything. Somehow, it bothered her to think

he'd kissed and caressed other women the way he'd kissed her only hours before. There was no doubt about it, though; Johnny Logan was a skilled lover.

"Angel," he said, "you can hang around the camp until I decide what to do with you."

"I'm a prisoner, then?"

"No, you can walk away any time you want."

"Walk? It's probably dozens of miles to town."

Johnny shrugged. "I can't help that." He pulled out the big gold pocket watch. "We've got to meet Doolin, Bill and Bitter Creek. What time's the train?"

"Three o'clock," Grat said.

Angie remembered then that part of the first John Logan's fortune had been made from gold and the railroads; she had read it in those old news clippings. Maybe she could catch the train back to Coffeyville; the secret to all this had to be in that town where she had first crossed the time barrier. "If you're going to meet a train, can I go along?"

"No," Johnny said. "You stay in camp."

"I don't trust her." Emmett glared at her. "Maybe we'd better take her along so we can watch her; we got an extra horse."

Johnny shook his head. "I hate to get her mixed up in it."

If she could manage to get on that train, she could escape from this bunch. "No, I'd like to go."

Johnny raised his eyebrows at her, as if he intended to object, but Bob said, "Emmett's right; if we leave her tied up here, she might get away. Besides, if she goes along, that makes her one of us and then she can hardly turn us in for the reward."

"You hear that, Johnny?" Dick crowed proudly. "You should see the posters. Most the law's ever offered for any gang; makes Jesse James look like a piker!"

Johnny swore under his breath. "Don't be proud of it; it only means trouble for us. But then, none of you have spent as much time in prison as I have."

Angie gasped. "You—you've been in prison?"

He nodded.

"Does John know about this?"

"Who?" He tossed the last sip of coffee into the fire.

"Your descendant; the one they call the outlaw of Wall Street."

"Who?" The other four sounded like a nest of owls to her.

Johnny laughed. "Lady, you are loco. Now hush up."

She studied his mocking face; the tiny mole next to his grim mouth that his descendant had inherited. When she figured out pieces of the puzzle, would they all fit together and make sense? No wonder John Logan VI was so secretive; he must know about this skeleton in the family closet.

The gang saddled up, including three extra horses: two chestnut geldings and a big blaze-faced bay. For her, they saddled a dainty paint mare Johnny told her was called Rosebud. Angie noted that there were a half-dozen different brands on the mounts. *Horse thieves, too,* she thought.

"Are we going to the station to meet some more of your scruffy friends?" she asked Johnny. "I presume it's not a meeting of railroad stockholders?"

He looked blank. "Now why would the likes of us know any stockholders?"

She wondered if John knew that his ancestor had been outside the law. Well, a lot of people had family scandals they didn't want to talk about. The finance magazines would have had a field day with this.

Angie patted Rosebud's velvet nose. "She's beautiful," she crooned. "I love horses. My folks were always being transferred, so I could never own one."

"You can have her," Johnny said. "She's too dainty for a man."

"You're making me a gift of a stolen horse?"

"I didn't steal that one; I bought her as a mate for Crazy

Quilt. Thought someday I might go straight; own a ranch and raise good horses."

"Fat chance of that." Dick laughed. "The law's lookin' for us everywhere."

"Shut up, Dick," Johnny snapped. "Let's make tracks." As they rode out of camp, he fell in beside her. "I don't like mixing a woman into this."

"Just consider it equal opportunity employment," Angie said.

"Besides being loco, you're too damned spirited," Johnny complained. "I pity the man who has to break you in."

Angie snorted. "That man isn't going to be you."

"Thank the saints for that!"

They rode many miles in silence. Somewhere in the distance, a train whistle echoed, and Johnny pulled out his big gold watch. "Looks like she'll be right on time."

Angie looked around, puzzled. She didn't see anything of a town or even a railroad station.

As they nudged their horses and rode toward a thicket of cottonwood trees, Johnny fell in beside her. "You stay out of sight and hold the horses; I wouldn't want you to get hurt."

"Is meeting a train dangerous in this time?" she asked.

He grinned at her. "It is the way we do it."

She got an uneasy feeling in the pit of her stomach and was surprised to realize she was as concerned for this lonely gunfighter as she had been for his descendant. "Johnny, maybe you'd better not do this."

He frowned and shook his head in dismissal. "The way I've come up, I've survived the best way I can; this life is all I've ever known."

Angie studied him and said softly, so the others wouldn't hear, "It doesn't seem like much of a life, Johnny; didn't you ever dream of something better?"

For a moment, as they rode, she didn't think he would answer. His eyes became softer, as if his mind was far away. "I used to dream of a peaceful life; a nice ranch, someone to love and kids; lots of kids.''

Once that had been her dream, too, but her life had turned into a domestic nightmare. ''They say it's never too late to make a fresh start.''

A flicker of hope shone a split second in his dark eyes, then was gone. He shook his head. ''No. I've cut my deal, and if it was a bad bargain, it's my own fault; I've got to live with it.''

''What kind of a bargain and who with?''

But the spell had been broken. He frowned at her, his face stone cold. ''You ask too many questions.''

The train whistle blew again, much closer this time; echoing across the endless prairie. Johnny urged his horse forward. ''Let's pick up the pace, boys.''

Angie looked around for a town or at least a railroad station. She didn't see anything except a stretch of track through a grove of trees. With Emmett leading the extra horses, they rode into the grove and dismounted.

''Here, Angel,'' Johnny said. ''You hold the horses.''

''But—''

''Just do it and don't argue,'' Johnny said.

The others were already dismounted, piling rocks on the tracks.

Angie stayed on her mare. ''What is happening? They'll cause that train to wreck!''

''No.'' Johnny shook his head. ''They'll just stop it; that's all.''

She could hear the train chugging toward them now and see it approaching over the horizon. ''Train robbers!'' she realized abruptly. ''Why, here your great-great grandson talks about your railroad interests and you're nothing but a train robber!''

Dick guffawed. ''He is interested in railroads; all of us are, especially the payroll car, hey, Johnny?''

''Shut up, Dick!'' Johnny snapped. ''You talk too much!''

"You two are gettin' too edgy," Bob complained. "There isn't gonna be any trouble; Doolin, Bill and Bitter Creek should be about ready to pull their pistols on the engineer and the conductor."

Angie glared at the scruffy bunch. "I think you're all terrible!"

Johnny looked up at her. "A lot of America's big fortunes have shady beginnings, Angel. A few generations later, nobody knows the difference, as long as they're rich."

"What about your dream, Johnny?" she argued. "What about—?"

"Shut up! Don't bring that up again!" he snarled. "I can't change the deal I made or he won't hold up his end of the bargain."

"Who, Johnny?"

The half-breed gunfighter didn't answer. *Damn!* he thought. *I almost mentioned the Gambler. Angie must not figure this mystery out.* Johnny turned and strode away to direct the others in placing rocks on the tracks. "Give the train plenty of time to stop, Bob. We don't want to hurt anyone unless we have to."

"Aw, who cares if we hurt anyone?" Dick growled.

"I do," Johnny said. "I only kill people in fair fights."

The train was coming closer. Angie could see it looming in the distance, black smoke billowing from its metal stack as it chugged toward them. The gang had the track piled with rocks and had hunkered down in the brush, putting bandannas over their faces and pulling their pistols.

Angie sat her mare, holding the reins of the other horses and staring in horrified disbelief. She was about to take part in a train robbery with a bunch of Western outlaws. That made her an accessory. She could go to jail; she who always obeyed speed limits and wouldn't drop a gum wrapper on the street. She didn't want any part of this!

The train rumbled forward now, beginning to slow as the

engineer seemed to see the rock barricade. He blew his whistle long and loud and hit the brakes. The big iron locomotive screeched, and sparks flew from the wheels as it slowed.

Angie surveyed the scene. All the outlaws were concentrating on the approaching train. Angie guessed that it would stop just short of the rock pile; then the outlaws would clamber on board and rob it. She decided suddenly that she wasn't going to be an accessory to robbery; it was wrong, wrong, wrong. None of the outlaws were looking her way. This was the perfect time to escape. She dug her heels into the startled mare and took off, leading all the other horses with her.

Behind her, she heard cries of surprise and protest. "Stop that little tart!"

"She's getting away with the horses!"

And Johnny's cry. "Angel! Damn it, Angel, come back here!"

She urged the little mare on, knowing from Johnny's voice that he was boiling mad. There was no telling what he'd do to her when he caught her. That thought caused her to slap Rosebud with the reins and ride as though the devil was on her coattails.

Now why had that comparison crossed her mind?

Chapter Ten

Angie didn't slow down for several miles, until all the horses were lathered and blowing. She was crossing rolling prairie with nothing in sight save a lone hawk dipping in lazy circles against a faded blue sky. There wasn't even a telephone pole or an occasional plane. Most of all, it was quiet except for a bobwhite calling in the tall grass and the wind rustling through stunted trees. Used to being constantly bombarded by the noise of traffic, piped-in music, televisions and boom boxes, the silence was both unnerving and soothing.

I could get used to this sort of laid-back, peaceful lifestyle, Angie thought. *Jiminy Christmas, are you nuts, girl?* She scolded herself as she stood up in her stirrups and looked around. *You're lost back in time over a hundred years ago with train robbers after your hide because you've stolen their horses and left them afoot in high-heeled cowboy boots. Peaceful lifestyle?* She snorted with laughter at the image of the ruffians limping back to camp. Then she imagined Johnny's face and stopped laughing. He would be furious with her, and she was more than a little afraid of that glowering, masculine bandit, yet tremendously attracted to him. Johnny was every bit as exciting and intimidating as his descendant.

Which direction to ride now? Angie had no idea where she was or where she was heading; she only knew that she had to find her way to civilization. Maybe she would ride into Coffeyville and find it exactly as she had seen it that first day—a nice sleepy town with pickup trucks parked downtown—and she'd be back in her own time.

Or maybe not. In the old West, a lone rider leading a bunch of horses with mixed brands would not only raise suspicions, it might get her thrown in some small-town jail.

Reluctantly, she let go of the other horses she was leading. They began to graze on the low grass and she smiled to think how long foot-sore men in boots would take to walk this far to retrieve these horses. At least she would be far enough away that she wasn't afraid the gang would catch up to her; at least, not any time soon. Maybe once they got their mounts back, the gang wouldn't bother looking any farther. The little mare she rode didn't look big enough that they'd pursue Angie to get Rosebud back.

Johnny might. He didn't seem like the kind of man you crossed and got away with it. She thought about him a moment, and the feeling that ran through her was the same as if she'd approached some wild thing—exciting and a little dangerous.

Angie nudged the little paint mare into a trot, leaving the other horses grazing prairie grass. Maybe since she'd interrupted the train robbery, she'd saved him from further outlaw activity. Why did she think he'd be less than grateful? In fact, there was no telling what he'd do to her if he ever caught up with her again. Angie intended to see that that didn't happen. As soon as she could figure out how, she was going back to the twentieth century. Johnny Logan would be on his own. She was surprised to realize that she had developed a certain fondness for the rough and rugged gunfighter.

In fact, now that she thought of it, when he had kissed her, it had been exactly like kissing John on the floating platform back at the lake. Surely she couldn't be mistaken about the way she had responded to him. Could he possibly be her Johnny Logan? Maybe he'd been hit on the head coming through the mirror, and now he had amnesia so he didn't remember her. Yet if this was true, what had happened to the scar on John's shoulder? Maybe time travel wiped out the memory. Yet she remembered everything, from the taste of his kisses to the thrill of his strong arms around her back at the lake, and again when he'd rescued her from Duke Babcock. It was all so confusing, and after all, she'd never time-traveled before, so none of it made sense.

It was almost dusk when she rode into a small town on the prairie. *Coffeyville?* No, this town was smaller. Angie rode down the dusty main street, trying to decide what to do next. A wooden sign swinging in the wind over a frame building read: PRAIRIE VIEW, KANSAS POST OFFICE.

It must be almost supper time; the sun was approaching the Western rim on the desolate prairie and there was no one on the dusty streets. She needed to do something about changing from jeans to a dress to keep from attracting unwarranted attention until she could decide what to do next. Thank goodness she still had her big purse with Father's antique coins.

Angie dismounted in front of the general store, whose owner was just coming out and locking up. "Please don't close yet; I'd like to buy some things."

The bent old man hesitated, looking her over. "You're dressed strange, ma'am."

She wasn't a good liar; never had had much practice. Could she tell the truth without arousing a lot of questions she couldn't answer? Like Johnny, people would think she was loco if she told them she'd time-traveled. "My suitcase has been lost. I've been stranded out in the country, trying to make it back to civilization alone."

He gave her a sympathetic look and his false teeth clicked. "These new big-city settlers; never prepared to deal with bad roads or country life. Come on in, ma'am." Shaking his head, he unlocked the door, and Angie followed him as he reentered the store and lit the kerosene lamps.

Angie looked around and took a sniff. It looked like a movie set for every old Western she'd ever seen. The general store smelled of dust, spices, leather and barrels of pickles. Stacked about were crates of crackers and barrels of sugar, bolts of calico, horse collars and boots. After a few minutes, she picked out a calico dress with tiny pink flowers and some pink ribbons to do up her hair. She bought some shoes, a lace petticoat and some bloomers. Angie hesitated, then couldn't resist a straw bonnet with pink and burgundy roses on the brim.

Without thinking, she plunked her credit card on the counter.

"What is this thing, ma'am?"

"Oh, never mind." Before he could pick it up and question her about it, Angie reached for the silver coins of her father's collection. Angie was amazed at how low the bill was, but still, her antique coins were running low. If she ran out of money before she discovered how to return to her own time, what on earth would she do? What she needed was a temporary job.

After paying for her purchases, she started to leave the store, wondering where to go from there. The sun would be setting soon, and she didn't want to be on the streets in case the footsore outlaws trailed her into town. She turned back to the old man. "You wouldn't know of any jobs, would you?"

He scratched his head. "We've got a bootleg saloon that the town just winks at, ma'am, but for a respectable woman; not much work."

"Why do they just wink at it?"

He cleared his throat and didn't meet her gaze. "Well, maybe because the owner is partners with the banker on the deal. Banker Hiram holds mortgages on most everything in town."

He hesitated, looking alarmed. "Please don't tell anyone I said that, ma'am."

"Of course not." She sighed and started out of the store. Well, she'd think of something.

"Wait, ma'am," he called behind her. "I just thought of one job; you wouldn't happen to be a schoolmarm?"

"Why, yes, I am!" Angie smiled as she whirled around, her heart beating with hope. "What grades?"

"All grades, ma'am. It's just a one-room schoolhouse. Our man teacher was called back to Omaha for a couple of weeks—his ma is ailin'—so we need someone to take his place for awhile."

"I would be *very* interested," Angie said.

His false teeth clicked as he smiled. "In that case, let me take you over to the hotel and get you a room; then I'll get the schoolboard together. I'm Luther Tuttle."

"Thank you, Mr. Tuttle!" Angie breathed a sigh of relief.

Old Mr. Tuttle walked her over to the hotel and left to gather up the other members of the schoolboard, making arrangements to meet her later in the hotel's lobby.

Angie got a room, although the clerk looked at her suspiciously when she said she was traveling alone. Respectable women didn't do that except in an emergency, she remembered, so she told him a vague tale without actually lying about being all alone in the world and left stranded on the prairie.

This town didn't even have running water in the hotel, but there was a big tin tub that the manager filled with buckets carried upstairs. Her room was small but nice enough, with Victorian wallpaper. After a good bath, she put on the new clothes and giggled at her image in the mirror when she raised her skirt to see the lacy bloomers. Actually, she decided she liked the clothes; they made her feel very dainty and feminine.

Later, when Angie went downstairs, she knew she looked properly demure and respectable in her full-skirted, pink-flowered dress, with her blond hair done up and tied with pink ribbons.

The schoolboard members were waiting in the hotel lobby with Luther Tuttle. "I'm sorry, ma'am; I've forgotten your name," he apologized, and his teeth clicked.

She didn't think she had given it, but she made the slightest curtsy and remembered that a proper lady didn't give a man direct and curious looks. "I'm Mrs. Angelica Newland," she said, "lately from Oklahoma Territory."

A pink-faced, potbellied man wearing a flower in his lapel and spats, nodded. "I am Wilbur Hiram," he said in a pompous tone, "the local banker and also the mayor of Prairie View."

His reddish hair was so greased down with macassar oil, she could almost see her reflection in it.

Angie nodded politely.

Mr. Hiram turned toward a man with white, bushy sideburns. "And this is Mr. Dudley, the newspaper editor, and Mrs. Mead, the head of the Prairie View Improvement Society."

"How do you do?" Angie curtsied. The newspaper editor looked middle-aged and had inkstains on his fingers, and plump, prim Mrs. Mead, in a large flowered dress, looked a bit like an overstuffed sofa.

They all sat down on the deep burgundy horsehair sofas in the hotel lobby, surrounded by potted ferns and stern portraits of Victorian ladies. Angie wondered briefly why no one ever smiled in those old pictures; then she decided it was because of the tight corsets. She hadn't bought one of those.

The group began asking Angie questions. She told them her father had been in the military. "He was formerly a pilot, but he and the Barbie doll were in Palm Beach when he died."

"What?" Mrs. Mead leaned closer and looked over her glasses at Angie.

Uh oh. Now she'd done it. Angie hated to lie, but she couldn't explain her stupid remark; they'd think she was crazy. "Uh, I said Father was farming a plot, out of reach, when he died; Florida, you know.''

"Ah," said Mr. Tuttle, "perhaps getting ready to be shipped to Cuba or the Philippines? We've heard there might be some trouble coming over there."

"But the *Maine* won't be sunk for several more years," she thought aloud.

"What?" the banker asked.

"I said my marriage sank several years ago," Angie blurted.

"Oh, your husband died at sea?" The newspaper editor leaned closer.

Angie didn't want to lie, but she knew divorce was scandalous in this time period. She looked sad and didn't answer.

The committee appeared very sympathetic.

"What about your mother?" Mrs. Mead asked.

"She and my sister were killed driving. . . ." Angie hesitated, trying to decide what to say next.

"Yes, buggies can be dangerous." Mr. Hiram nodded. "Women shouldn't really be allowed to take the reins."

Oh, brother. Angie dabbed at her eyes. "So you see, I'm a respectable woman, trying to make it alone in the world. I really do need a position so I can support myself."

They were all looking sad and nodding approval, and the pompous banker asked if she was engaged.

"No." She shook her head, thinking of Logan and wondering where he was and if his law-breaking ancestor, Johnny, had gotten himself shot in the attempted train robbery.

"Ah!" Wilbur Hiram rubbed his soft, pink hands together. "May I be the first to suggest that Mrs. Newland seems perfect for the position?"

The others had evidently been waiting for the banker to make his feelings known. Now they all joined in with murmurs of agreement.

"Maybe with a woman teacher," Mrs. Mead said, "we can attract a better element to our town. That bootleg saloon is attracting such a rough crowd." She looked pointedly at the banker, who stared off as if he had no idea what she was talking about.

"Rough crowd?" Angie asked. "You don't mean outlaws?" *Was this a town where Johnny Logan and that gang hung out?*

"Mrs. Mead is exaggerating," Wilbur Hiram said smoothly. "The Lady Luck Two is only providing what people want."

The others looked at the floor and didn't say anything. Evidently, Mr. Hiram controlled this town with his money and mortgages.

The newspaper editor cleared his throat. "Let's get back to the subject. Mrs. Newland will need a place to stay."

"I hold the mortgage on this hotel." Mr. Hiram puffed out his chest with importance. "I'm sure they will be happy to give our new teacher a reduced rate." He smiled at Angie. "I move we hire this pretty young lady."

"I second that," said the store owner.

The vote was unanimous.

Mr. Hiram stood up, took Angie's hand in his soft, pink one and kissed it. "Now that everything's settled, Mrs. Newland, you may start tomorrow. I'll drive you to the school myself in my new buggy."

Everyone exchanged glances and smiled at each other, evidently relieved that Mr. Hiram approved of her. The arrogant banker must control this town and everyone in it. Well, if she was going to be trapped back in time for the rest of her life, she could do worse than marry a rich, small-town banker, even if he did wear his hair greased down and parted down the middle.

The rest of her life? She couldn't stay; John needed her help, wherever he was. However, right now, all she could do was take care of herself.

The next morning, bright and early, Wilbur Hiram was waiting out in front of the hotel with his shiny new buggy. It had bright red wheels, silver on the harness and a fine black horse to pull it. Wilbur wore spats, a derby hat, a silk vest over his little pot belly and a flower in his lapel. Worse yet, his slickly oiled head reeked of rose hair tonic. He helped her in, his hand lightly brushing her waist. "It's been a long time since we've had such a lovely lady in our midst here in Prairie View."

"I'm happy to be here." She tried to listen to his chatter, mostly about himself and his success as they drove, but her mind was on her own problems.

". . . Autumn Festival," he said.

"What?" She realized he was staring sideways at her.

"I said, in late September we always have an Autumn Festival to raise money for the school. There'll be a dance and social and a basket supper auction."

She must have looked blank, because he explained. "You know, the ladies all prepare a box or basket and the men have to bid on them." He winked at her. "I'm sure you're an excellent cook, my dear."

Angie smiled uncertainly. She hoped by late September she would have figured out a way to return to her own time and John Logan. "I'm so sorry, Mr. Hiram"—she gave him her sweetest, most demure smile—"but without a kitchen, I will have a difficult time preparing food to bring."

"Do call me Wilbur," he said as the buggy moved along. "My dear, you really must take part; it's for the benefit of the school. Why, every cowboy and clerk in the county will be bidding up those baskets, hoping to have a chance to share supper with you. Of course, I have the most money, so may I hope you'll be looking forward to having supper with me?"

Well, as a matter of fact, no, Angie thought, but she let her eyelashes flutter demurely. "Mr. Hiram, you surprise me with your boldness!"

His pale eyes bore into hers. "I apologize, but I am so looking forward to getting to know you better."

She smiled back at him. Angie didn't know how long she

was going to be in Prairie View, but she'd better stay on the good side of the richest man in town.

"Here we are at the school." He reined up before a small, weather-beaten building just outside town on the edge of a pecan grove. Children of various sizes ran about the schoolyard, chasing balls or swinging in an old-fashioned rope swing. Banker Hiram raised his voice. "Here, kiddies," he shouted. "I've brought a new teacher, Mrs. Newland, to substitute while Mr. Jones is gone."

The children ran to gather around the buggy.

Angie gave them her warmest smile. "Hello, children, I'm so pleased to meet you."

The children laughed and pushed forward eagerly.

Mr. Hiram shooed them away. "Here, now, everyone into the building." He turned to Angie. "Such adorable tykes." His lips smiled, but his face didn't. It was clear the banker didn't really like children.

"I'd better go in now," Angie said as one of the bigger boys began to ring the school bell.

"Here, let me help you."

In the full-skirted long dress, she couldn't move fast enough to get down alone. His soft pink hands felt sweaty through her dress. She wondered if she could avoid the obligation of accepting rides with Mr. Hiram every day. "Thank you for the ride, but if it's nice tomorrow, I think I'll walk to school," she said.

Before he could answer, she grabbed her purse, turned and hurried toward the weather-beaten building.

"Toodle loo!" he called behind her.

She tried to imagine Johnny Logan saying "Toodle loo," and smiled. Funny, he was in her thoughts now almost as often as John Logan VI.

Inside the school, she saw she had about twenty students of all ages and sizes. She did a quick appraisal as she greeted the children: blackboards, a few McGuffey readers, small slates and chalk. No computers, no movies, no extras. This was going to be teaching in its purest form. "Now, class, I am Mrs. Newland."

"Good day, Mrs. Newland," the children said politely, in unison.

She was thunderstruck at the respect in their voices. Maybe she was going to like teaching in the Gay Nineties. *Don't start liking it too much,* she reminded herself; *you're only here temporarily . . . I think.*

However, the days passed peacefully one into another as the leaves turned yellow and autumn came on. She loved working with the children, but banker Hiram was becoming a pest, making no bones about his interest in her. The townspeople seemed nice enough, but from what she heard, there was a rough crowd that hung out at the Lady Luck Two, though they didn't come into the respectable part of town.

On a Friday afternoon in late September, Mrs. Mead and the ladies of the town arrived with crepe paper and ribbons to help the children decorate the school for tomorrow night's Autumn Festival.

"Mrs. Newland," the plump dowager said, "what are you putting in your basket?"

"I—I really haven't given it much thought, having no kitchen." Angie paused in hanging the ribbon.

"Oh, but you must," one of the others giggled, and the ladies exchanged glances as they pushed the desks back so there'd be room for dancing. "We hear Wilbur Hiram is planning to bid on your basket."

She wondered if he'd like baloney sandwiches, and decided she was expected to do better than that. "Remember, I don't have a kitchen, so—"

"Oh, but the hotel will lend you theirs," Mrs. Mead said. "The money's for the school. Why, last year, the top basket went for two dollars!"

"Two dollars?" Angie said.

"Yes, isn't that something?" The others chortled. "But that was Mildred Fenney's daughter, and Joe Williams was absolutely crazy to marry her."

Mrs. Fenney smiled with superior smugness.

Mrs. Mead exchanged a glance with the others. "I wouldn't be surprised if we don't get banker Hiram to pay maybe three dollars to share Mrs. Newland's basket."

"That's a lot of money," said another.

"But he can afford it," said a third.

"I'll do the best I can," Angie said. It occurred to her that these Western men expected women to be fine cooks. If she fixed something that would make a hog sick, maybe Greasy Hair Hiram would stop pursuing her.

Mrs. Mead patted her arm. "I'm sure you'll fix something larruping."

"Larruping?" Angie said. "That sounds like something out of an old Roy Rogers movie."

The ladies looked at each other blankly.

"A what?" Mrs. Mead asked.

"Never mind." Angie shrugged. "I promise Mr. Hiram will never forget my basket supper."

The ladies returned to their decorating. In a couple of hours, the room was transformed with bright yellow and orange ribbons and crepe paper. Scarlet autumn leaves had been arranged artistically, and around the room, pumpkins and hay bales vied for space. Angie was pleased when she stepped back and surveyed the results. "Ladies, we've done ourselves proud!"

They all went their separate ways, but banker Hiram was waiting out front of the school with his buggy to drive Angie home. His hair was so shiny, she could almost see her reflection in it.

"My dear, do give me a hint as to how you'll decorate your basket so I'll know which one to bid on," he wheedled.

"Now that wouldn't be fair," Angie protested. "You're

supposed to bid on a basket without knowing who it belongs to.''

He winked at her. ''With my money and power, my dear, I don't have to play by the rules. And I expect to become ever richer; I've been investing with those railroad and banking tycoons, Morgan and Rockefeller.''

Suddenly he didn't seem so very different from John Logan VI, except that there was something vulnerable about Logan in spite of his hard exterior. Johnny, too. It occurred to her that it was becoming more difficult to distinguish in her own mind between the outlaw and his descendant. She had tried to put both men out of her thoughts, but she had failed.

They reached the hotel, and Angie hopped out before he could come around and help her down. ''If you don't mind, Mr. Hiram, I'll get myself to the festival tomorrow evening. I have to be there so early.''

''I don't mind going early, and you must call me Wilbur.''

Mrs. Wilbur Hiram. She ran the name through her mind and gagged. ''Nevertheless, I want my basket to be a surprise, so I'll catch a ride with Mrs. Mead.''

Evidently he did mind. His expression turned pouty. ''Very well, my dear, but once I buy your basket, I'll expect the first dance, too.''

She nodded and ran inside. She decided right then and there that her cooking was going to give him such indigestion, maybe he wouldn't feel like dancing after he ate. That thought cheered her. However, she'd have to share that food. She decided she'd get around that by eating just before she went to the festival and merely nibbling out of her box. Suppose someone outbid him? Everyone had made it clear that was very unlikely.

Early Saturday, she borrowed a corner of the hotel kitchen and fried some chicken almost black, then oversalted it. She made some potato salad and loaded it with mustard. Finally, she baked a chocolate cake, disregarding a recipe. It fell, and was so sweet she shuddered when she tasted it. If her horrible cooking didn't discourage Wilbur Hiram, nothing would.

At last she put all the food in a beautifully decorated basket wrapped in pink tissue paper with pink blossoms and ribbons on the top.

"There now." She stepped back and took another look. Surely there wouldn't be a prettier basket there, even if the food inside would give an elephant indigestion.

That done, she went upstairs, took a bath in the big clawfoot tub and sprayed herself with a dainty cologne from the general store. With her teaching salary, she had bought a new pale blue cotton frock that matched her eyes. Frankly, she was getting attached to these frilly clothes with all the lace and ribbons. Angie had never felt as feminine as she did now, looking in the mirror. In fact, she was beginning to feel right at home in the Gay Nineties. Maybe she'd been born in the wrong time period. That made her think of Logan and Johnny and the mess she was in. Darn, it was getting difficult to remember which guy was which; she really liked them both the same. That realization surprised her.

When she was dressed, she took one last look at her yellow hair, done up in curls and tied with a blue ribbon, gathered up her pretty basket and walked to the schoolhouse.

Mrs. Mead and several of the other ladies were already there.

"My! Don't you look fetching!" Mrs. Mead said. "Some of the local cowboys and businessmen may decide to bid against Wilbur Hiram for the privilege of sharing the evening with you."

Angie blushed. "You think so?"

"Let's hope so." Mrs. Mead went back to decorating the front of the room. "Hardly any of the baskets ever bring more than fifty cents or a dollar, and the school could use a lot of repairs."

Angie put her basket down on the table with the early arrivals.

"What a pretty basket!" they all said.

"Thank you." *But my cooking would choke a horse,* Angie thought.

Within an hour, families were arriving in buggies and wagons. Kerosene lights shone brightly through the windows. The front table was soon covered with decorated baskets. Giggling, blushing girls stood nearby, waiting to see who would bid as the room grew more and more crowded and noisy.

Wilbur Hiram pushed through the crowd to her. He wore a new suit and a bright yellow silk vest over his round pot belly. His hair was shiny enough to see her face in and he reeked of rose oil hair tonic. "Ah, there you are, my dear. I hope you're ready to eat with me; I've already asked around until I found out which is your basket."

She thought about the food in it. Her idea didn't seem so clever now. She was going to be humiliated in front of this whole crowd. "Wilbur, you don't want to bid on my basket; I'm a terrible cook."

"Don't be silly, my dear." He caught her hand and kissed her fingertips. "It's not the food, it's sharing your company all evening and dancing with you; that's what I'm buying."

She extracted her hand from his soft, pink one. "You're awfully sure of yourself. Maybe someone will outbid you."

"They wouldn't dare." The banker looked grumpy. "Besides, I've brought ten dollars. In all the years we've been doing this, no basket has gone for more than three."

"Ladies and gentlemen." Mrs. Mead stepped up on a little stool and rang a bell for attention. "We're going to auction the baskets now, and remember, it's for a good cause. So you young men who have managed to find out which basket belongs to the girl you favor, get your money out!"

The bidding started, with the young ladies looking a mite embarrassed. Most baskets went for under a dollar. One thin, homely girl got no bids until her father stepped in and bought hers. She looked crimson with embarrassment. As the bidding progressed, Mrs. Mead selected basket after basket, held them up, commented on them and made the men bid. Finally, there was only one basket left: Angie's. She took a deep breath as a murmur ran through the crowd. Evidently, she had taken the eye of several young men, and Mrs. Mead had obligingly leaked the ownership of the decorated pink basket. Wilbur Hiram caught Angie's eye and gave her a smug, assured nod.

Mrs. Mead announced, "I've been saving the best for last. Now you gents get your money out, and Mrs. Newland, you come up here and stand by me. I reckon everyone's heard there's a new schoolmarm in town, and a pretty one she is, too."

An appreciative murmur ran through the crowd. One thing about this time period, Angie thought, they liked their women plump and dimpled.

Mrs. Mead gestured for silence with her gavel. "Now remember, fellas, the highest bid gets to eat this supper with the lady."

A cowboy on one side immediately offered fifty cents. A merchant yelled, "Seventy-five cents!"

The old postmaster, who was a widower, raised his hand. "I'll give a dollar."

"A dollar and a half," yelled the cowboy.

"Two dollars," said a leather salesman.

"Five dollars!" sang out the banker in a confident tone. A buzz went through the room, and then there was only silence.

"Are there any other bids?" Mrs. Mead raised her gavel. Angie looked over at the banker. He was pleased with himself; that was evident. Tomorrow, everyone would be talking about what a grand gesture he'd made in paying so much for the new teacher's basket. He looked so confident and smug, pushing through the crowd to claim the victory.

Mrs. Mead raised her gavel. "Are we all finished? All right, then, going once, going twice—"

"I bid a twenty-dollar gold piece!"

The masculine voice came from the very back of the room. For a moment, there was stunned silence as the bid registered, and then came a buzz of excited conversation. "Twenty dollars! Did you hear? Some fella bid twenty dollars!"

Banker Hiram turned, his face angry, to look at the newcomer as everyone else craned to see who'd dare defy Wilbur Hiram. Angie gasped. She didn't need to look; she'd recognized that arrogant, confident voice.

It was Johnny Logan.

Chapter Eleven

Angie stared in disbelief at Johnny. With his Stetson pushed back at a jaunty angle, he was striding toward the front of the schoolhouse. The stunned crowd made way for him.

Mrs. Mead seemed speechless, her gavel still half raised.

Johnny swaggered past banker Hiram, almost pushing him aside as he walked up to the front of the room and flipped the gold piece onto the table, where it rang loudly. "Sold!" he shouted.

Angie wasn't quite certain what to do. Nor did anyone else seem to know. The crowd stared in mute disbelief at this arrogant gunfighter, his pistol strapped low on his lean thigh as he picked up the basket and announced to the crowd, "I'm sure the food is equaled only by the lady's beauty."

The banker's pink face had turned a mottled red, but when he started to speak, his gaze went to the pistol Johnny wore, and he gulped and said nothing.

Johnny reached out and took Angie's numb hand. "What is

everyone gawking at?'' he asked. ''I think it's time we all had supper. Shall we, my dear?''

Was there a way out of this? With no other man in the crowd armed, there seemed to be nothing to do but let Johnny lead her across the floor. Around her, she caught the hushed whisper, ''That's Johnny Logan!''

''The gunfighter?''

''Of all the nerve, showing up among honest folks!''

''Poor Mrs. Newland! Too bad the sheriff's out of town!''

Johnny led her to a bench in the corner. ''Sit down, my dear, and let's enjoy this larruping supper you've fixed.''

He really was going to sit and eat in front of all these staring people. Angie could only gape at him as he laid out the food on the bench.

He grinned at her. ''Aren't you going to say anything, Angel? I've never known you to be speechless before.''

Under her breath, her lips barely moving, Angie said, ''You cocky son of a bitch! How dare you?''

''So you do know how to swear,'' he answered softly, and winked at her. Then, in a loud voice, he declared, ''This looks mighty tasty, my dear Mrs. Newland. Yes, I'd love a glass of lemonade to go with it.''

This would give her a chance to escape. Angie hopped up and hurried toward the lemonade table. The banker, standing nearby, reached out and caught her elbow. ''My dear, this is outrageous! If only the sheriff was here!''

''I don't know what he wants,'' Angie said, watching Johnny out of the corner of her eye. ''Maybe he's just showing off. Maybe he'll eat and leave.''

''It makes me sick to see him be so familiar with you,'' Hiram said self-righteously.

''Just wait until he eats the food I brought,'' Angie said.

''What?''

''Never mind.'' Johnny was looking her way and frowning at the banker. ''If I don't return, he's going to come over here.''

"Do you think I'll have to defend your honor?" Sweat broke out on Wilbur's face, and he ran his finger around his collar as if it was choking him.

Angie took a deep breath of rose oil hair tonic and decided eating with the cocky gunfighter wasn't so bad. Besides, Wilbur didn't look as if he was any match for Johnny. "Let it go, Wilbur," she said. "He'll just eat and then maybe he'll leave."

"Be brave, my dear," said Wilbur. "I'll figure out a way to save you. I have many friends at the Lady Luck Two."

"That isn't much help right now," she said. She looked at Johnny. He gestured to her. She picked up two glasses of lemonade and walked back to join him.

"Who's the prissy guy?" Johnny said.

"The local banker. You've got a lot of nerve showing up here."

He shrugged and unwrapped the chicken she had cooked. "I understood it was open to the public. My money's as good as any. Besides, I'm enjoying his outraged glare."

"Be careful, Johnny. You've really made him angry," Angie cautioned. Wilbur Hiram wasn't someone to be trifled with.

The local band began to play a lively tune loudly but not too well: *Oh, dem golden slippers! Oh, dem golden slippers! Golden slippers I'm goin' to wear to walk the golden street. . . .*

Johnny took a big bite of her charred chicken. "I hope they play a waltz; that's my favorite dance."

It was John Logan's, too. Angie caught her breath. "I thought you'd be leaving after you ate."

"Now sweet, why would you think that?"

"Because you aren't welcome here."

He actually grinned. "I'm not welcome most places. You disappoint me, Angel. I thought you'd be glad to see me."

"Jiminy Christmas, why would you think that?" She watched him grimace as he bit into her potato salad.

He gave her a long look. "Because we have so much to talk about, like stealing horses."

She was a little afraid of him, the way he was looking at her. Still, what could he do in this crowded room? "I didn't steal the horses; I borrowed them."

"You still have Rosebud."

Angie gulped. "Well, yes, I do."

"You know what they do to horse thieves out here?"

"But not to ladies," she answered primly.

"Oh, so now you're hiding behind that. I'll bet you've gone to wearing bloomers, too."

She felt her face flame. "It isn't polite to discuss a girl's unmentionables."

He made a face as he took another bite of her food. "Speaking of unmentionables, suppose I told your love-struck banker about you and you lost your job?"

Now she really was afraid. Maybe if she was civil to him, he'd go away.

People had returned to their own food and conversation, casting only an occasional curious glance toward the pair in the corner.

"Johnny," she whispered, "how did you find me?"

"Gossip travels. When I heard there was a pretty new school-marm over at Prairie View, I knew it had to be you."

"Pretty? They're calling me pretty?" She'd never get used to that; it was a heady feeling.

"What else? I know I never met a beauty like you before, even if you are loco." He looked at the chicken doubtfully, then took a bite. "Damn, Angel, it's a good thing you're pretty. If this is the best you can do, you'll never get a husband."

She took a bite off a chicken leg. It was really awful. "I was trying to discourage the banker's attentions. I figured if he ever tasted my cooking, I'd lose a suitor."

"You figured that right. And to think I paid twenty bucks for this."

"No one asked you to show up and bid." She sipped her lemonade and watched him, more than a little annoyed with herself that she still found him so attractive. Wilbur Hiram was watching them, looking jealous and angry.

Johnny took a big bite and smiled as if it was delicious. The banker looked even more upset.

"Oh, stop deliberately annoying Wilbur," Angie said. "My cooking would make a hound dog sick and you know it."

"Umm! Ummm!" Johnny said loudly. "I'll bet Lassie would love it."

"What'd you say?" A startling thought crossed her mind.

"I said, lass, I love it."

Of course it had been a stupid thought; she had merely misunderstood him . . . or maybe not. Could it possibly be? But if so, and he still had his memory why would he try to fool her? No, he couldn't be John Logan VI . . . or could he? "I hope it chokes you! What are you doing here anyway? I thought you might have been caught in that train robbery."

"We had to give it up." Johnny snorted and took another bite. "It's a little hard to pull off a train robbery without horses to get away on."

"Didn't you catch the horses later?"

"Yeah, after we limped about five miles. Cowboy boots weren't made to walk in. If I'd had you within reach that day, I'd have broken your pretty neck. You got anything to say for yourself?"

"Yes; don't finish the potato salad and definitely don't eat the cake."

He took a tentative bite, shuddered. "The banker ought to thank me for saving him from this."

"He looks like he'd like to kill you instead." She watched Wilbur Hiram glaring in their direction.

Johnny shrugged. "He's the type who gets someone else to do his dirty work."

Angie gave up attempting to eat the salty chicken and nibbled on a biscuit. "So what is it you want? Rosebud?"

"Of course not! I—I simply wanted to see you; that's all."
He wiped his mouth.

"Well, I don't want to see you," she said primly, then
realized she was lying. She was attracted to this man, as attracted
as she'd ever been to his great-great-grandson, but that
attraction would all be futile. "Look, Johnny, I know you think
I'm loco, but I really am from the future. I can't get mixed up
in a relationship with any man because I'm trying to get back
to my own time."

He cocked his head and looked at her for a long moment.
"Okay, so you're from the future. You don't like this time
period well enough to stay?"

Angie considered a long moment while the band played
noisily in the background. She did love the old West. All those
times she had read Western romances, she had dreamed of
finding a cowboy, imagined living with him on a ranch in the
wide-open spaces. "I—I don't know if I can stay back here
or how I'm supposed to get back to my own time. Besides,
I'm worried about your descendant."

Johnny sighed and shook his head.

"Now, don't be thinking I'm loco," Angie insisted. "I do
work for him."

"Is he an outlaw, too?"

She remembered the headline across the magazine cover.
"Well, kind of. But he's respectable; sort of like banker Hiram.
He's in some sort of trouble and I'm trying to help him."

Johnny's eyes betrayed no emotion. "You in love with this
guy?"

She looked away, not wanting to admit how attracted she
was to the gunfighter sitting across from her. How could she
be in love with a man and his great-great grandfather at the
same time? "I—I don't know for sure." She gave up on the
food and pushed it to one side.

The band ended its tune and began a new one.

*After the ball is over, after the break of morn, after the
dancers leaving, after the stars are gone . . .*

She couldn't stop the tears from overflowing her eyes.

"Now what's the matter?"

"That's John's favorite song."

"So what? It's mine, too. It's everybody's favorite tune this
year."

"He waltzed with me once to that song." Angie sobbed.

He handed her his bandanna. "Stop crying, will you? The
banker's looking at me like it's my fault. Would you like to
dance?"

"No, of course not." She dabbed at her eyes, remembering
that time she had danced this same number in Logan's penthouse.

"I bought a basket supper," Johnny said easily. "I see the
other gentlemen are dancing with the ladies whose baskets they
bought."

"You aren't a gentleman," she protested.

"No, I'm a gunfighter," he snapped and yanked her to her
feet, "and I dare anyone to interfere."

He pulled her out on the floor, and she didn't know what to
do without making a scene except go into his arms.

He was a big man. She couldn't see past his shoulder when
he pulled her close, and her hand seemed to almost fit into the
palm of his. She was acutely aware of the warmth and strength
of his body as he held her in a virile embrace, the slight scent of
tobacco, leather and an expensive cologne. Funny, that smelled
almost like the cologne John Logan VI favored. Of course, that
was only wistful thinking on her part.

Then she forgot about everything but being in Johnny
Logan's embrace. He was an excellent dancer. Around them,
people were giving way as he whirled her about the school's
floor.

*. . . many a heart is aching; if you could read them all; many
the hopes that have vanished after the ball. . . .*

Johnny put his face against her hair and sang the words ever so softly. He had a good baritone voice, and the warmth of his breath stirred the hair next to her ear and sent delicious little thrills down her body.

Without meaning to, she closed her eyes and let him hold her even closer as they waltzed. The thought crossed her mind that she cared about this man; really cared. If he were an honest rancher, it would be so tempting to stay back in this time, marry him and bear his children. After all, she had no one in modern times, not even a relative. If she never returned to Oklahoma City in the year 1999, who would know or care?

Johnny kissed her ear ever so gently.

"You shouldn't do that," she whispered, upset with herself because she liked it. "That will cause gossip."

"If you wanted to avoid gossip, Angel, you should have refused to eat with me."

"I was trying to avoid trouble."

"The banker doesn't have the guts to challenge me for you. A man who won't fight for a woman doesn't have any right to her."

"You don't have any rights to me."

"Don't I?" He was holding her so close as they danced, she could feel his hard body all the way down her torso.

"People will talk."

"Let them." His face was buried in her hair.

Angie glanced around. "Well, at least Wilbur Hiram has left the school."

"Good, then after a while, I can take you home . . . or somewhere."

Angie didn't answer. She was keenly aware of the hostile looks the people were giving her and the scandalized whispers as Johnny held her in a lover's embrace on the dance floor. Even as she tried to decide what to do next, Johnny whirled her out the open rear door of the building.

"What are you doing?" Angie demanded as she looked back toward the school.

"It was getting hot in there," he said and took her hand, leading her out into the night.

"This will cause a lot of talk." But she let him lead her.

"Let 'em talk." Johnny shrugged and led her into the shadows of the autumn evening.

"Where are we going?"

He stopped in the shadows of some trees, took off his gunbelt, tossed it to one side. Then he sat down, pulling her down beside him. "I wanted to talk to you without a bunch of people watching."

"I'm not sure we've got anything to talk about." His nearness was making her nervous. *This is insane,* she thought. *I can't fall in love with a man who lived more than a hundred years before my time.*

He reached out and brushed a stray curl from her cheek. "I never met a girl like you before, Angel. If you had come along sooner, maybe I would have given up my outlaw ways, gotten myself a spread some place that would be good for kids."

"It's not too late." Angie looked at him, knowing this romance was impossible. "The Cherokee Strip will be opening in 1893; I remember that from American History class. You could be part of that land rush, get yourself a nice ranch."

He sighed loudly and looked up at the sky. In the background, lights shone from the schoolhouse windows, and the little band played "Camptown Races."

"Angel, do you ever think about dying?"

It was a totally unexpected question from this tough gunfighter. "Not much; I think about living, Johnny. After all, we all have to die."

He started to say something, then seemed to rethink it. "What if you could figure out a way you didn't have to die?"

What was on this lonely gunfighter's mind? "Are you talking about religion; going to heaven?"

He laughed cynically. "Not hardly! Never mind, Angel. Even if I got that ranch in the land rush, it wouldn't matter if you wouldn't stay and be my lady."

"I told you, I've got to go back, if I can figure out how. John Logan's in trouble."

"Logan, Logan, Logan! It's loco, but I'm actually jealous of the guy! Why don't you think of Johnny for a change?"

"I am thinking of Johnny; maybe way too much," she admitted.

"Could you—could you care for me?"

She shook her head. "I couldn't live the way you live, Johnny. I have old-fashioned values. Could you go straight?"

He sighed. "No, it's too late; way too late. I'm damned to stay on this same path forever." In the moonlight, his face was a study in sadness.

She reached up and touched his cheek. It didn't make any sense that she was falling in love with an outlaw who had lived a hundred years before she did; but then, being tossed back in time didn't make any sense, either. "Johnny, suppose instead of trying to return to my own time, I elected to stay back in this century with you?"

"You may not know it, sweet, but you don't have any choice in whether you stay or go." His voice was bitter.

"How do you know that?"

"Let's just say I do, okay?"

She was mystified at his answer, but at least maybe he believed now that she was a time traveler. "But if I stay and you became an honest rancher—"

"It's too late, I tell you, Angel. I've sold out. Besides, this would never work for us."

"Why, are you afraid the law won't leave you alone?"

He lit a cigarillo in the darkness. In the flare of the match, she saw his hands trembled. "No, there's something else; a deal I've made that I can't change."

He didn't care as much for her as she did for him. A great sadness washed over her. "And even for me, you wouldn't?"

"Damn it, it's not that I wouldn't. I—can't. Look, Angel, this is new to me. In all my years, I've never been honest with a woman. They were all just conquests to me." He smoked, his cigarillo glowing in the darkness, illuminating his tortured face as he seemed to struggle with some terrible inner torment. "I can't offer you anything but a little more than a week."

"A week?" She pulled back in shock.

"Believe me, I'd give you a lifetime if I could." He stopped to consider his words, then laughed, but there was no humor in the dark, tormented eyes. "A lifetime. I've outsmarted myself; I've got forever, but I can only promise the woman I love a few more days."

He tossed the smoke away and she reached out and put her hand on his arm. It was as tense as a coiled spring. This man was wrestling with some horrible mental conflict.

"It's okay, Johnny," she whispered. "I trust you. If that's all the time we've got, I won't ask any questions; I'll take it and be glad for it." Instinctively, she leaned over and kissed his cheek to comfort him.

With a soft cry of anguish, he took her in his arms, pulled her to him and kissed her.

For a second, she resisted; then her attraction for him was too strong and she melted against him, letting him mold the soft, rounded curves of her body against the hard planes of his.

His hot mouth dominated hers, forcing her lips open so his teasing tongue could explore and taste there. His hand went into the lacy bodice of her dress, touching and squeezing her breasts possessively. "I've wanted you," he whispered, "from the first time I saw you. Tell me you don't feel it, too."

Jiminy Christmas, it was true! And she knew in that moment that he was *her* John Logan, even if he didn't remember her. She could hear her own pulse pounding in her ears as he pushed her skirt up, ran his hands up her thighs under her lace bloomers.

"Johnny," she whispered, "this can't happen. I told you, I don't belong in this time."

"You belong wherever I am," he insisted, and he kissed her again.

Maybe she should tell him he didn't belong in this time, either, but if he was suffering from amnesia, he'd be upset and confused. Did he even remember how to return to the twentieth century or know any way through besides the mirror? She put her hands on his temples, feeling for a bump that might have wiped out his memory, and found no telltale injury. *Was she going to have to take the responsibility of attempting to get them both back to their own time?*

Then Angie forgot everything but the sensation of being in his arms. She had never believed in one-night stands, quick sexual encounters with no emotional attachments; but then, that had been before she met the gunfighter called Johnny Logan. Johnny had taught her what real desire was, and he was stroking the flames of passion within her with his hard, masculine hands caressing her skin.

She had so many unanswered questions, yet nothing mattered now but this man and this moment. The outlaw kissed his way down her throat and she sighed and let him do as he would. It seemed almost like a dream, the way the stars twinkled above them in the black night, the soft music drifting from the schoolhouse. Angie ran her hands through his black hair. Maybe she could jog his memory. "Johnny, I know so little about you."

"Does it matter?" His lips brushed into the valley between her breasts. "I never felt this way about a woman before. If I'd met you before I made that deal—"

"Deal? What deal?" She reached out and touched his lips with the tips of her fingers.

"Never mind." He caught her hand, kissed her fingertips ever so gently. She could not care about this man; would not care about him, and yet, when he pulled her to him, she went into his arms willingly, savoring the taste of his mouth. Maybe her kisses would remind him of that day at the lake and he would suddenly recognize her and remember the secret of sending them both back to the future.

His hands cradled the back of her head, holding her as if she were a china doll that might be easily broken. She slipped her arms around his neck, returning his kiss with mounting ardor, encouraging him to kiss her deeper still. His weight pushed her gradually to the grass and she lay there with him, letting him kiss her in a deepening frenzy, his hot hands pushing up her skirt to stroke and tantalize her thighs.

His mouth kissed down the line of her jaw in a tender way that surprised her, like a butterfly's velvet wings brushing against her skin.

She threw back her head, offering him her throat in a gesture of surrender to his masculine strength. The tip of his tongue kissed down her neck toward the hollow and she knew she would not try to stop him when his warm fingers pushed the front of her lacy bodice down and his lips sought her breasts.

She caught his head and pressed his mouth hard against her nipple, encouraging—no, *demanding*—that he taste and tease there, even as his callused hand played with the lace of her pantalets. His fingers felt like fire and she let her thighs fall apart, wanting him to reach up under the lace and touch her in that softest, most sensitive part of her very being.

Angie put her hand over his manhood. Even inside his jeans, she could feel the throbbing hardness pressing against the denim. He was going to make love to her; she knew that, and she could no more stop him than she could keep the sun from rising each morning. She did not want to stop him. The tide of passion was sweeping her toward a tumultuous ending and there would be no turning back.

"I'm going to take you, Angel," he promised. "I'm going to love you like no man has ever loved you; I'm going to make you totally and completely mine."

Maybe in the throes of passion he would remember that sun-

kissed afternoon at the lake, when their passionate coupling had been interrupted.

"Then do it!" she commanded, arching her back so that his mouth could better explore her nipples.

She thought she heard footsteps on the grass, but before she could do more than pull her bodice closed, a hostile man's voice thundered, "Just what in the hell is going on here?"

Banker Hiram.

Angie sat up suddenly. Behind Johnny in the darkness, she could see the shadowy forms of the banker and a crowd of tough-looking men. Farther behind them, some of the men from the town stood silently.

Johnny's dark eyes flashed alarm. He reached automatically for his pistol, but his gunbelt lay a few feet away, where he had tossed it. Even as Angie watched helplessly, he dove for his gun, but the banker had already put his foot on the holster. "Not so fast!"

Jiminy Christmas, the whole town seemed to be there. Angie pulled her skirt down.

Johnny stood up, gestured. "Look, the lady didn't want to come out here; I'm responsible."

He was trying to protect her reputation. It had been a long time since she'd met a man that chivalrous.

"That's not true!" Angie stood up, rearranging her mussed clothing, "I came out here with him of my own free will—"

"You slut, you!" The banker slapped her.

Johnny swore and went for his throat. "I'll kill you for that!"

Even as Johnny took him to the ground, punching him hard in the face, the toughs behind them moved in, dragging Johnny off Hiram.

Hiram stood up, wiping the blood from his prim mouth. His eyes gleamed with vengeance. "Maybe the outlaw was right; maybe he was raping her!"

"Yes, she's innocent. I was taking advantage of her!" Johnny struggled to break away, but two big men hung on to him.

"No, he wasn't!" Angie shouted, but no one seemed to be paying any attention to her. A rumble began to build in the crowd, of harsh words and liquor-fueled courage.

The banker smiled and dusted the dirt from his coat and shiny spats. "Let's show him what we do to rapists around here!"

A man said, "Shouldn't we wait 'til the sheriff gets back to town?"

"We can take care of this ourselves," the banker said, rearranging the natty flower in his buttonhole. "Someone get a rope!"

"No," Angie screamed, and threw her arms around Johnny's neck. "He wasn't forcing me, I swear it!"

No one seemed to hear her in the hubbub—or, at least, no one paid any attention. The noise was building and the crowd grew larger and more unruly as men arrived with torches. "The banker's right! We can handle this ourselves! Get a rope and bring his horse!"

Angie whirled on Hiram. "Please, Wilbur, don't do this! He doesn't even belong in this time, and neither do I! Do you hear me? Let him go! I love this man!"

The pot-bellied banker pulled her hand off his arm with a sneer. "Do you hear her, men? Poor thing's hysterical from the ordeal!"

"Let's lynch him!" Someone in the crowd shouted, "Get a rope!"

"Oh, please, no!" Angie screamed and turned to the crowd. "He didn't do anything! You hear me? Oh, please don't do this!"

Johnny seemed strangely calm, although his face was set. "Don't beg, Angel. They've made up their minds. Get out of here while you still can!"

"You slut!" The banker turned on her. "You should have fought and screamed when this outlaw grabbed you. You're no better than he is!"

A chorus of agreement went up from the crowd. Someone was leading that fine paint stallion of Johnny's forward in the torchlight.

Angie looked around at the crowd, gesturing frantically and shouting. "Isn't anyone going to do anything? Isn't anyone going to—?"

"Sure we are," Hiram said. "Throw me that rope!"

The crowd pressed forward with a shout. Someone tied a hangman's noose in the rope and with a quick motion, Hiram knocked Johnny's Stetson from his head as he slipped it around the half-breed's neck and tightened it.

"No! Don't!" Angie tried to throw herself forward to stop them, but someone was holding her back. The noise of the crowd seemed to grow. Shadows from the torches danced across faces, distorted in the darkness. She could smell the scent of burning pitch as she gasped for air and struggled to stop them.

Johnny's face was set. "Get out of here, Angel. We'll meet again in another place and time; I promise that."

"No!" She fought to get away. "I'm not going to let them kill you!"

But even as she said it, the crowd pressed forward, grabbing Johnny, tying his hands behind his back. His face seemed pale but calm in the garish torchlight. Then a couple of the toughs lifted him up on his horse.

"Stop!" Angie screamed. "Oh, please, I'll do anything! You can't kill this man!"

"We're only doing justice," Hiram said smoothly. "Someone get that slut out of here." He leaned over and picked up Johnny's pistol and holster. "I reckon I'll keep this. Okay, someone toss that rope over a limb."

With a cheer, the mob watched one of the saloon toughs grab the end of the rope and throw it up over a limb of the very tree under which Johnny had been making love to her.

No, this couldn't happen, Angie thought as she fought to get away from the men who held her. Johnny Logan couldn't be lynched; he had to return to his own time period.

"Don't kill him," she begged and fought to break away. She must stop them from murdering Johnny. But the crowd ignored her, pushing forward eagerly to watch the hanging.

The banker turned, and his expression was evil. "Someone get that slut out of here."

Even as she struggled, two men grabbed her and carried her to Hiram's buggy. They both got in, one to hold her, the other to drive. He snapped the whip and the horse started off at a trot while the other man held on to her.

Angie screamed and tried to get out of the buggy, but it kept moving. She looked back at the eerie scene; the mob with their flaming torches, Johnny sitting the paint stallion in the moonlight, the stars twinkling overhead in the black velvet night, oblivious to the killing that was about to happen.

Johnny's face was set, yet calm. He did not struggle, perhaps deciding to meet his death with dignity. He looked toward her, smiling ever so slightly. His lips moved and formed the words, "I'll find you again someday; remember I love you."

Even as she watched the scene growing smaller and smaller in the distance, the crowd fell back and grew silent as Hiram stepped forward with a whip.

"No!" she screamed as the whip came down across the paint's rump. The stallion bolted and galloped away. Johnny hit the end of the rope with a jerk and then hung there, swinging in the wind. For a long moment, the crowd fell silent, watching the man dangling between earth and sky.

"Johnny!" she screamed in disbelief. "Oh, my God, Johnny!"

But Johnny Logan did not answer. He swung motionless in the torchlit darkness at the end of the rope.

Chapter Twelve

The men put Angie, still kicking and screaming, out of the buggy in front of her hotel. "For shame! Wantin' to save that outlaw! What kind of a woman are you, anyway?"

"And what kind of people are you," Angie screamed at them, "lynching a man because he made banker Hiram mad?"

She must have hit pretty close to home because the men ducked their heads, cracked the whip and drove away in a hurry.

Two women passing by, escorted by the old postmaster, clicked their tongues with disapproval. "You shameless hussy! We all saw what was going on."

"And he's a known gunfighter," said the postmaster. "We was doin' you a favor."

"This is a terrible place!" Angie screamed back. "A town of lawless people."

"You get out of town, you trollop!" a passerby yelled. "We got a right to keep law and order here!"

God save the world from self-righteous prigs, Angie thought, blinded by tears as she ran into the hotel and began to pack. She couldn't bear to look any of these people in the face again; besides which, if she was here tomorrow, they'd probably run her out of town.

"Johnny, why did you have to come here?" she sobbed as she packed. She hadn't realized how much the arrogant gun-slinger had come to mean to her until she'd seen his limp body hanging from that limb.

Well, she couldn't do anything for Johnny now; she could only look out for herself. Her mind dull with anguish, Angie counted her money. It was almost gone, but she might have a little more than enough for a train ticket out of this terrible town.

And go where? She was trapped back in time, and as far as she knew, there was no way to return since that sinister mirror had been broken. Johnny might have known another way out, but the crowd had just lynched him. At the moment, Angie didn't care much what happened to her.

Maybe it didn't matter which way she went, as long as she left. It was late and dark as she picked up her small suitcase and walked to the station. There was no one on the streets; perhaps they were all hiding inside, ashamed of themselves for turning into a lynch mob, or maybe some of them had had the common decency to stay behind and bury the dead man. Wilbur Hiram had been the ringleader. She could only hope God's justice caught up with the pompous banker for what he had done. Angie entered the train station and went to the lone ticket agent, a middle-aged fellow with red wattles of skin like a turkey gobbler.

"I'd like a ticket."

"To where, ma'am?"

She hesitated. The pain of seeing Johnny Logan lynched had left her completely numb; she couldn't even think. Angie counted out her money. "I—I don't know. Where's the next train headed?"

"Comin' through toward daylight; going on to Oklahoma Territory."

"That'll be fine." It also left her a couple of dollars for necessities. She bought the ticket and sat down to wait. Oklahoma would still be a raw territory only three years after the first land rush. Had Johnny's death altered the future? Now he would never go up to the Klondike and strike gold to begin the family fortune, or have a descendant who would become the Outlaw of Wall Street and build his skyscraper in Oklahoma City or make megadeals.

Johnny. She must not think about him or the tears would come again. She had to pull herself together and decide what to do next. But all she could remember was the way she had fitted into his arms and the taste of his lips. Despite her sorrow, she would concentrate on how to return to 1999 and the new Millennium. Too late, she realized that her love had truly belonged to Johnny Logan, as the swaggering, arrogant, yet oh-so-vulnerable gunfighter. Yes, she would have been willing to stay back in time with him if he never regained his memory and returned to his other life. For a long moment, she wondered why he had told her he could only promise her a little more than a week. Well, now there would never even be another night in his arms.

The hours seemed to crawl by, but finally, a long, lonesome whistle announced the arrival of the train pulling into the desolate little station. No one else got on or off. Angie grabbed her bag, handed the conductor her ticket and hurried into the old-fashioned parlor car with its brass trim and red velvet seats. The car was only half full, and most of the occupants looked asleep. Only one or two stirred with sleepy curiosity as she came down the aisle and found a seat alone. In her sorrow, she did not want to have to talk to anyone. The engine blew a warning blast and then began to move. Angie breathed a sigh of relief and leaned back against the seat. The car smelled of stale cigar smoke and fried chicken lunches.

Angie tried to sleep, but when she closed her eyes, she saw the half-breed gunfighter and remembered the precious moments in his arms, dancing and whirling to the song he loved so well. Johnny Logan was dead and she would never kiss or dance with him again.

Stop it, Angie, she scolded herself. *You're a strong person; you will survive and do whatever it is you were left on earth to do.* She thought of the car wreck she had lived through. Maybe her survival hadn't had any rhyme or reason to it, though Grandmother would have thought otherwise. What was it she had said? *God moves in mysterious ways his wonders to perform.* Surely Angie hadn't died and been revived just to wander around without purpose a hundred years before her own time? She had to move ahead on faith; to do otherwise would make her question God and her own sanity.

Rosebud. She had left Rosebud behind in the Prairie View stable. Angie sought out the conductor. "How do I get off this train? I left something behind—"

"I can't stop this train, 'cept for emergencies."

Was this an emergency? She didn't think the conductor would think so. Besides, if she got off the train out in the middle of nowhere, how would she get back to Prairie View? "How far to the next stop?"

"Less than an hour, ma'am," the old man assured her. "I'll let you know when."

Relieved, Angie returned to her seat. She couldn't afford the luxury of another ticket back to Prairie View, and she wasn't sure what would happen when she showed up there. Still, the little mare meant a lot to her; Johnny had given it to her. She had to go back. The wheels clicked rhythmically: *trapped in time, trapped in time, trapped in time.* Then: *Johnny's dead, Johnny's dead, Johnny's dead.*

Day broke all pale pink and lavender as the train chugged south toward Oklahoma Territory. People in the swaying car were beginning to wake up. Around her were immigrants and their families, several farmers, drummers with their sample cases, a shady character or two, a cowboy, several old men, and a couple of painted women who might be whores.

One of the old men, who had been dozing, suddenly came alert and pointed out the window. "Hey, riders coming!"

Other heads turned curiously in the direction in which he pointed, but Angie half-yawned and turned away. What did she care about cowboys riding along the tracks?

"Hey!" yelled a cowboy. "Somebody get the conductor! I think they're tryin' to board!"

Now Angie turned to see what everyone else was looking at. Racing alongside the train were half a dozen riders. She wouldn't have paid any attention, except that the riders wore bandannas over their faces. The horses suddenly looked familiar, and now she noted that one of the riders wore fancy cowboy boots.

"Jiminy Christmas, it's Bob, Grat and the boys!" Even as she recognized them, the riders pulled pistols and began firing at the train.

"Holdup!" a woman shrieked. "They're going to hold up the train!"

Abruptly, the whistle blasted a warning; then the engine hit its brakes. The big iron wheels locked and shrieked in protest as they slid along the rails, throwing everyone forward. Angie grabbed for the back of the seat ahead of her, tensing and gritting her teeth. Were they all going to die? She'd almost died once in the car wreck; surely she hadn't survived that only to be killed on an antique train! Suitcases and boxes fell from the brass luggage racks, and women screamed as the train slid along the track, wheels locked. It was sheer pandemonium around her. The outlaws must have piled rocks on the track like they did last time. For another second, people screamed and luggage flew through the air.

Angie hung on and gritted her teeth. After a long moment,

she realized the train had stopped and she was still alive. Maybe God had saved her a second time. But to what purpose?

Then there was no more time to think, for through the dirty window she could see some of the bandits reining in, masks over their faces, as they began to board the train.

"Bandits!" a drummer gasped. "And they're getting on!"

That set up a fresh chorus of screams. Angie felt someone had to do something, and she'd never been a shrinking violet. She jumped to her feet and stepped to the front of the car. "Everyone be still," she commanded, "and you ladies stop that caterwauling."

"But we're about to be ravaged by outlaws!" one of the whores shrieked.

"In your dreams!" she quipped, and then remembered the time period. "They're probably just after the express box gold," Angie assured everyone. "Stay calm."

She was afraid herself, her heart beating hard, but she felt panic would only make things worse. At her words, the other passengers looked around at each other. "That's right; they're after the money in the express car, that's all."

She returned to her seat and sat down. Behind her, she heard the outlaws clamoring aboard the train. *I can't believe this,* she thought. *I'm stuck back in time on a train that's about to be robbed by Western bandits. It feels like one of those virtual-reality games.*

"All right!" shouted a baritone voice behind her. "Everyone stay calm and be quiet! As soon as the boys get the express box, we'll be on our way!"

The voice was familiar; too familiar. No, it couldn't be; she had to be imagining it. She turned to look as he came down the aisle. As he drew close, he started, and she saw his dark eyes widen in surprise above the red bandanna. At that moment, Angie came to her feet, reached out and jerked the bandanna down. "Johnny?"

Angie stared with disbelief into a rugged, familiar face with a tiny mole next to a hard mouth. Then she fainted dead away.

She was only vaguely aware that he caught her gently. For a split second, she was in his strong embrace, and she breathed the wonderful scent of leather, fine tobacco and the warmth of his skin. He lifted her easily, cradling her in his arms for a long moment. Then he eased her back down onto the seat and began backing down the aisle. "Everyone stay in your seats and no one will get hurt!"

Her senses began to return and her eyes fluttered open. She heard his boots as he ran, and then he was gone. A moment later, she heard the sound of horses galloping away. She jumped up and ran down the aisle. "Johnny! Don't leave me! Take me with you!"

But the riders were already disappearing, fading into the landscape. *Had she really seen him, or had she wanted to see him so badly, she had conjured him up as a phantom?* When she turned back around, everyone in the car was staring at her in dour disapproval.

"Did you hear that? She knows them bandits!"

"Maybe she was the lookout and they double-crossed her!"

Angie shook her head. "No, you don't understand; that man is dead! I saw him hanged myself."

Now they really stared at her, and began to whisper among themselves. "Poor thing's loco!"

"Well, reckon she had quite a scare just now when that hombre put his hands on her; you know how delicate ladies are."

"Or maybe she's plain crazy; a crazy woman can't be held accountable for thinking she knows a bandit."

The conductor came into the car just then. "Everyone sit down and take it easy," he gestured. "You, too, ma'am. I reckon the law'll want to talk to everyone at our next stop."

The train began to move again and Angie slumped down in her seat, putting her face in her hands. Was she loco? She would have sworn that man had been Johnny; yet she'd seen him lynched. Nothing was logical anymore; first she'd been lost in time and now she'd seen a dead man alive and robbing a train. None of this made any sense. Or maybe her eyes were playing tricks on her. She closed her eyes and recalled the startled feeling of looking into the half-breed outlaw's dark face. No, there was no mistake; nobody but Johnny Logan had eyes as sensual as those.

For a few minutes, the train rattled on down the tracks, the passengers mumbling to each other, but no one talked to her.

"Coming into Coffeyville," the conductor yelled. "Coffeyville next!"

This was where it had all started, Angie thought, so maybe this was where she would find the answers to all the mysteries. Maybe she should get off here and try to retrace her steps, find some answers.

That was decided for her. When the train pulled to a stop, the marshal and several deputies, as well as a gaggle of curious townspeople and a newsman, were waiting at the station.

"Everybody off!" the conductor yelled. "The marshal will want to talk to you."

Angie took her time getting her things together as she watched the others leave the train. She wanted answers, too, and didn't want to be questioned about something she didn't understand herself. Maybe she could sneak away in the confusion. She tiptoed across the platform, hoping to melt into the crowd, but a deputy yelled at her, "Sorry, miss, but would you come back please? We want to talk to everybody."

With a sigh, Angie went into the station and sat down on a bench, away from the crowd.

"That's her!" An old man with a long beard pointed an accusing finger at Angie. "That's the girl who seemed to know the robbers!"

Immediately, a crowd formed around her. A lawman with a big belly squatted down beside her. "Who are you, miss?"

"Angie; Angie Newland."

"And where were you going, Miss Newland?"

She spoke without thinking. "I'm just trying to get back to the twentieth century."

"Did you hear that?" Someone in the background whispered. "I told you she's just loco."

She heard a flurry of whispers. "That poor thing's had a bad scare, bein' handled by that outlaw."

The marshal had joined the crowd. "I reckon, ma'am, what the deputy meant was, what town are you going to?"

"I—I'm not sure. Oklahoma City, maybe; I don't remember."

She saw some of the men exchange glances.

The marshal gave her arm a reassuring pat. "Now, miss, I realize you've had a bad scare, but some folks thought maybe you recognized one of the bandits."

"I did." Angie looked up at him. "But he's dead, you see."

"Dead?"

"Yes. They hanged him at Prairie View."

The marshal scratched his head and looked around. "But you say he was robbin' the train?"

Angie nodded.

The marshal turned away and made a motion to disperse the crowd. "Well this pore thing is addled; anyone can see that."

"Sorry, marshal," said the big-bellied deputy. "We didn't realize she was half-witted."

Angie started to protest that she wasn't half-witted, but then kept silent. She didn't want to have to be interrogated again on how a dead man could be robbing a train. "May I—may I go?"

The marshal nodded. Angie picked up her purse and her little suitcase and went outside to look around. The train didn't look like it was going anywhere for awhile. The crew were all talking to the law and the newsman inside the station.

Now she had time to reason. Of course her mind or her eyes must be playing tricks on her. Be reasonable, Angie, she scolded herself; how could Johnny Logan still be alive? Did he have a twin brother? No, Logan had told her he had no brothers and sisters. Could she have wished him up out of her grief-stricken imagination? Angie was beginning to doubt her own sanity. The whole thing was a big mystery that Angie wanted solved for her own peace of mind. The adventure had started here; the answer to the puzzle had to be right here in Coffeyville.

She started down the street, not certain what to do next. The photography shop—she would go back there where this weird chain of events had begun. Maybe the shop would be open and she could walk in, step back through that mirror and find herself in the twentieth century, with cars honking and teenagers sauntering down the street carrying blaring boom boxes. No, the mirror had been broken, but surely there was another way to get back to her own time. Or at least get some answers from the owner. With Johnny dead, there was no reason to stay in 1892, and yet with his death had gone the possible alternative way of returning to 1999.

Angie crossed a street. Within a couple of blocks, downtown began to look familiar, with all its horse troughs and brick streets. Yes, here was the harness shop and the general store. That meant the photography shop should be in about the middle of the block. There were two banks; she remembered they were right across the street from each other. The dirt street was torn up and bricks stacked nearby, as if they intended to pave the street soon.

She paused in front of the Condon Bank and looked about, confused. There was no sign of a photography shop. She walked on slowly, looking for familiar landmarks. Yes, that was the horse trough that had gotten shot full of holes. She could see the patches on it and the bullethole in the wall nearby. This store right here had to be the place. The door was open. Her heart beating faster, Angie opened the screen and went in. Her heart sank. It was now a boot shop. Had she only imagined the photography store?

A pudgy man came out of the back wearing a dirty apron and holding a boot in one hand and some polish in the other. The shop smelled of leather and polish. "Yes, ma'am, may I help you?"

"I—I suppose I'm in the wrong store. I thought this was a photography studio."

"I wouldn't know about that." He shrugged. "It was empty when I rented it a few days ago."

Maybe the owner of the building could shed some light on the previous tenant. "Do you know where I might find the owner of this building?"

"Sure. He owns the Lady Luck Saloon. I wouldn't advise a respectable woman going in there, though."

Angie nodded and went out, ignoring the dour warning. There were two Lady Lucks? Did the same owner control both of them? This might be another wild goose chase, but she was too stubborn to give up. Whatever it took, she had to get to the bottom of all this. She went down to the livery stable and tried to rent a rig, but when the man found out where she wanted to go, all his rigs were busy.

"That's way out on the outskirts of town, across the state line in Indian Territory, where there ain't much law," he cautioned. "I'd advise you to stay away from that place, ma'am." He didn't look her in the eye. "Lots of questionable folks hang out there in South Coffeyville. Things go on there we frown on in law-abidin' Kansas."

Angie was tired, hungry, confused and frustrated. He might be willing if she had more money, but she was almost broke. Did Wilbur Hiram own this saloon also, or was he only a partner? And what about Rosebud? The banker had probably confiscated the little mare by now. Maybe she should get back on the train and go on to Oklahoma City, although what she would do when she got there, she wasn't sure.

Without Johnny, she had no reason to stay in 1892 but no knowledge of how to get out. Somehow that photography shop and its owner were involved in this mystery, and Angie was determined to solve it before it drove her over the brink. She picked up her suitcase and began to walk. The Lady Luck was in wild-and-woolly Indian Territory, outside the jurisdiction of the local law. There was no telling what she would find there, but she had to take that chance.

It was farther than she'd expected. Angie walked a long time, the road dusty in the late September morning. Eventually, she rounded a curve and came upon a large Victorian mansion. Even in the daylight it looked sinister and evil. On this warm day the windows were open, and she could hear a piano playing, women laughing and cowboys singing in drunken, off-key voices.

Angie paused and stepped into some bushes, watching the place and having second thoughts about why the boot maker and livery stable operator had warned her against coming here. Two bad-looking thugs stumbled out the door and got into a fistfight out front. Gunslingers and gamblers brushed past the fighting pair, paying them no heed as they entered. From somewhere, gunshots rang out and a woman screamed. Next, a big rough bouncer carried a smaller man out by the scruff of his neck and threw him in the street. "Don't be a sore loser and accuse us of cheatin' at cards. Next time, we'll kill you rather than throw you out!"

Angie watched and listened. Maybe this really was no place for a lady. On the other hand, if she didn't take the bull by the horns, she might never solve this mess. Angie took a deep breath and picked up her purse and her suitcase. All she wanted was a little information. Surely a lady could walk into a saloon and gambling hall in broad daylight and get that without much trouble.

Or maybe not. Well, if she didn't go in, she'd never know.

She marched up to the front doors and entered. Even in broad daylight, the place was packed, and so noisy, no one seemed to notice Angie. She took a deep breath and looked around. The place smelled of whiskey, cigar smoke and cheap perfume. The large room was richly decorated in gaudy Victorian style, a stage with scarlet velvet curtains, roulette wheels, poker tables, a bald man playing a piano and scantily dressed girls sitting on the arms of chairs with their arms around drunken gamblers. Along the wall ran a fancy carved bar with a brass rail and mirrors, where three bartenders were working hard to get the drinks out. Pretty girls in bright, scanty costumes rushed up and down with trays, serving beer. Over the bar hung a painting of a voluptuous nude. The nude made Angie feel skinny.

The piano banged away loudly: . . . *Oh Susanna! Oh, don't you cry for me; I'm goin' to Alabama with my banjo on my knee. . . .*

Three dancing girls high-kicked across the stage to the music. A scantily dressed redhead carrying a tray of beer brushed past her. Angie caught her by the arm. "Where can I find the owner?"

The girl tucked the tip she'd just gotten into her red lace garter. "You wantin' to work upstairs or down?"

Angie didn't have any idea. "I don't know for sure," she shouted over the noise. "I need to see him about it."

The redhead nodded toward a hallway near the bar. "Office is back there."

A gambler grabbed Angie's arm as she started past. "Hey, honey, you new here? Let's go upstairs."

She thought quickly. "I'm a downstairs girl! Get your hands off me!"

He hesitated, and she slapped him.

The other men standing nearby laughed. "Hey, Al, you should listen to the lady."

"If she's a lady, what's she doin' in here?"

Angie pulled her demure blue dress back up on her shoulder and headed toward the hallway. With almost no money, she wasn't certain what she was going to do after she got her information and left here, but she'd worry about that later. Right now, nothing mattered but asking the important questions and hoping the owner could clear up the mystery.

It was much quieter walking through this back hall. Angie stopped in front of the closed door. Who was she going to meet in here? Surely it couldn't be Wilbur Hiram! Could he own both saloons even though they were miles apart? She took a deep breath and knocked.

"Who is it?" The voice was gruff and angry, but slightly familiar.

"I—I need to talk to you."

"Go away. I got all the girls we need here right now."

"I'm not looking for a job. I just want information."

"You think I'm a God-damned library?"

"You shouldn't swear like that!"

"I don't need any choir girls, either!"

She wasn't going to be scared off. Angie took a deep breath and opened the door. The room was richly decorated in bright scarlet and black. There was a fine desk and a big leather chair turned away from her.

Her heart pounded with trepidation. "I—I know you told me to go away, but I need some answers, and—"

"I was wondering just when you would find your way to me." The chair whirled around and the man in it smiled in triumph.

Angie could only stare in disbelief. "I—I thought this place might be owned by banker Hiram."

"No, *I* own banker Hiram."

Angie gulped and blinked as she stared. It couldn't be, but it was. Looking back at her from the big leather chair was Nick Diablo.

Chapter Thirteen

"You!" Angie was taken aback; then she recovered from her shock and advanced to the desk to stare and make sure. Same penciled mustache, same dark hair and hard mouth. Eyes as black as obsidian under arched eyebrows. Only now he was dressed like a riverboat gambler, with a black coat and a string tie. He still wore the diamond pinkie ring.

It was Nick Diablo, all right. But it couldn't be. Maybe it was Nick Diablo's great-great-grandfather. "I thought maybe—no. I just thought for a minute you were someone I knew."

He leaned his elbows on his desk, steepling his fingers, a slight smile on his thin lips. "I make the acquaintance of lots of people; many go into partnership with me."

Not me, Angie thought. His eyes were too cold and remote. She licked her lips for courage, reminding herself that he was only a man, after all, and he might have the answers she needed. "I—I need to know about the photography shop."

"Sit down, my dear. You look faint." His voice almost

purred as he gestured her to a chair across from him. "Perhaps you need a glass of sherry?"

She did feel exhausted, and remembered she hadn't had any breakfast. "That would help, thank you."

He got up and went to a carved Victorian sideboard and picked up a fine crystal decanter and tumblers, then paused to look at her. "And to what do I owe the honor of this visit?"

"My name is Newland. Angie Newland. I need some answers."

He poured the sherry and handed her a fragile cut-glass goblet. Angie sipped it gratefully.

The gambler sat on the corner of his desk across from her, holding his own goblet, and smiled. "I'm in the pleasure and instant gratification business, not the answer game, but for a charming lady like yourself . . ." He let his words trail off as he toasted her silently with his drink. The diamond on his hand sparkled.

For a moment, Angie could only stare at him, mesmerized. There was something about his eyes and the way he smiled that made her feel like a butterfly tangled in a giant spiderweb. In the background, music drifted faintly from the saloon outside, and a woman laughed.

Jiminy Christmas, this all seemed so unreal. "You own buildings in Coffeyville?"

His brow wrinkled in thought. "I probably own several. I'd have to ask my accountant. Matter of fact, I own property all over the globe."

Angie thought about the other saloon. "You own another Lady Luck in Prairie View?"

He nodded. "I also own a partner there. We're doing well together, Hiram and I. Very successful concept; indulging people's so-called sins. I'm thinking about franchising."

Angie leaned toward him. "The building I'm asking about was in Coffeyville; a photography studio."

He shrugged, boredom in his black eyes. "I don't remember;

tenants come and go in strip malls and shopping centers. Some of the shops I own myself—tax write-off, you know—some I sublease.''

She hadn't realized they had strip malls and tax write-offs in these days, but this man was so sophisticated and debonair, if there were such a thing, he'd know it. Angie's heart fell with disappointment at his words. ''You don't remember anything about a photography shop?''

He shrugged. ''I owned some that were making huge profits in porn—never mind; that wasn't in Coffeyville. Are you wanting to open a photography shop?''

Angie shook her head. ''No, I'm just trying to get information on the one that was there. It's been replaced by a boot repair business.''

The gambler seemed to stifle a yawn. ''I don't remember; you'd have to talk to my accountant. I may have sold it. Is that all, my dear? I'm terribly busy.''

She suspected he wasn't telling everything he knew, but her reasoning was none too clear. Angie had drunk the sherry too fast. She felt light-headed and dizzy. She set down her goblet, discouraged. ''I don't know what to do or where to go next; you were my last hope.''

He smiled, and his eyebrows arched expressively. ''I'm a lot of people's last hope; more fools they.''

He meant the gambling tables, she thought; desperate people losing their money trying to get something for nothing.

His hands were fine and graceful, as if he'd never done a moment's work in his whole life. When they moved, the light caught the big diamond on his finger. ''Why the interest in photography?''

Angie shook her head. ''I'm just trying to find some answers.'' She toyed with her glass. ''There was a big, oval mirror there; it was broken in a million pieces by a gunshot.''

He grinned, but there was no warmth in his hard face. ''You're wanting to buy furniture?''

"No!" Angie felt increasing frustration. "I wanted to know about *that* mirror; you could step through it and end up in another time. . . ." She let her voice trail off when she realized he was staring at her as if she were crazy. "Oh, never mind."

"Mirror, mirror . . . ah, yes, I remember now!" A light broke over his sinister face. "I doubled the insurance value; made a profit; cleaning lady swept the broken glass up and dumped it in the trash." He rubbed his hands together. "I could get you a similar one for a small markup."

Something about his enthusiasm made her wonder if he also had some descendants who were used-car salesmen.

She was wasting her time here; this ancestor of Nick Diablo either didn't know or wouldn't tell. On the other hand, why should he try to hide information about a mirror? It had been a long shot anyway. She was going to have to look elsewhere for clues.

With a sigh, Angie set down her glass on a chair-side table and stood up. "Well, thank you for your time."

"Wait, my dear." He reached out and caught her arm, and she was astounded at how cold his hand was through the sheer pink fabric of her sleeve. "Maybe I can help you."

The sun came through the window behind him, and she saw her shadow across the pale cream carpet. Funny, this man threw no shadow. There was something eerie about him in more ways than one. Angie shook his hand off. "I'm afraid there's nothing you can do; I'm caught in a mess that if I tried to explain it, you'd think I was loco."

He clucked sympathetically. "I've heard some pretty sad tales, and occasionally I help someone out, offer them a deal too good to refuse. Met a lot of congressmen that way. Besides, it's a great tax write-off."

"I can't afford whatever you're talking about; I'm all but broke."

"Ah!" His black eyes gleamed. "Would you be looking for a job then?"

"Here?" Her expression must have telegraphed her alarm.

"Well, with your buxom good looks, I'm sure the cowboys would—"

"My grandmother would roll over in her grave," Angie said and started for the door.

"Wait!" he called after her. "Your grandmother must have been terribly old-fashioned with middle American values. Surely you're more of a realist."

"I'm afraid I have middle American values, too."

"Tsk! Tsk! Too bad!" He cocked his head at her. "Remember my dear, modern mores say that there is no right or wrong but thinking makes it so; every issue is a shade of gray."

That conflicted with everything Angie had been taught, but she was too sad and tired to argue and she was getting a headache. If the gambler wouldn't or couldn't help her, she didn't know what to do next. She had a feeling he knew much more than he was telling. Maybe if she went to work here, she'd finally find out. Uncertainly, Angie paused with her hand on the doorknob. "Work here and wear those skimpy costumes? I don't think so."

She started to leave, but he held up his hand.

"Wait! Consider this: I'm an honest businessman, and this business pays taxes that the town wants and needs. My customers are here of their own free will, and the employees are earning a living; so who's hurt by victimless crime?"

What he was saying sounded so logical. "Well, I do need a job, but I feel like I'd be selling out," Angie admitted.

He stood up, rubbing his hands together again. "Everybody's doing it," he said. "Why be an old stick-in-the-mud?"

"You sound just like some of the kids in the high-school I attended," Angie said. A thought crossed her mind and she paused. "Do you know a man named Logan?"

"Who?"

"Johnny Logan?"

"Ah, the gunfighter." The gambler smiled. "I know him well. He comes in here once in awhile to drink and gamble."

Tears came to her eyes and she blinked them away. "He—he's dead; at least I think he is."

"Is that a fact?" His cold black eyes didn't register any emotion.

She considered telling him about Johnny being hanged, and then her seeing him alive again. But she decided the gambler would think her loco. "This mystery is too complicated to explain. I've run out of leads; I don't know where to go or what to do."

He returned to his drink and gave her a charming smile. "Maybe I could be persuaded . . ."

She waited hopefully. "Yes?"

He shrugged. "I don't know if I can help, but your innocence appeals to my soft heart."

He looked like a man with a heart of cold steel, but she didn't say that.

She hesitated in the doorway.

"I could offer you a job as a waitress; serving beer, carrying sandwiches to the cowboys who don't want to walk away from a winning hand of cards long enough to eat."

"I'm thinking it over," Angie said again. "Does Johnny Logan have a twin brother?" No, of course not. There wasn't any logical answer to this puzzle except her own grief.

"Brother? How should I know?" The gambler shrugged with impatience.

That seemed to be the most logical answer to seeing Johnny on the train. However, nothing about this mess had ever seemed logical. In the romance novels she loved, they would call this paranormal. Right now, her only clues were this gambler and his connection with Johnny Logan . . . or his twin brother. Angie had reached a dead end; if she couldn't find the answers here at the Lady Luck, she might as well hang it up.

He must have seen she was desperate and wavering, because

Nick said, "You wouldn't have to dance or entertain, just serve tables. And you'd have a room with your own key, so you'd be safe enough."

"I'm not sure—"

"Think about it. The tips are good here and jobs are scarce."

From the saloon came the sounds of a piano, a roulette wheel whirling and a woman's drunken laughter.

"No, I—I just can't." Angie shook her head and left the office, walked through the saloon and out the front door.

However, walking back toward town, she reconsidered and rationalized. The gambler had been quite charming and persuasive. Maybe she and her grandmother had been old-fashioned and judgmental. As the gambler had said, all the customers and employees were there of their own free will.

Uncertainly, Angie turned and looked back toward the Lady Luck Saloon. The only leads she might find were connected with that place. In the meantime, she was low on money and she had to eat. Being a waitress wasn't the same as being an entertainer or a lady cardsharp, was it?

Angie closed her mind to the small protesting voice inside, turned around and went back to the saloon.

The gambler was still in his office. "Ah, come in, my dear."

"You don't seem surprised to see me."

"I knew your common sense would overcome your silly moral inhibitions."

Angie decided not to argue the point. "No skimpy costumes, I'll only have to work as a waitress and I'll get a room with a lock on the door?"

He nodded and held out a big brass key. "You have my word on it. Now get a uniform from Tom, the main bartender. And welcome aboard, my dear."

Nick Diablo smiled to himself as the girl accepted the key and went off to find Tom. She'd given him quite a start by turning up in this time period. Why and how had that accident happened? However, the girl was blond and innocent-looking as an angel; attractive enough to put some money in Nick's pocket.

Not that it mattered how she had traveled back through time. Angelica Newland was stuck back here because, of course, she hadn't unraveled the secret of how to return to the twentieth century. And Nick wasn't about to tell her unless she was willing to sign a contract with him. She didn't seem like the type; but then, that made her an even bigger challenge. It would be so entertaining to tempt her. Very few people had the will and the moral fortitude to resist his offers.

Such a luscious morsel! He licked his lips with anticipation, remembering the girl's full, soft curves. His sex came up hard and throbbing as he imagined her at his mercy. Such a naive and trusting little fool she was!

Nick walked over to his desk, set his tumbler down and opened the drawer, making sure he had the identical key to Angie's room. Perhaps tonight he would sneak in, catch her asleep and enjoy those soft charms. The thought made him smile with pleasure.

Later, he'd ply her with drugs and alcohol like he'd done to a million women. After he tired of her, he would put her to work as a whore here in the Lady Luck, earning money for him. She'd find that she wouldn't be able to escape, and after awhile she would give up and stop trying.

Nick lit an expensive cigar and considered. There was only one fly in the ointment. Well, in a few days, that fly would be gone and Nick would have the girl all to himself. After all, Nick could move through time whenever he wished, but Logan couldn't return for a hundred years, so the girl would be at Nick's mercy.

He shut the desk drawer with a shiver of anticipation. He had written the book on kinky sex and domination, and he could hardly wait to pleasure himself with the voluptuous blonde. Yes,

she was a very rare girl indeed; naive, trusting and incorruptible
. . . or maybe not. It would be a challenge and fun to find out.

This first day had been harder than she had expected, Angie
thought with a sigh as she went upstairs, entered her room and
carefully locked the door behind her.

She'd been at a dead run all day, serving beer and carrying
heavy trays of dirty dishes. She almost envied the pretty, painted
dolls who danced on the little stage or decorated the arms of
gamblers' chairs, urging them to drink and bet even more.

Now it was late evening and her shift was over, although
the Lady Luck still seemed to be full of raucous cowboys and
drunken toughs. She had a twinge of conscience, then reminded
herself that she needed a job. Angie went into the bathroom,
turned on the water in the big clawfoot tub and added some of
the perfumed bath oils she found in the cabinet. With a sigh,
she peeled off her soiled uniform and laid out a fresh lace
nightgown. What the future held she didn't know, but at least,
for the time being, she had a job; even if it was in the kind of
place she felt uneasy about.

Tonight she would try not to think about her dear Johnny or
how she was going to get back to the twentieth century. The
thought crossed her mind again that she might be stuck perma-
nently back in the old West, and it surprised her to realize she
wouldn't really care, if only she could have that beloved man
by her side. She liked this time period with no world wars,
airplanes, atom bombs, missiles, computers or fax machines.
Life in the twentieth century had gotten too complicated for a
girl of simple tastes.

She admitted to herself that the fiery and unpredictable gunfighter had stolen her heart. If only Johnny was alive to share
life with her. She swallowed the lump in her throat. Obviously,
she'd been mistaken about seeing the arrogant gunfighter on
the train; or maybe she had yearned to see him so badly,

she'd imagined that another man looked like him. Angie busied herself brushing her hair and piling it on top of her head while the bathtub filled.

Damn it, what was she doing on this train? That had been Johnny's first thought as he strode into the railroad car wearing a mask and pointing his pistol. Even as they stared at each other in shock, a split second before she called his name and reached out to yank his mask down, he realized just seeing her made him feel warm inside in a way he'd never felt before. No woman had ever affected him this way; no, not in all these long, long years. He must not fall in love with Angel, he reminded himself. That would make him vulnerable. Women were to be used and thrown aside, not cherished.

So here she was on the train they were robbing. Even as she stared up into his face in disbelief, Angel had crumpled in a faint. Johnny caught her gently, lifted her, still keeping his pistol trained on the occupants of the coach. *Now what was he going to do with her?*

She felt so warm and soft in his arms. Moreover, she looked so young in that blue flowered dress with ribbons in her hair; the same dress she'd worn last night at the school festival, when the banker led the lynch party.

Johnny glanced down into her pale face, wanting to kiss those full, soft lips, wanting to hold her forever. He glanced out the window, knowing Bob and the boys would frown on him taking her along. A woman riding with them would slow them down and put them all in danger.

Instead, very gently, Johnny laid her back on the seat, turned and strode out of the rail car without robbing anyone. Maybe if he was lucky, she would think she had only imagined him when she woke up. It was better that way.

He hesitated a split second as he swung up into Crazy Quilt's saddle and looked back toward the train. Everything in him

screamed for him to run back in there, scoop her up and take
Angel with him.

"Come on, Johnny!" Grat yelled. "We've got the express
box; let's get the hell out of here!"

The others spurred their horses and took off at a gallop. Yet
Johnny paused to look back toward the train as he turned Crazy
Quilt to ride out. He would be leaving the first week of October,
so this was probably the last time he would see Angel ...
unless he could figure out a way. . . . Was he crazy? All women
were the same, and they brought a man nothing but added
danger and trouble. All he needed was a trip into town. Sadie,
that red-haired whore at the Lady Luck, would give him what
he needed and wipe the memory of the little blonde from his
mind.

Back at the camp, the others were in high spirits, drinking and
counting the gold. Johnny sat morosely, stirring three spoons of
sugar into his coffee and staring into the fire.

"Hey, Johnny," Emmett called, "why so sad? This was a
big haul."

"Nothing." He was sick of them in a way he'd never been
before. Maybe if it hadn't been for Angel's influence, he would
never have realized how wicked and cruel they were. *Careful
Johnny,* he reminded himself as he sipped his coffee, *you're
about to develop a conscience, and that would never do.* Thinking about right and wrong would make him vulnerable. Angel
had done this to him. He tried to be angry with her about it,
but all he could do was worry about her future and what would
happen to her after he went away forever.

As for the gang, he didn't have to put up with them much
longer. In a few more days, most of them were going to die.

Chapter Fourteen

"You know, Johnny"—Bob paused in polishing his fancy boots—"one more big job and we could go to South America."

Johnny didn't answer. He knew what lay ahead for Bob.

"What's in South America?" Grat asked.

"Hot women and booze and lots of good weather." Bob winked.

Grat snorted. "We got that here."

"I tell you what *ain't* in South America," Bill said. "Tough lawmen. I'm with Bob. I hear there's a big posse lookin' for us down in the Indian Territory."

Dick nodded and scratched himself. "They're closin' in on us, all right. It's only a matter of time now."

Emmett looked toward his big brother. "Bob, what's this about South America?"

"We'd be out of the law's jurisdiction down there, and I got me a big idea," Bob said as he lit a cigar. "With Doolin and Bitter Creek talkin' about quittin' us, that'd be less to divide the loot with."

Johnny looked around. Doolin and Bitter Creek had gone their own way after the robbery.

Emmett began to load his rifle. "I don't trust Doolin no how; too much of a taste for women."

Johnny stood up and stretched. "Speaking of women, I got a need for one; it's been a long time."

Bob shook his head. "You loco? Goin' to town after we've just robbed a train ain't so smart."

Johnny checked his Colt to make sure it was loaded, then pulled out his gold watch and looked at the time. "It's late; maybe nobody will expect anything so bold."

Bob stood up, glowering. "I tell you, you ain't goin'!"

Johnny reached for his saddle, but Bob stepped between Johnny and his horse. "Didn't you hear me?"

"Bob," Johnny said, so softly it was almost a whisper, "I'm going into town. Now you get the hell out of my way before I kill you!"

"Damn!" Dick said, "he must need a woman bad. Let him go, Bob."

Bob, looking as if he might argue, took a second look at Johnny, standing there with his hand on his holster. "I believe you'd do it."

"Don't try me," Johnny said.

Dick shook his head and scratched himself. "He ain't been the same since that little blonde rode with us."

"No, I haven't, but that isn't your lookout." Johnny finished saddling up, angry with himself that he'd let the girl get to him. A night in Sadie's bed would make him forget Angel.

"Maybe I'll go with you," little brother Emmett said.

"You ain't welcome," Johnny snapped.

Bill rubbed his hand across his unshaven face nervously. "You ain't fixin' to turn us in for the reward, are you, Johnny?"

He paused as he checked his girth, glaring at the other man. "You want to take that back now, don't you, Bill?"

Bill gave a choked, embarrassed guffaw. " 'Course I do; I know you wouldn't turn on your old pards.''

Johnny paused, almost wishing he could save them from their coming fate; but the future was set in stone and he couldn't change it. "I wouldn't do you in, Bill. It's your own reckless judgment that'll finish you."

Dick frowned. "He's probably got something there. Why don't we forget about that one more big haul and hightail it for South America with what we got now?''

"Now?" Grat paused in cleaning his rifle. "We ain't got near enough gold yet.''

"Dick's giving you good advice.'' Johnny shrugged and mounted up. "You'll find that out too late.''

"Now how would you know that?'' Emmett sipped his coffee and looked up at Johnny.

Johnny hesitated. He knew, but they would not believe him even if he told them how he knew. "It's bound to happen; that's all.''

Grat said, "You don't sound like you're plannin' to go to South America with us.''

Johnny shook his head. "You ain't going to South America.''

"Says who?'' Bob challenged, bristling. "I'm boss of this gang.''

"Never mind." There was no point in telling them what he knew; they'd never believe him. "You all do what you like.'' Johnny wheeled his horse and rode out, calling back over his shoulder, "I'll be back by morning.''

Bill laughed. "Mount a pretty one for me, Johnny!''

Johnny didn't answer as he rode out into the darkness. His mind was on Angel.

An hour later, Johnny was riding into the outskirts of Coffeyville. Thirty minutes after that, he strode into the Lady Luck and looked around.

Over at the crowded bar, a pretty red-haired whore in tight

green satin pulled out of a cowboy's arms and came running toward him. "Johnny! Long time no see!"

"Hi, Sadie." Somehow, she didn't appeal to him anymore, even though she was good at what she did. And where she had once seemed pretty, now she looked like a cheap slut. Any man with money could crawl between Sadie's thighs. He wanted a woman who couldn't be bought; who'd belong only to him.

Sadie threw her arms around him, rubbing her voluptuous body against him, but he paid little attention, his dark gaze sweeping the room, seeking only one face.

"Well, you ain't very glad to see me!" She pouted and rubbed her body against him. Sadie reeked of men and strong perfume.

"I've been busy."

She wore too much face paint, he thought, remembering the clean, shiny face of a certain blue-eyed blonde. He wondered now how he could have ever taken this red-haired whore to bed.

"I bet I know something you ain't too busy for." Sadie grinned as she put her hand on the swell of his trousers. "That gun hard and long and loaded like always?"

He caught her hand and pushed it away. "Maybe. But not for you."

Her painted eyes widened with jealousy. "Who is she, Johnny?"

"None of your business."

Sadie looked up at him hopefully. "Nobody can do it to me like you do, Johnny. Maybe later?"

"No." Johnny shook his head as his gaze swept around the room, looking for that one dear face. He realized at that moment that there would never be another woman for him—only Angel. She had a hold on him that no one had ever had before. To be beholden was a weakness. Johnny didn't like weakness and dependency; he'd been on his own too long. "Where's your boss?"

Her painted face turned into an ugly pout as she gestured. "In his office, counting the gold me and the other girls bring in like always."

Johnny pushed through the crowds, strode into Nick Diablo's office and slammed the door. "All right, where is she?"

The gambler blinked. "Who?"

"You know damned well who!" Johnny's hand slid automatically to his holster.

"Don't pull that macho stuff on me!" Diablo sneered. "That's no good against me. You should know that."

Johnny sighed and pushed his hat back. "Okay, where is she? In Coffeyville some cowboys told me they saw a new, pretty blonde here."

The other threw back his head and laughed. "You must have galloped all the way to get here this fast. She that good under a man?"

Johnny reached out and caught him by the shirtfront, jerking him to his feet. "You sorry son of a bitch!"

Nick pulled out of his grasp and smoothed his shirt, his face more annoyed than angry. "This is French silk and you wrinkled it. Such a fuss over a woman!"

Johnny leaned on the desk with both hands. "If she's here, you'd better tell me, damn it, or I'll rip that fancy shirt off your back and shove it down your throat!"

"Do you realize who you're talking to?" The gambler's face turned dark and ugly. "I don't know what's got into you, Johnny."

"Sorry." Johnny shrugged and turned away, not wanting the other to see his face. He'd been a fool to challenge Nick, who held such power over him. "It's the girl; she's changing the way I think about everything."

Nick threw back his head and laughed. "Such a softie you've become. I never would have believed it of the deadliest gunfighter in the West. Yes, she's here. She's upstairs."

"You son of a bitch, if you've put her to work as a whore—"

"Now, now"—Diablo made a soothing gesture and went to the sideboard—"don't be so rash. She's working as a waitress; that's all. You want a drink?"

Johnny ignored the hospitality. "You're sure that's all?"

Diablo grinned and nodded. "She has some very old-fashioned ideas about morals, not at all sophisticated and worldly."

"That's what I like about her," Johnny admitted. "She's honest and innocent as her name."

"Angel," Diablo sneered. "A little ironic, considering."

"I know; must be God's joke on me."

Diablo winced. "Don't mention Him. The Big Guy and I haven't been on the best of terms since He kicked me out of His bailiwick and I had to go it alone."

Johnny didn't answer.

Diablo poured two whiskies, handed one to Johnny and returned to sit down at his desk. "Be careful, Johnny. You're an outlaw, remember? You can't open yourself up to really care about her. Romantic love is silly stuff for weepy ladies."

Johnny sat down on the edge of a chair, sipping his whiskey. "I didn't mean to care about her; it just happened, that's all."

"How touching!" A sneer played across Diablo's thin mouth. "Women are playthings; remember? Toys to be tossed aside when you tire of them. You mustn't get too attached to a plaything."

"I never have before," Johnny said defensively. "There've been hundreds of women over the years; I've used them and left them without a second thought. But this one's different."

"Yes, she is," the gambler admitted.

"After all, it's my fault she's here," Johnny said.

Diablo shrugged. "She loves you, which makes her rash. People in love are willing to do anything, sacrifice everything for the other. Quite stupid, if you ask me."

"I didn't ask you," Johnny snapped. "What's to become of her?"

Diablo laughed. "Can't you guess? Frankly, you ought to be relieved. She might have guessed your secret, but now she'll never be able to tell what she knows."

An agony of uncertainty gripped Johnny. "I—I want her. I want to take her with me when I go."

"Easier said than done."

"But you're telling me it can be done?" Johnny leaned forward eagerly.

The other shrugged, his expression bored. "For all intents and purposes, she's going to spend the rest of her natural life around here."

Johnny stood up. "Then I'll stay with her."

"Impossible!" The gambler sipped his drink. "You can't stay. You've got a date with destiny on October 5. It's set in stone."

"No!" He buried his face in his hands. "There's got to be a way!"

"I can assure you, the cost is more than you'd be willing to pay; more than she'd be willing to pay."

"Damn you!" Johnny glared at him.

The other laughed. "No, that's my line. What kind of a guy are you, Johnny? Haven't you had all that any man could desire—long years of pleasant debauchery, riches, luxury, beautiful women, power?"

"I thought I had all I could want until I met Angel; now, none of it means anything without her."

The other man lit a fine cigar. "Spoken like a lovesick fool. Don't look so upset, Johnny; she's just a woman, after all. You'll find a prettier one; a dozen sexier ones. Forget about Angel; count yourself lucky that she can't go spill your secrets."

Johnny stood up and paced the floor. "She wouldn't do anything to hurt me."

"Ahh! Now you're even beginning to trust her; that's bad,

Johnny. Trust leads to real love and finally to marriage. You don't dare marry, and you know why."

Johnny slammed his glass down on the desk. "I thought when I made that deal with you, I was getting the best of the bargain."

Nick Diablo threw back his head and laughed. "That's what everyone thinks, but only the Big Guy can outsmart me." He glanced skyward. "And He doesn't seem too interested in this case. Maybe because you've always been such a rotten, selfish bastard that you don't deserve His help."

"I wonder if rotten, selfish bastards can ever change," Johnny muttered. "I wish now I'd never become an outlaw; just been a regular, law-abiding guy."

"Oh, spare me that schmaltz!" The gambler sneered. "Give up all the good things I've given you for the life of an ordinary schmuck sweating on some dusty ranch, branding cattle and working seven days a week until you drop dead at a too early age? I don't think so!"

Johnny sat there for a long moment, thinking. He'd made a mess of it, all right. He'd shown no mercy and now he'd get none. His clever bargain was not a bargain after all. He'd always looked out for Number One and no one else. Now, for the first time in his sorry life, he was thinking about someone else's welfare. "Can I renege on my deal?"

"Are you loco? Think, Johnny, think! It's too much of a sacrifice. Put yourself first, like everyone else does!"

"You're right; I—I don't know what came over me for a minute."

"Glad to see you come to your senses." Diablo looked relieved. "Look at the bright side, Johnny. You've still got a few days until the fifth. You can seduce her and enjoy her until then with no strings attached, like you've always done with women."

"For the first time, it seems rotten."

Diablo's eyebrows arched and he grinned. "Watch out. You're beginning to develop a conscience; that's bad, Johnny."

"Is it? Angel wouldn't think so."

The gambler reached into his desk drawer, leaned over and tossed Johnny a big brass key. "Stop lusting after her and go up and get her. After you've topped her three or four times, you'll see she's just another tart, after all."

Angel. In his mind he saw that sweet expression, those serene blue eyes, that soft, rounded body. His manhood swelled. Johnny reached out and picked up the key. "What room is she in?"

"Now you're talking! I'll see you aren't disturbed until late tomorrow morning. By then, you should be tired of her." He stood up and gestured. "Second door to the left, upstairs."

Johnny turned and went out, climbed the stairs. The gambler was right. She was just a woman, after all. After Johnny had vented his lust, he'd be as bored with her as he had been with all the others. Women were only created for a man's amusement. After all, it was Angel's own fault she'd gotten herself into this predicament, but Johnny was going to take full advantage of it. Just enjoying her ripe body a few times should cure this terrible yearning. He closed his heart to the still, small voice, so unfamiliar to him, that reminded him that she'd gotten herself in this spot trying to help him. "Everyone should look out for Number One," he said to himself as he went down the hall. "That's what I'm about to do."

Angie leaned back in the tub with a sigh, the hot water relaxing her tired muscles. She was up to her shoulders in scented soap bubbles, and she played with the foam as she washed herself and then leaned back again to enjoy the sudsy hot water. From somewhere downstairs, the faint melody of the piano drifted up the stairs and under the door.

After the ball is over,
After the break of morn,
After the dancers leaving,
After the stars are gone,
Many a heart is aching . . .

Johnny. She winced at the pain, thinking she would never get over his loss. The man she had seen on the train must have been the product of her imagination, she had wanted Johnny to be alive so badly. She didn't know what she was going to do in the future, and with her inner pain, she didn't really care. For now, she had a job, even if it was in a gambling joint.

Angie heard a slight noise in the bedroom and looked up. Johnny Logan came through her bedroom door, closed it behind him, locked it. He stood there now staring at her.

"Johnny?" Even as she asked it, she shook her head. No, it couldn't be. Yet the apparition tossed his Stetson on a chair and strode toward her.

She couldn't move; she could only stare at that broad-shouldered form with disbelief, tears of joy filling her eyes. "Johnny?"

And then he was kneeling beside the bathtub, gathering her into his arms, kissing her lips, her eyes. "Oh, Angel, I've missed you so!"

She threw her arms around his neck, leaving a trail of soap-suds as she pressed her bare body against his black shirt. "How can this be? I saw them lynch you! I saw—"

"It's okay, baby, it's okay." He held her against him so tightly, kissing her, running his hand through her hair as if he couldn't get enough of the touch and taste of her. "I'm alive, see? When they tied that knot, why, they—they didn't do a good job and it slipped, so I was slowly strangling. Then they walked away and that little limb bent to the ground, enough so that I could stand on my tiptoes until they were out of sight. That gave me time enough to untie my hands."

She ran her hands up around the open neck of his shirt, discovering the raw rope burn there. "God must really be looking out for you."

He hesitated. "Well, maybe not God." He pulled her soapy body into his embrace, kissing her deeply as he reached to lift her out of the tub. She hung wet and naked in his arms as he kissed her. Angie slipped her arms around his neck, thrilled he was alive and in her embrace. She put her arms around his neck as he carried her in and laid her across the bed.

"You'll get the covers wet," she cautioned.

"I don't care; I don't care about anything but loving you. All these times we've come close, but tonight we won't be interrupted. Tonight, I possess you at last!" He bent his head and kissed her mound.

Angie moaned softly and twisted against the sheets as he separated her thighs. Perhaps she should object to him kissing her there, but even as she thought that, his tongue traced along the ridge of her femininity, gently sucking, and it was like being touched by fire. The flames seemed to spread up her belly and down through her loins. Instinctively, she reached to hold his mouth against her while he tasted and teased her with his lips. He stabbed deep with his tongue and she could only writhe, wet and soapy beneath him.

"You like that, Angel?"

"You know I do."

"Good! Because I intend to do it a lot." He began to kiss up her wet belly as she reached to unbutton his shirt.

As he paused over her, she caught his nipple in her teeth and nibbled it.

He swore softly under his breath and clasped her head to him. "You've made me want you as I've never wanted another woman."

"And I want you, Johnny! I don't care whether you're an outlaw with a price on your head. We'll take whatever time we have together and be thankful for it."

"Yes," he agreed, "whatever time we have." Then his lips found her wet breast and he covered it with his hot, eager mouth.

Oh that felt so good. She caught his dear face between her two hands and encouraged him to taste and torment her with his tongue. She writhed under him, trying to pull him between her thighs, but he resisted, intent on tasting and caressing her breasts.

"Not so fast, baby," he commanded. "I've dreamed of what it would be like to make love to you, and now that I'm finally doing it, I'm going to make it last."

She wanted him inside her. Angie reached to unbutton his pants, release his turgid member. She ran her finger across the tip, felt the hot wetness of his seed. She wanted that; she wanted to feel him exploding deep inside her.

"You're mine now," he whispered in fierce possessiveness, "and I'll move heaven and earth to keep you!" He sucked her lower lip into his mouth as he pressed against her.

She was trembling and aching with her own need as she clawed at his back, trying to hurry the meshing of their two straining, eager bodies.

"Take me!" she demanded. "I can't take any more of this teasing!"

He needed no further urging. He was still clothed, although his shirt and pants were undone, but she was wet and slick and naked beneath him. She spread her thighs wide and arched up to meet him as he finally entered her.

They had come close so many times, and now he was throbbing inside her. Angie gasped and arched her back as he plunged deep. She felt him pull back and enter her again more slowly, stabbing into her very depths. He was hard and throbbing as he lay on her, tasting and caressing her breasts. She locked her legs around him, urging him deeper still as her excitement mounted.

"Take me, Johnny," she gasped, "take me now!"

He needed no further urging. She met him thrust for thrust. He was trying to hold back, make it last longer; she could see it in his face and hear it in his gasping breath, but her own need was building to a crescendo, her body locking onto his, demanding what he had to give. She dug her nails into his lean hips, raking him with her desperate hunger, helping him ram down into her.

Angie had never known lovemaking could be like this. For her, it had never been like this before. And maybe not for him, either, if she could judge by the look on his face. For the first time, his remote features were alive with emotion.

"I love you, Johnny," she whispered against his mouth. "I love you!"

"You mustn't love me; this is something else—"

"Not for me! I love you, Johnny, only you! Now ride me! Ride me hard!"

He obliged her with a slamming rhythm that threatened to bring the bed down, but they were both oblivious to anything but the meshing of their bodies and souls.

She gasped, and at that moment he plunged into her one more time and they went into spasms of mutual ecstasy. The world seemed to stand still. There was nothing but the pleasure and the emotion she felt for this outlaw who clasped her so tightly as they strained against each other.

It had never been like this before for Johnny; never. It was more than sex; it was as if he was putting his soul and his very being into this woman who locked him to her with her long legs. He was helpless in her grip as she used him for her need, and he didn't ever want to be free of her.

"Angel, oh, Angel . . ." He tried to pour every drop he had into her, wanting to fill her, pleasure her, give her his very soul, put his child in her belly.

He could feel the deep, hot velvet of her grasping him,

squeezing every drop he had to give in the depths of her womb. He put his tongue deep in her mouth as they strained together and she sucked it deeper still. He could feel her nails tearing up his body, wanting still more, and he put all his weight on her, giving her everything he had to give as she began to climax all over again, exciting him into a frenzy so that he, too, rebuilt his desire and exploded harder yet inside her. It was like tumbling into a dark, wonderful passion that he had never experienced and couldn't have imagined was possible. And it was all because of her.

After a long moment, Johnny gently kissed her cheek and pulled her to him, looking down into her sweet face as he kissed her eyelids. He had never, never felt like this about any other woman, wanting her as he had never known he could want a woman. He had never been in love, and maybe this wasn't what he was feeling; except that he still wanted to hold her even though his passion was spent. He kissed the tip of her nose and held her protectively against him. She was his, all right, in a way that she had never belonged to another man; he could see that wondrous surrender in her blue eyes.

"I love you, Johnny."

He didn't answer, although he knew what she wanted to hear. Because of the mess he had made of his life, he couldn't commit to her. "Don't say that," he whispered. "You won't mean it tomorrow."

"And you're too independent to say it at all."

He looked down into the hurt in those wonderful eyes and didn't answer. He would kill the man who hurt her, yet he was the one who was going to hurt her worst of all on October 5, when he deserted her. He had never really known love before and now that he did, he was going to lose it. Maybe it was only justice . . . or God's revenge.

"Make love to me again," she murmured, reaching up to trace the small mole by his mouth with her finger.

He turned his head and caught the tip of her finger in his

mouth, sucked on it and licked it with his tongue. "You just had me twice. You know how long it's been since I could top a woman twice in ten minutes?"

Her face was flushed with passion. "I never knew it could be like this; I want you to do this all night."

He sighed and didn't answer. Tired as he was, he yearned to make love to her again and again. Of course it was understandable that he was weary; after all, he was one hundred forty-one years old.

Chapter Fifteen

He held her close for a few moments, kissing her face gently. He couldn't tell her his secret; she might not believe him, and anyway, they were both powerless to change the deal he'd made.

"Oh Johnny, I've waited a long time for a love like this," she whispered.

"And I've waited forever, baby," he murmured as he kissed her again, then seemed to catch himself. "This isn't love, Angel. We were just two people pleasuring each other; that's all."

She shook her head and reached up to run her finger down his face. "No, it's more than that; much more."

"You're right," he answered, and he began to kiss her again. "Oh, baby, I've never had anything like this before; never!"

He hadn't pulled out of her and now, to his surprise, he found himself hardening with passion, wanting her again. She began to buck under him, locking him against her with her thighs, using him for her pleasure.

It excited him to have a woman need him; *really* need his

body that badly. He pulled her to him and their passion flamed anew. Again they embraced in a torrid mating and clung together when it was over.

Johnny looked down at the girl under him, already dozing off to sleep in his arms as if content to be there forever, trusting him to take care of her. *Was he out of his mind?* He couldn't complicate his life with a woman. He would be leaving in a few days and he couldn't take her with him; Nick had made that clear, while encouraging Johnny to use her for his lust.

Angie was the personification of everything that was good in the world and he was the essence of evil, always looking out for himself. Yet now he was looking out for her, determined to protect her from her fate at the Lady Luck.

You sorry, rotten hombre, he scolded himself. *If you must leave her and break her heart, the least you can do is keep Nick from turning her into a whore here in this bordello.*

"Sweet," he whispered, "we've got to get out of here."

She smiled in her sleep. "Make love to me again."

"I'd like nothing better," he murmured against her ear, "but there's something more important right now."

"Nothing's more important than your loving me."

She was right, he thought in wonder. Nothing else mattered; not money, not power, not luxury. He'd heard an old man preaching on a street corner in a wild boom town once and remembered the words the man shouted at the bored passersby. *For what doth it profit a man to gain the whole world and lose his only soul?* No, more than his soul—the love of the only woman in all eternity who had ever meant anything to Johnny.

"You do love me?" Her trusting eyes flickered open.

"I want you," he admitted after a moment.

"I suppose that will have to do."

He almost told her then; told her of the mess he was in that he couldn't get out of. *Nobody makes a deal with the devil and wins,* he thought. "Come on, sweet." He stood up and began to button his shirt. "You're in danger here; I'm taking you out of here."

She lay there naked, smiling at him from the damp sheets. "I feel perfectly safe when you're around."

"And you are," he promised. "I'll never let anyone hurt you; not as long . . ."

She waited for him to continue, but instead, he sighed and pulled on his boots. She watched him, all muscle and sinew and built like a stallion; more than enough to satisfy any woman. "Come to think of it," she said, "how'd you get in my room, anyway?"

"Angel, you're so naive." He leaned against the bedpost. "Didn't you figure Nick would have a second key?"

She sat up suddenly. "But he promised—"

"You are too trusting; that's why I'm taking you out of here." He caught her hand, pulling her off the bed. She stood there naked, leaning against him, safe in the circle of his strong arms. He would kill any man who touched her; his possessive embrace told her that. She had pleasured him and he had more than pleasured her.

Johnny kissed her forehead, then whirled her around and gave her a smack on her bare rear. "Get dressed before we end up on that bed again."

Her eyelashes fluttered innocently. "Would that be bad?"

He shook his head. "Baby, you don't know the meaning of 'bad.' Your mama surely gave you a name that fits—innocent as an Angel, but makes love better than the best tart I ever had; but there's no time now."

She dug out a skirt from her little carpetbag and began to dress, feeling all warm and loved. "Later, there'll be lots of time. We've got the rest of our lives; half a century, at least."

Instead of answering, he looked away, and his rugged face grew troubled.

"What's the matter?" She paused in slipping on her clothes.

"Nothing. Just get dressed."

Something had changed; something that she'd said. "Oh, I get it; this was just a one-nighter. You don't want me for keeps."

"Angel, I—" He didn't meet her eyes.

"What is it, Johnny?" She came over to him, put her hand on his arm. "There's something troubling you."

He swore under his breath, turned and went over to stare out the window. "You're getting to know my every thought, my every emotion, baby. It makes me vulnerable."

"That's not bad. It just shows you trust me." She had not put on her blouse yet. She went over to him, leaned against him, pressed her naked breasts against his chest. "I trust you, Johnny. I'd trust you with my life."

For just a moment, he pulled her to him, running his hands up and down her back. Then he seemed to regain his self-control and pushed her away. "Don't trust me, Angel. I'm evil; no good."

She shook her head. "No, I don't believe that; everyone has some good in them—"

"Not me."

"My grandmother said love could bring out the good in people."

He laughed. "Suppose it's not there to bring out?"

She reached up, took his face between her two hands. "It's there; somehow, I know it. Look into my face, Johnny, and tell me you don't care about me."

He went rigid and slapped her hands away, looking out the window again, his face contorted with warring emotions. "I can't care about you," he whispered.

Angie shrugged. "Then I'll take whatever I can get. Maybe me caring about you is enough."

She thought he had tears in his eyes, but he blinked rapidly. "You are the most unselfish person I ever met."

"Love does that, Johnny." She swallowed hard, unwilling to believe that he did not love her as much as she cared about him. "Love makes a person willing to sacrifice all for the other."

Now he shook his head in fierce denial. "I've always looked out for me and nobody else. I can't change that; I'm sorry."

"End of discussion." She reached for her shirt and her shoes.

"So you hate me?" He was staring at her.

"No, I love you. I'll take whatever you have to offer; go wherever you decide to go. For me, just being with you is enough."

He gestured helplessly. "Angel, it's not as if I don't care. It's just that . . ."

"Yes?" She waited, hoping to hear him say he loved her as she loved him.

"Never mind. Get your stuff together; we're getting out of here."

She didn't question him as she finished dressing and gathered up her few things. Wherever he was going, she was going, too. It was as simple as that. She watched him pick up his gun and holster off the bed, not even remembering him taking it off. "I thought banker Hiram had your gun."

"He did. I climbed up to his bedroom late at night and got it back."

"You didn't kill him, did you?"

Johnny laughed. "No. He sat up in bed, stared at me, screamed and toppled over, and banged his head loud on the headboard. I reckon he thought he'd seen a ghost."

"Was he all right?" Angie put on her shoes.

Johnny shrugged. "How should I know? It would serve him right if the scare gave him a heart attack. Did you know he wears a striped nightshirt and a nightcap? And his bedroom reeked of rose oil hair tonic."

Angie laughed as she imagined the scene Johnny was describing. "Hiram deserves a bad scare at the very least, if there's any justice in this world."

Johnny opened the window out onto the upstairs porch.

"He'll get justice. Hiram will lose his fortune next year in the big financial panic and depression of 1893."

She stared at him. "Now, how would you know that?"

"What?" He reached for her little carpetbag.

She grabbed her big purse, wanting him to trust her enough to admit that he had time-traveled, too. "You know what I mean. You're evading the issue."

"I don't know what you're talking about. Let's get out of here before Nick comes up here." He held out his hand to Angie, helped her out onto the roof.

Maybe he really had amnesia. In that case, maybe he couldn't remember what he had to do to return to 1999. As long as they were together, she didn't care whether they returned to the future or not.

From the roof, it looked like a long way down to the dark street below. She forgot about Johnny's remarks and focused on the dark roof. "I'm scared of heights."

"You'll be all right, Angel," his voice was so gentle, it surprised her. "I won't let anything happen to you."

He pitched the carpetbag over the edge of the roof and she heard it land on the ground below. She peered over. Crazy Quilt's bright spotted coat was visible below. "There's no steps."

"We'll go down the drainpipe. Do you trust me?"

"You know I do."

"Nobody ever trusted me before." His hard eyes softened as he reached out for her. She went into his arms, knowing his strength would protect her. "Are you sure you're all right with this?"

Angie closed her eyes and clung to him as they went over the edge of the roof. "As long as I'm with you, everything's all right."

He kissed her forehead. "Don't say that, baby. You make me feel like the worst kind of heel."

"Good. That shows you've got a conscience after all, even

though you deny it.'' She looked at how far it was to the ground and automatically crossed herself.

''I don't want to hear anymore,'' he snapped at her. ''I might decide to drop you as we go down.''

''You wouldn't do that.''

''You're too damned trusting, lady.'' He laughed. ''You gotta have that damned big purse?''

''It's got stuff I might need.'' First aid things might be even more important in this time period, where aspirin hadn't even been created yet.

''Okay, have it your way.'' Johnny started climbing down the drain pipe, holding her close and telling her where to put her feet.

She wasn't afraid with his strong arms around her, protecting her, shielding her.

Johnny carried her over and put her up on the back of his horse, then swung up behind her, holding her close. He buried his face in her damp hair for a long moment. ''If only . . .''

She waited for him to continue, but he only sighed and clucked to Crazy Quilt. They rode out of town through the dark night at a walk.

''Nick is going to be upset that I've taken you.''

''I don't know why; I was just a waitress.''

He nudged Crazy Quilt away at a gallop. ''Angel, you're so innocent. I think he had something else in mind.''

''I left Rosebud in Prairie View.''

''I've bribed a cowboy to go steal her back. She should be in camp by the time we get there.''

''Steal her? You are just terrible!''

''I told you that, but you insist on hanging out with me.''

''Maybe I can salvage you.''

He held her close against him. ''If only you'd come along sooner, you might have.''

Angie hardly heard him. It was enough to be with Johnny, riding across the prairie in the golden swirl of autumn leaves.

Nothing mattered to her anymore except being with him. "I never thought I could be so happy," she murmured.

Johnny hugged her to him and kissed her hair but said nothing. When she glanced up, she saw his dark face was troubled. Why had he taken her? Was he already regretting it?

They rode for an hour and met the cowboy in a grove of trees. Angie cried out when she saw her little mare. "Rosebud! Oh, I missed you so much!"

"Great!" Johnny grumbled as he reined in. "Now I'll have to give the hombre twice as much."

Only as she slid from his horse did she see that in spite of his grumbling, he was grinning at her honest joy.

Rosebud nickered a welcome as Angie threw her arms around the paint mare's dainty neck.

Johnny paid the rustler and Angie swung into the saddle. "How will I ever repay you?"

He smiled. "Watching your pleasure is payment enough for me; I'm glad I could do it for you."

"See? Those aren't the words of a selfish, self-centered man."

"Baby, you're seeing something in me that isn't there." His voice was gruff. "If I make you happy, you'll be better in bed to me."

"Liar! You can have me anytime you want me; you did it because you care about me."

"Angel," his voice held a warning, "stop trying to fence me in; tie me to you. I don't like it."

"All right." Maybe she had been wrong; maybe she was only a moment's amusement for a jaded gunfighter. If it was no more than that, she'd have to love enough for both of them. There wasn't anything in this world she wouldn't do for this man, she loved him so.

Neither said much as they rode back to the outlaw camp. The boys were gone and Angie was relieved. "You ought to ditch this bunch,'' she said as they dismounted. ''They're going to bring you nothing but trouble.''

''Don't I know it!'' He pulled her to him and kissed her, tenderly brushing a wisp of blond hair away from her face. ''But I'm stuck with them; I can't change that.''

''Yes, you can, Johnny!'' She stepped away from him. ''They're bad, and I know that deep down, you're good.''

He laughed softly, almost bitterly, and began to unsaddle Crazy Quilt. ''If only you had come along before I made that deal. Now my path is set; I can't change it.''

''Johnny, it's never too late to make a fresh start. You're young; you've got maybe a half century of life left. We could—''

''Shut up, Angel. I don't want to hear any more!'' He cut her off abruptly as he staked the paint out to graze, then unsaddled Rosebud and did the same. ''I've done a deal that I can't get out of. If you knew my past, you'd know how and why I came to this point.''

She took his hand and pulled him down beside her on a blanket. ''Tell me, Johnny. I want to know everything about you.''

He shook his head. ''You'd be shocked.''

She reached up and ran a finger down his rugged, high-boned face. ''I love you, Johnny; nothing you say is going to make any difference.''

His jaw worked for a long moment and he swallowed hard. ''I don't know what I've done to deserve your coming into my life. Nobody ever cared about me.''

''Your mother must have cared about you,'' Angie protested.

He shook his head. ''My mother was a Kiowa whore who drank too much. I was just an added problem for her. She abandoned me in front of Logan's Saloon when I was only three or four years old.''

There was a long pause and he frowned. From the expression

on his features, she knew he was reliving some terrible memories.

"But didn't your father—?"

"I never knew my father." Johnny caught her hand and kissed her fingertips. "I think he was some soldier who slept with my mother once."

Angie made a sound of sympathy, but Johnny squared his shoulders proudly. "I didn't need anyone; I could take care of myself. Old Logan took pity on me, fed me for sweeping up. The customers weren't always so nice to a half-breed bastard. When I was big enough, I drifted on."

"To where?"

Johnny shrugged. "Anywhere. I tried to work as a cowboy, but most ranchers didn't want a half-Injun kid on the place. Finally, some outlaws befriended me, taught me how to handle a gun, change a brand, play poker."

Her heart went out to the poor, friendless child he had been. "Didn't you ever try to go straight again?"

"Yes." He nodded. "I bought a few cows, tried ranching in Nevada, but some big cattleman said I stole them from him. Nobody would listen to me. I ended up in the state prison."

It was worse than she thought. No wonder he had been such a hard case. "And then?"

"There was a guy in prison, Nevada Randolph; he was the half-breed son of a powerful family who owned a big ranch, the Wolf's Den, in Arizona. I thought maybe I could go to work for him when we both got out. But then I figured maybe he was just being nice and didn't mean it, so at the last minute, I didn't go there. I drifted on."

"You should have taken that chance; you're afraid to trust anyone, aren't you, Johnny?"

He didn't appear to have heard her, his mind was focused on the past. "While I was in Arizona, a rich landowner tried to outdraw me. I didn't want to shoot him, but I had to. His friends said it was murder. They sent me to Yuma to hang."

"Yuma Territorial Prison?" She'd heard how tough the place was.

He nodded. "A hellhole. Only a handful of men ever escaped that place, and most who tried died out in the desert. Several of us escaped at the same time; don't know where the others are now. I made my way to Texas. Early this past spring, word got around that some men in Wyoming were recruiting gunfighters, so I went."

"Why did they need gunfighters?"

Johnny shrugged. "I didn't ask; I needed money and I was one of the best. Maybe fifty of us went up."

"And?" she prompted.

He lit a cigarillo, then glanced at her ruefully. "I didn't know until it was too late that it was a range war; some of the richest, most powerful ranchers in Wyoming were determined to scare the little ranchers out. It turned into the Johnson County War; they had to call the troops out to restore order. I didn't want any part of terrorizing small ranchers, so I drifted on."

"You see, Johnny?" She put her hand over his big, rough one. "Deep in your heart, there's some good and decency left there."

He pulled his hand away. "You don't know anything about me, Angel, what a bad guy I really am. When I left Wyoming, I drifted down to Oklahoma Territory, hoping to get a job on a ranch, but with my past, nobody would hire me. So I took up with this gang."

"But you keep trying to go straight," Angie argued. "That has to mean you're not past saving; you just need some encouragement and help."

He shrugged and smoked, his face bitter. "Once an outlaw, always an outlaw."

She had to let him know that she knew. If he didn't learn to trust, he was lost. "Maybe a corporate outlaw, and as hard and ruthless as they come?"

She saw the sudden pain in his eyes. He didn't have amnesia; he was John Logan, all right.

"Baby, if I told you . . ." A long pause.

"What?" she persisted.

He wavered, looking into her trusting blue eyes. Did he dare trust her? He had never trusted anyone in his whole life. He must not fall in love with this sweet, naive girl, he reminded himself. In a few days, he would be leaving forever, and he wasn't sure how to take her with him, or if he should. She knew enough of his secret to be dangerous to him if she returned to 1999. "Never mind; you wouldn't believe my preposterous story anyway."

"Try me."

He shook his head and forced himself to smile. He must get her off this subject before he weakened and told her everything. Even if she did believe him, the die was cast; history was written in stone. The only one who might be able to change things was Nick Diablo, and of course, that gambler wouldn't. "So, Angel, what's your story?"

She shrugged and leaned back against his knee, her eyes closed, relishing the feel of his fingers stroking her hair. "One of two daughters. My younger sister was petite, beautiful and popular."

"You're beautiful."

Angie flinched. Of course he was being polite; she knew she was nothing compared to her sister. "Mother was always throwing my sister up to me; telling me how much more everything Barbara was than me."

"That must have hurt."

Of course it had hurt. After all, Angie couldn't change her looks much, and Barbara's simpering smile was not straightforward Angie's style at all. "You get used to it. Not being the favorite child is something you can't change, no matter how hard you try. And believe me, I tried."

"What about your father?" He stroked her hair.

For a long moment, her throat closed up and she wasn't sure she could speak. "He—was in the Air Force and left Mother for a younger, prettier woman when I was in grade school."

She waited for him to ask about the Air Force. After all, in this time period, airplanes hadn't been invented yet. Maybe he was only being polite and not really listening, because he didn't ask. Instead, he said, "Tell me about your mother and sister."

Even now, she couldn't believe it. Angie had been in college and Barbara in high school when it happened. "Barbara was always winning something or being voted queen of something. I was just her plain, pudgy sister whom Mother pretty much ignored. That rainy night, we were on our way to one of Barbara's pompom competitions when we were in a car wreck."

She waited for him to ask what pompoms and cars were, but he said nothing, only smoked and stroked her hair. He was from the future, all right. Why was he so afraid to trust her?

Angie said, "They were both killed and I nearly died. In fact, the paramedics said I died and came back." Angie closed her eyes. Even now, that moment seemed so real to her. She had been moving toward the light, feeling a tremendous peace and calm. Then there had been a roll of thunder and that tremendous voice, commanding her to go back.

She laughed without mirth. "I dreamed God was telling me I couldn't go; I wasn't finished yet. There was something I had to do. When I opened my eyes, it was only a truck driver with a deep voice, shining a flashlight in my eyes, trying to keep the rain off my face, and telling me to hang on; the paramedics were on the way."

He laughed softly. "With a name like Angel, I could believe God would speak to you."

"Don't be silly"—she sat up and kissed his cheek—"my name is Angelica, and so far, nothing has happened that makes me think it was anything but delirium and a thoughtful truck driver."

After that, she, too, had learned CPR and always carried a

small first-aid kit in her purse. She had been saved that way; she intended to return the favor if she ever happened on the scene of an accident.

Johnny sighed, pulled her to him and held her for a long moment, kissing her face in a gentle way that surprised her. "So, what am I supposed to do with you, baby, now that I've got you?"

"Love me," she said lightly. "Love me and promise you'll stay with me until we are very old people. And then be buried next to me, so our children and grandchildren can come put flowers on our graves."

She had said the wrong thing. She knew it from the expression on his suddenly troubled face. Abruptly, he stood up. "Don't ever talk about death."

"But everyone dies."

He turned away with a curse. "Then life has no meaning, does it? If we are born and then we die?"

"Of course it has meaning if you leave descendants to carry on your bloodline, if you've left the world a better place because you lived."

There was actual fear across his rugged countenance. "Seventy or eighty years isn't enough time."

She stood up and tried to put her arms around him. He was actually trembling. "It's enough, Johnny," she whispered, "if you spend it with the right person."

He shook his head. "No, it isn't enough; what I want is to live forever!"

Chapter Sixteen

"Forever?" Angie blinked, puzzled. Johnny didn't seem like the religious type. "I—I don't understand—"

"Never mind. Forget I said anything." His dark, rugged face was closed, devoid of emotion.

"I'm sorry I upset you, Johnny."

"Forget it, I said." He ground out his cigarillo under his boot. "Let's talk about something else."

"Okay." She laughed to ease the tension that was suddenly in the air. "Let's talk about us. Now that I'm here, what do you intend to do with me?" She went into his arms and he held her against him for a long moment, as if he never intended to let her go.

"I—I don't know. There's no real future for us, Angel. I told you, I've made a bad deal. A real Faustian bargain."

She didn't stop to ask what he meant by his last words. She was too scared. She reached up and took Johnny's face between her hands. "No future? Are you going to desert me?"

"Don't say that!" He pulled her to him and kissed her with

a fierce passion. "I wouldn't leave you of my own free will, Angel. I want you to know that."

"Tell me where you're going," she pleaded. "You won't be rid of me so easily. I intend to stay by your side always."

"But what if you can't?" He looked down into her eyes, and she saw the barest hint of emotional agony in his dark ones.

She was puzzled. "Of course I can . . . unless you don't want me."

"Want you? You're tearing me up, baby. I never wanted anything so much in my life, but—"

She cut off his troubled torrent of words with her lips. He pulled her to him like a drowning man grabbing onto a life preserver, kissing her as if he might never let her go. They clung together for a long moment before she broke free.

"Do you love me?" she demanded.

He shook his head. "I don't know for sure. I never loved anyone before and no one ever really loved me."

She turned away. "If you don't know for sure, then I suppose the answer is no."

He caught her arm. "What is love besides sex and silly stuff for songs?"

"When the other person means more to you than anything; more than yourself, more than your own life. When you would do anything, sacrifice anything for that special one; that's love. True love is so powerful, so pure and good that nothing can withstand it!"

"Nonsense!" His lip curled with bitter knowledge. "Nothing is more powerful than evil! I don't know anything about love; I only know I want you in my arms always," he said, pulling her to him. "I want to possess you over and over; I hunger for you in a way I've never hungered for another woman."

She looked up at him. "That's lust, and it's not enough, Johnny."

"You want too much, baby. That's all I can offer."

Angie buried her face against his shirt and let him hold her. He wouldn't or maybe couldn't make a permanent commitment. Maybe it was because, as he said, he had never loved anyone or had anyone love him; or maybe the permanence and the obligation of it scared him.

"Well," she whispered, "maybe that has to be enough for now." She didn't know what was troubling him or the source of this inner agony he was enduring, but she was ready to close the door on 1999 and stay in this time forever, if she could only stay with Johnny Logan. What mattered was this man and this moment.

"That's what I wanted to hear, Angel." He turned her so that he had her up against a tree trunk, tilting her head back, kissing her throat. Angie ran her fingers around the open collar of his shirt, feeling the rope burn there, grateful that somehow he had survived. There were a lot of things about Johnny Logan that she didn't understand, but she loved him, and she would close her eyes to his faults.

He opened the neck of her blouse, kissed the rise of her breasts. "I wish you could have my children," he whispered. "I'd like to have a little girl just like you."

"Why can't we?" she whispered, but he didn't answer. It occurred to her then that they couldn't end up together, not if the gravestones in the Logan family cemetery were to be believed.

The thought of this man in another woman's arms made her flinch, she loved him so, but she mustn't think of that. Nothing mattered but the way Johnny was holding her now. "Don't talk, just kiss me," she whispered against his mouth. She teased his lips with the tip of her tongue.

With a sigh, he sucked her tongue into his mouth and began to unbutton her blouse, making love to her as she leaned against the trunk of the giant cottonwood tree. He had her pinned against the trunk with his virile body and she spread her thighs slightly so that he was pressed against her mound. Her blouse was completely open and he ducked his head to kiss and caress her breasts.

With a groan of surrender, she threw back her head and closed her eyes, holding his dear face against her breasts as he nuzzled and caressed her nipples.

His hand began to slide her skirt up. She wasn't wearing any bloomers. When his hands discovered that, they grew feverish with warmth. He stroked her bare thighs, cupped her bottom and, finally, began to tease between her legs. She let her thighs fall open slightly, leaning back against the tree as his fingers stroked and teased her silky wetness. He leaned against her, running his fingers inside her as he sucked her breasts.

Angie threw back her head, breathing hard through her mouth as she reached out to open his pants. His pulsating maleness came free and she held it in her hand, feeling the heat and the hardness there. "Now. I want you now."

"Now, baby; right now," he promised fiercely. "I'm going to take you this way." He gasped, and then he bent his knees slightly, coming up into her, his mouth still suckling her breast as she wrapped her legs around his lean hips. She locked her thighs around him, impaled on him as they stood there, his hot hands on her waist, his mouth still sucking her nipple. She could feel the heat of him pulsating within her. Very deliberately, she locked her body onto his, sending spasms of pleasure through them both.

Still against the tree, he slammed her into it over and over as they coupled. She had her arms around his broad shoulders, holding him to her. The mating was fierce and primitive as she moved her hips to take the ultimate advantage of his ramming force. The tree they leaned against shook with the power of his male thrust.

"More!" she said. "I can't get enough of you!"

He slammed her up against the tree one more time, and it seemed she could feel him pulsating deep in her most secret place. Angie buried her face against his massive shoulder and sank her teeth into his brawny muscle in this most primitive of mating urges, wanting to hold him to her even as he shuddered and began to give up his seed.

Angie could almost feel him coming deep inside her as he pressed her against the tree in a violent, passionate coupling. Even as he climaxed, Angie reached that same pinnacle of desire, holding him inside her with her own convulsing body until she had taken everything he had to give.

Then he leaned against her for a long moment, reluctant as she was to break apart, dissolve this magic. She relished the feel of him inside her, relished the thought that even now, her womb was full of his hot, virile seed. She might yet have his child, even if she could never keep Johnny for her own. She hung on to him until they both ceased convulsing and trembling. Her breasts were damp with dewy perspiration against his naked, brawny chest, his two big hands clasping her waist.

After a long moment, she slid her legs down his trim hips, standing on her feet and hanging on to him, trembling.

"Angel, did I hurt you? I didn't mean to. It's just that wanting you drives me loco."

"I know; I know. I—I feel the same. I never climaxed with my husband, did you know that? That makes me almost a virgin."

"*My* virgin, because I taught you pleasure," he whispered against her mouth and kissed her again, tilting her head back and tangling his hands in her hair so he could thrust deep with his tongue, tasting and teasing her.

Angie pulled away from him, gasping for breath. "I can never get enough of you! After while, will you make love to me again?"

"That's a promise."

She reached out to jerk her skirt down and smiled up at him. "I hope a dozen years from now, you'll still want to do that to me."

His face grew troubled. "Let's not think past today, okay?"

"You're still planning on leaving me, even after the way we have loved together?" She was incredulous.

"I told you, baby, I was going to be leaving. What are you trying to do, obligate me?"

Angie shook her head to hide her tears. "Is that what you think?"

He ran his hand through his black hair in distraction. "Look, Angel, if I could find a way to take you with me; I'm not sure you'd go."

"I'd go anywhere with you," she assured him quickly.

He turned his back on her, walked over and sat down on the blanket. "I don't even know if I could take you."

"You could at least give it some thought—"

"I am thinking about it. I'll ask Nick—"

"I knew it! Nick Diablo's mixed up in this, isn't he?"

He raised his head, looking at her. "How'd you know that?"

"I didn't. You just told me." Angie sat down beside him. "Johnny, what kind of hold has this gambler got on you?"

"The worst kind." He stared at the toe of his boot, rather than look at her.

"Isn't there anything you can do?" She put her hand on his arm, but he shook it off.

"I made the deal; I've got to fulfill the contract."

He looked so depressed that her heart went out to him. "What if you refuse?"

Johnny shrugged. "Then I die. It's as simple as that."

"Sign or die? Those are the choices?"

He nodded. "I can't explain. You'd think me loco."

Angie was too shocked to speak for a moment. She'd seen movies and read stories about gangsters killing people because they reneged on deals, but she'd never believed them. But they didn't have gangsters back in the old West, did they? "Maybe you could tell the law—"

"Angel, do you hear what you're saying?" His voice rose. "I'm an outlaw; the law won't help me on this one, even if they could. Neither can you. That's why I tried not to drag you into this. Why did you have to follow me through that mirror—?''

''What?'' She stiffened, her attention suddenly caught by his words. She'd been right all along; he didn't have amnesia. ''The mirror; you know about the mirror.''

''What mirror? I know one got broken in that shootout with Duke Babcock, that's all.'' He didn't look at her.

''You're lying,'' Angie insisted. ''I know you well enough now to know that. Look at me!''

His head came up slowly and she stared into his eyes, reached out to touch the tiny mole by his mouth. An outrageous idea dawned on her and she shook her head. Of course it was preposterous, and yet . . .

''Logan, once you asked me if I'd ever seen the movie *The Highlander,* and I didn't understand what you were driving at.''

''That makes two of us, baby, because I don't know what a 'movie' is and I never heard of this *Highlander* guy.''

If he really loved her, he'd trust her; he'd believe she would never do anything to hurt him. The movie was about a man who had the power to live forever. Could Logan possibly be like the *Highlander?* Then she laughed and shook her head. ''I must have been crazy to think that such a thing could possibly be.''

He didn't answer, only pulled her to him and put his arm under her head. He smelled of tobacco and leather, good mannish scents like sun and campfire smoke.

They settled down together on the blanket, curled up in each other's arms.

He kissed her forehead. ''You through asking questions?''

''Yes.'' What she didn't tell him was that she was determined to help him in his trouble, go with him on the day when he had to face Nick's henchmen or go into hiding. If they had to live life on the run, maybe it was worth it if they could just be together. "If you'd just let me help you . . ." she murmured.

He smoothed her hair with a gentle hand. "You can't help me, baby, but thanks for the thought."

"When do you have to leave? Is there a set date?"

He hesitated. "October fifth."

She did some quick figuring. That date was only a few days away. "And you won't take me with you?"

"I told you I can't, Angel, not unless you're willing to make the same deal I did; and I wouldn't let you do that. Now let's stop talking about it."

"Whatever you say." She'd sign it, she thought, anything to stay by his side. Wherever he had to be on October 5, Angie intended to be there, too. "I'm sleepy," she yawned. "You want to rest for awhile?"

"Sure, as long as I've got you in my arms."

They curled up together like two cuddling kittens, and Angie smiled as a red-gold leaf swirled down from the tree and floated onto her face. She had this man and this moment in time; she could ask for nothing more—except to spend the rest of their lives together. Maybe, because of his background, he was afraid of commitment; afraid to give her his whole heart and trust. She would change his mind; she was sure of it. She would help him deal with his trouble, whether he wanted her to or not.

They had a delightful couple of days. The weather was mild for late September. Every morning while the dew was still on the grass and the sun was turning the sky pink with a fresh dawn, they went riding, galloping across the prairie. Every afternoon, when the day warmed, they swam naked in the nearby creek, and afterwards, they made love under trees that were scarlet and gold with the coming of autumn. Late in the lazy afternoon, they would curl up together and nap. At night, they lay together on Johnny's blanket and watched the stars overhead and made love again. And after he had drifted off to sleep, she would hold him to her and pray that he would change his mind about taking her with him, wherever he was going, whether he was returning to the future or not.

One crisp morning as they rode across the prairie and stopped to survey the landscape, Angie said without thinking, "I wish this could last forever!"

He didn't smile in return. "For the most part, nothing lasts forever, Angel."

"Jiminy Christmas, I didn't mean literally," Angie said, thinking about *The Highlander*. "Nobody would want to live forever."

He cocked his head at her. "You mean, if you got the chance, you wouldn't want to?"

Rosebud stamped her feet, impatient to run again, but Angie reined her in. "Don't be silly, Johnny; if I lived forever, I'd outlive you and my children and grandchildren. I'd be afraid to love anyone because I'd know I was going to be around to watch them die. I'd be so alone."

He looked off into the distance, as if lost in thought. "So alone," he murmured. For a long time, he said nothing, then seemed to shake off his melancholy thoughts. "Come on; I'll race you to that tree over there."

"You're on!"

The two horses took off at a gallop, apparently enjoying the morning as much as their riders. The horses reached the big elm tree dead even.

Angie dismounted. "No fair! You held Crazy Quilt back and didn't outrun me."

He swung down and laughed. "Would you like it better if I beat you? I was trying to do you a favor."

"Why?"

He hesitated, and she thought for a moment that he would tell her he loved her. She had not mentioned his leaving her in October, but it was always on her mind. Maybe if she talked from the depths of her heart, he'd trust her enough to do the same. They walked the horses over to a small lake to water them.

"Johnny, I want to tell you how I came to be here."

"You told me." He patted his stallion's neck.

"I meant the details. At first, I hesitated; I was afraid you wouldn't believe me."

He looked at her levelly. "What makes you think I would now?"

Was she assuming too much? "Because we've come to care about each other; trust each other."

He made a gesture of dismissal. "I'd really rather not get into anything that might tie me down."

"Okay." She shrugged as she tied Rosebud to a nearby bush so the mare could graze. "I'm not asking for anything from you, but I trust you enough to tell you this without worrying or caring whether you'll think I'm loco or not."

He tied his horse to the bush, too, and said nothing.

She waited in vain. "Aren't you going to say anything?"

Johnny shrugged and reached in his pocket for a slender cigarillo. "I'm waiting to hear you out."

"Okay, here goes; I followed you through some kind of a magic mirror and back into the past."

He laughed and lit the cigar.

"I was hoping you wouldn't laugh." She felt crushed by his attitude.

"Now, baby, what do you expect? What time are you from?"

"You know as well as I do; 1999. The Millennium is coming."

"So what?" He blew smoke toward the sky. "It's 1892. The new century is only eight years away. It might be just as exciting to see the new century dawn."

"Why are you doing this?" She felt tears come to her eyes.

He looked haunted and trapped. "I—I can't tell you."

"Please trust me! I love you," Angie said.

No answer.

She was getting desperate. "Look, Johnny, next year there'll be another Oklahoma land run, this one in the Cherokee Strip. Johnny, if we stay in this time period, we could take part in that land run, get ourselves a little ranch. You could start over."

He sighed and shook his head, and she thought she saw tears in his eyes. "Damned cigar smoke," he muttered.

"Don't be afraid to be sensitive, Johnny. Don't be afraid of loving me."

"I'm not afraid of anything except dyin'!" he snapped. "Look, baby, I can't start over, I've got to walk the path I'm already on; it's too late for me."

She grabbed his arm, looking up at him, pleading. "Johnny, I'll help you. We'll do it together."

He shook her hand off. "I told you I didn't want to discuss this anymore. Wouldn't you want to go back to your own time if you could? It's bound to be better than this."

Angie thought for a minute. "I don't know whether it is or not; we've still got lawlessness, evil and misery. Some things don't seem to change. But yes, some of it is much better."

He was staring at her keenly. "And you'd give that up to stay back here?"

She nodded. "For you, I would. I love you, Johnny."

"Don't say that," he snapped and turned away. "You know I'll be leaving soon."

"After you sign that contract?"

"We've covered this ground too many times already, baby. Stop bringing it up."

"If you'd only tell me why—"

"Damn it! Let it lay, Angel!" He blew smoke like an angry dragon.

She licked her lips and took a deep breath, willing to brave his anger because she loved him so. "I want to be with you, wherever that is."

He sighed loudly and stared off into the distance, as if looking over the horizon. "You wouldn't be willing to do what it would take to go with me."

She stared at him, puzzled. "Johnny, I'd do almost anything."

He turned away, crushed out his cigarillo, leaned against the tree. His shoulders shook ever so slightly.

"Johnny? Are you all right?"

There was a long moment before he answered. "Sure, I'm okay." He straightened up and took her in his arms. "You're one in a million, Angel, but you'd have to sign a contract that would shock you—"

"I don't care!" She laid her face against his shirt. She could feel his heart beating there.

His arms came up almost automatically to enfold her, hold her close. "My dear, dear Angel. I'm a rotten, no-good hombre; how rotten you will never know."

She wasn't certain what he meant, but maybe she was breaking through that tough veneer of his. "I trust you, Johnny, to do what's right."

He held her very close and kissed her hair. "Don't ever trust anyone, baby, and you won't be disappointed."

She looked up at him. "I trust you, Johnny; you won't disappoint me."

"Damn it, I will! Now stop it, will you?" He pulled out the big gold watch, glared at it. "It's getting late; we ought to head back to camp."

"All right." She'd done the best she could to reach him and it didn't seem to be enough, Angie thought sadly as they mounted up and started back to camp. She had declared her love and willingness to make any sacrifice, while he held back. There was nothing else she could do. Now he would have to make the important decisions for himself.

They rode back to camp, not saying anything. Angie was disappointed in his attitude. Still she couldn't resist him when he took her in his arms on his blanket in the shade of the tree and they made frenzied love as if for the very first time. Afterwards, they took a nap, curled up together.

They were just waking when Bob and Grat and the rest of them came riding in at dusk.

"Well"—Bob smiled as he dismounted—"look who's back."

"I went and got her," Johnny said with a yawn.

Dick smirked and stared at her. "Looks like you've been making good use of her."

Angie glanced down, realized her bodice was open, and quickly buttoned it.

Johnny glowered at him. "Watch your mouth, Dick; she's no slut."

"Well, now, ain't that a disappointment!" Grat said, and he sounded like he'd been drinking. "I was hopin' for a little of that action later tonight."

"I've said this before, and I don't want any mistake about it," Johnny said, his voice like ice—cold and hard. "I'll kill the man who touches her."

She laid her hand on his arm. He was fast with a gun, but it would be deadly to go up against the whole gang. "It's okay, Johnny."

"Are you goin' soft on us, Johnny?" Bob grinned and paused to dust off his shiny boots. "Next thing we know, you'll be talking about vine-covered ranch houses and babies."

Angie laughed. "I'm all for that."

Johnny didn't laugh. He gave her a troubled glare and went to poke up the fire.

Emmett shook his head. "I don't like having a woman around; she's liable to lead the law to us for the reward."

"She wouldn't do that," Johnny said.

"You trust her too much," Dick grumbled.

"I'd trust her with my life," Johnny snapped, and then looked surprised at his words, as if he had realized it for the first time.

Angie knelt by the fire and reached for a skillet. "Here, let me see what I can do about some food."

"Now you're talkin'!" Bob grinned.

Johnny pulled out his watch as Angie busied herself slicing up bacon. "Where you guys been all this time?"

"Around." Bob glanced at Angie with a look that said he didn't trust her even if Johnny did.

"We're lookin' for our next job," Grat said. "With the law all over the trains now, we figure we'd better lay off them awhile."

Angie sliced bacon and made biscuits without saying anything. These outlaws were up to no good and would finally end up in jail or go out in a blaze of glory. She didn't intend that Johnny be with them when that happened.

Johnny sighed. "Civilization is even coming to Indian Territory. The handwriting's on the wall, boys; law and order are taking over. The old ways will soon be gone."

Bob shook his head. "There'll always be men like us, no matter how civilized things get. I want to live well, but I don't want to sweat for starvation wages on some hardscrabble farm, like my folks."

Angie looked up. "You don't get something for nothing."

"Who asked you, sister?" Bob snapped.

"Watch you mouth," Johnny warned. "I don't want you talking to my woman that way."

"Well, she's as pious as a church choir," Bob complained as he reached for the bottle of whiskey in his saddlebags. "Next thing we know, she'll have old Johnny here hanging up his guns and plowing on some little spread."

"Sometimes that don't sound half bad," Bitter Creek said softly, his expression regretful. "A woman like that one could make any man want to reform."

"I'm not changing, I tell you." Johnny swore under his breath.

Angie watched his stoney face. Maybe he didn't know how

to return to the future and was afraid to tell her. Why didn't he understand that she'd be happy to stay back here in time with him? She had hoped against hope that he might finally love her enough to give up his outlaw ways, but probably, after his wild and rugged past, a life on a settler's small ranch would seem too tame for him.

She served up the grub and the gang sat around until dark, talking about what project they might take on next. They didn't mention specifics, and Angie figured it was because she was there and they didn't trust her.

Johnny yawned. "Let's give it up and get some shut-eye."

"Easy for you to say," Bob snorted, "with a pretty gal to sleep with. I'm disappointed with you, Johnny. Partners always share and share alike."

"She's something I don't share," Johnny snapped. "Get your own woman."

Was that all she was to him, a convenience to warm his blankets? Angie didn't say anything as they let the campfire burn to nothing but glowing coals and settled down to sleep. Johnny pulled her protectively against him and drew up the blanket. "I like the feel of you in my arms," he said.

She snuggled down against him, feeling safe and protected as she dropped off to sleep.

In the middle of the night she awakened, wanting to relieve herself. She raised herself up on one elbow, looking around. The campfire was only a handful of glowing coals, throwing long shadows across the clearing. Johnny slept peacefully next to her, and she smiled as she looked at him. The worry had left his face and the lines had smoothed, so that he looked much younger. Around her, she could hear the others' snores.

She went off into the dark woods, relieved herself and started back, her mind busy with her dilemma. As she passed through a spot of bright moonlight, she saw the sudden shadow and opened her mouth to scream, but a hand clasped over her mouth.

In sheer terror, Angie fought to get away, or at least to scream to awaken Johnny, but she was powerless against her assailant's strength. She could hear him panting with effort as he subdued her and began dragging her into the woods. *Was she about to be murdered or raped?*

Chapter Seventeen

Angie went limp as her attacker dragged her toward the brush. Maybe he would relax his grip, thinking she had fainted. Whoever he was, he was a heck of a lot stronger than she was; since she couldn't overpower him, she'd have to outsmart him.

She willed herself to wait a few seconds until she felt his grip relax a little. If she could just get her mouth free to shout for Johnny . . .

Now! she thought and came alive, fighting and scratching, trying to twist away from her assailant, but he was strong. She could feel his hot breath on her bare neck as he dragged her through the brush. If she could just scream for Johnny; but she couldn't get that hand off her mouth.

"Now, you little slut, stop strugglin' and give me what I want!"

Bob. It was Bob. The realization caused her to freeze momentarily.

"That's it, honey," he breathed heavily against her hair as he dragged her deeper into the trees. "You know me and you been wantin' me, too, ain't you? And even if you ain't, too bad.'' His wet, sloppy kisses were on her neck, moving down her shoulder. She shuddered and tried to pull away from his mouth, but he only laughed.

"You just let me have you and then go back and keep quiet so I won't have to kill that damned half-breed. After all, he's bein' selfish; partners are supposed to share.'' He snickered softly as he dragged her.

What should she do? Angie cringed at the feel of his body against hers. If she managed to scream, would Johnny come running right into Bob's ambush? Angie's heart pounded so hard, she was sure Bob could feel it; he had his hand up under her breast.

"Now, honey,'' he crooned, "don't you be scared of old Bob. I'm just gonna do what Logan's been doin' to you all these nights, and you're gonna keep quiet about it and lay still while I do it, you hear?''

Angie managed to nod, acting as if she had decided to cooperate. *What to do?*

"That's the girl.'' He paused in the shadows of a tree, and his hand crept up and cupped her breast. "You're something; you know that? I can hardly wait to get my mouth on these.''

Angie wanted to retch or make a noise of disgust as she felt his dirty hand squeeze her breast. She must wait until he took his hand off her mouth. Angie stopped struggling completely and made a soft sound, as if she liked the way he was touching her.

"Like that, do ya?''

She nodded.

"I knew you was a slut; Johnny thinks you're so good. Well, you're gonna feel good under me, all right.'' His breathing came in short gasps as he pawed her with his free hand. "I'm gonna put it in you so deep, you'll think you been had by a bull, and I'm gonna suck these off!'' He squeezed her breast hard.

Angie had never felt such anger and outrage as she did at that moment, but she forced herself not to fight or struggle. Once he took his hand off her mouth . . .

Abruptly, Bob pulled a bandanna from his pocket. "I'm not stupid enough not to keep you from yellin,' " he muttered. "Once I've had you, you won't dare tell; that half-breed doesn't trust anyone, especially women. He'd believe you'd lay down for any hombre that wanted you."

For a split second, Bob took his fingers away and tried to shove the dirty rag in her mouth, and in that moment, Angie twisted her head to one side and screamed. The sound was choked off by Bob's hand as he hit her hard. Her own blood tasted rusty warm in her mouth.

She came alive, fighting and trying to jerk out the rag, but Bob was throwing her down on the grass in the shadows, falling on top of her. He crammed the bandanna in her mouth so her cries of protest were muted moans. "Oh, honey, what a mattress you make!"

She struggled to escape, but he was tall and wiry, and she couldn't get out from under him. He pinned her arms above her head with one hand while the other reached to rip open her bodice. With revulsion, she felt his rough hand pawing her breasts. *How dare he!*

"Now you just lie still, honey, 'til I finish," Bob panted as he tried to get her dress up, "then we'll both go back to camp as if nothin' happened. From now on, you're gonna meet me out here every night, or I'll tell that half-breed of yours that you been doin' me on the side. He'd kill you for that."

Or you, if he truly trusts me, Angie thought as she fought to get out from under Bob. His dirty hands and mouth were all over her as he tried to open his pants.

Bob could never take Johnny in a fair fight, Angie thought, but he wouldn't have any qualms about shooting Johnny from an ambush if the gunfighter tried to rescue her. Bob bent his head to her breasts.

She would not let him put his mouth on her or rape her, no matter if he killed her. She turned her head in a quick motion, raking the rag across a rock. It scratched her skin, and she could feel the sting of the rough stone, but the bandanna was out of her mouth. "Let me go!" she shrieked. "Let me go!"

"You little bitch!" Anger etched his lean face in the moonlight as he brought back his hand to strike her again.

Angie shied away from the blow, but even as Bob brought his hand back, someone reached out of the darkness and grabbed it, twisting it backward.

Bob screamed long and loud. "My arm! You're breaking my arm!"

Johnny stepped out of the shadows, twisting Bob's arm even more. "You bastard, I'll tear it off for touching her!"

Bob jerked his arm away and stumbled to his feet, favoring his injured hand. "I wasn't doin' nothin', Johnny. She offered and I was just—"

"You liar!" Johnny hit him then, his fist landing a solid blow that could be heard as it connected with Bob's chin. They meshed and fought as Angie scrambled to her feet, gasping and sobbing while she pulled her torn bodice to cover her naked breasts. The two men fought and tumbled in the clearing, the bright moon throwing long, distorted shadows across the grass.

The others came running, rubbing their eyes sleepily. "What in tarnation is goin' on?"

Neither man answered as they fought. The others formed a ring and watched. Bob landed a blow and Johnny stumbled backward, tripped across a downed tree branch and fell. Bob charged at him, roaring like a wounded bull. In the bright moonlight, Angie could see the dark smear of blood down Bob's face and shirt.

"Look out, Johnny!" she screamed.

Johnny came to his feet, quick as a cat. He tackled Bob's legs and they went down, tumbling over and over. Johnny came up on top, reaching for his knife. "You stinking bastard, I'll make sure you never attack another woman!"

But Doolin and Dick waded in, grabbing Johnny's arms. "Okay, that's enough, Johnny. You've taught him a lesson."

Johnny struggled a long moment, then seemed to get control of his anger and stopped fighting. He look a deep, shuddering breath and stood up, then shook off the men's restraining hands. "I warned him about touching her."

"We know you did," Emmett said, reaching to help his older brother to a sitting position.

"The slut offered it to me!" Bob screamed. "You know how women are, Johnny!"

"Not her!" Johnny attacked him again with both fists. "Not Angel! She wouldn't do that!"

The other brothers grabbed Johnny again.

"Bob couldn't help hisself," Grat whined. "He likes women, and that one's just almost more temptation than a man can stand."

"That's right," Bob was almost sobbing as he wiped blood from his face. "I'm not responsible if she keeps flaunting herself in front of me."

"I wasn't flaunting," Angie snapped, "and everyone is responsible for his own actions."

Emmett helped Bob to his feet. "You okay, brother?"

"Of course I am!" Bob snarled, "I'm older than you. I don't know why you feel you always got to look out for me."

Grat, the grumpy one, made a face and yawned. "All that woman's been is trouble. I say we send her away before she breaks up the gang."

"I'll be glad to go!" Angie snapped. "And you'll go with me, won't you, Johnny?"

There was a long pause as all eyes turned toward the half-breed. He hesitated.

"Johnny?" she asked again.

The silence was broken only by a distant night bird's lonely cry. The bird mirrored Angie's suddenly bereft feelings.

Johnny cleared his throat and didn't look at her. "Angie, I'm sorry, I can't. I—"

"Never mind; I've got my answer." She straightened her shoulders and walked away from the silent group, toward the horses. She was so blinded by tears, she almost couldn't see to bridle Rosebud.

She put on the saddle blanket and reached for the saddle. It was heavy, and she struggled with its weight as she lifted it.

"Here, let me do that," Johnny said, coming up behind her.

He tried to take it from her, but Angie shoved him away. "I can do it. Don't act like you care about me; you've made your choice."

"Angel, you don't understand. I can't change; my course is set."

"You mean, you don't love me enough to change." She struggled with the saddle, throwing it up on the mare's back.

"Where are you going?" Johnny acted as if he might block her from mounting her horse.

"What do you care?" Angie said bitterly as she cinched the girth. "I'm just one of all those faceless women you've slept with; nothing more."

"Baby, that's not true," Johnny protested.

The others had come over to stand and watch.

Bitter Creek said, "Maybe we shouldn't let her ride out; she might turn us in for the reward."

"She would never do that," Johnny said, and his eyes looked deep into hers.

She returned the look for a long moment. "You trust me." It was a statement, not a question.

"With my life," he said.

"Let her go," Grat grumbled. "She ain't gonna call the law on us. Can't you see by her face she loves you, you stupid half-breed?"

There were sudden tears in Logan's dark eyes. Angie could see them shining in the moonlight.

"Yes, I love Johnny," she whispered, "but Johnny doesn't love me."

"Maybe I do," he protested.

"But not enough."

"How much is enough?" His dark face mirrored emotional turmoil and confusion.

"You shouldn't have to ask." Angie walked across the camp, grabbed her little carpetbag and purse and swung up on the mare. "I'll be in Coffeyville if you change your mind."

She started to ride out, but Johnny reached up and caught her bridle.

"Get your hand off my horse, you rotten, miserable SOB!"

Johnny's eyes widened in surprise. In truth, her outburst of anger had surprised her, too, but he had hurt her for a final time and she was lashing out at him.

Slowly he turned loose of the bridle and stepped back. "Okay, if that's the way you want it."

"It is." Angie lashed her startled little paint mare and Rosebud took off at a gallop. Angie rode out, tears streaming down her face. He didn't care enough to either go with her or stop her from leaving. And after all, a handsome, skilled lover like Johnny Logan could pick up a willing woman in almost any saloon.

Johnny watched her ride out. Everything in him screamed for him to call out to Angel, beg her to stay, but it would be useless. He could not change what was going to happen on the morning of October 5. He simply had to play his role in history and endure the deal he'd made.

Doolin spat to one side. "Well, that's that. Let's get some shut-eye, and in the morning, we'll talk about our next job. Right, Bob?"

Bob rubbed his fingers across his mouth and smiled, as if remembering the taste of Angel's lips. "Right!"

"Okay," Johnny said and shrugged. "We'll let bygones be bygones." He still wanted to kill Bob for touching Angel, but he couldn't; it wasn't part of recorded history. As for the others, if he could warn them, change the outcome, stop the killings, he would, but nothing could change what was going to happen. Besides, if he told what the future held, the gang would think he was loco.

Angie rode into Coffeyville, checked into the hotel and cleaned up. She went to bed but couldn't sleep. What was she to do now? Whatever Johnny was involved in, she intended to try to be there for him, even if he didn't care enough about her to trust her with his secrets or take her with him when he went. She spent a sleepless night dreaming that she ran after Johnny screaming, "Don't leave me behind!" as he ignored her and rode away without looking back. Finally he was only a small figure on the horizon, growing smaller and smaller until he was gone completely, leaving her alone in a time and place that was more than eighty years before her own birth.

The next morning she put on her most prim dress and the straw bonnet and went to the city hall to meet the mayor.

"I'm Mrs. Newland and I was on my way from Indian Territory," she said, "but I've lost my luggage and my money. I'm well-educated; perhaps I could get a temporary job teaching school?"

The mayor had red jowls and a fringe of white hair. He seemed to look her over and nodded as he asked questions. Then, seemingly satisfied, he said, "We can't offer you a permanent job, but would you be interested in a part-time position for a few days?"

"I don't know; I might."

He scratched his bald head. "We've been trying to get school started, but our last schoolmarm ran off and got married a couple of weeks ago. The new one isn't due in town until the end of the first week in October.''

October. Johnny had once mentioned some date in October that was important. She couldn't remember now what it was or why it stuck in her mind. ''I may only be temporary myself, but yes, I'll take the job.''

''Good! I'll talk to the schoolboard this morning.''

By noon, she was in the small brick school, teaching all grades. Her heart ached over Johnny, but he had made his choice. Anyway, most outlaws lived short, violent lives. She didn't want to be there to see Johnny gunned down on a street somewhere. Yet she didn't know how to return to her own time. If only she had Johnny by her side as her husband, she wouldn't care if she stayed back in 1892. As he had said, it would be fun to welcome in the new century, especially knowing everything that was going to happen for the next hundred years. Or was he cold-bloodedly planning to return to the future without her? He'd never trusted anyone in his lonely life and didn't seem able to believe she'd never do anything to hurt him.

At lunchtime on her second day of teaching, Angie was writing on the blackboard and the children were copying everything down on their slates. ''Oh, if we only had some computers,'' she thought aloud.

''What?'' Several of the children raised their heads.

''Nothing.'' She must be more careful about giving herself away. ''Has anyone read a book they'd like to share with us?''

Little Ben with the freckles on his nose held up his hand. ''I just read a book by Jules Verne. Do you think any of the things he talked about will ever be invented?''

''What do you think, children? Maybe in a hundred years, people will be going to the moon or driving around in horseless carriages.''

''You mean,'' asked Winnie Sue, ''send a balloon into space?''

"No, something more advanced than that. The next fifty years are going to be very exciting for you children. You'll live to see some thrilling inventions." *And the Panama Canal, Teddy Roosevelt and two world wars.*

"Flying machines?" little Ben suggested.

"I think so." Oh, if she could only tell them about the Wright brothers and trips around the world by jet. "And oil will be important. Do any of you children have oil on your land?"

Willie was evidently poor, judging by his worn clothes. He scratched his head with his stick of chalk. "You mean that black stuff Pa greases buggy wheels with? It's seeping up and killin' the grass in our pasture."

"Well, someday, when the flying machine and the horseless carriage are invented, oil is going to be very important," Angie said. "Tell your daddy not to sell that land and maybe you'll be rich."

This started a big discussion among all the children about inventions and future possibilities. It occurred to Angie that if she was stuck back here in this time forever, she knew enough about the future to make some wise choices. *Knowledge is power.*

"Class, it's time for lunch."

"Gosh, Mrs. Newland, I hope you stay in teaching," Millie, one of the older girls gushed. "You've made me want to be a teacher, too."

Angie smiled as she shooed everyone to take their lunch pails out under the trees. "I may stay in teaching, Millie. I do like it. You're the oldest girl in school, aren't you?"

Millie nodded shyly. "Sixteen, ma'am."

"Then I'll let you help out with the lessons some. However, I'll only be here 'til Wednesday. The new teacher comes Thursday morning."

The class moaned.

"Now, now, that's not nice," Angie scolded. "Everyone eat

and enjoy the playground; then we'll have some more discussion and a spelling bee.''

About the time lunch hour ended, little Susie with the dark pigtails, fell off a playground swing and scraped her knee. Millie picked her up while the children went running for Angie.

Thank goodness she still had her first-aid kit. Angie grabbed her purse and went out. Responsible Millie had dusted the little girl off and soothed the sobbing child while Angie dug around in her big purse for a bandage and some disinfectant.

"You gonna put coal oil on it, teacher?'' The children clustered around.

"Jiminy Christmas, no!'' It occurred to her that medicine of that day was pretty primitive. People died of common ailments because penicillin, antibiotics or even aspirin were not available yet.

It was a good thing she had some first-aid training if she was going to keep teaching school. She bandaged Susie's knee after putting disinfectant and ointment on the scrape.

The bell rang and the children trooped back inside. She loved children, but she could hardly keep her mind on her work for worrying about Johnny. Angie let Millie lead a spelling bee; then she assigned the children some reading. Angie returned to her desk and sat down. School would be out in a few minutes.

Her gaze fell on a large dictionary lying on her desk. She remembered then the word that Johnny had used. Faustian. Surely he didn't mean that literally. Maybe there was another definition. Curious, she pulled the big dictionary to her and began to flip through its pages. Finally she found what she was searching for:

Faust, a German legend of a man who enters into a compact with the devil. Faustian: belonging to, resembling or befitting Faust, sacrificing spiritual values for material gain.

Angie blinked and reread the definition. *What had Johnny been trying to tell her? Or keep her from knowing?* Nick Diablo's grinning, evil face came to her mind. In Spanish, *diablo* meant . . .

''Mrs. Newland,'' Millie asked anxiously from the front row, ''are you all right? You look sick.''

''I—I'm fine.'' Angie took a deep breath, swallowing hard to keep from retching. She was still sitting there staring at the definition when the bell rang and the children whooped with delight and ran out of the school.

She sat and stared at the print until it blurred before her eyes, and then, without thinking, she crossed herself. Her unconscious gesture surprised her. It had been a long, long time since she'd even been to mass. Angie hadn't really been religious since her mother and sister had been killed and she had lived. Hadn't that proved that there wasn't any justice or rhyme or reason to the universe?

Slowly she closed the book and stared unseeing across her empty classroom, struggling with her decision. Shadows were lengthening into twilight before she gathered up her things and locked the schoolhouse door behind her.

Tonight, she was going to call on that gambler and demand to know just what hold he had on Johnny, and what she could do to free him from that obligation. She loved Johnny enough to do anything it took. Anything.

Oklahoma Territorial Marshal Heck Thomas leaned on his desk and looked at the new reward posters that had just been brought into his Guthrie office.

Ritter, a deputy with a long, sweeping mustache, stuck his head in the door. ''What's new, Heck?''

Heck's steel gray eyes narrowed. ''The railroad's raised the reward again. Five thousand dollars apiece now.''

Ritter whistled long and loud. "Isn't that the most that's ever been offered for outlaws?"

Heck nodded as he took the new poster over to the bulletin board and nailed it up, using the butt of his revolver. "It sure is; but considering the havoc they've been playing with the trains, you can see why."

He stepped back and studied the grainy photos. "Don't know what went wrong with Grat, Bob and Emmett; I knew them and their big brother well. Frank was killed in the line of duty, tryin' to arrest some lawbreakers. He must be rolling over in his grave there in Coffeyville at his little brothers turning outlaw."

The deputy looked at the poster. "Wasn't they once ridin' on the side of the law?"

Heck nodded. "That's what makes them so dangerous; Grat, Bob and Emmett know every trick in the book about how we work. It's been keepin' them one step ahead of us."

"Who else is riding with them?"

"Hard to tell." Heck sighed, and turned to look out the dirty window into the busy streets of the territorial capitol. "Maybe Doolin and some of the other hard cases. I hear tell they've added a new gunfighter."

The deputy spat into the spittoon. "Maybe they ain't our worry no more; maybe by now, the brothers have vamoosed to Texas or farther west."

Heck took out his Colt and checked it to make sure it was fully loaded. "I don't think so. That's a big family, most of them farming up near Kingfisher. I figure the boys go home to visit now and then. Besides, Oklahoma and Indian Territories are the last lawless places an outlaw can hit four trains in one summer like they've done and still manage to avoid bein' captured."

"What do you think they'll do now?" The deputy reached up to the gun rack for a Winchester rifle.

Heck thought a minute. "If I were them, I'd be tryin' to

make one last big haul and quit. It's gettin' too hot for them with settlers comin' in.''

''Civilization's comin','' the other man agreed. ''There's not gonna be room for outlaws; just ranchers and settlers.''

''I'm ready for it,'' Heck said. ''Let's get a posse together.''

''We're ridin'?''

Heck reached for a Winchester as he nodded. ''We'll go up to their old stompin' grounds near the Kansas border, see if anybody's seen them or if we can pick up their tracks.''

The deputy paled. ''They say Bob is a crack shot.''

Heck paused. ''One of the best. But then, nobody ever said bein' a lawman was gonna be easy.''

The deputy started for the door. ''I'll round up the boys and get us some rations.''

Heck went over to his desk to pick up his saddlebags. ''Tell them we'll be on the trail until we get them this time. We just can't allow Grat and his brothers to ride roughshod over northeastern Indian Territory.''

The other man nodded and went out. Heck reached down and ran his sleeve over his badge to shine it a little. He was getting old and tired; but then, so were the other two lawmen who'd help him tame the Territory. The Three Guardsmen, the public called them, after the heroes in that *Three Musketeers* novel.

Hell, the marshals weren't heroes. They were just doing their jobs, attempting to bring law and order to this wild, lawless country. To do that, they had to kill or capture men who were as dangerous as wolves. He took one last look at the reward poster with the grainy photos of the three brothers. Yes, the size of the reward was a new record, all right; more than had ever been offered for outlaws before, even the James boys and the Youngers. Emmett, Grat and Bob were cousins of the Youngers.

Because Heck knew the brothers, he didn't want to kill them. But he didn't think they'd come peacefully. He was a lawman;

he was going to do his job. He grabbed his saddlebags and his Winchester and started for the door. He turned once to look back at the big poster: WANTED: $5000 REWARD. THE DALTON GANG. ARMED AND DANGEROUS.

They were that, all right. Heck sighed and strode out the door to join the posse that was even now gathering on the Guthrie street.

Johnny stared into the campfire and listened to the brothers talk.

Grat grumbled and took another drink. "We could knock over another train; it's easy to catch them away from a station. Out on a lonely stretch of track, they're sitting ducks."

"But," Emmett said timidly, "the railroad's gone to expecting that, and sooner or later we're gonna run across a boxcar load of lawmen with good horses and we'll be ambushed."

Bob looked over at Johnny. "You're awful quiet, Logan. What do you think?"

Dick sneered. "He ain't thinkin' about anything except that gal of his."

"Leave Angel out of this," Johnny snapped.

"Well, Logan," Bob persisted, "what do you think?"

Johnny hesitated, lighting a cigarillo to stall for time. He knew what was going to happen in a few days; he'd lived through it all before. He knew he could do nothing to change history, yet he must try. "Why don't we leave this country? There's lawmen behind every bush. Doolin heard in South Coffeyville that Heck Thomas may be on our trail."

Doolin nodded. "That's right, Bob, and I'd rather have a rattlesnake in my blankets than be trailed by any of the Three Guardsmen."

"Aw," Emmett said with a dismissive gesture, "those lawmen ain't much."

"Now, Emmett," Dick said, "you and your brothers know him; ain't he one of the toughest?"

Nobody said anything, because they all knew it was true. The trio of lawmen known as the Three Guardsmen were bringing law and order across the whole of this lawless territory.

Johnny could not change the history he knew lay before him, but he must try. "Why don't we just lay low for awhile, or go off to Mexico?"

Bill smiled. "Now that do sound good, don't it? Cool drinks and hot señoritas."

Bob snorted. "All that takes money, and where do they keep money?"

"Banks?" Grat said.

"Right!" Bob leaned back against his saddle and stared into the campfire, looking pleased with himself.

"Wait a minute," Doolin protested. "Banks are in towns, and towns are full of people."

"So what?" Bob said.

Johnny didn't say anything. He knew he could not change the events that were being set in motion.

"Bob," Dick said, "I ain't hankering to ride into no town and run up against a bunch of angry citizens. Half the men in these towns are Civil War veterans and can handle a gun."

"Well, but if they ain't expectin' us. We might can ride in, hit a bank and be gone before the townfolk know what's goin' on."

The others looked dubious. They all turned to look at Johnny as if to get his opinion. Johnny shrugged.

"Now what are you lookin' at him for?" Bob snarled, anger in his blue eyes. "I'm the leader of this gang, and I say we do it."

Emmett, the youngest brother, hesitated. "I don't know, Bob. It's pretty daring."

"Everything we've done is daring." Bob took out his bandanna and rubbed the toes of his shiny new boots. "We've got to pull one last big job and then we'll have money to go off to South America, where we can live like kings.''

Doolin played with a twig. ''What are our other choices?''

Bob cursed under his breath. ''You know, Doolin, you're beginnin' to get on my nerves. I'm not sure I want you in on this.''

''And I'm not sure I want any part of it,'' Doolin threw back. ''There's reward posters out everywhere; you'll be recognized the minute we ride into a town. Besides, I hear Fred Dodge may be on our trail, too.''

Again there was silence. Fred Dodge was relentless about bringing in wanted men for the company he worked for, Wells Fargo.

''Well, then, you yellow belly,'' Bob sneered, ''you can just sit right here by this campfire until old Heck Thomas rides up and slaps the cuffs on you.''

Emmett cleared his throat. ''We could maybe put this robbery off for awhile.''

Bob shook his head. ''If anything, we got to speed it up, before Heck and his posse search us out.''

The others looked at Johnny again. ''What do you think?''

''Damn it,'' Bob said, ''he ain't the leader. Don't ask him.''

''I think it's inevitable.'' Johnny sighed and smoked.

Grat and Emmett blinked and looked at each other. ''What does that mean?''

''It means,'' Johnny said, ''what's going to happen is bound to happen and nobody can change it.''

They all looked at each other, their faces puzzled, as if no one was quite sure what he meant.

Bob shrugged. ''Anyway, here's my plan.'' He reached for a stick and began drawing in the dirt. ''We all know a sleepy little town with two fat banks, just waitin' for us to come take their money.''

Grat's eyes widened. ''You don't mean—''

''Sure I do.'' Bob chuckled. ''That will be the last place

they'd expect us to hit, and it ain't in Indian Territory, neither, so they won't be expecting us to cross the river into Kansas.''

"But," Emmett hesitated, "brother, we used to live there. They'll recognize us."

Bob laughed. "We'll wear disguises and take them by surprise. They only got one old marshal, and he's no threat."

Everyone looked at each other.

"Think about it," Bob wheedled. "Two fat banks. Enough money for us to live like gentlemen in South America. The other choice is to keep pulling nickle-and-dime holdups until someone like Heck Thomas tracks us down and throws us in the pen or hangs us."

There was a reluctant murmur of agreement.

Johnny closed his eyes and winced. He had lived through this once and must live through it again every hundred years; it was part of the bargain.

Bob Dalton looked around the circle. "Well, since nobody's objectin', I reckon it's settled. We'll make our plans, and in the middle of the week, when there's not much goin' on, we'll ride in and rob both banks at the same time."

"Excuse me for bein' a stupid galoot," Dick grumbled, "but I don't know what town you're talkin' about."

Bob grinned. "Coffeyville!"

Chapter Eighteen

"Coffeyville!" the gang all shouted in unison.

Grat shook his head, his face grumpy. "What a fool idea!"

Emmett, always the adoring brother, said, "Now maybe Bob's got a good reason for—"

"Crazy galoot!" Grat spat into the fire in disgust and glared at Bob. "What a damn fool idea!"

The others looked at each other, then at Johnny, but he said nothing, staring into the fire and smoking.

Dick cleared his throat. "Bob, I ain't one to question your leadership, but it do seem a mite foolish—"

"Damn it! It's a great plan and here's why." Bob reached for a stick and began drawing in the dirt. "They're expectin' us to keep hittin' trains 'cause that's usually what we do, but most of the money is in banks. Coffeyville is a rich little town, less than a couple a miles across the state line, and they got two banks. Since we used to live there, they won't expect us to come to Coffeyville."

Grat scratched his head. "Can't decide if it's a smart plan or the stupidest thing I ever heard tell of."

"If Bob thinks it's a good idea," Emmett said, "I'll back him."

"Oh, hell!" Bill snorted. "You'd back your big brother, no matter what he thought."

"If y'all shut up, I'll tell you some more," Bob said.

They all leaned in closer, listening attentively, except Johnny. Bob drew in the dirt with his stick. "Here's the layout of downtown. The banks are across the street from each other. There's hitchin' posts right outside both. Since they won't be expecting us, we can rob them both in a couple of minutes, swing up on our horses and skedaddle before anyone can raise the alarm. By the time that old sheriff hears about it, we'll be gallopin' out of town. We'll get back across the line into Indian Territory before they can figure out what happened."

"That sounds okay." Dick grinned. "Once we're back in Indian Territory, it's lawless enough, we can lose ourselves."

"Who are we kidding?" Grat snorted. "We heard Heck Thomas is lookin' for us, among others, and he's stubborn as a bulldog. He'll stay on our trail until he's got us all in a hangman's noose."

"That's the reason we got to take this one last big chance," Bob argued. "Because of lawmen like Heck and all those bounty hunters who're greedy for those big rewards." He paused and grinned with pride. "We outdone Jesse James and the Youngers. Nobody ever offered that kind of money for their hides."

"So why do *we* have to take this big chance?" Grat took another swig out of his whiskey bottle.

"Because, big brother," Bob said, "once we make that double bank haul, we can head for Mexico or South America."

Emmett nodded, always eager to agree. "See, Grat? You know Bob's always thinkin' ahead."

"Thinkin'?" Red-haired Doolin spat to one side. "What

about the fact that the folks in Coffeyville know the Daltons on sight?"

Bob shrugged. "We'll disguise ourselves; put on fake mustaches and beards."

The others looked at Johnny. "What do you think?"

He still had enough of a conscience that he had to warn them, even if he knew it would do no good. Johnny looked at the tip of his burning cigar and spoke slowly. "I think Bob's plan will get you all shot to pieces on the street."

Bob snorted. "You're just mad that you didn't think of it first, Mr. Big-Time Gunfighter. I'm sick of you, Logan, and I don't trust you. After we pull this job, I hope I've seen the last of you."

"You will have." Johnny nodded.

Doolin stared at Bob's drawing in the dirt. "Hell, I don't know, Bob, I ain't so sure I want any part of this—"

"You a coward?" Bob asked.

"Watch who you're callin' a coward." Doolin's voice held a sharp edge.

"Now, fellas," young Emmett said, "let's not fight among ourselves. Anybody wants to fight, he can wait for Heck Thomas to catch up to our trail."

"I don't think I want in," Doolin said. "What about you, Johnny?"

"I'm bound to go along; I got no choice," Johnny said truthfully.

Dick thought for a moment and scratched his scraggly mustache. "So when we gonna do this, on a Saturday?"

"Hell, no," Bob said. "There'll be too many folks in town on a Saturday. Middle of the week would be better. What about Wednesday?"

"Day after tomorrow?" Bill asked. "That don't give us much time."

"It's enough," Bob said.

"But don't we want to ride in, have a look-see?" Dick looked dubious. "Just to check things out?"

"No need," Bob said. "Me and my brothers been in that town a hundred times. We know it like the backs of our hands."

"But you ain't been there lately," Doolin argued.

"Well, no," Bob's tone was irritable, "but just how much could a sleepy little town change, and what difference would it make anyhow?"

Nobody challenged that.

"Okay," Bob said, "we're agreed, then."

Johnny sighed and tossed his cigarillo in the fire. He would be returning to the twentieth century at sundown, Wednesday, October 5, for another hundred years, and most of this bunch was headed straight to six feet of dirt and a trip to hell. He shuddered at the thought of dying. Well, it wasn't going to happen to him; he had a contract to live. The only other thing he had any feelings about was Angel. He wanted to take her with him; he couldn't imagine life without her now. And after all, he told himself, it was his fault she had followed him through the mirror and gotten stuck in this time period. Maybe Nick Diablo would grant Johnny a special favor.

". . . you aren't hearin' a thing I say," Bob snapped.

"What?" Johnny started out of his thoughts.

"I said I'll want you to go in a little earlier, Johnny, maybe hang around that saloon, play cards, listen for any gossip about posses lookin' for us."

Johnny nodded and pretended he didn't see the look that passed between Bob and Grat. They didn't trust him, he knew; but then, the brothers were mistrustful of Doolin, too. Once the robbery was over, they probably intended to double-cross him. There was no honor among thieves.

"You know," Doolin said, "I been thinkin' it over, and I don't think I want any part of this; what about you, Bitter Creek?"

Bitter Creek had not said a word during the long discussion.

He sat chewing on a twig. "We've been runnin' mates a long time, Doolin. If you think it's a bad idea, I'll go along with you."

Bob spat in the dirt. "Are you two loco? There's a lot of money in those two banks!"

Doolin and Bitter Creek got up and began to collect their stuff.

Doolin said, "There may be, Bob, but the fact that they know you in that town makes me skittish as a colt. Count me out."

The others watched as Doolin and Bitter Creek grabbed their gear and began to saddle up.

Grat took a big drink out of his bottle and wiped his mouth with the back of his hand. "That's okay. With fewer of us, there'll be more money for each."

"And less guns to back us up," Johnny reminded the gang.

"Aw," Bob gestured, "this is gonna be like takin' candy from a baby."

"I wouldn't count on that, Bob." Doolin finished saddling and swung up. "We'll head off deeper into Indian Territory and maybe rejoin you later. No hard feelin's?"

Bob shook his head. "No hard feelings."

Emmett said, "You two will regret not comin' along; Bob has always done a good job of leadin' us."

The two didn't answer the younger brother. Doolin leaned on his saddle horn and looked at Johnny. "You comin' with us?"

Johnny shook his head. "I—I can't; I'm bound to be part of this raid."

"All right, then; good luck to you all." Doolin and his quiet friend turned their horses and rode out south toward Indian Territory.

For a long moment, no one said anything as the hoofbeats faded away. There was no sound save a hoot owl somewhere and the crackle of the fire in the darkness.

"Injuns say hoot owls are a sign of death," Dick said.

"Oh, hell!" Bob snapped. "You believe what a bunch of crazy redskins say?"

Bill looked up toward the distant tree for a long moment, then off to the south. The firelight threw distorted shadows across his worried face. "You think Doolin and Bitter Creek got the right idea?" He was looking at Johnny.

Bob kicked dirt at him in disgust. "Now, why are you askin' him for? I'm the leader of this gang."

Johnny didn't say anything. He sat staring into the fire for a few minutes. Then he got up and began to saddle his horse.

"Where you goin'?" Dick asked.

"Well, Bob just said he wanted me to go into the Lady Luck," Johnny said laconically and kept saddling.

Bob glared at him. "I didn't mean tonight."

"I better scope things more than once," Johnny said.

"Scope things out?" Grat scratched his head. "What kinda talk is that?"

He'd have to be careful about using slang from the twentieth century. "I meant, I might have an early look-see and maybe do a little gambling."

Bob leaned over and wiped the dust off his shiny boot. "You wouldn't be thinkin' about goin' with Doolin and Bitter Creek?"

"No, I'm in this; I've got to finish it."

Grat frowned and took another drink. "You ain't never really been one of us, Logan. I hope you ain't thinkin' about that five-thousand-dollar apiece reward."

Johnny looked at him patiently, as if explaining to a child. "Grat, you think they'd give a big reward to another outlaw? I just want to have a few drinks, and I have a yen for a woman."

A couple of the others snickered. "We can shore understand that."

Bill said. "With all that money, I want to buy two or three hot señoritas."

"All you're gonna buy," Johnny said coolly as he mounted up, "is a cold grave."

"Stop that kind of talk!" Grat was more irritable than usual as he guzzled whiskey. "It's bad luck."

Johnny started to ride out, but Bob caught his bridle. "It's that little blonde, ain't it?"

"Let go of my bridle, Bob, or I'll shoot your arm off." Johnny kept his tone soft but firm.

Bob hesitated, then turned loose the bridle. "Just be careful you don't give us away to nobody."

Dick laughed. "All old Johnny's thinkin' about is climbin' on that Angel girl; nothin' else."

"Don't let her name cross your dirty lips," Johnny said. "She's respectable."

"Then what in the hell is she doin' hangin' out with the likes of you?" Bob sneered.

Johnny hesitated. "I don't know; I'm just lucky to have met her, I guess."

Grat said, "When'll you be back?"

Johnny shrugged. "I'm going in to tell her good-bye. I can't just leave without her ever knowing what happened to me."

"Be careful you don't tell her too much," Grat warned.

"Don't worry. I don't want to make her an accessory; she'd try to stop us."

"The devil himself couldn't stop us!" Bob crowed.

"The devil won't try," Johnny said with certainty and rode out of the camp.

Angie paced the floor of her hotel room, trying to make sense of everything and attempting to decide what to do. It was late and very dark when she sneaked out of the hotel, saddled Rosebud and rode down to South Coffeyville to the Lady Luck Saloon.

This late, the place was wild and loud, music and laughter

drifting through the open windows. It was warm, even though it was now the third day of October. The hitching rail was full. Angie rode around back and tied Rosebud up, patted her absently, returned around to the front and entered.

A rinkey-tink piano banged away on "Ta-ra-ra-boom-de-ay" while dancing girls kicked their heels, turned to flip up their skirts and show the back of their bloomers to cheering, rowdy cowboys and gamblers. The place reeked of smoke, beer and cheap perfume. It was surely no place for a respectable woman, but Angie was desperate. Taking a deep breath, she threaded her way through the crowd toward the back office.

Her heart was pounding in her ears as she stopped in front of the door and knocked.

"Damn it, go away and come back later! I'm busy now!"

Angie hesitated. If she told him who she was, he might not see her at all. Instead, she opened the office door. Nick Diablo sat in his big leather chair, a half-naked girl on his lap, her lip rouge all over his face, his shirt half-buttoned. He had both her breasts in his hands and her dark hair was down. She looked very young and more than a little drunk.

The gambler came to his feet, cursing, the girl sliding onto the floor. "What the hell do you want?"

Angie tried not to look at the girl, who was swaying to her feet, pulling her clothes up to cover herself. "Mr. Diablo, can we talk?"

"I don't want to talk to you." Diablo gestured irritably and began buttoning his silk shirt as the girl scurried out a side door. "Can't you see you're interrupting?"

"She's too young," Angie protested.

"Mind your own business, you Goody Two-shoes. Young ones are the best."

"You're a sorry excuse for a man!" Angie confronted him.

He grinned. "I've got the worst traits of all men; it's my job. Like a drink, my dear?"

"No, I want some information and I want it now!" Angie

leaned with both her hands on his desk and glared back at him, but her heart was thudding with a sense of foreboding and evil.

He poured himself a drink and flopped back down in his chair, the diamond pinkie ring twinkling in the light. "I told you before, I'm not a God-damned library!"

From somewhere, there was an ominous rumble of thunder, although Angie thought the sky had been clear when she entered the saloon. "You shouldn't swear," she said primly.

"Shut up! I ought to throw you across my desk and—" He said something unprintable.

Angie winced. "You try it, and you've got a fight on your hands."

Nick Diablo gave her a charming, easy smile. "That's what I like about you, honey. You're spunky; a real challenge for me."

She didn't want to talk about anything but Johnny and his problems. "You're going to think I'm loco, but I don't belong in the Gay Nineties. I stepped through a mirror in your photography shop and back into this time."

Whatever she had expected, she hadn't expected him to sit there calmly regarding her over his drink. "I know," he said.

"You know?" She was taken aback.

"You weren't meant to do that. It was set up for Logan."

"Logan? John Logan of Logan Enterprises?"

"Certainly!" Nick laughed. "That's what you get for sticking your nose in things that don't concern you."

She was both bewildered and angry. "There's so much I don't understand."

"What does it matter? You don't know how to return, so you can't tell the world Johnny Logan's secret."

Abruptly she faced what deep in her heart she had known all along. "Just as I thought! Johnny Logan, the gunfighter, is in reality John Logan the Sixth!"

Nick grinned. "And also the second, third, fourth and fifth.

You see, I've given Johnny eternal life and all the good stuff that everyone wants.''

Eternal life. So this was the terrible secret Logan was hiding. She had to swallow twice to ask, ''And—and what did he give you?''

His eyebrows arched upward and he grinned. ''I think you know, honey, so why do you ask?''

Chapter Nineteen

Angie started and automatically crossed herself.

"Damn it!" he said. "Don't make obscene gestures like that around me!"

Somewhere outside, the thunder rolled even more ominously.

Angie began to back away slowly, shaking her head. "No. Johnny wouldn't do that; he's not that evil."

"Tsk! Tsk!" the gambler clucked in disapproval. "Such an old-fashioned word. There is no such thing as evil, honey, just small, narrow minds who think in old-fashioned terms of black and white instead of gray."

She had never felt such horror and disgust as she backed toward the door. "He—he signed a contract with you?"

Nick nodded. "Good for one hundred years, with an option to renew. He re-signs on October fifth."

She saw it all then. "And when he re-signs, what happens?"

"He gets whisked back to 1999."

"But the mirror's broken," Angie protested.

Nick shrugged. "He doesn't really need the mirror like you do; he goes back automatically the moment he signs."

"And I'm left behind." The hard truth dawned on her.

"Not necessarily." He rubbed his hands together. "Honey, have I got a deal for you! You sign the same contract, you get all the good stuff, too, and after all, isn't that what people hunger for and spend every minute chasing—the good life?"

"But at what cost?" Angie asked.

He made a gesture of dismissal. "Nobody ever asks that, and they don't really care. Play now, pay later—like credit cards, you know."

Angie was shaking as she reached for the doorknob. "No. I'd never go for that."

"Too bad!" He grinned like a used-car salesman. "You're going to be left back here alone."

"Suppose Johnny doesn't re-sign?" she challenged.

"Then he dies; simple as that."

"But how—?"

"Look, honey"—he stood up, his hard eyes irritable—"if you don't want to deal with me, there's plenty who do. I've got two young innocents waiting in my bedroom right now, eager to please me; one wants to be the next Lillian Russell, the other wants me to marry her to a millionaire robber baron. I can do that for them."

"You are heartless, bad and sinful!" Angie screamed at him.

"Sinful? Such an old-fashioned, out-of-date word," he snickered, "and you are a naive, stupid girl!" Then his mood changed abruptly. "Now get the hell out of my office!" His face was as dark as his heart.

Angie turned and ran blindly out of his office, slamming the door behind her.

Nick grinned and watched her go. She was going to be a real challenge, all right. It wasn't likely she'd sign a contract, so she'd be stuck back here in time without Johnny to protect her. Once Nick got that damned gunfighter back to the twentieth century and out of the way, Nick intended to grab the little innocent and use her for his pleasure for a while before he put her to work as a whore in one of his saloons.

He laughed at the thought as he got up and went to pour himself a whiskey. Johnny wouldn't be able to help her; once he was gone, he couldn't return to 1892 until it was contract renewal time again. On the other hand, Nick could and did travel to any era and place he wanted. Yes, he'd enjoy that Angie girl as much as he liked, and Johnny would never know.

The thought of what he intended to do to Angie made him want a woman. Nick sipped his fine liquor and gave some thought to the pair of young innocents upstairs. He'd have one and then the other, thrown across his desk, and they'd submit to any perversion. Stupid females. They'd trade their virginity, the most precious thing they owned, for gold and fame and the other things Nick could offer. Maybe he'd have the young brunette first. With a smile, Nick reached for the bell cord.

Johnny rode into the outskirts of Coffeyville. It was a sleepy little town at night, peaceful and law-abiding. He realized he didn't even know where Angie was staying.

Give it up, Johnny, he said to himself. *She doesn't want to see you again, and you're leaving in a couple more days anyway.* Yet he couldn't bear to leave her behind. Maybe he should ride across the river to South Coffeyville and see if Nick Diablo could be persuaded to send her back in time with him.

The Lady Luck was making money tonight, catering to human weakness, Johnny thought as he approached. From a long way, he could hear drunken laughter and music drifting out the open windows as he reined in. There were many horses tied to the hitching rail out front. He dismounted and tied Crazy Quilt, patted his nose and turned toward the noisy saloon. As he started through the swinging doors, two drunks pushed past him and got into a loud argument that became a fistfight.

Nobody tried to break it up. Instead, the crowd of sluts and ne'er-do-wells began to make bets on the outcome.

Disgusted, Johnny pushed on through the doors. The place was crowded and loud, and cigar smoke swirled like fog. Music and roulette wheels added to the confusion. He elbowed his way to the bar. "Joe, is the boss in?"

The bald, mustachioed bartender paused in filling beer mugs. "I saw a blonde headin' into his office. You'd better wait until she comes out. You know how he hates to be disturbed when he's got some pretty innocent in there."

"Okay." It occurred to him that if he really were the gallant knight Angie thought he was, Johnny would go back there and save the stupid girl from becoming Nick's latest toy. Why had that thought even crossed his mind?

Johnny pushed his Stetson back in disgust. He'd never looked out for anyone but himself until Angel came along. If the gambler seduced some innocent, it wasn't Johnny's business.

"Hey, Johnny!" Sadie pushed out of the crowd and came over to the bar. She wore green satin and too much lip rouge. "You here to see me?"

"In your dreams, honey."

"What?" Her painted eyes grew puzzled.

"Never mind. It's just a saying. I'm waiting to see your boss." He pulled out his gold watch and checked the time.

She grabbed his hand, pulling him toward a poker table. "In that case, why don't you play a hand or two? Maybe I'll bring you luck and you'll stay."

"I don't think—"

But she was already pulling him to a table.

"Oh, what the hell?" He might as well sit down while he waited to see Nick. Johnny took a seat and Sadie perched on the arm of his chair, rubbing her big breasts against him. He could feel her nipples through the tight green satin.

The dealer had bags under his eyes and a crooked cigar in his mouth. "You in?"

"One hand," Johnny said, looking toward the office door.

Sadie put her arm around his shoulder and her lips against his ear, kissing up and down the side of his face. "You win, you can have me for a prize."

His mind went to Angie. "Sorry, Sadie, no can do."

The small band struck up a song:

After the ball is over,
After the break of morn . . .

Sadie began to sing along, but her voice was off-key. *"After the dancers leaving, after the stars are gone; many a heart is broken . . ."*

Johnny winced at the memories. "Sadie, see if you can get the band to play something else."

She was pouty. "But it's a big hit. Anyway, I thought you liked that song."

"Reminds me of someone I'd rather forget." As if he could.

He heard a commotion and looked up. A blonde was threading her way through the crowded tables from Nick's office door. Johnny could barely see her in the swirling cigar smoke. She was moving blindly, as if she was crying, and as she passed a table, a drunken cowboy reached out and grabbed her arm.

Angie had run out of Nick's office in horror. She had to get out of this terrible place! Maybe the whole thing was a nightmare; certainly it couldn't be real. The saloon was crowded with tables and the smoke was thick. She was trying not to cry, but the tears were blinding her as she hurriedly threaded her way through the tables, running for the door.

Halfway there, a drunken cowboy reached out and caught her hand. "Hey, honey, you're new here, ain't you?"

"Let go of me!" She tried to pull out of his grasp, but he

laughed and pulled her down on his lap while the crowd around him turned to look and laugh at the sport.

"Let go of me!" She tried to scratch him, but he grabbed her other hand and held her, pulling her even closer. "How about a kiss, sugar, and then we'll go upstairs and see if you're as good as you look!"

She struggled while the crowd watched and laughed, but no one made any move to help her.

"Let go of her, cowboy!" a male voice commanded over the laughter.

She looked up. Johnny was seated only a few tables away, a painted redhead hanging on his shoulder as she perched on the arm of his chair. Even from here, Angie could see the lip rouge smeared down his face.

Both she and the cowboy stared at him as the band stopped playing and the crowd grew quiet. The cowboy still held her wrists.

Johnny stood up suddenly, his movement overturning his chair and dumping the saucy redhead to the floor. "Maybe you didn't hear me, cowboy. I said let go of her!"

"Now, stranger, you got no right to mix in this. I'm takin' this slut upstairs and give her a good—"

"No, you aren't." Johnny moved so that his feet were slightly apart, his hand hovering just above his gun. "Now you let go of her and let her up. Apologize to the lady and I'll forget—"

"Lady? This slut ain't no lady!" the cowboy said.

"You're wrong, cowboy. She's *my* lady. Now let go of her or I'll kill you."

He meant it. She could see the deadly anger in his dark eyes and she had seen him handle a gun.

Evidently so had a lot of others, because someone whispered, "Jed, let her go, for God's sake! That's Johnny Logan, the gunfighter!"

The cowboy's ruddy face turned white as a fish belly. "J-J-Johnny Logan?" He let go of Angie and she scrambled off the cowboy's lap. He stumbled to his feet, taking his hat off apologetically. "Gosh, I'm sorry, Mr. Logan. I didn't know she belonged to you!"

"I don't!" Angie snapped and pushed past them both, threading her way through the crowd toward the door. She had seen that redhead draped all over him, and Angie was so angry and so hurt, all she could do was think about getting away.

"Angel, wait up!" She heard him coming after her, but she ignored him and pushed blindly through the swinging doors and out into the fresh night air.

Her horse. Jiminy Christmas, she had left Rosebud tied around back so no townspeople would notice that the new schoolmarm was inside. Even as she started down the steps, Johnny strode up behind her and grabbed her arm. "I said, wait up!"

"Let go of me!" she raged, and tried to pull away.

"Baby, listen, give me a chance to explain!"

"I've talked to Diablo and I saw you with that slut!"

"Then you know about the contracts? We could be together forever, Angel, go back to Oklahoma City or any place you'd like, live forever, have anything your heart desires. Between me and Nick, we'll lay the world at your feet."

"Let go of me, I said! It's too high a price to pay; have you no conscience?" She was struggling to get away from him, her anger blinding her. She wanted to hurt him in the worst, deepest way. "Let go of me, you evil, sinful bastard!" And she slapped him hard.

His head snapped back, the sound ringing loud. Even in the darkness, she could see the marks her fingers left on his high-boned face. His eyes were as hard as granite. "If you were a man, I'd kill you for that!"

She crossed herself without thinking and backed away from him. "I pity you, John Logan. I hope you go back to the twentieth century and I never see you again!"

Angie turned and ran down the steps, then hurried around

back to mount her horse. She didn't know whether she hoped or feared he would come after her, but he didn't. When she rode out, he was standing all alone on the porch of the Lady Luck, staring into the darkness.

Johnny watched her ride out, still feeling the sting of her hand and the humiliation of her words. She was right; he was all the things she had said. His gut churned as he turned and strode back into the saloon. People, seeing the look on his face, made way for him as he strode toward the back office.

Johnny banged on the door with his fist.

"Go away! I'm entertaining company!"

A woman giggled.

Johnny was in no mood for subtlety. He drew back his boot and kicked the door open, then burst into the room.

Diablo stood up, dumping a naked brunette on the floor. "What in hell's the matter with you?"

Johnny ignored the cowering girl.

"Angel was here." It was a statement, not a question.

"Yes."

"You better not have touched her—"

"Do you realize who you're threatening?" the gambler shouted. "Anyway, she wouldn't let me."

Somehow in his heart, he had known that. Angel was his woman; only his. "How much does she know?"

"Almost everything. So what?"

Johnny swallowed hard and closed his eyes. So now she knew just how rotten Johnny really was. He'd never cared what anyone thought of him before, but her opinion mattered.

"She knows I'm leaving?"

"Yeah. But I didn't tell her how." Diablo turned to the girl on the floor. "Get outa here, slut. I'll do you later upstairs!"

She grabbed her clothes and fled, giving Johnny an inviting smile as she left.

Johnny frowned at her.

"I don't know what it is about you," Nick grumbled. "All the women want you."

And he only wanted one woman. It was both an exhilarating and a miserable feeling.

Nick seemed to take a good look at Johnny for the first time and whistled long and low. "The blonde do that to you?"

Johnny reached up and touched his face, knowing she must have left the red marks of her fingers there. "So what if she did?"

"I think you've met your match, Johnny. She's got a lot of fire to her." Lust and maybe a little admiration shone in his hard black eyes.

"She'd be more than a match for almost any man. What sons she could give a man. . . ." He didn't finish the sentence, remembering. A man who was immortal didn't want to fall in love, watch the woman he loved age and die, father children he would live to bury as they died of old age. "I want to take her with me, Nick. Can you do that?"

Nick shrugged and sat down on the edge of his desk. "I offered, but she didn't go for it."

"I knew she wouldn't," Johnny said, and he was suddenly proud of her. "She's good, Nick; good and honest, too."

The gambler made a dismissive gesture. "You're gettin' soft, Johnny. She's doin' that to you."

"Yeah, she is."

Nick looked at his fingernails, his diamond ring sparkling. "Forget about her, Johnny. In a couple more days, you'll be back in Logan Towers with wealth, power, prestige and everything else."

"But I won't have her."

"Spare me the schmaltz," Nick said. "You can buy the prettiest, sexiest women in the world; they'll do anything, and I do mean *anything,* you want to satisfy your lust."

Johnny walked over, leaned against the window and stared

out into the darkness. From the saloon drifted the faint strains of his favorite song. For a moment, he had her in his arms again, waltzing her around his penthouse. . . . *Many a heart is broken, if you could read them all; many the hopes that have vanished after the ball. . . .*

How right that was. Nothing meant much to him without her.

"Look"—Nick came over and put his hand on Johnny's shoulder—"you're tired and upset. You'll see things differently tomorrow. Think about the big Millennium party you can throw in three months; biggest in the world. Turn it into a real orgy; charter the Concorde and take a bunch of movie stars to Paris or London, buy truckloads of the world's best champagne, set off millions of dollars' worth of fireworks. You can buy a dozen beautiful cover models and sleep with two or three at the same time in the same bed. Think of the fun!"

Johnny didn't answer. Without her, nothing sounded like fun. "On the other hand, it's only eight years 'til the new century dawns. I could be on my own ranch, sitting in front of a crackling fire with her—"

"No, you can't," Nick snapped. "Barring a miracle, which, of course, we're all too cynical to believe in, you're scheduled to die, remember? That's why you signed my contract."

Johnny rubbed his hand across his forehead to clear his mind. "I know you're right, but I just keep thinking that if I had a chance to do things differently—"

"Well, you don't. Only religious idiots believe you can clear the slate, make a fresh start. You're tired and not thinking straight, Johnny. Go get some rest."

"Yeah," Johnny nodded and shook Nick's hand off, "you're probably right. It wasn't meant to be; we're worlds apart."

"And more than a hundred years in age," Nick reminded him.

"Yeah, that, too. Well, no, back in this time, I'm only thirty-four."

Nick groaned. "You can already imagine little kiddies around the ranch dinner table and her serving up food while you all sing 'Home on the Range.' Forget it, Johnny. It ain't gonna happen."

"I know." Johnny sighed and started for the door, then paused with his hand on the knob. "The Coffeyville thing— is it still going to happen exactly the way it did before? I can't change any of the details?"

"Exactly the way it happened before. No changes."

Johnny gritted his teeth. "Okay then. I'll see you Wednesday, just before sundown."

The gambler smiled. "I'll bring the contract."

"Fine," Johnny said and turned and strode out of the saloon. Diablo was right. The sooner he forgot about Angel, the better. After all, it was her own fault if she got left back in time.

Chapter Twenty

Tuesday seemed like a long day to Angie, even though she enjoyed the children and the teaching. As she locked up after the final bell, she thought she might enjoy continuing to teach in some distant frontier school. She was going to need something to do if she was left back in time alone.

However, tomorrow would be her final day in this school. The new schoolmarm was expected to take over on Thursday morning. She decided she would use some of the old coins she still had in her purse to buy candy to give out tomorrow.

The weather was balmy for early October, she thought as she walked downtown. If only Johnny was here with her. No, she shook her head, she must not think about what might have been.

Where was he now? She thought about the things he had said, the offer Nick Diablo had made her. Maybe none of that was real; maybe she had only imagined all of it, or maybe it had been a bad dream.

Downtown, Walnut and Union streets connected with each

other in a "Y." The Condon Bank was located where the two streets met. She stopped in front of it. Workmen stacked bricks from a cart near the sidewalk and the dirt street was torn up for several blocks. "What's happening here?"

A short workman raised his head and smiled, touching his cap politely. "Progress, ma'am. We're paving this whole street these next few days before bad weather comes."

Angie looked around for the usual horses tied to hitching posts out front of this and the other bank, the First National across the street. There weren't any horses. "What happened to the hitching posts?"

"Sorry about that, ma'am." The laborer looked up from unloading the bricks. "Hitchin' posts had to come down temporarily so we could lay the street. We'll put 'em back up in a few days."

A young man came out of the Condon bank and stopped to watch. "Be nice, won't it, ma'am, not to have all that mud on a rainy day? You're the temporary schoolteacher, aren't you?"

"Yes, I'm Mrs. Newland."

"Pleased to make your acquaintance, ma'am." He touched the brim of his hat. "I'm Tom Ayers, the cashier here at the Condon. Sorry for the inconvenience, but it'll be worth it when the street's finished."

"I'm sure it will be." Angie nodded. She looked around and saw other horses tied in the alley about half a block west of the bank. As she watched, she saw the town marshal, Charles Connelly, come out of the jail, which fronted the alley, and walk down toward the bank. He must be almost fifty, she thought. A sprinkle of gray peppered his mustache and goatee.

"Evenin', ma'am, and Tom." He touched the brim of his Western hat.

"Hello, marshal," Angie said. "Nice day, isn't it?"

"Certainly is." He watched the laborers for a moment. "How's business, Tom?"

"Couldn't be better! Why, the *Journal* says Coffeyville is

growin', and things are certainly good at the bank. The First National, too, I imagine.'' He nodded toward the building across the street.

''Well, I must be going, gentlemen.''

''Glad to make your acquaintance, ma'am.''

Angie nodded politely and walked away, leaving the marshal and the bank cashier gossiping about local events. Her mind was on her own problems as she paused in front of Isham's Hardware Store. Through the windows, she could see barrels of nails, tools, farm implements and even a showcase full of pistols and rifles for sale. She nodded politely to a lady coming out of the First National Bank next door to Isham's and then walked on down to Read Brothers' Dry Goods.

A handsome young clerk with a nice smile came out of the store. ''Evenin,' ma'am. Were you wantin' to come in and look at some of our ladies' clothes? Got the latest fashions from back East.''

Angie smiled and shook her head. ''Not today. I don't think we've met. I'm the temporary schoolteacher, Mrs. Newland.''

''Glad to make your acquaintance. I'm Lucius Baldwin. If you're not comin' in to shop now, I might close early; I've got choir practice at the church.''

''No, go ahead and close,'' Angie said. ''I wouldn't want to keep you from choir.''

Angie walked on. From the shoe repair shop, old Mr. Brown waved at her, and she waved back.

She bought some candy and put it in her big purse, along with her first-aid kit and her dwindling funds. Then she walked over to visit Rosebud at John Kloehr's livery stable. The stable was on the same alley as the city jail. She had to walk past all the horses, tied to a long pipe in the alley, to get there.

The stable smelled like hay and leather. She enjoyed the scent as she went inside. ''Good evening, Mr. Kloehr.''

''Evenin', ma'am. Street's quite a mess, ain't it, all torn up like it is?''

She nodded. "And all the horses blocking the alley because there's no place else to tie them."

"Long ways to walk to get to the bank and the stores," he agreed, "but they'll have it fixed soon. I was just finishing feeding and gettin' ready to lock up; I want to go out and do a little target practice."

"You a pretty good shot?" She walked over to Rosebud's stall. The mare greeted her with a whinny.

He hesitated. "Well, now, I reckon I'm a pretty fair shot."

Angie patted Rosebud's velvet nose, her mind on Johnny. "I'll bet you're being modest."

He colored and pulled at his mustache. "Some say there's none better than me with a rifle."

Angie chatted with him about the town for a few minutes, then said good-bye to Rosebud and left the mare contentedly munching oats while Angie headed back to the hotel. She had an early supper in the dining room and went to bed, but she could not sleep, wondering what to do next and how this whole drama was going to play out. Most of all, she thought of Johnny. Somehow, he seemed warmer and much more human than he had been as business mogul John Logan VI. Passing time and his bargain would make him heartless and jaded. She had liked him better as the gunfighter. There seemed to be a little good left in Johnny Logan. But he wasn't her concern anymore, and she must stop caring about him. Finally, she drifted off to sleep.

In a few more hours, he was going to be lying on a Coffeyville street, badly wounded and near death, but tonight Johnny followed the same routine he had the night before the robbery, over a hundred years ago. He rode to the Lady Luck and played cards for hours, dreading what was coming tomorrow morning. More than the physical agony he would have to endure a second time was his inner pain at never seeing Angel again.

Nick dropped by his table, ignoring the other players and

the dancers cavorting across the stage. "You used to be a fair poker player, Johnny, but you're losing badly tonight."

"And you know why." Johnny shuffled the deck with a sigh, handing it to the dealer.

"Oh, hell." Nick's eyebrows arched into a devilish grin, but he kept his voice low. "The pain won't last but a few hours, and then you've got a hundred years of debauchery and riches ahead of you before you have to come back again."

"That's not what I'm talking about." Johnny frowned up at him. "I can't seem to forget the girl."

"What is it with you? There's women aplenty waiting for the 'Outlaw of Wall Street,' " Nick reminded him as he fingered his penciled mustache.

"Not like Angel." Johnny shook his head.

"Now why would she want a sinful loser like you?" Nick laughed.

"She said she loved me; nobody ever really loved me before." Johnny picked up his hand halfheartedly, and looked at his cards, but his mind wasn't on the game.

"Love? Hah, it's only a savvy way to sell more candy and flowers," Nick sneered. "Look out for Number One like you've always done." The big diamond on his pinkie flashed in the light.

"Somehow, that doesn't give me much satisfaction anymore." Johnny frowned and tossed in his hand.

"Don't go soft on me, Johnny."

Soft. Soft was Angel's lips, the way she felt in his arms, the way her blue eyes looked up into his. How could he live without her? He feared he could do nothing else. Johnny pulled out his gold watch and checked the time. "It's not long 'til dawn. I'd better be going if I'm going to ride into town with the boys."

Nick grinned. "Right! I'll see you tomorrow; same time and place as last time." He turned and walked away.

Johnny went outside, then paused to look up at the sky. Was there anything out there beyond those stars? Tomorrow night at this time, he would be back in Logan Towers as John Logan VI, with money and power and everything else his heart could desire. Except Angelica Newland. He'd been smugly satisfied with his life until she'd come along and showed him how empty it all was.

You stupid jackass, he reminded himself as he untied Crazy Quilt. You ought to be relieved that she's going to be stuck back in the Gay Nineties. She won't be able to expose you as an eternal outlaw who's made an unholy deal.

He didn't feel relieved; he felt empty. Nothing seemed worthwhile, not even living forever, without Angel by his side. He mounted, then paused to look up at the starry sky. "Hey, God, if You're up there, why don't You do something about this mess? Is Old Nick more powerful than You are?"

He thought he heard the distant rumble of thunder over the music and drunken laughter drifting from the saloon. Johnny paused, feeling a bit foolish for shouting at an empty sky. Nothing. Nothing but the echo of a woman singing in an off-key voice and the whirl of roulette wheels. The sky was clear and full of stars. He must have imagined he heard thunder; it was probably some drunken cowboy shooting off a pistol.

Anyway, if God was out there somewhere, He surely hadn't given any time or thought to a second-rate gunfighter, Johnny thought bitterly as he rode out. Nick was right, there was no justice or mercy; it was every man for himself in this dog-eat-dog world. And surely there was no one more powerful than the Lord of Darkness.

Once Johnny had sensed light and hope because of the trust in a girl's eyes, but there was no hope and no redemption, either, for a rotten hombre like him.

You've got to stop thinking about her; you've got a bank robbery tomorrow, he scolded himself as he nudged Crazy Quilt into a lope and started back to camp. In the east, dawn would soon begin to turn the eastern sky pale gray. In a few short hours, Johnny would re-sign his contract and be back in Logan Towers. He must not think about what might have been.

Before dawn, Heck Thomas and Fred Dodge, the Wells-Fargo man who had joined the posse, drank a quick cup of coffee around the fire. The Indian scout had just come in with a report of fresh tracks. They doused their fire and within minutes they were in the saddle again in northern Indian Territory.

"It's gonna be a nice day," Heck said as they rode out.

"Be a lot nicer if we were headed home," one of his deputies said, "I'd like to sleep in my own bed for a change."

"Just keep following the tracks," Dodge said. "It's almost light; make it a lot easier."

It did make it easier. Just after dawn, they found the empty camp.

"Deserted." Heck sighed. He dismounted and looked around, watching his famed Sac and Fox Indian scout, Talbot White, check every bent twig, every horse dropping, to see how fresh it was.

Dodge grumbled, "Missed them again."

Heck conferred with his scout, who gestured. "Maybe one full day behind them."

Dodge raised his eyebrows. "Could he be wrong?"

"Not likely," Heck said. "He's one of the best trackers in the business. Let's ride over to the Sac Fox Indian agency and see if anything new's come in on the telegraph."

The Indian pointed. "Tracks lead north."

"Where in the hell do you suppose they're headed?" The Wells-Fargo man sighed.

Heck shrugged. "Surely they ain't about to rob a train. They must know we're hot on their trail."

"And we ain't the only ones." Burrel Cox, famed posse man, leaned on his saddle horn. "With five thousand apiece on their heads, everyone's gunnin' for them. Hear Chris Madsen's got a posse, too.''

Chris Madsen was one of the other two of the famed Three Guardsmen.

''Chris is a good man; rode many a mile with him.'' Heck swung up on his horse. ''You'd think the Daltons would be tryin' to clear out of the country with the net closin' in on them the way it is.''

''Maybe they ain't got enough money,'' the deputy suggested as he nudged his horse into a walk. ''They'll have to get some somewhere.''

A worried look crossed Heck's weathered face.

The Wells-Fargo agent glanced at him as the posse urged their horses away from the abandoned camp. ''What's the matter?''

''Nothin'.'' Heck shrugged. ''I was just wondering what they might be desperate enough to do for that getaway cash.''

''Hell,'' the deputy, Cox, spat in the dirt, ''we're only a few miles from the border. Maybe they're headin' into Kansas.''

''Reckon so.'' Heck glanced back at the deserted outlaw lair. ''I'd feel bad if we didn't ride to the nearest telegraph and alert the Kansas authorities that the Daltons are comin' their way.''

''You know, the direction those tracks were headin' ''—the deputy paused to light a cigar—''looked like they might be goin' toward . . .''

''Toward where?''

''Naw, they wouldn't do anything that loco. The Daltons grew up there; they'd be recognized in that town.''

''Who knows what Bob Dalton's liable to do?'' Heck took off his Stetson and scratched his head. ''The trap's closing on them and Bob knows it, so he's desperate.''

A third man asked, ''What's the town?''

Heck answered as he nudged his horse into a lope. ''Coffeyville.''

* * *

Angie began her final schoolday with a heavy heart.

After she had breakfast, she stopped to watch the men beginning to lay bricks on the street in front of the Condon bank, then walked on over to the school. By eight-thirty, the children were beginning their prayers and opening ceremonies. "Now we'll do some arithmetic," she said and began to write on the blackboard. "What's the date, children?"

"Wednesday, October fifth," Millie, the oldest girl volunteered.

"Good." Angie wrote the date on the blackboard and then began to copy arithmetic problems for the children to work. *October fifth,* she thought. *Today is the day. What can I do to help Johnny?* She shrugged off the thought and tried to concentrate on the arithmetic, then glanced up at the big schoolroom clock: 9:00 A.M. The day had barely begun, and already it seemed months long.

Now that Doolin and Bitter Creek were gone, it was only going to be the three Dalton brothers, Dick Broadwell, Bill Powers and Johnny to take part in the action.

The night before, the gang had moved their camp closer to town and suppered on biscuits and hard-boiled eggs. Now in the predawn darkness on Onion Creek, they drank a quick cup of coffee.

Johnny shook his head, dreading what was coming. "Bob, I wish you'd give this up."

Bob dusted the toe of one of his shiny boots. "I hope you didn't tip off the law when you was in town last night."

He decided to overlook the not-so-subtle accusation. "I wasn't really in town, remember? I was at the Lady Luck, like you told me."

Grat was already sipping whiskey and as mean-tempered as a snake. "I don't trust Logan."

"The feeling's mutual," Johnny said.

Dick and Bill looked uneasy. "Maybe Johnny's got a point. With you Daltons from Coffeyville, they may recognize you, sure as shootin'."

Before Bob could answer, Emmett piped up. "If Bob thinks it's a good idea, I'm for it." He patted his own unshaven face. "See? I been growin' a beard so they won't know me."

Bob pulled something out of his saddlebag. "Here's my idea so they won't recognize us."

"What in the hell you got there?" Grat snapped.

"He's got fake mustaches and beards," Johnny said without even looking Bob's way.

"Now how the hell did you know that?" Bob asked.

Because I've lived through this once before, Johnny thought. He should have kept his mouth shut. In a couple of hours, the streets of the town were going to be running red with blood. "I could see what they were when you pulled them out."

Bob shrugged, satisfied. "See?" He held up the disguises. "With these, no one will recognize us when we ride into Coffeyville." He began to put on a fake mustache and goatee, and tossed Grat fake black side-whiskers and a mustache.

Bill eyed the fake hair with skepticism. "Tell me again why we're hittin' the banks so early instead of late in the afternoon, when we could have darkness to cover our tracks."

Bob snorted. "I told you; the banks'll be stocked with money early in the morning and nobody will have had time to make big withdrawals yet. We'll get a good haul."

Johnny kicked dirt over the campfire. "If we don't get a move on before it gets daylight, we won't get there when the banks first open up."

"Right!" Bob said with satisfaction. "Now here's the rest of the plan. We'll tie up right in front of the banks. By the time the employees spread the alarm, we'll be on our horses and gone; outa town before they know we're there. We'll head for the Osage Hills. Later, we'll meet up on the Cherokee Strip. I got a Texas cowboy named Amos Burton who's gonna meet us with a wagon and team.''

"Amos Burton?'' Grat said. "Ain't he black?''

"Even so, he's trustworthy,'' Bob assured him. "We'll hide the money in the wagon, change clothes and start drivin' west. We'll look like a bunch of farmers if anyone should see us.''

Dick nodded. "Don't sound bad. Where do we go from there?''

"Seattle.'' Bob grinned. "From there, we can get a ship outa the country. See what a great plan? The law'll probably expect us to head down through Texas into Mexico.''

"Cole Younger thought it would be easy to get away when he and his brothers and Jesse James robbed the Northfield, Minnesota, bank in '76,'' Johnny reminded Bob. "As I recall, Bob's still sittin' in prison for that crime sixteen years later.''

Bob Dalton frowned. "Well, I always said we was better than either the James boys or our cousins; that won't happen to us. Now let's stop jawin' and get a move on.''

They all checked their weapons to make sure they were loaded. Each was carrying a Winchester on his saddle and plenty of ammunition. Because of the danger of what they were about to undertake, Bob had bought ten new Colt revolvers and passed them out to everyone, but Johnny elected to carry only his own regular pistol. Bob had a Colt in his holster, another in his boot and a .38 Webley British Bulldog pistol in his vest pocket.

Bob looked about the camp as they mounted up. "In a few hours, we'll have plenty of money and be headed for safety.''

Johnny sighed as he nudged his horse and they all rode out. "In a few hours, most of you are headed straight to hell.''

"Hush that talk!'' Emmett said. "If Bob thinks this is a good idea, it'll work.'' He didn't sound too certain, but he would have followed his older brother into hell, Johnny thought.

"Let's just get this over," Grat grumbled and fingered his fake mustache. "I heard a rumor yesterday that Heck Thomas's posse is ridin' hard; lookin' for us."

Bob laughed as he mounted up in the darkness. "Hell! Everybody's lookin' for us! It's that big reward. That's why we got to make this last big hit and skedaddle."

Dick spat to one side. "I just wish we'd had more time to plan it."

Emmett said, "You heard Bob; the fact that posses are closin' in is the reason we ain't got time to waste."

Grat might have been a little drunk. "Coffeyville, here we come!"

Johnny took a deep breath and swung into the saddle. He dreaded the pain and yes, the betrayal he would be facing in a few minutes, but he would have to endure this re-enactment so he could sign Nick's contract later that evening. It was either that or bleed to death out there on the town garbage dump.

They were heavily armed and tough looking, Johnny knew. It was long past dawn as the group rode into the southern outskirts of Coffeyville along Buckeye Street. James Brown's young daughter would remember later that she had seen them as she rode toward town. The six hardly gave her a look as they passed her.

William Gilbert recalled afterward that the dusty, heavily armed group had ridden past his house on the outskirts of town. He remembered that they had passed a bunch of sheep and laughed and baaed at the animals. He didn't give the group another thought.

The group had swung around to approach town, riding east on Eighth Street. They passed Mr. and Mrs. R. H. Hollingsworth in their rig, less than a mile west of town. The couple looked at them curiously, and would say later that the six were heavily armed. The riders kept their eyes on the dusty road ahead. In a few minutes, they passed two men, John and J. L. Seldomridge, riding out of town. Like the Hollingsworths, the Seldomridge men would remember there were six men and six horses and that the men were heavily armed and seemed to be on some kind of mission. Neither group of citizens was concerned enough to turn around and ride back to warn anyone.

After they had passed the two men riders, Bill said, "I wonder what those people were thinking? You suppose they know we're going in to rob the banks? Especially with all the weapons we're carryin'?"

"Naw," Bob said with a shake of his head. "They probably just think we're a posse ridin' in from Indian Territory. After all, that wouldn't be so far-fetched."

They would be in the heart of town soon; less than two blocks away. Johnny took a deep breath as Crazy Quilt moved to the front of the pack. He only had a little time now until it happened.

Bob asked, "What time is it, Johnny?"

The moment was set in history, and he couldn't stop it, no matter how hard he tried. Johnny pulled out his gold watch. "9:20 A.M." He put the watch back in his pocket so it wouldn't be damaged when he fell.

"Bank ought to be open by now," Bob said, riding close behind Johnny. "Logan, I want you to keep a sharp lookout for us while we go in."

"Okay, Bob, anything you say." He felt Bob's presence behind him and didn't turn his head. He couldn't change what was about to happen. The first time he had been both stupid and trusting, not thinking his partners would double-cross him. At least he wasn't going to take part in the killings that were only minutes away from happening.

Funny, he thought, until Angel entered his life, it hadn't mattered to him who or how many people were shot down in this historic incident. Now he would stop the whole thing if he could. Nick was right; Angel was changing him.

It was coming any second now; they were almost to the alley. He braced himself for the pain as he rode along and closed his eyes. In his mind, he saw Angel's innocent blue eyes, and he finally admitted to himself that he loved her. *Too late,* he thought, *her love might have saved you, but you're the devil's own now.*

At that moment he felt, rather than heard, Bob's movement. Then the pain exploded against the back of his head and he grabbed for the saddle horn, but he was already falling toward the dirt street.

Chapter Twenty-one

"God damn!" Dick swore. "What'd you do that for?"

The five drew in and looked at Johnny Logan sprawled unconscious in the dirt of the street, his faithful horse standing near him.

"I don't trust that half-breed." Bob slipped his Winchester back in its saddle scabbard. "So I knocked him out."

Grat pulled his pistol. "Let me finish him, Bob."

Bob swore and reached out to grab Grat's hand, looking around as he did so. "You loco? Anyone hears a pistol go off this close to downtown, everyone'll come to see what's happenin'. We don't want the law alerted."

Bill Powers surveyed the area. "We're lucky there's nobody on the street right now." Then he stared at the unconscious man lying in the dirt beneath their horses' hooves. "What'll people think if anyone comes along?"

Bob shrugged and urged his horse forward. "They'll think a drunk cowboy fell off his horse and maybe call the marshal to throw him in jail. Come on; time's awastin'."

"Aw, you ain't gonna let me kill him?" Grat reholstered his pistol reluctantly.

"Tell you what," Bob said with a grin, "when we come back this way on our way out, you can plug him then."

That seemed to satisfy Grat. He said, "A shame to leave his horse; I'd like to have him."

"Who you kiddin'?" Emmett snickered. "You can't handle that stallion; nobody can but Johnny."

"That's right," Bob snapped. "Now leave the damned horse be and come on."

The other four obeyed and rode at a slow trot down Eighth Street toward downtown.

"Now, I'll go over it once more," Bob said. "We tie up out in front of the banks. It's just a few steps inside. Emmett and I will go into the First National. You other three go in the Condon. We move fast, sack up the money and we'll be on our horses and gone before anyone can spread the alarm."

"Sounds good," Emmett said. "As I recall, Marshal Connelly don't even carry a pistol most of the time."

Bob laughed as they rode. "As you remember from livin' here, nothin' much ever happens in this sleepy burg. But we're about to make it happen!"

Emmett fell in alongside him. "They'll be talkin' about us tomorrow, huh, Bob? Jesse James and our cousins never did nothin' this bold."

Dick spat on the ground. "Maybe because they had better sense. I think I'm sorry I let you talk me into this, Bob."

Emmett rushed to Bob's defense. "Now hush that kind of talk. We're about to make history here."

They rode down to Walnut Street and into the *y* where the two streets, Union and Walnut, converged. The Condon Bank was at that intersection, the First National across the street next to Isham's Hardware Store. They reined in and paused.

"Uh-oh," Grat said, looking around. "What happened to the hitchin' rails?"

"Look." Emmett gestured. "They're pavin' the street; they've taken the hitchin' rails down."

Bob swore under his breath. "Now if that don't beat all."

The others looked at him. "What do we do now, Bob?"

Bob chewed his lip, taking in the scene. It was a warm, busy morning in the main part of town, farmers and tradesmen going about their business. Up on the side of Condon Bank, two men on a ladder were painting a sign. "We ain't beat yet. We'll just tie up wherever we can."

Dick leaned on his saddle horn. "I don't see no place to tie up horses. I got bad feelin's about this; let's forget it."

"Damn it!" Bob snapped. "I didn't come this far not to do it; not with all them posses on our tail."

"Bob'll figure out something," Emmett assured them.

"Oh, shut up!" Grat snarled. "You always take his part."

"That's 'cause I'm usually right," Bob said. He looked around again and gestured. "How about that alley to the west of the Condon?"

They all turned to look.

"Ain't that a little far from the banks?" Bill asked uncertainly.

Grat nodded. "He's right. And as I remember, ain't the jail down that alley?"

"For bein' the oldest," Bob snapped, "Grat, you ain't never got any ideas, you just belly-ache about mine."

"Bob's right," Emmett said, "it ain't so far."

"Unless we run into trouble," Dick argued.

Bob swore. "Well, you got any better ideas? The horses'll be out of sight there. Besides, that marshal ain't nowhere to be seen and he don't carry a gun no ways."

Grat laughed. "All these soft, civilized town people just waiting like fat geese for us to pluck 'em."

"Let's quit jawin' and get to it," Bob ordered.

There was no hitching rail in the alley, where Kloehr's livery stable and the jail were located, but there was a heavy pipe along the front of a vacant lot. They tied up the five horses to that pipe and took their Winchesters from their saddles.

"It seems a mighty long way from here to the banks," Dick said uncertainly.

"Oh, stop belly-achin'!" Bob answered. "Just slip them rifles under your coats and walk along pleasant-like. Nobody's gonna pay us no never mind."

Dick snorted. "Five strangers in a group walkin' toward the banks? You think they won't notice?"

The group started out of the alley, headed toward the banks.

Bob shrugged. "Hush your jawin', Dick. They'll think we're a hunting party or maybe a posse."

Everyone laughed at the irony of that.

They walked into the busy plaza where Walnut and Union streets converged. As Bob had predicted, although there were people on the street, no one paid any attention to them as they headed toward the banks. Bob and Emmett walked into the First National, and the other three went into the Condon Bank.

Down the block, out in front of McKenna and Adamson's Dry Goods store, Aleck McKenna was sweeping the sidewalk. He started in surprise and stared again at the men leaving the alley and walking across the plaza. He thought he recognized some of the Daltons from the old days, when the boys had lived in Coffeyville. He leaned on his broom and peered through the Condon's plateglass windows. From here, he saw hands going up in the air and the sudden gleam of light on the long barrels of rifles. McKenna dropped his broom and ran to spread the word that the Daltons were robbing the bank.

In the next two or three minutes, word spread up and down the street like wildfire. Of all the citizens, only George Cubine had a weapon. He had brought his Winchester to his uncle's boot and shoe store the day before, just to keep it away from his children. The others rushed into Isham's Hardware Store, where a clerk began handing out weapons and ammunition to eager volunteers. Someone ran to alert the sheriff. The painters heard the confusion and scrambled down from their ladders. Men began overturning wagons to give themselves cover.

Inside the banks, the robbers were blissfully ignorant that they'd been recognized.

Bob and Emmett strode into the First National.

"Okay, this is a holdup!" Bob held his rifle on the surprised people inside. "Get your hands up, give us the money and no one will get hurt!"

Stunned clerks and customers started, then began to raise their hands. Bob could see he and Emmett were going to have their hands full. After all, there were only two of them, and there were already three employees and three customers in the bank. Of course, all six were unarmed. So far, so good. Bob turned and glanced back at the plateglass windows. Because the First National fronted on Union Street, he couldn't see anything but the side of the Condon Bank across the street.

A Mr. Boothby came into the bank unexpectedly, saw everyone with their hands in the air and tried to retreat back out the door. Emmett pointed his Winchester at the surprised customer. "Get in here and be quick about it!"

Now they had seven people under their guns.

Bob said, "Emmett, keep an eye on everybody. I'll see if I can find someone to open the safe." He strode to the back office of the bank.

In minutes, he herded Bert Ayers up to the front of the bank. "Open the safe and be quick about it."

"All right, all right; take it easy." Ayers began to carry packets of bills from inside the vault to lay on the counter. As nervous as he was, it seemed to Bob the bank employee was taking an awfully long time to get the money out.

"Come on! Come on!" Bob snapped.

"That's all there is." The employee stepped back.

"Is there any more in the vault?"

Ayers shook his head.

"Damn it, I don't trust you! I'll see for myself!" Bob pushed past him and went into the vault, then came out cursing. "Here's another ten thousand in cash! Thought you'd fool me, did ya? I ought to blow your brains out!"

All the hostages began to sweat as Bob waved his Winchester.

"Bob," Emmett said, "we gotta get outa here!"

Bob tossed Ayers a grain sack. "My brother's right; I ain't got time to kill you. Here, put the money in this so we can clear out!"

Johnny came back to consciousness slowly. His head felt as if someone were using it for a drum and he was facedown in the dirt. He managed to raise his head and groaned aloud at the pain. *Where was he?* He remembered now: Bob Dalton had double-crossed him and hit him from behind. He lay in the middle of the street with Crazy Quilt waiting patiently for him to get up and remount. The street was deserted for the moment. No doubt when the gang thundered back through here on their way out of town, they planned to finish Johnny off—if they got here before some curious citizen spotted Johnny and called the law.

He had to get up. Easier said than done. With his head pounding, he drifted in and out of consciousness, knowing he couldn't get on his horse. He could barely raise his head.

The banks. The Daltons were going to rob the banks. He had to stop them. *Stop them?* The unfamiliar thought gave him pause. Angel Newland had been more of an influence on him than he had realized.

At least he had to get out of the road, where he'd be at their mercy when they came galloping back. As ornery as Grat was, he'd probably try to trample Johnny with his horse. Johnny couldn't reach his watch. He could only guess how long he'd been unconscious; maybe only a few minutes.

He struggled to get to his knees and failed. He must stop massacre that was about to occur. *Are you loco? You're reliving history and you can't change it.* Angel would want him to try. It took all his willpower, but he dug his fingers into the dust and began to crawl toward town. *How far was it, a block? Maybe two?* He'd never get there in time. His head pounded, but he kept crawling, his horse patiently following along. It was a wonder no one had come by and noticed Johnny lying in the street. If they did, they'd pick him up as a drunk and throw him in jail. He couldn't go to jail; he had to spread the warning.

You can't change history, he told himself again, *but you've got to try; it's the right thing to do. The right thing to do? Who are you kidding, you half-breed loser? You never did anything right in your whole life.*

No, I did one thing right, he thought and he smiled to himself. *I loved a girl named Angel Newland, and I think she loved me, too. I must have some good left for a girl like her to care about me.*

He managed to get to his knees. *If I can just get on my horse, I can get downtown in time to stop them.* But he couldn't mount up; he didn't have the strength. Instead, Johnny grabbed the stirrup. "Go on, boy, go on."

The horse hesitated, then began to walk, dragging Johnny along the ground. It hurt his shoulders and his hand to be dragged along the dirt. He lost his grip and fell facedown in the street. His horse kept walking forward.

"Whoa, boy," he whispered, but the paint stallion did not seem to hear Johnny's faint voice. The horse continued walking toward town.

Abruptly, he heard a shot and then another. *Too late,* Johnny thought, *too late to do anything except try to save my own neck.* The echoing shots spooked Crazy Quilt and the stallion took off at a gallop out of town.

Helpless, Johnny stared after his galloping horse. It was too late to warn anyone and he couldn't escape now, not without a horse. All he could do was try to save himself. Where was he? The alley near the jail. From here, he could see the gang's horses tied to a pipe. He crawled out of the middle of the road and under an outside stairwell. He was partly hidden here; no one would see him unless they were really searching for him. Bob and the boys wouldn't know he was here.

His brain told him he couldn't change history, but his heart told him he had to try; Angel would want him to. His Winchester was on his horse, but he still had his Colt if he could reach it. Maybe he could stop the gang when they came back for their horses. With only a pistol, he didn't have a chance against five heavily armed men. His head pounded with pain, but he saw her lovely face in his mind as he reached down and drew his Colt. *Are you loco? This isn't the way the event is supposed to play out.* He must have more decency in him than he had thought; or maybe Angel had encouraged whatever little good was buried deep within him.

Inside the Condon Bank, Grat, Dick and Bill had leveled their Winchesters at the surprised clerks and customers. "Get the money and get it fast!" Grat shouted profanity at a bank employee, Charles Carpenter, tossing him some sacks. About that time, an elderly customer, John Levan, walked into the bank, and Grat ordered him to the floor.

Bank cashier Charley Ball, who heard the confusion and came out of his office, was forced to the floor to join Mr. Levan.

While Carpenter sacked money ever so slowly, Grat tossed a sack to Charley Ball. "You get the money out of the vault."

Ball held the sack and stared into the barrel of the Winchester. "I can't get the money. There's a time lock on the safe."

Grat cursed. "How long before it goes off?"

"Nine-thirty," the clerk said without thinking, then began to sweat as he looked up at the bank clock. It was already 9:40 A.M. If the bewhiskered robber noticed that, the man might be angry enough to kill him. There was forty thousand dollars in the safe and it wasn't insured.

However, the robber must not be too smart. He didn't seem to notice the clock. "And how long is that going to be?"

"Uh, it's only nine-twenty," lied the clerk, pretending to glance at his watch. "You've got ten minutes yet."

"Then we'll wait," Grat said.

He leaned against the counter as the minutes ticked by.

"Grat, we ain't got time to lollygag around here," Dick finally protested. "Bob and Emmett'll be finished and ready to leave!"

"You're right!" Grat began to curse and waved his Winchester in Charley Ball's face. "Damn you! I think you're lyin' to me anyways. Open that safe!"

Sweat began to roll down Ball's forehead. He looked around at the other white-faced, silent clerks and customers. He stared past the three robbers. Behind them and through the plateglass window, he could see the plaza and men running and pointing. Obviously someone had sounded the alarm that the bank was being robbed. Maybe if he stalled them long enough, this bunch could be stopped. "I tell you, I can't open the safe!"

"You wanta die? Give me the money now!" Grat shouted.

"Okay, okay." As slowly as possible, Ball took the sack and went back to the vault, taking his time twirling the knobs. "There's a bunch of silver dollars—you want them, too, don't you?"

"Sure!" Grat said. The silver would be heavy and he wasn't certain how he was going to get it completely across the plaza to his horse, but he was too greedy to leave it behind. He watched the clerk putting money in the sack. "Bill, you and Dick keep your eyes on everyone; I don't trust them."

Luther Perkins, a citizen who had offices over the bank, threw open the side door and stuck his head in. "Hey, the First National's being robbed—"

He broke off in confusion as he stared at the white-faced

people with their hands up, and the gleaming Winchesters. Before Grat could order him in, the man jerked his head out and slammed the door behind him.

"Well, if that don't beat all," Grat snapped. "Now they'll know." He looked around at Dick and Bill. "Let's get the hell outa here!"

They turned to stare at the running crowd and confusion out on the plaza.

"I think it's too late, Grat! We're done for!"

Chapter Twenty-two

"The hell you say!" Grat grabbed the bulging bank sack. "Let's clear out!"

But even as they started out the front doors, the armed citizens outside began firing. Glass shattered in the bank windows and came crashing down on the brick sidewalk and showered those inside the building.

Cursing, the trio retreated back through the doors to crouch down out of sight.

"Now what do we do?" Dick poked the barrel of his rifle through the broken window.

"We'll scatter them and then run for the horses!" Grat began to shoot through the window and was answered by return fire. Suddenly, those horses a few hundred yards away in the alley seemed like a million miles from here.

Inside the First National, Bob listened to the shooting outside and thought quickly. "Damn, they've spotted us! We'll use hostages."

At gunpoint, he and Emmett herded three bank employees

and four captive customers ahead of them out the front doors onto Union Street and were met by gunfire. The bandits retreated back inside the bank.

"Okay," Bob hissed, "it's too hot to go out the front, but I know this bank." Bob nodded to Emmett. "We can get out the back door and go around behind the Condon, get to the horses without crossin' the plaza."

"Ain't that farther?" Emmett asked.

"Damn it! You got any better ideas?"

"No, Bob, I wasn't questionin' your lead—"

"Then get the money! Here, you!" Bob pointed his Winchester at bank teller W. H. Shephard. "You're gonna be our hostage. Now you go out that back door right ahead of us."

"Okay, okay, just don't shoot!" Sweat ran down the man's pale face as the trio started for the back door, Emmett protecting the retreat by facing the silent employees and customers.

Lucius Baldwin, the young clerk at Read Brothers Dry Goods Store, watched out the window of the business. "I ain't gonna let them get away with this!"

"Boy," yelled his boss, "stay inside. You don't know anything about guns!"

"I'm as good as any of those others!" Disobeying the older man, young Baldwin ran out the door and down the street to Isham's. "Gimme a pistol."

In truth, he was young and reckless and didn't know much about guns, but he imagined his photo in the *Coffeyville Journal* and how everyone would think he was a hero. Baldwin took the pistol and ran out and around the building to the alley. Coming out of the back door of the First National were three men. He recognized Shephard, an employee of the First National, but the other two he didn't know. At least he'd have three men to back him up. One of the men was yelling something at him, but over the gunfire out front, he couldn't be sure what it was.

Bob Dalton yelled at the boy again to drop his pistol. The

young man stared at him as if he didn't understand. Then Bob put a bullet in his chest. The young clerk stared at Bob for a long second, as if he couldn't quite understand what was happening. Then he dropped the pistol and crumpled into the dirt of the street.

Bob prodded the bank employee with his rifle. "Now get movin'. It's a long way to them horses!"

Marshal Connelly heard the gunfire break the pleasant morning from his office over in the jail. "What in tarnation?"

A man stuck his head in the door. "The Daltons! They're robbin' the bank!"

Connelly jumped to his feet, pulling at his goatee. "Alert the town and the telegraph office! Dagnab it, where did I put my gun?"

Johnny lay hidden under the outside stairwell, listening to the shouts and echo of gunfire. Only a few yards from him, the robbers' horses stamped their hooves and snorted at the noise. Pain pounded in Johnny's head so badly he could barely see, but he had drawn his Colt. When the Dalton gang ran back here in the alley to get their horses, he intended to change history; he intended to try and stop them. Right now, it sounded like people were bleeding and dying out there, and he was helpless to do anything about it.

The first sounds of gunfire echoed like thunder through the open windows of the little school. All the children looked up from their books, chattering excitedly.

Angie stood up from her desk so fast, her chair overturned. "Jiminy Christmas! What's happening?"

She heard running footsteps, and a cowboy stuck his head in the door, so breathless he could barely speak. "Dalton gang is robbin' the banks! Keep the children inside! I'm on my way to the telegraph office!''

"What?'' Angie asked, but the cowboy was already gone.

Again the children chattered and confusion reigned.

Automatically, Angie rapped on her desk with a ruler for order. "Children, get back to work and be quiet!''

The room quieted down, but Angie's thoughts were in turmoil. The Dalton gang—that meant Johnny was there. He was with the Daltons and even now might be lying dead in the middle of a botched robbery. She had to go see about him.

"Children,'' she kept her voice calm, even though her heart was racing, "I'm going to see what's happening.'' She called the oldest girl, Millie, the one who wanted to be a teacher, up to her desk and spoke in a low tone. "There's candy in my desk that I intended to give out at the end of the day. Remember, Mr. Jones is due in class tomorrow. If I don't come back, read to the children, then hand out the candy and dismiss the class at noon. Tell them to go straight home. Tell them not to go into town.''

With those words, Angie slipped out the door of the school and ran for town. She knew Johnny had warned her to stay away, but if he was in danger, she intended to be there to help him.

Bob Dalton was a crack shot, and if he had to kill half the male citizens of this town to fight his way to the tethered horses, he intented to do so. "Come on, little brother, and don't leave the money behind!''

Emmett followed Bob blindly, knowing they were going out into a barrage of gunfire. Bob was a top shot, but there were men in this town who were good shots, too. "I never thought they'd put up a fight; I thought they'd step back and let us rob 'em!''

"You loco?'' Bob yelled as they ran behind the Condon

Bank. "This town's like most Western towns—full of Civil War veterans, and they know how to fight!"

Over at the Condon Bank, Grat looked out the shattered window at the plaza outside. To venture out there was certain death. "Is there a back door to this place?"

"No," lied the bank personnel.

Grat was as gullible now as he'd been about the time lock on the safe. Or maybe he just wasn't too smart. He didn't bother to send either Bill Powers or Dick Broadwell to check to see if the employees were lying about the back door. "Okay, then there's no help for it; we'll have to go out the front. You two"—he gestured toward Ball and Carpenter—"you carry that sack of silver out ahead of us."

The two bank employees did as they were told, but the barrage of gunfire sent all of them stumbling back inside the bank. Grat looked around uncertainly. *Now what to do?* Brother Bob had always been the leader, but now Grat was on his own.

Dick screamed out suddenly, "I'm hit! I can't use my arm no more!"

Grat knew they were in trouble. As greedy as he was, they weren't going to be able to take all that heavy silver with them. He ordered Ball to pass him the currency, which Grat stuffed inside his vest. "Leave the hostages, boys! Let's clear out!"

The other two obeyed and they lay down a barrage of gunfire as they ran out the door of the Condon Bank, running with their heads down, hoping to make it to their horses, tied up in that alley that abruptly seemed so far away.

Bob and Emmett, once they cleared the back alley, left Shephard and ran around the building, hoping to cross behind the plaza. Bob was an expert shot. From here, he could see boot-maker George Cubine holding a rifle and standing in front of

Rammel Brothers Drug Store. Cubine had been a friend of his in years past, but now Bob Dalton was desperate. He cut down Cubine in a hail of gunfire.

Another citizen, Charles Brown, an older co-worker of Cubine's, grabbed Cubine's rifle. Bob shot him down and Brown fell within two feet of Cubine's body. Now Bob saw his comrades running from the Condon Bank and opted to give them a covering fire, shooting with expert and cool accuracy at the citizens crouched behind every wall and overturned wagons out front. He shot at everything that moved and knew he was wounding some of them, but there were too many armed citizens to deal with.

He tried to give covering fire to the running trio of robbers, but there was too much gunfire for them to make it to the horses. Even as Bob watched, Grat and Powers were hit, dust flying from their clothes at the bullets' impact. Both stayed on their feet, staggering toward the alley where their tied horses reared and neighed, struggling to break free. Then Broadwell was hit by a shot from the second floor of the Condon.

Powers, staggering toward the horses, tried to find shelter in the doorway of a building on the alley, but the door was locked. Pinned against the door by the merciless gunfire, he died right there, only a few feet away from the horses. Grat stumbled to a stairway and hid behind a post, trying to return the fire, but he was hurt too badly. Without Bob to tell him, he wasn't sure what to do next. He only knew that he must get to his horse. He took a stumbling step away from the stairs, saw the movement and the flash of Johnny's pistol and fired. His shot caught Johnny in the shoulder, spoiling the gunfighter's aim. He realized in that moment that Johnny was trying to protect Marshal Connelly, who had run out into the alley and was facing the horses, his attention on the gunfire from the plaza and his back toward Grat. Grat shot the lawman in the back. Then Grat staggered past Marshal Connelly's body toward the rearing horses.

Liveryman John Kloehr, an excellent shot and armed with a borrowed .44 Winchester, and local barber Carey Seaman, who had just returned from a hunting trip and still had his shotgun in his wagon, ran into the alley. Kloehr put a slug through Grat's neck and Grat collapsed near the marshal's body, blood gurgling from his throat into the dust of the alley.

Dick Broadwell was wounded, but he still managed to stumble to his horse and mount up. He turned to gallop away, but he wasn't fast enough. Both Kloehr and Seaman shot him. Still, Dick hung on to his saddle horn and galloped away, leaving a trail of blood in the dust of the alley as he went.

Bob and Emmett ran south on Eighth Street, still trying to get to their horses. Along the way, they almost collided with a youth named Bob Wells, who was armed only with an almost useless .22 pistol. Now the boy stared up into the outlaws' Winchesters and froze.

"Get outa here, kid!" Emmett whacked the boy across the rear with the butt of his rifle and sent the youth scrambling for safety.

Bob yelled encouragement to Emmett. "Look, there's the horses. We're gonna make it now!" They ran into the alley, Bob looking up toward the offices above the Condon Bank, expecting more gunfire from there. Instead, someone fired a shot from inside Isham's Hardware Store that slammed into Bob. He staggered over and sat down hard on a stack of rock near the rear door of the jail. Gamely, he kept firing, but he did not even have the strength to bring his rifle to his shoulder.

Emmett had now made it to the horses with his vest full of money. He mounted up. "Come on, Bob!"

Kloehr's borrowed rifle roared from the protection of the stable and hit Bob in the chest.

Emmett hesitated. He was hurt, but he could ride, and he had the money. Ahead of him lay the end of the alley. He might have a chance if he spurred his horse. Behind him, Bob was sitting in the dirt, leaning against the wall, blood running down his chest as he tried to fire.

He couldn't leave his brother behind. Emmett galloped back to Bob. "Here, brother, grab my hand. We can ride double outa here!"

Bob shook his head. "I'm done for. Save yourself, Emmett." And he died.

Even as Emmett stared down at his dead brother, Carey Seaman stepped out into the alley and put two loads of buckshot into Emmett's back. The outlaw dropped the money and slid from his horse, a pistol still in his hand.

From where he lay hidden, Johnny watched the last scene of the tragedy. He had tried in vain to save the marshal and had taken a slug in the arm for his trouble. Now, no doubt, the armed citizens would find him and finish him off.

"They're all down!" someone shouted, and the townspeople began to converge on the alley. There were four dead men lying there: Bob and Grat Dalton, Bill Powers and Marshal Connelly. The area would be known ever after as Death Alley.

A dignified man approached the wounded Emmett. The outlaw held out his pistol. He was bloody and barely conscious. "Here, Colonel Elliott, take it. Don't let them kill me." Then the outlaw passed out.

The man Emmett had recognized took the pistol and bent over Emmett. "Someone get Doc Wells."

"No, somebody get a rope!" another man yelled.

Dr. Wells came running, looking over the fallen to see who still breathed. He ordered Emmett carried to his office.

A citizen protested. "Doc, we was gonna lynch him!"

"He isn't going to live to be hanged," the doctor assured him. "There's no point in hanging a dying man."

Cooler heads prevailed, and from his hiding spot, Johnny watched as four men carried the wounded Emmett up the nearby stairs to the doctor's office and gathered up the bodies. He was bleeding and in a lot of pain, but he wasn't going to surrender. If he did, angry as the crowd was, they'd surely lynch him without benefit of trial. When the crowds moved away from the area, he could crawl out and escape.

Escape? He laughed without humor through a haze of pain. He was wounded, lying under a stairway in the heart of town and he didn't have a horse. It had taken less than fifteen minutes from the time the robberies began until the last of the outlaws lay bloody and dead in the alley. There was nothing Johnny could do but lie here and try to stop his own bleeding. When the crowds moved away he would crawl out. There was no way for him to escape his fate and he knew it.

Angie ran toward the plaza, heedless of her own safety. All she could think of was Johnny. Ahead of her, behind the First National Bank, a crowd was gathered around a prone body. Johnny? She pushed through the crowd and knelt there. It was young Lucius Baldwin, and he smiled up at her, blood on his lips. "Hello, miss."

"Oh, Lucius, what happened?" She gathered him into her arms, wiping the blood from his mouth.

"I—I was tryin' to be a hero, I reckon. Three men came out of the back of the bank. I thought they were all citizens. Instead, it was some of the Daltons with a hostage."

"Don't try to talk," she whispered. "Just take it easy." She looked over at the men surrounding the young man. One of them gave her the slightest shake of his head.

"One of them shot me," young Baldwin said. "I never even got to fire my pistol. . . ."

"Lucius?" Angie stared down into his blank eyes in horror. "Lucius, answer me!"

"It's too late, ma'am," an old man said softly. "He's gone."

Angie began to cry as someone helped her to her feet. She

looked around. Downtown had been shot to pieces. She saw shattered windows and bulletholes in walls. There were dead men lying out on the sidewalks and wounded men sitting on curbs while others tried to help them. There was a lot of confusion and shouting, and women crying. She began to walk aimlessly. "Who—who all was killed?"

A passerby shook his head. "From what I understand, there's four citizens dead and three wounded. There's four robbers dead and one up in Doc Wells's office, not expected to live."

"Only five robbers?" She looked at him hopefully. "Who's the wounded one?"

The grizzled old man looked at her strangely. "There was only five robbers, ma'am—"

"That's not true," a passerby objected. "At the height of all the shooting, I saw a horse galloping out of town."

Johnny. Could it be Johnny?

Angie took a deep breath. "What—what color was the horse?"

The man scratched his head. "I'm not certain; the confusion and shootin' and all. It might have been a paint."

The two men hurried on, leaving Angie standing there breathing a sigh of relief. *A paint. Crazy Quilt.* So Johnny had escaped after all. She could cry for all the snuffed-out lives lost here today, now that she was sure Johnny hadn't hurt anybody or taken part in the robbery. Deep in his heart, there was still some good in the gunfighter.

In the meantime, there were people to comfort and children at the school who needed her. She stood in the middle of the plaza for a long moment. Then, regretfully, she turned away to see about the living.

Johnny watched her from under the stairwell. How he wanted to cry out to her, comfort her. But even as he watched the sad emotion on her tearstained face, he knew it was futile. All he could do was watch her as she walked away and disappeared up the street. He closed his eyes, remembering every detail of her beloved face. It was the last time he would ever see her in all eternity, he realized.

Now he lay there, bleeding and in pain, knowing that at sundown he had to keep his appointment with Nick Diablo. Angel was going to be left back in time and there was nothing Johnny could do about it.

Chapter Twenty-three

Late in the afternoon, Johnny's wound began to bleed again. He tried to stop it with his bandanna, but he hadn't the knowledge or skill to stop the hemorrhaging. If he crawled out of the stairwell and tried to find a doctor, he risked being lynched by angry citizens. He could only lie there as the shadows lengthened, knowing he had to make it to sundown. He had an appointment with the gambler, but without a horse how was he going to get there?

The late afternoon sun threw distorted shadows across the deadly alley where dark bloodstains still soaked the dirt. The bodies had long since been carried away and the whole of downtown seemed empty as townspeople gathered in their homes to mourn the dead who had thwarted the bank robbery at the cost of their lives.

What time was it, anyway? With great effort, Johnny reached for his gold pocket watch. His bloody hand smeared it so badly, he had a difficult time seeing the face. Less than an hour to sundown. Somehow he had to get out of Coffeyville undetected and to the town garbage dump to meet Nick. Just how was he going to do that? Tentatively, Johnny looked up and down the alley. Nothing moved. It took all his strength to drag himself out from under the stairs. *Now what?*

At that moment, he heard footsteps. Alarmed, he grabbed for his pistol, wondering if he could bring himself to shoot some innocent person who might have come into the alley. While he never would have questioned it before, now he was not so sure he could. Yet he didn't have the strength to crawl back under the stairs. He held his breath and listened to the sound moving closer. Crazy Quilt turned the corner and nickered at Johnny.

"Good boy!" Johnny gasped and held out his hand. "You came back for me after all!"

The big paint stallion walked toward him, stopping before him. Johnny reached up and patted the paint's muzzle. "Just don't move, boy. Maybe I can make it."

Easier said than done, Johnny thought.

The horse snorted at the scent of blood, but it must have sensed Johnny's desperate need, for it didn't move away. Johnny craned his neck and looked up. From down here in the dirt, it looked like a long mile up to that saddle. Yet he had to do it; otherwise, he'd bleed to death right here in the alley, as Grat and Bob had done. For a moment, he wondered if Emmett was still alive. Emmett had always liked Johnny better than his brothers did. Maybe he wouldn't tell the law about the sixth outlaw if he regained consciousness.

Johnny took a deep breath and reached up for the stirrup with his good arm. His fingers clenched on it. So he had it; now what? He couldn't expect the horse to drag him all the way out of town without someone noticing, even if Johnny had the strength to hang on that long—which, of course, he didn't.

He had to get to his feet. Gritting his teeth, Johnny grabbed the stirrup and pulled hard. Damn, it hurt. He felt sweat break out on his face from the superhuman effort, but gradually he stumbled to his feet and leaned against the stallion, feeling faint and breathing hard.

Crazy Quilt snorted at the scent of blood and stamped his hooves.

"Whoa, boy, don't move. For God's sake, don't move!"

God. He hadn't thought about God in a long, long time. Angel had changed him, all right. He leaned against the horse, trembling. If the horse moved, Johnny would crumple to the ground again, and he knew he didn't have the strength to get up a second time.

The horse seemed to sense Johnny's trouble and calmed, waiting.

All he had to do now was mount up. But he wasn't sure he could do it, not with his arm bleeding and hurting like it was. *If you stay here, you're going to die,* he scolded himself, *but if you can rendezvous with Diablo, you can live.* Funny, he'd always been terrified of dying. Now he thought there were worse things; like life without Angel. Strange, he had never really lived until he had met her, only existed, but he hadn't known it until now. *What on earth was he going to do without her when he got back to his fine penthouse in Logan Towers?*

"You mustn't think about that right now," he mumbled. "You mustn't think about anything but getting into this saddle."

He might pray for a miracle, he thought, but he didn't know how to pray. Besides, would God listen to a bad hombre who had sold his soul to the devil? Of course not; Johnny was on his own now, as he had always been since he was a hungry, abandoned kid.

Johnny clenched his teeth to hold back any cry of pain as he pulled himself up onto the horse. For a moment, the effort sent such spasms of pain through his muscular body that he thought he would black out. He grabbed onto the saddle horn, willing himself to stay conscious. If he fainted and fell, he wouldn't have the strength to remount.

It seemed late. He must not miss the meeting at sundown. With a trembling hand, Johnny pulled out his pocket watch and looked at it. He only had a few minutes left. Even as he tried to put the bloody watch back inside his vest, it slipped from his hand, slick with his own scarlet blood. As it fell, he grabbed for it, almost falling from the horse. He saw the watch slide down his leg and drop in the soft sand under Crazy Quilt's hooves.

"I'll be damned!"

In response, he thought he heard a roll of thunder and looked up. The sky was clear, though the long shadows of dusk were beginning to spread. On the ground, glinting in the last rays of sun, lay his gold watch. It was not more than four feet to the ground, but it might as well be a mile. He couldn't get it from here and he didn't have the strength to dismount, get the watch and remount. There was no help for it; he'd have to leave it.

Regretfully, Johnny nudged his horse and rode out at a walk. If he was lucky, no one would notice him—or if they did, maybe they wouldn't see the blood and might think he was some stray cowboy leaving town.

So far, so good. Johnny held on to the saddle horn, gritted his teeth and kept riding. He was in a race against time to be at the town dump before sundown, but he dare not urge his horse into a lope; he might not be able to bear the pain or stay on the paint. Yet he had to renew the contract before sunset or die. No, he wasn't going to die, he promised himself; he was going to live forever. All he had to do was get to the town dump in time.

Angel. There was nothing he could do for her. He didn't even know where she was. Angel Newland was going to be left back in time when he returned to 1999. If he could, he would take her with him. But hurt as he was, it was all he could do to save himself.

* * *

Angel sat in her empty classroom for most of the afternoon, but her mind was a blank. What to do? Finally, grabbing her big purse, she returned to downtown. The ravaged streets were deserted now, and it was difficult to believe that such violence and tragedy had played out here only that morning. There was shattered glass, bulletholes in walls and even blood on the brick sidewalks. But maybe Johnny had gotten away.

She paused, then climbed the stairs to Doc Wells's office. Emmett Dalton lay under a blanket, barely breathing.

"How is he, Doc?"

The old man nodded. "I think he'll make it, but don't tell anyone. Some of the townfolk want to lynch him."

Maybe Emmett could give her a clue.

"Did he—did he say anything about those in the robbery?"

"No," Doc sighed, "just managed to hold up his hands in surrender and handed his pistol to Dave Elliott, the editor of the *Journal.* Emmett knew Dave from a long time back. You know, the editor is also an attorney, and he represented the boys' mother when she divorced their pa."

"No, I didn't know."

Doc shrugged. "Old man Dalton wasn't much good. Poor Mrs. Dalton! I reckon they've notified her by now. She and some of her other children will come soon."

She was almost afraid to ask. "Do they—do they think any of the bandits got away?"

"Funny you should ask." Doc leaned back in his chair. "We've had two reports of folks who saw six riders coming into town, but witnesses at the robbery said there was only five. That fella who thought he saw a paint horse galloping away from town must have been mistaken."

"A paint horse?"

"So he says."

Angie said a silent prayer of thanksgiving.

Doc hooked his thumbs under his suspenders. "One of the robbers did manage to mount up and ride out, though."

Again Angie held her breath. "Oh?"

"Yes." Doc nodded. "They found him lying in the road a half mile away, dead, his horse standing next to him."

Dead. She felt her heart plunge. She didn't want to ask, but she had to know. "Did they identify him?"

"They say it was Dick Broadwell. Hurt too bad to ride very far without bleeding to death."

Angie heaved a sigh of relief. At least Johnny might still be alive. "Doc, can I get you something to eat?"

"No, thanks just the same. Someone's comin' to spell me in a minute and I'll go get some rest." He looked up at her. "I'd say, young lady, just looking at you, you need some rest, too."

"You're right. Well, I'll be going then." Angie turned and left, closing the door behind her. She went down the stairs and into the stable. She wasn't sure what to do except go look for Johnny. She saddled up and mounted Rosebud, slanting her hand against the sun, so low on the horizon.

What to do now? Curious, she rode into the alley where so many had died. There were dark spots of dried blood in the dirt. And a few spots of fresh blood. *How could that be?* Even as she stared hard at the ground, a glint of metal caught her eye. A bullet? No, it was bigger than that.

Angie dismounted and reached for it. Her heart almost stopped as she clasped it. Johnny's gold watch, and the blood on it seemed almost fresh.

Oh, dear God. Johnny was hurt after all, and in dire straits or he would never have left his watch behind. She looked up and down, and realized the blood droplets led out of the alley. Had Johnny been here lately and, if so, how had he left and how badly was he hurt?

She bit her lip to keep from weeping as she swung back up

on her horse, still clutching the bloody watch. If he was out here somewhere, maybe she could find him. She slipped the watch into her big purse and nudged Rosebud forward. She'd have to hurry. Once it got dark, she wouldn't be able to follow the blood trail anymore.

Yet she couldn't ride faster than a walk and still follow the scarlet drops. Angie kept her gaze on the ground and urged Rosebud on. The slanting rays of the Indian summer sun threw long shadows as she rode slowly out of town.

October fifth. She remembered what Johnny and Nick Diablo had said. If she didn't get there first, Johnny Logan was going to sign that contract with Nick Diablo. She wasn't sure what she believed about what he'd told her, but in her heart, she knew she had to save him from Nick!

It was all he could do to stay on his paint stallion as it slowed to a walk. Only a couple of miles behind him in the frontier town lay the botched bank robbery, citizens and outlaws dead or dying in the streets. Soon Johnny would be dead, too . . . unless a posse got here first.

He put his hand to his bloody, gunshot arm and winced as the horse stopped. God, he hurt so! Crimson blood dripped dark and wet onto the saddle, ran down the stallion's black-and-white hide and into the prairie dust. *What a miserable end to a miserable life.*

Johnny struggled to stay conscious, hanging on to the saddle horn, his head whirling. *Where was he?* He looked around at the desolate prairie. He saw a broken chair, some empty boxes, garbage, shattered dishes and other refuse.

He threw back his head and laughed. "Yes, the garbage dump! This is Coffeyville's ash heap! How ironic! How funny!" His laughter choked off into a weak cough as he reeled in the saddle, the stallion looking back at him as if questioning his sanity. "Don't you get it, Crazy Quilt, old boy? I'm just human trash myself. I've sure proved that, the way I treated her. Fittin', ain't it, that I'm scheduled to die here?''

The horse snorted and stamped its hooves, as if awaiting orders to move on.

Johnny glanced at the sun, soon to set on the western horizon. "No, I ain't gonna die, even though posses and vigilantes may be lookin' for me. Reckon all the others are already dead."

Johnny attempted to urge his horse forward, but he no longer had the strength. Instead, he felt himself falling. He hit the ground hard and shuddered for a long moment, willing himself back into consciousness despite the pain. He lay in the midst of the rubble, his blood-smeared horse now munching stray blades of grass growing through the trash.

Where was Nick? Maybe Johnny was in the wrong place. If he could just stand up and get back on the horse . . . Johnny struggled, but he was growing weaker by the moment. He couldn't even get up, much less mount and ride across the border into Indian Territory, where he might find refuge among the Kiowa. It would be dark soon, and Johnny was afraid of the dark; silly weakness for a tough, half-breed gunfighter. No matter; if he didn't find Nick in the next ten minutes or so, he wasn't going to be alive to see the sun set.

"What a rotten end to a rotten life," he muttered, and tried to staunch the flow of blood from his arm. But he had lost his bandanna. "The fastest gun in the West dies amid a pile of trash."

Well, he was human garbage himself. Then he laughed, remembering. No, he wasn't going to die; he had relived the terrible tragedy and now all he had to do was wait for the gambler to show up with the contract. In a few minutes, he was going to be whisked back to the twentieth century and his rich lifestyle in Logan Towers.

There was no sound save the softly blowing wind. Maybe the gambler wasn't coming. Johnny licked his cracked lips in desperation, cursed God and screamed at the sky, "I don't want to die! I want to live! I'd do anything to live!"

Abruptly, a tall, lean rider seemed to appear out of nowhere, loping toward him. Maybe it was a deputy or a bounty hunter. If it was a posse, they'd string him up right here. Johnny managed to turn his head and look around, chuckling softly. "No tree," he whispered. "Can't lynch me; no tree."

The stranger reined his shadow gray horse to a halt and leaned on his saddle horn, looking down at Johnny. "You've left a blood trail. I'm surprised no one but me has noticed it yet."

Johnny stared up at him. The somber rider's voice was deep as a tomb and seemed to echo through the stillness. His eyes glowed dark and hard as obsidian over a small mustache and a mouth like a hard slash. He was dressed all in black, with the finest boots, Western hat and long frock coat. Something about him sent a chill up Johnny's back. "Hello, Nick. I was afraid you wouldn't come."

The sinister stranger nodded and lit a cheroot as he stared down at Johnny in the twilight. "And miss the chance to reclaim you? Once mine, I don't like to give souls back, although, once in awhile, the Big Guy steps in and wins a round." He glanced up at the sky and then down at Johnny. "You really messed up back there, trying to stop the robbery. What's wrong with you?"

"I—I'm not sure. Maybe it was the girl; she thought I was worth salvaging."

The other sneered. "Forget that. You were always a loser. Without me, you're nothing; with me, you're a winner."

"Hot; so hot. Help me," Johnny gasped and ran his tongue over his dry lips again. "You've got a canteen; give me just a sip of water."

Nick shrugged as he dismounted. "You'll think hot and thirsty when you get where you're going if you don't get the contract renewed."

"Going? I can't even ride. I—I don't want to die," Johnny begged, holding out a bloody hand in appeal. "Please, get me to a doctor—"

The gambler yawned and squatted down next to Johnny, then looked at the setting sun. "Stop whining, Logan. You've always been brave, no matter what."

"I—I've never been this hurt before."

"It's almost over; you'll be dead when the sun sets unless you play ball with me."

Johnny stared up into the soulless dark eyes and then at the ghost-gray horse. An eerie, troubling memory came to him of an old preacher on a street corner in a lawless trail town shouting scripture at the sinners passing by.

. . . and I looked up and beheld a pale horse and his name that sat upon him was Death and hell followed with him.

Johnny fumbled for his Colt. "Help me, damn you, or I'll—"

"You'll what?" The gambler blew cigar smoke into the air. "Your pistol is empty."

"How—how do you know—?"

The other only smiled.

Of course his Colt was empty. The bank robbery had been an inferno of gunfire. Ironic. He had not planned to die like this. Handsome, tough gunfighters went out in a blaze of bullets in some wild saloon with half the town and all the pretty, adoring whores watching. "What about the contract, or have you come for me?"

"Of course I brought the contract." The other nodded and tossed away his cigar.

"Hurry up then." Johnny looked at his life running out, mixing with the dust beneath him. "Anything," he gasped, "I'd do anything—"

"Fine." Nick Diablo pulled a paper from his black frock coat and knelt next to Johnny. "Here's the contract. You know the

drill—good for one hundred years with option to renew again."
He laid the ancient parchment next to Johnny's hand.

"The girl," Johnny gasped. "What about the girl?"

"The hell with her!"

"I—I was hopin' to have one last chance to take her with
me."

"Forget about her, I tell you! Leave her here in the Gay Nineties
where she won't be any threat to you by telling your secret. There
are plenty of women waiting for the rich outlaw of Wall Street
to get back to the twentieth century."

Johnny was in pain and growing weaker. "I don't want any
other woman. I want Angel."

"Are you loco?" The gambler made an annoyed gesture and
the diamond on his hand winked in the fading daylight. "Look,
all you do is re-sign and you're outa here. Why do you have to
make it so difficult?"

Johnny turned his head and looked toward the sinking sun. Its
light glittered on something in the garbage dump. "What—what
is that?"

"What? The bits of that old mirror?" Nick yawned. "You
remember, it got broken when Duke Babcock's shot went wild."

"Angel followed me through that mirror," Johnny remembered
aloud.

"Well, and she could go back that way, too, but she doesn't
know that. You don't need the mirror; this contract fast-
forwards you right back to the future. Now hurry up and sign.
I've got one of the president's appointees to meet this evening."

Johnny ignored the proffered paper, his mind on the girl.
"How—how could she go back through a broken mirror?"

"She doesn't need the whole thing, idiot, only a piece big
enough to see herself with a ray of sun directly reflecting into
her eyes. The eyes are the window to the soul, you know. Now
just sign," the gambler snapped. "I'm running out of patience
and you're running out of daylight."

They heard a sound that seemed to float on the still air, and both of them looked toward town. In the distance, they could see Angel's horse coming toward the dump. The girl's blond head was down as she followed the blood trail.

"Angel." Johnny managed to pull himself up on one elbow. He tried to call out to her, but his voice was too weak.

Diablo swore. "Now what's she doing out here?"

"Tryin' to save me, I reckon," Johnny whispered. "She loves me, and you know what? I love her!"

"Oh, balderdash!" Diablo said. "You mean you lust after her. I'll get you a prettier one back in Oklahoma City. We'll ship one of those wild dames in from Dallas. Now sign while you can or die right here."

Johnny shook his head. "I can't leave her back here alone."

Diablo swore under his breath. "I don't know what you can do about it. There are only two ways to return; the mirror or the contract. She won't sign; I've tried to tempt her. She's a good person, a truly good person."

Johnny was dying; he knew it. He could feel himself getting weaker as Angie rode toward them. "I—I'm going to tell her how to go back through the mirror."

"You don't have time!" Nick yelled. "Don't you realize that? Look at the sun! In a couple of minutes, it's going to be below the horizon and your chance will be gone. You idiot! Do you love her enough to throw it all away; trade your life for hers?"

He thought about it for less than a heartbeat, and then Johnny made his choice. "Yes, I love her more than I love myself and I'd do anything for her, even die for her!"

In that moment, the sun brightened with a blinding brilliance and in that light, she seemed to see him on the ground and was off her horse and running toward him. "Johnny! Johnny, are you all right?"

"Now that you're here, I am." He smiled up at her.

With a cry of dismay, she knelt and took him in her arms, holding his bloody body close as she glared at Nick. "He's hurt. Why aren't you helping him?"

"He won't let me," Nick grinned, looking toward the setting sun, "and he'll be dead in less than a minute."

"Angel," Johnny gasped and brought up his hand, pointed. "Mirror . . . see the mirror pieces over there?"

Angel turned and looked. Across the dump, she could see the sun glinting on the shards of broken mirror.

"Angel," Johnny gasped, "you can get back to the twentieth century! Pick up a piece and look into it, that's the secret!"

She hesitated only a moment, looking toward the broken glass.

Diablo laughed. "He's right, you know. Look out for yourself for a change and hurry! The magic's only good this one time. Go back to your own time; he's dying anyway."

"No, I can't leave him this way." She shook her head and began to dig in her purse.

"Baby," Johnny whispered in disbelief, "don't you understand? I've given up my chance to go back, and you're about to be trapped back in time with a dead man."

"Not if I can do anything about it!" she snorted. "Jiminy Christmas, Johnny, I love you!"

Abruptly, the thunder rolled and echoed though the fading sky was clear and Angie knew at that moment why she had been spared from that car wreck. It hadn't been an oversight. She'd been sent back for one purpose: to save this one black sheep called Johnny Logan. She reached for her little medical kit and made a tourniquet to put on his arm.

Nick Diablo laughed with delight. "You can't save him, you know! He wouldn't sign my contract to save himself and you wouldn't go through the mirror to save yourself! Now you're both in bad trouble!"

Angie looked up at the sky, shouting an appeal. "Hey! I'm doing the best I can! Now if You sent me back, can't You at least give me a little help down here?"

And out of a clear sky, lightning suddenly flashed and hit Nick. Even as they watched, he disintegrated into a little pile of smoking ashes.

Angie crossed herself and nodded with satisfaction. "Now that's more like it!"

She wrapped the tourniquet around Johnny's arm and found a bandage and some antibiotic ointment, working hurriedly. "You aren't going to die, Johnny. Somebody up there is looking out for us!"

"Now why do I suddenly believe that?" he whispered, and he smiled at her as the sun sank below the horizon. He watched it sink, the twilight all calm and pink behind it. "Do you realize you're stuck back in this time period now?"

She shrugged and inspected the finished bandage. "So are you. And you've just given up everything old Nick gave you. Will you be content with only another half century to live?"

He took her hand. "If I can spend the next fifty or sixty years with you, baby, it'll be worth it."

She leaned over and kissed him. "Do you think you can ride if I help you?"

"I don't know; I'll try."

"By the way, I found your watch. That's how I knew you were at that robbery."

"I tried to stop them."

"I know, Johnny. There's some good in you after all." Very slowly, she helped him to his feet.

"They all dead?"

She nodded. "Except Emmett, and he may not make it." She helped him get up on his horse. Then she swung up on Rosebud. "Let's ride down to Indian Territory. The Cherokee Strip will open up next year and maybe we can get a homestead in the land run."

He looked at her in the last rays of daylight, loving her as he had never known he could love a woman. "You'd settle for being a poor rancher's wife?"

"You just gave up a fortune and eternal life for me," she reminded him.

"Without you, baby, I had no life but didn't know it."

"We get a fresh start from here on out," she said. "We can do it, Johnny, without selling out! Good can beat Evil, but it takes love and commitment." She glanced skyward and smiled. "And a little help from the Big Guy upstairs."

The thunder rolled again, almost in agreement. Across the horizon, light gleamed for a moment, then faded, leaving them in the peaceful lavender dusk of twilight.

Angie looked over at Johnny, loving him as she had never thought she could love a man. "We've got to ride. Think you can make it?"

His voice was stronger now, his rugged face full of love and hope. "I've got you now. I can make it!"

And with that promise, they turned and rode off into the coming darkness, losing themselves forever in the safety of Indian Territory.

To My Readers

The legend of the sixth outlaw in the Coffeyville bank raid is one of the West's most enduring mysteries and the reason I wrote this novel. As I told you in my story, four witnesses reported seeing six riders just outside town minutes before the bank holdups. Another witness recalled seeing a rider galloping away at the height of the gunfight downtown. Yet numerous witnesses said there were only five men involved in the actual robberies.

Some have said that if there was a sixth man, he might have been Bill Doolin, whose horse went lame; while he went to steal another, he arrived too late to participate. One author has even suggested the sixth man was actually a woman. We will probably never know if indeed there was a sixth rider and who it might have been.

My main characters, Logan Enterprises, its building, Logan Parkway and the towns of Osage and Prairie View are all fictional. However, every time I open a newspaper or turn on the television, I get a sense that Nick Diablo is still around, and doing a landslide business in silent contracts with many of the world's people.

The town of Coffeyville, Kansas, about a mile across the Oklahoma line on Hwy 169, has grown from a town of about 3,000 to 13,000. It's a pleasant place to visit, especially during Dalton Defender Days, held the first week of every October to re-create the famous raid and honor the four citizens who died defending their town against the outlaws.

Before writing this novel, I went to Coffeyville and walked the streets and Death Alley. However, only two of the original buildings that played a major part in the action, the Condon Bank and Isham Hardware Store, are still standing. While visiting Coffeyville, you will want to go to the museum that holds Bob Dalton's saddle, many of the weapons and other objects related to the infamous raid.

You'll also want to visit the Elmwood Cemetery and the graves of three of the outlaws. Grat and Bob are buried there, along with Bill Powers.

The fourth dead outlaw, Dick Broadwell, was taken by his brother, a respectable businessman, to be buried in Hutchinson, Kansas. Broadwell was the outlaw who managed to mount and ride out of town although severely wounded. He was found lying dead in the road about half a mile west of town while his horse grazed peacefully nearby.

Also in Elmwood Cemetery is the grave of Frank Dalton, one of the fifteen Dalton children, who was killed in the line of duty as a U.S. deputy marshal. His brothers, Grat, Emmett and Bob all worked on the right side of the law for awhile.

Of the four citizens killed, Charles T. Connelly was the town marshal and a veteran of the Civil War; Lucius Baldwin, the clerk who mistook the Daltons and their hostage for local citizens, was only twenty-three years old; and the other two, Charles Brown and George Cubine, worked together. Brown and Cubine are both buried at Elmwood Cemetery. Marshal

Connelly was buried in Independence, Kansas, and young Baldwin was buried in Burlington, Kansas.

Three citizens, Charles Gump, T. Arthur Reynolds, and Thomas Ayres, were also wounded. The editor of the *Coffeyville Journal*, David Elliott, walked into Death Alley and accepted Emmett's pistol as he surrendered. While the *Journal* is still the local newspaper, Elliott himself was killed in 1899 in the Spanish-American War and is also buried in Elmwood Cemetery.

Charles Ball, the gutsy bank employee who delayed Grat for a fatal ten minutes with his tale of the time lock on the vault, would eventually become president of the Condon Bank.

John Kloehr, the expert shot who played such a major role in stopping the bandits, was later presented with a fine engraved rifle from the Winchester Company.

The lawmen, Heck Thomas and Fred Dodge, arrived in Coffeyville on October 8, after getting word at the Sac and Fox Agency that the gang had been wiped out. Fred Dodge wisely let the citizens of the town decide who got the reward. The fine citizens divided it fairly between the wounded and the survivors of the slain heroes. However, Heck Thomas was given a share for his diligent pursuit of the gang.

As I told you in my story, the Daltons were related to another infamous outlaw gang. The Dalton boys' mother was Adaline Younger Dalton, an aunt of the Younger brothers. It is interesting that all the worst outlaws of that time period, the James boys, the Daltons, Youngers and Belle Starr had their earliest roots in southern Missouri.

Emmett was so badly wounded, with twenty-three chunks of lead in him, that Dr. Wells did not think he would live through the night, which was the only thing that kept irate citizens from lynching him. However, Emmett survived his wounds and was sent to prison. He was pardoned by the governor of Kansas in 1907 and married Julia Johnson Lewis. It is an interesting side note that Julia was the widow of one of three men killed in the first gunfight in the new state of Oklahoma, on Statehood Day, November 16, 1907, in the town of Bartlesville. Emmett went straight after he got out of prison and wrote two books: *When the Daltons Rode* and *Beyond the Law*. Emmett starred in the movie version of *Beyond the Law*. *When the Daltons Rode* became a 1940 Universal Studios Western movie starring Randolph Scott, Brian Donlevy and Broderick Crawford.

Emmett came back to Coffeyville for a visit in 1931 and had a headstone engraved and placed on his brothers' graves, which until that time had been marked only with the rusty piece of pipe the outlaws had used for a hitching post in Death Alley. Emmett died in Hollywood, California, in 1937, and is buried in the family plot in Kingfisher, Oklahoma. Julia is buried in Dewey, Oklahoma.

Another Dalton brother, Bill, also became an outlaw, riding with Bill Doolin after the Coffeyville raid. Bill Dalton was shot and killed on his own porch in Oklahoma in 1893.

Bill Doolin, who might have been the "sixth" man, continued to wreak havoc across Oklahoma Territory after the Coffeyville raid. While hiding out in New Mexico, he reportedly became a friend of and saved the life of Western writer Eugene Manlove Rhodes. Doolin's colorful career was ended by a lawman's shotgun blast in 1896.

Bitter Creek Newcomb would be killed in Oklahoma Territory in 1895 by the Dunn brothers, who, some say, did it for the reward.

The black cowboy from Texas, Amos Burton, faithfully carried out his part in the plan, waiting in vain for the Daltons to join him.

If you're interested in the Dalton boys or Bill Doolin, other books you might find at your public library are: *Daltons! The Raid on Coffeyville, Kansas,* by Robert Barr Smith, University of Oklahoma Press, and *Bill Doolin, Outlaw, O.T.,* by Colonel Bailey C. Hanes, University of Oklahoma Press. A reprinted version of David Stewart Elliott's small book, *The Last Raid of the Daltons and the Battle With the Bandits,* written in 1892, is available at the Coffeyville Museum.

About gunfighters in general: Most of what you read about gunfighters is Hollywood bunkum. In the first place, they were generally called shooters or gunmen, not gunfighters. They didn't wear their pistols strapped low (just try mounting a horse with it in that position). As far as I have been able to discover, there was never a single "gun duel" as we see in the movies about the old West. Nobody cared whether you were the "fastest draw"; it was only important to be the most accurate shot. As a matter of fact, for all the pistols the Dalton gang carried, it was later found that none of them had been fired. They had taken their deadly toll with rifles and had been done in with rifles and shotguns.

Most of the "gunfighters" you've heard about are terribly overrated. Billy the Kid? Credited with only four kills, five possible kills or assists. Wyatt Earp? No confirmed kills, five possible kills or assists. Bat Masterson? Only one confirmed kill, no possibles or assists. Doc Holiday? Only two confirmed kills, two possible assists.

So who was the champion killer? Jim Miller, also known as "Killin' Jim" and "Deacon Jim," holds that dubious record, with twelve confirmed kills and one assist. In fact, it is possible he was guilty in 1908 of gunning down Pat Garrett, the sheriff who killed Billy the Kid. Miller was taken out of jail and lynched, along with three other outlaws in an Ada, Oklahoma, livery stable on April 19, 1909, two years after Oklahoma became a state.

Finally, two other statistics that might interest gunfighter buffs: the *year* that holds the record for the most gunfights is 1878. Texas was the state with the *most* gunfights: nearly 160 during that violent era of the Old West. If you're interested, a fascinating source is *Encyclopedia of Western Gunfighters* by Bill O'Neal, University of Oklahoma Press.

The song, "After the Ball," was a hit of 1892, and an even

bigger one the following year at the Columbian Exposition, better known as the Chicago World's Fair. "After the Ball" ushered in the period of multimillion-dollar sheet music sales, eventually earned more than five million dollars, an unheard of sum for that time.

Eternal Outlaw is my seventeenth novel for Zebra Books. If you've read the others, you know they all connect in an ongoing saga called *The Panorama of the Old West.* How does *Eternal Outlaw* connect with the others? Remember Johnny Logan said he served time in the Nevada State Prison with Nevada Randolph? Some of you will remember Nevada Randolph as the hero of an earlier book, *Nevada Dawn*.

Unfortunately, many of my early novels are out of print, and I'm sorry, but I don't have any extra copies. However, Zebra Books has just re-released one of my readers' all time favorites, *Comanche Cowboy*. Look for it in your local bookstore.

Since some of my books are written out of sequence, you can read them in any order. If you'd like a newsletter and an autographed book mark explaining the series, you may write me at: Box 162, Edmond, OK 73083-0162. Please include a #10, self-addressed, stamped letter-sized envelope. Foreign readers need to send a postal voucher, available at your local post office, which I can exchange for proper postage. U.S. regulations do not allow me to use foreign stamps. If you're on the Internet, you can visit my Web Page at: http://www.nettrends.com/georginagentry.

Let me leave you with something to think about—a quote from President Teddy Roosevelt: "Only those are fit to live who do not fear to die. And none are fit to die who have shrunk from the joy of life and the duty of life."

So what story will I tell next? My readers will be pleased to know I have another Indian romance coming out early in the year 2000. I wrote this story because I was so intrigued by a black, tear-shaped gem stone that is found in Arizona. Because of an ancient legend, the stones are known as Apache Tears.

The U.S. Cavalry used a lot of Indian scouts in the Old West. Among the best and most deadly were the Apache. It is a fact of history that only once in all the annals of the Indian Wars did Native American scouts ever mutiny. The Apache scouts turned on the soldiers in August 1881.

Our virile, half-breed hero is Ndolkah, which means "Cougar." This rugged Apache scout wears a necklace of Apache Tears. Ndolkah is a friend of Cholla, the hero and fellow scout from my earlier book, *Apache Caress*. Despite his good intentions, Cougar is about to get caught up in the historical mutiny against the U.S. Cavalry.

The heroine is a flame-haired society beauty with green eyes who is visiting her fiancé at the Arizona fort. Elizabeth Winters is better known as Libbie. The Apache warrior renames her Blaze. What an apt name for the elegant red-haired beauty! The dark and dangerous Apache hungers for the spoiled and willful Blaze and gives her his necklace of Apache Tears, even though he knows she is promised to the blue-blooded officer, Lieutenant Phillip Van Harrington.

Cougar and his little band of renegades swoop down out of the mountains and kidnap her. He tells himself it's only because he needs a hostage, and later he will trade Blaze to Mexican banditos for weapons and gunpowder, or maybe hold her for ransom. In the meantime, he'll use this fiery seductress as his personal slave and to warm his blankets. Of course he has underestimated the fiery and rebellious Blaze, who will not submit meekly to any man!

Come along with me to relive the excitement and romance of old Arizona in this story I call *Apache Tears*.

Eternally Yours,
Georgina Gentry

<u>BOOK YOUR PLACE ON OUR WEBSITE</u> AND MAKE THE <u>READING CONNECTION!</u>

We've created a customized website just for our very special readers, where you can get the inside scoop on everything that's going on with Zebra, Pinnacle and Kensington books.

When you come online, you'll have the exciting opportunity to:

- View covers of upcoming books

- Read sample chapters

- Learn about our future publishing schedule (listed by publication month *and author*)

- Find out when your favorite authors will be visiting a city near you

- Search for and order backlist books from our online catalog

- Check out author bios and background information

- Send e-mail to your favorite authors

- Meet the Kensington staff online

- Join us in weekly chats with authors, readers and other guests

- Get writing guidelines

- AND MUCH MORE!

**Visit our website at
http://www.zebrabooks.com**